The Masterful
Mr. Montague

BY STEPHANIE LAURENS

The Cynster Novels
Devil's Bride • A Rake's Vow • Scandal's Bride
A Rogue's Proposal • A Secret Love
All About Love • All About Passion
The Promise in a Kiss • On a Wild Night
On a Wicked Dawn • The Perfect Lover
The Ideal Bride • The Truth About Love
What Price Love? • The Taste of Innocence
Temptation and Surrender

The Cynster Sisters Trilogy
Viscount Breckenridge to the Rescue
In Pursuit of Eliza Cynster
The Capture of the Earl of Glencrae

The Cynster Sisters Duo
And Then She Fell
The Taming of Ryder Cavanaugh

The Masterful Mr. Montague

From the Casebook of Barnaby Adair

Stephanie Laurens

HARPER LUXE

An Imprint of HarperCollins*Publishers*

THE MASTERFUL MR. MONTAGUE. Copyright © 2014 by Savdek Management Proprietary Ltd. All rights reserved. Printed in the United States of America. No part of this book may be used or reproduced in any manner whatsoever without written permission except in the case of brief quotations embodied in critical articles and reviews. For information address HarperCollins Publishers, 10 East 53rd Street, New York, NY 10022.

HarperCollins books may be purchased for educational, business, or sales promotional use. For information, please e-mail the Special Markets Department at SPsales@harpercollins.com.

FIRST HARPERLUXE EDITION

HarperLuxe™ is a trademark of HarperCollins Publishers

ISBN: 978-0-06-232682-9

14 ID/RRD 10 9 8 7 6 5 4 3 2 1

The Honorable Barnaby Adair's
Previous Investigations

Cornwall, June 1831
Assisting Gerard Debbington, brother of
Patience Cynster, brother-in-law of Vane Cynster,
and Miss Jacqueline Tregonning
In: The Truth About Love

Newmarket, August 1831
Assisting Dillon Caxton, cousin of Felicity Cynster,
brother-in-law of Demon Cynster,
and Lady Priscilla Dalloway
In: What Price Love?

Somerset, February 1833
Assisting Lord Charles Morwellan, Earl of Meredith,
brother of Alathea Cynster, brother-in-law of
Gabriel Cynster, and Miss Sarah Conningham
In: The Taste of Innocence

London, November 1835
Assisting Miss Penelope Ashford, sister of Luc,
Viscount Calverton, sister-in-law of Amelia Cynster
In: Where the Heart Leads

The Masterful
Mr. Montague

Prologue

October 1837
London

"I'm dying and I want to do the right thing." Agatha, Lady Halstead, set her lips in a determined line.

Straightening from plumping Lady Halstead's pillows, Violet Matcham laid a reassuring hand over her ladyship's frail one where it lay atop the counterpane. "You're in perfect health—you know you are. The doctor said so only last week."

It was midmorning, and the curtains were tied back, allowing weak autumn sunshine to wash into the large bedroom. The soft light was kind to Lady Halstead's papery, mottled skin, to the fine, silvery wisps of her thinning hair, to the milkiness that was dulling her once-bright blue eyes.

"And what would he know, heh?" Lady Halstead slanted a shrewd if peevish look at Violet. "Young men—they always think they know. But I'm very old, Violet dear, and I feel the chill of death in my bones." Sinking back onto the pillows, Lady Halstead looked up at the ceiling. "People used to say that, and I always thought it was pure fancy, but now I know what they meant—I feel it, too." Without moving her head, Lady Halstead looked at Violet; turning her hand, she briefly—weakly—squeezed Violet's fingers. "Most of my friends are long gone, and it's been nearly a decade since Sir Hugo, bless his soul, passed on. I'm very ready to join him, my dear, but first I must do as he asked."

Accepting that no good would come of trying to jolly Lady Halstead out of her mood—indeed, she seemed sober and composed and as rational as ever—Violet inquired, "What did Sir Hugo ask of you?"

She'd been employed by her ladyship as her companion since shortly after Sir Hugo's death; she'd therefore never met the gentleman—a paragon by all accounts—but she had heard so much of him from Lady Halstead that Violet almost felt that she knew him, certainly well enough to ask her question without fear the answer would be something nonsensical. And so it proved.

"The dear man made me promise that before my time came, I would ensure all my affairs—both my personal affairs and those of the estate—were in order. He set great store by such things."

And, Violet thought, *you treasure his memory, so it's important to you that you do as he wished.* Her previous employer, Lady Ogilvie, had been devoted to her late husband, too.

Lady Halstead raised her head, sitting straighter in the bed, her voice strengthening as she continued, "So despite my current health, as I know my time is approaching, I wish to ensure that all is as it should be regarding my will and the estate."

Sir Hugo had made his fortune in India, and had been knighted for services rendered to the Crown on the subcontinent. Consequently, the Halsteads inhabited that nebulous social stratum of upper gentry-lower aristocracy, and were, in common parlance, comfortably well off. The Lowndes Street house reflected that; a highly respectable address in a well-to-do neighborhood. Even Lady Halstead's bedroom, with its large modern bed, damask curtains, matching upholstery and counterpane, and the well-polished, good-quality furniture, attested to the family's standing.

Although she didn't know the finer details of the Halstead estate, Violet understood that on his death, Sir Hugo's holdings had passed entirely to Lady Halstead for her use through her lifetime; on her death, the estate would be divided according to the provisions of Sir Hugo's will, which gave equal portions to each of the four Halstead children. His request, therefore, and Lady Halstead's desire made perfect sense.

Violet nodded. "Very well. What do you want me to do?"

Although her mind was still clear and surprisingly shrewd, Lady Halstead had grown increasingly frail and now remained abed for much of her days. Managing the stairs was an effort, one she undertook only when she deemed it necessary. Violet routinely managed the small household in Lowndes Street, just south of Lowndes Square. With only herself, Lady Halstead, Tilly, her ladyship's maid, and Cook, it wasn't an onerous duty, especially as all four women got along well. Violet's years with Lady Halstead had been peaceful and untrammeled, a gentle, undemanding, if unexciting existence.

Sinking back once more, Lady Halstead sighed. "Sadly, old Runcorn, too, passed on last year, so I suppose we must summon that young son of his." A frown passed over Lady Halstead's face. "I really must decide if the boy is up to the task of managing my affairs."

The late Arthur Runcorn had been the Halsteads' man-of-business for many years. Violet had only met Mr. Andrew Runcorn—the boy—once, when he'd come seeking her ladyship's signature on some form; although young to the extent of being several years shy of Violet's own thirty-four years, she'd formed a favorable impression of the earnest Mr. Runcorn Junior. He'd seemed honest and sincere, and willing to please, but as to whether he was capable of managing finances, she had no way to judge. Moving to the tall-boy in which Lady Halstead's traveling writing desk was stored, Violet bent and drew out the deep bottom drawer. "When would you like to see him?"

"Tomorrow." As Violet straightened, the portable writing desk in her hands, Lady Halstead nodded decisively. "Write a note and ask him to call tomorrow morning. And he should bring a listing of all the properties and investments that make up the estate. Tell him I wish to conduct a full review."

Violet carried the writing desk to the small table before the armchair on the other side of the bed. After laying out paper, ink, and pen, she looked at her ladyship. "Would you like to dictate?"

Lady Halstead waved the suggestion away. "No." Her lips lifted in a smile. "You know how to phrase things better than I."

Violet smiled back, dipped the nib in the ink, and bent to her task.

Lady Halstead had been frowning for the last five minutes.

In the sitting room downstairs, seated in an armchair to her ladyship's right, Violet wondered what in Andrew Runcorn's summation of Lady Halstead's estate was at fault.

The young man-of-business had responded immediately to the summons Violet had dispatched yesterday with a brief note, and, today, had duly presented himself at the house on the dot of eleven o'clock, as requested. Of medium build, with a boyishly round face, brown hair, and wide brown eyes, the younger Runcorn had lost none of the eager sincerity Violet recalled from earlier in the year, and to her ears, at least, his recitation of the details of Lady Halstead's estate had sounded confident, and remarkably clear and concise.

He had, she'd thought, made a good fist of it, and, indeed, Lady Halstead had seemed to concur, nodding in gracious approval. But then her ladyship had asked to go over her current finances—the state of her various deposits in the Funds, and her account with Grimshaws Bank.

Seated bolt upright in the straight-backed carver she preferred, still frowning, Lady Halstead lifted one sheet from the five spread over her shawl-draped lap. "The balance of my bank account is not correct."

Young Runcorn looked shocked. "It isn't?" Lady Halstead held out the sheet and he took it, briefly perused it, then, slanting a glance at Violet, somewhat diffidently said, "This balance has been confirmed by the bank, my lady."

Lady Halstead's frown deepened. "I don't care if some clerk said it's right—it's not." She waved. "Go and get it checked properly."

Detecting the querulous note in her ladyship's voice that indicated true upset, Violet reached out and laid one hand over her ladyship's fingers, now restlessly picking at the shawl. "Is everything else as you believe it should be?"

"Yes, yes." Her fingers stilling under Violet's, her frown lightening, Lady Halstead unbent enough to say to Runcorn, "You've been most precise. I have no fault to find with any other aspect, but that bank balance is not correct."

"Perhaps," Violet said, catching Runcorn's eye, "you might recheck with the bank?"

Runcorn got the message; in the wider scheme of the Halstead estate, checking a bank balance was a minor thing. "Yes, of course. No difficulty at all." He reached for his satchel and stowed the offending statement. "I'll go around to the bank immediately."

That was exactly the right thing to say. Lady Halstead calmed and graciously nodded. "Thank you, young man."

With Violet's help, Runcorn gathered the papers he'd brought, then very correctly took his leave of Lady Halstead.

Violet took pity on him and showed him out.

Somewhat to Violet's surprise, by the time she returned from seeing Runcorn out, Lady Halstead appeared to have put the question of the bank account balance out of her mind; Violet got the impression that her ladyship was certain that, when Runcorn questioned the bank more thoroughly, he would receive a revised balance and all would be as her ladyship had expected.

Consequently, when Runcorn returned at three o'clock the next day with the news that the bank insisted the account balance as he'd originally reported it was correct, Violet was somewhat taken aback.

Having descended the stairs for luncheon, Lady Halstead was once again seated in her carver in the sitting room. On hearing Runcorn's news, her expression grew oddly blank. "That's . . . *most* unsettling."

Runcorn hurried into speech. "My lady, I do assure you we—that is, my firm, Runcorn and Son—haven't touched the account at all. The bank will confirm. Other than requesting statements from time to time, as per our duty as your agents, we have never drawn so much as a penny, I swear—"

"Young man!" Lady Halstead spoke with the authority of a woman who had sons; Runcorn's panic had snapped her out of her abstraction. "Do compose yourself—and do sit down. I entertain no suspicion whatever of your honesty—I do not for a moment believe Runcorn and Son have stolen from me. That, sir, is not the problem."

Subsiding onto the edge of a chair, Runcorn blinked. "It isn't?"

"No, indeed. The problem with that account balance is that it is too much—significantly too much—not too little. Money is being paid into that account by someone, presumably for some reason, but who that someone is or what that reason might be, I have no notion."

"Ah." Rather than looking mystified, Runcorn's expression lit with relief. "There must be some long-ago investment that has only recently started paying dividends—that happens quite frequently. Sir Hugo might have bought into some concern two decades ago and it's only just started paying a return."

Reaching for his satchel, Runcorn rose and bowed, his youthful face radiating his signature eager earnestness. "Rest assured, my lady, that I will review the account, identify the unexpected payments, and trace them to their source."

"Hmm." Lady Halstead was frowning again. "I suppose it might be some mistake—that someone in the bank has mistaken the account."

Runcorn dipped his head. "That, too, is possible, but considering the breadth of Sir Hugo's investments, I suspect the former possibility will be found to be the case. Regardless, I shall analyze the account and make the appropriate inquiries, and will report to you once I have identified the source of the unexpected funds."

Lady Halstead's expression suggested she wasn't quite as convinced as Runcorn of his prowess, but she graciously inclined her head and bade him a good day.

That evening, when Violet went to check on Lady Halstead before retiring to her own bed, she found her ladyship uncharacteristically fretful. Since Runcorn had left, she'd grown progressively more unsettled.

Straightening the coverlet over Lady Halstead's gaunt form, Violet soothingly murmured, "Are you still worrying over that money in your bank account? I'm sure Mr. Runcorn will get to the bottom of it."

Leaning forward to allow Violet to rearrange her pillows, Lady Halstead humphed. "Would that I had your confidence." Then she sighed. "No, that's not fair. The truth of it is that I do have confidence in Runcorn and Son, possibly more confidence than young Mr. Runcorn himself, and it's precisely because of that that I cannot see how these payments could possibly be due to some overlooked investment."

Sinking back onto her resettled pillows, Lady Halstead met Violet's gaze. "I may not know everything about financial dealings, but I do know that investments have umpteen pieces of paper attached—certificates, notices, statements of their own. If some investment had started paying a return, Runcorn and his people would have known. They would have seen the notices or been advised in some way. Perhaps if we had changed our agent, something might have slipped past, but Runcorn and Son have been our agents since we returned to England, and that was nearly thirty years ago. I can't imagine Hugo would have missed passing any advice of investment to Runcorn, so . . . well." Lady Halstead spread her hands. "Where is this wretched money coming from?"

Soothingly, Violet murmured, "I daresay Mr. Runcorn will report in a few days, then we can see what he's found. No need to borrow trouble, as my father always said."

Lady Halstead grimaced. "The late reverend was no doubt wise, but that money isn't the only odd thing."

Detecting a certain grimness in Lady Halstead's eyes, Violet realized that there was, indeed, something else contributing to her ladyship's anxiety. "What else has happened?"

Lady Halstead regarded her as if debating whether or not to reveal what she so clearly wished to share. Then her lips firmed and she tipped her head toward the tallboy. "Bring me the writing desk."

Violet obliged. When she set the cedar box with its sloping lid beside Lady Halstead and opened it, her ladyship reached in, rummaged for a second, then drew out a creased sheet covered in cramped writing. "This came a week ago. I still don't know what to make of it."

She paused, staring at the letter clasped in her gnarled fingers.

Half a minute ticked past, then Violet gently prompted, "Tell me. If it's worrying you, perhaps we can work out what to do about it."

Lady Halstead blinked, met Violet's eyes, then smiled. "That's why I mentioned it—you're always one who will do what you can to make things better." She glanced at the letter, then tucked it back in the box and closed the lid.

"It's from the vicar's wife who lives near The Laurels, our country house. Even though I haven't been back to the village since Sir Hugo passed, and the house has been closed up for all those years, she and I exchange letters every now and then. She wrote to tell me about the new occupants of the house, who are apparently reclusive, and to ask to whom we'd let the property, or whether we'd sold it." Lady Halstead met Violet's eyes. "I haven't sold the property, and I haven't leased it, either. As far as I was aware, the house was still closed up. So who is living there, and what are they using my house for?"

Violet held Lady Halstead's anxious gaze. She had no reassuring answer to her ladyship's question.

Worse, she had no idea how to easily get one.

In the end, she lifted the writing desk and returned it to the bottom drawer of the tallboy. Straightening, she went back to the bed, smoothed the covers, and reached for the lamp on the bedside table. Before dousing the light, she met Lady Halstead's eyes. "Let me think about it overnight, and tomorrow morning we'll discuss what to do."

Lady Halstead's lips twisted, but she nodded. As Violet turned the tiny wheel and the light faded, Lady Halstead closed her eyes.

Satisfied, Violet quietly left the room. With conjecture as to the deepening mystery of the Halstead estate circling in her mind, she walked slowly down the corridor to her own bed.

"I've come to a decision."

Lady Halstead made the announcement the instant Violet, accompanied by Tilly, came through her ladyship's bedroom door the next morning.

Hurrying to open the curtains, then to help Lady Halstead into a sitting position and resettle the pillows at her back, Violet smiled. "You can tell me while you eat breakfast."

As Tilly stepped forward and set the breakfast tray across Lady Halstead's lap, her ladyship waved Violet away. "No. That will keep you from your own breakfast, and I will require your assistance in doing what I wish. And"—Lady Halstead pounced on the copy of *The Times* Tilly had ironed, rolled, and set to one side of the tray—"I have to do some research first."

Reassured by the enthusiasm lighting Lady Halstead's face, Violet acquiesced. "Very well—I'll come back as soon as I've broken my fast."

"Hmm." Lady Halstead was already engaged in searching through the news sheet.

Violet retreated, closing the door and following Tilly downstairs.

Stepping off the stairs, Tilly glanced back at Violet. "She seems in fine fettle again—not like the last few days."

Violet nodded. "It sounds as if she's thought of a solution—of a way to learn the answers to the questions that have been plaguing her."

"Good. Don't like to see her bothered."

"No, indeed." Smiling, Violet followed Tilly into the kitchen. Tilly and Cook were as devoted to Lady Halstead as Violet was. The old lady was the lynchpin around whom the household revolved, and she'd always been a kind mistress, one who attracted affection, loyalty, and respect purely by being herself.

Half an hour later, their breakfasts consumed, Violet and Tilly returned to Lady Halstead's room. Lady Halstead looked confident, even smug, but she had Violet and Tilly help her out of bed and assist her to wash and dress for the day, then instructed Tilly to make up her bed, all without a word regarding her new tack.

But when Tilly left, bearing away the breakfast tray, Lady Halstead lay atop her smoothed counterpane, a shawl over her legs, and smiled at Violet. "I really do feel so much better now I've decided what I should do."

Sinking into the armchair beside the bed, Violet murmured supportively and prayed that whatever her ladyship had decided was a reasonable course of action; if it came to it, there was no one she could appeal to for help should her ladyship decide on some less-than-wise course. Although she had four children, Lady Halstead allowed none of the four to influence her in any way, despite this one or that attempting to do so every now and then. Having known the Halstead children for nearly as long as she had known Lady Halstead, Violet considered her ladyship's stance fully justified. "So," Violet prompted, "tell me what you want to do."

"I have decided," Lady Halstead said, "that while I do not expect any blame in this situation to attach to Mr. Runcorn or his associates, the bald truth is that he is as yet inexperienced, and clearly this matter of the monies being paid into my bank account, especially if in any way connected with the people at the country house, might have quite complex implications, ones young Runcorn might well fail to see, inexperienced as he is. I need to be sure about what is going on—I need to be certain we've got to the bottom of it—and I doubt I will ever feel that degree of certitude in young Runcorn's conclusions.

"So!" Lady Halstead lifted her chin. "I propose to engage the most experienced man-of-business in London to consult on this matter." Lady Halstead paused, then looked at Violet. "What do you think?"

Violet blinked, then refocused on Lady Halstead's face. "I think . . . that that's an excellent idea." Now her ladyship had mentioned it, Violet, too, had harbored a niggling doubt, not of Runcorn's expertise but of his ability to reassure Lady Halstead. Regardless of whatever Runcorn found, her ladyship wouldn't be completely reassured. . . . Violet nodded. "I can't see any reason you shouldn't ask some more-experienced person to consult in this matter. Defining their role as a consultant purely engaged to look into this strange business should smooth the way with Runcorn—he seems the sort who would welcome advice from a more senior practitioner."

Lady Halstead was nodding. "Indeed—that was a point I considered. I quite like young Runcorn and don't want to put his back up." Her chin firmed. "But I must have certainty, or I won't feel I've kept my promise to dear Hugo."

And that, Violet fully understood. "Very well. So who is this more-experienced man-of-business you wish to engage?"

"That," Lady Halstead confessed, "stumped me for a while, because, of course, I have no notion about other such agents. But then"—reaching out, she picked up the news sheet that she'd left on her bedside table—"I recalled that there is a column in the financial section of *The Times* where the correspondent urges readers to write to him with questions that are pertinent to managing finances." Unfurling the paper, she pointed to a column. "See? There."

Taking the paper, Violet scanned the column. It wasn't long; the enterprising columnist had taken three questions and provided a paragraph-long answer to each. "So . . . you want to write to *The Times* for a recommendation?"

"Well, in a manner of speaking." When Violet glanced up, Lady Halstead informed her, "I'd thought to write and ask who, in the columnist's erudite opinion, is the most experienced and most trustworthy man-of-business in London."

Chapter 1

A week later

Heathcote Montague was sitting at his desk in the inner sanctum of his suite of offices a stone's throw from the Bank of England, the gloom of an October evening closing in beyond the window, when he heard an altercation in the outer office. Deep in the ledger of one of his noble clients' enterprises, he blocked out the sounds of dispute and worked steadily on through the figures.

Numbers—especially numbers that represented sums of money—held a near-hypnotic appeal; quite aside from being his bread and butter, they were his passion.

And had been for years.

Possibly for too long.

Certainly too exclusively.

Ignoring the niggling inner voice that, over the last year, with each passing month, each successive week, had grown from a vague whisper to a persistent, nerve-jarring whine, he focused on the neat rows of figures marching down the page and forced himself to concentrate.

The hubbub by the main office door subsided; he heard the outer door open, then shut. Doubtless the caller had been another potential client attracted by that wretched article in *The Times*. A terse note to the editor had resulted in bemused bafflement; how could Montague not be pleased at being named the most experienced and most trustworthy man-of-business in London?

He had refrained from blasting back an excoriating reply to the effect that he and his firm did not require, much less appreciate, public referrals. Which the plain truth; he and his small staff were stretched to their limit. Experienced agents as skilled with figures as he was were thin on the ground, yet the reason his practice was universally held in high esteem was precisely because he refused to hire those who were not as pedantic about business, and especially clients' money, as he was; he had no intention of risking his firm's standing by hiring less-able, less-devoted, or less-trustworthy men.

He'd inherited a sound client list from his father some twenty or so years ago; in his father's day, the firm had operated principally as agents assisting clients in managing the income from their estates. He, however, had had wider interests and greater ambitions; under him, the firm had expanded to become a practice dedicated to managing their clients' wealth. With protecting their money and using it to make more.

His direction had drawn the attention of several noblemen, especially those of a progressive stripe, those lords who were not content to simply sit back and watch their assets stagnate but who, instead, shared Montague's personal conviction that money was best put to use.

Early successes had seen his firm prosper. Managing investments with consummate skill and knowing the ins and outs of money in all its varied forms were now synonymous with his name.

But even success could ultimately turn boring—or, at least, not be as exciting, as fulfilling, as it once had been.

Peace had returned to the outer office; he heard his senior clerk, Slocum, make some dry comment to Phillip Foster, Montague's junior assistant. A quick laugh came from others—Thomas Slater, the junior clerk, and the office boy, Reginald Roberts—then the usual calm descended, a quiet broken by the shuffling of paper, the turning of pages, the soft clap as a file box was shut, the shushing slide as it was returned to its shelf.

Montague sank deeper into the figures before him, into the world of the Duke of Wolverstone's sheep-breeding business, one Montague had overseen from inception to its present international success; the results, if no longer as exhilarating as they might once have been, were nevertheless gratifying. He compared and assessed, analyzed and evaluated, but found nothing over which he felt moved to take action.

As he neared the end of the ledger, the sounds from the large outer office where his staff performed their duties changed. The working day was drawing to a close.

Distantly, he registered the sounds of drawers being shut, of chairs being pushed back, heard the exchange of pleasantries as his men shared what waited for them at home—the small joys they were looking forward to. Frederick Gibbons, Montague's senior assistant, and his wife had a new baby, adding to the two youngsters they already had. Slocum's children were in their teens now, while Thomas Slater and his wife were expecting their first child any day. Even Phillip Foster would return to his sister's house and her cheerful brood, while as for Reginald, he was one of a rambunctious family, the middle child of seven.

Everyone had someone waiting at home, someone who would smile and kiss their cheek when they walked through the door.

Everyone but Montague.

The thought, clear and hard as crystal, jerked him from his complacency. For one instant focused him on the utter loneliness of his existence, the sense of being singular, unconnected with anyone in the world, that had been steadily growing within him.

Good-byes were called in the outer office, although none were directed at him; his staff knew better than to interrupt him when he was working. The outer door opened and closed, most of the men departing. Slocum would be the last; any minute, he would appear in Montague's doorway to confirm that the day's work was done and all was in order—

The outer door opened.

"Your pardon, ma'am," Slocum said, "but the office is closed."

The door shut. "Indeed, I do realize it's the end of the day, but I was hoping Mr. Montague would therefore be able to spare me a few minutes—"

"I'm sorry, ma'am, but Mr. Montague isn't taking on any new clients—*The Times* should have said as much and saved everyone a lot of bother."

"I quite understand, but I'm not here to inquire about being taken on as a client." The woman's voice was clear, her diction precise, her tones well modulated, educated. "I have a proposition for Mr. Montague—an offer to consult on a puzzling financial matter."

"Ah." Slocum was unsure, uncertain what to do.

Curiosity aroused, Montague shut the Wolverstone ledger and rose. Although Slocum had apparently not yet registered the oddity, ladies were not customarily the ones who, at least initially, approached a man-of-business. Montague couldn't recall ever being engaged by any female directly—at least, not about business.

Opening his office door, he walked out.

Slocum heard him and turned. "Sir, this lady—"

"Yes, I heard." His gaze fixing on the lady who stood, spine straight, head high, before Slocum, Montague knew he said the words, but they seemed to come from far away.

Of average height, neither slender nor buxom but perfectly proportioned, the lady regarded him with a frank directness that instantly captivated, and effortlessly commanded, his attention. Beneath the soft wave of her dark brown hair, from beneath finely arched brown brows, eyes of a delicate light blue held his gaze.

As he neared, drawn across the room by some power far more potent than politeness, those eyes widened fractionally, but then her chin rose a notch, and lips of pale rose parted on the query, "Mr. Montague?"

Halting before her, he bowed. "Miss . . . ?"

She extended her hand. "My name is Miss Matcham, and I'm here to speak with you on behalf of my employer, Lady Halstead."

He closed his hand around hers, engulfing long, slender fingers in a momentary—sadly brief, strictly businesslike—clasp. "I see." Releasing her, he stepped back and waved toward the door to his office. "Perhaps you would take a seat and explain in what manner I can assist Lady Halstead."

She inclined her head with subtle grace. "Thank you."

She moved past him, and the scent of roses and violets speared through his senses. He glanced at Slocum. "It's all right, Jonas. You can go home—I'll lock up later."

"Thank you, sir." Slocum lowered his voice. "Not our usual sort of client—I wonder what she wants."

Anticipation rising, Montague softly answered, "No doubt I'll find out."

With a salute, Slocum gathered his coat and left. As Montague followed Miss Matcham, who had paused in the doorway to his office, he heard the outer door close.

With a wave, he indicated Miss Matcham should enter, then he followed her in. The question of the propriety of meeting with a young lady alone rose in his mind, but after one searching glance at his visitor, he merely left his office door open. She wasn't that young; although he was no expert on ladies, he would put Miss Matcham somewhere in her early thirties.

Her walking dress of fine wool in a pale violet hue and the matching felt bonnet neatly enclosing her head were stylish, yet not, he thought, in the current height of fashion. The reticule she carried was more practical than decorative.

Halting before his desk, she glanced at him. Rounding the desk, he gestured to one of the well-padded chairs set before it. "Please, be seated."

Once she'd complied, her movements as she drew in her skirts again displaying the inherent grace he'd noted earlier, he sat, set the Wolverstone ledger aside, leaned his forearms on his blotter, clasped his hands, and fixed his gaze on her fascinating face. "Now—how do you believe I might help you, or, rather, Lady Halstead?"

Violet hesitated, yet she and Lady Halstead had plotted and planned to gain access to Mr. Heathcote Montague, and now here she was . . . she heard herself say, "Please excuse my hesitation, sir, but you're not what I had expected."

His brows—neat, brown brows arched over unexpectedly round eyes that, in her opinion, would have made him appear trustworthy even were he not—rose in surprise.

The sight made her smile; she doubted he was often surprised. "The most experienced and most trust-worthy man-of-business in London—I'd expected to have to deal with a cranky, crusty old gentleman with ink-stained fingers and bushy white brows, who would glower at me over the tops of his half spectacles."

Montague blinked, slowly, lids rising to re-reveal his golden brown eyes. He was brown and brown—brown hair of a shade lighter than Violet's own, and hazel-ish eyes that were more brown than green. But it was his face and his physical presence that had struck her most forcefully; as her gaze once more passed over the broad sweep of his forehead, the strong, clean planes of his cheeks, his squared jaw, he shifted. He caught her gaze, then held up his right hand, fingers spread.

There were ink stains, faint but discernible, on the calluses on his index and middle fingers.

As she registered that, he reached to one side and picked up a pair of gold-rimmed spectacles.

"I have these, too." He waved them. "If it would help, I could put them on. Glowering, however, might be beyond me."

She met his eyes, saw the lurking smile, and laughed, smiling, too.

He joined her in her laughter and his smile became manifest, his face creasing in a way that made him seem years younger than the midforties she guessed he must be.

Sound, solid, dependable; everything about him—his features, the shape of his head, his build, his attire—underscored that reality. The accolades of "most experienced" and "most trustworthy" bestowed by *The Times* weren't at all hard to believe.

"I do apologize." She let her laughter fade, but her lips remained stubbornly curved. She straightened on the chair, surprised to discover she'd relaxed against its back. "Despite my unbecoming levity, I am, indeed, here to speak with you on behalf of Lady Halstead."

"And your relationship to her ladyship?"

"I'm her paid companion."

"Have you been with her for long?"

"Over eight years."

"And what can I do for her ladyship?"

Violet paused to reorder her thoughts. "Lady Halstead already has a man-of-business, a Mr. Runcorn. It was the current Mr. Runcorn's father the Halsteads originally engaged, and the younger Mr. Runcorn has only recently taken his late father's place. That said, Lady Halstead has no specific fault to find with young Mr. Runcorn's abilities. However, a situation has arisen with Lady Halstead's bank account that she believes Mr. Runcorn lacks the experience to adequately resolve. At least not to her ladyship's satisfaction." Violet met Montague's golden-brown eyes. "I should mention that Lady Halstead is a widow, her husband, Sir Hugo, having died ten years ago, and her ladyship is now very old. Indeed, the problem with her bank account only came to light because, in keeping with a promise she made to Sir Hugo, she decided that it was time she ensured that her financial affairs, and those of the estate, were in order."

Montague nodded. "I see. And what is it her ladyship believes I can do?"

"Lady Halstead would like you to look into the puzzling question of what is going on with her bank account. She requires an explanation, one she can be certain is correct. Essentially, she wishes to engage you to give a second opinion—a consultation on this matter, nothing more." Violet held Montague's gaze and calmly added, "I, on the other hand, am here to ask you to help give reassurance to a gentle old lady in her declining years."

Montague returned her regard steadily, then the ends of his lips quirked. "You have a way with an argument, Miss Matcham."

"I do what I can for my ladies, sir."

Devotion, in Montague's opinion, was a laudable trait. "What can you tell me about the . . . irregularities afflicting this bank account?"

"I will leave that to Lady Halstead to elucidate." As if sensing the question rising in his mind, the intriguing Miss Matcham added, "However, I have seen enough to verify that there is, indeed, something odd going on, but I haven't studied the statement Mr. Runcorn provided so cannot put forward any definite opinion."

Would that all his clients were so circumspect. "Very well." Looking away from Miss Matcham's remarkably fine eyes, Montague drew his appointment book closer and consulted it. "As it happens, I can spare Lady Halstead half an hour tomorrow morning." He glanced across the desk. "When would be the best time to call?"

Miss Matcham smiled—not a dazzling smile but a gentle, inclusive gesture that somehow struck through his usually impenetrable businessman's shields and literally warmed his heart. He blinked, then quickly marshaled his wits as she replied, "Midmorning would be best—shall we say eleven o'clock? In Lowndes Street, number four, just south of Lowndes Square."

Gripping his pen firmly, Montague focused on his appointment book and wrote in the details. "Excellent."

He looked up, then rose as Miss Matcham came to her feet.

"Thank you, Mr. Montague." Meeting his gaze, she extended her hand. "I look forward to seeing you tomorrow."

Montague gripped her fingers, then had to make himself let go. "Indeed, Miss Matcham." He waved her to the door. "Until tomorrow."

After seeing Miss Matcham out of the office and on her way down the stairs to the ground floor, Montague closed the door, then stood stock-still, his mind replaying the interview, dwelling on this aspect, then that . . .

Until he shook free of the lingering spell and, wondering at himself, strode back to his desk.

His eagerness, the ready-to-be-engaged enthusiasm that carried him to Lowndes Street at eleven o'clock the following morning, was, he tried to tell himself, engendered more by the sense of fate dangling something new—some financial irregularity outside the norm, a tantalizing prospect certain to excite his jaded inner self—than by any lure attached to the lovely Miss Matcham.

She opened the door to his knock, instantly obliterating his attempt at self-deception. He would have sworn his heart literally sped up at the sight of her. Then she smiled. "Good morning, Mr. Montague. Do come in."

Reminding himself to breathe, he stepped forward as she stepped back. He walked into a narrow front hall; a quick survey showed decent artwork, good-quality furniture, polished woodwork, and painted walls. All was neat and tidy. The sight confirmed that, as he'd suspected from the address, Lady Halstead wasn't short of funds. She might not rank as high in wealth as the majority of his clients, but she would have assets worth protecting; in consulting for her, he wouldn't be wasting his time.

Miss Matcham closed the door and joined him. With one hand, she directed him to the room on their right. "Lady Halstead is waiting in the sitting room."

He inclined his head and gestured for Miss Matcham to precede him, seizing the moment to wonder anew at the effect she had on him. He didn't quite understand it; she was lovely to look at—he could, he felt, stare at her for hours—yet she was no raving beauty. Today, she wore a pale blue morning gown that skimmed her curves in a distracting way—at least, he found it distracting. Being indoors and thus bonnetless, her coiffure was on display, so he could better appreciate the thick lushness of her hair, the dark locks confined in a bun at the back of her head but with one sweeping wave crossing her forehead, softening the line of her brow and emphasizing her pale, flawless, milk-and-roses complexion.

Following her through the doorway, he forced his gaze from her and scanned the room. A very old lady with wispy silver hair and refined features sat in a straight-backed chair, her forearms resting on the padded armrests. She was dressed in dark bombazine, with shawls draped about her shoulders and also over her legs. An ebony cane with a silver head rested against the side of the chair.

Miss Matcham went forward. "This is Mr. Montague, ma'am." She glanced at Montague. "Lady Halstead."

As Miss Matcham moved to take the armchair to Lady Halstead's right, her ladyship, who had been shrewdly studying him, held out her hand. "Thank you for calling, sir. I'm sure you are a very busy man—I will endeavor not to take up too much of your time."

Taking her hand, Montague bowed over it. "Not at all, ma'am. I'm keen to learn what the issue with your bank account might be."

"Is that so?" Lady Halstead waved to the armchair to her left. "In that case, please sit."

As he did, Miss Matcham passed several documents to her ladyship. Turning to him, Lady Halstead held out the papers. "This is a copy of the bank's statement of the payments into and out of my bank account over the last six months."

Accepting the sheets, Montague scanned them as Lady Halstead continued, "You will see I have circled various deposits. Those deposits are a complete mystery to me—I have no notion whatever of who is paying that money into my account, much less why."

Montague inwardly blinked. Flicking through the five sheets her ladyship had supplied, doing calculations in his head . . . "I have to admit"—he looked up at Lady Halstead, then at Miss Matcham—"that I had imagined your irregularities would prove to be some confusion on the bank's part, or else a matter of embezzlement." He looked again at the statements. "But this is quite different."

"Indeed." Lady Halstead sounded vindicated. "Young Runcorn, my man-of-business, believes the payments must derive from some old, forgotten investment that has only now started to pay a return."

Studying the figures, Montague shook his head. "I know of no financial instrument that pays in this manner. The payments are roughly monthly but are not regular enough to be specified by any financial contract—for instance, the repayment of a debt. Such payments would come in on a fixed date of every month. And as for investment dividends, I know of no company that pays monthly amounts. Insurance companies might pay certain stipends monthly, but again, they would be on a fixed date." He paused, then added, "As for the size of the payments, they amount to a considerable sum."

He looked at Lady Halstead. "How long has this been going on?"

"Fourteen months, I believe."

He glanced again at the amounts. "At a similar rate?"

"More or less."

Montague's head was whirling, his financial brain trying to find some pattern that these payments would fit, but there wasn't one. He was sure of it. As for the total sum paid into her ladyship's account over the past fourteen months, would that he could find an investment for his clients that returned such a result.

"I'll have to look into it." His financial self wouldn't be able to let the puzzle lie.

"Thank you. I will, of course, meet your customary fee."

"No." He looked up, the underlying boredom—ignored, suppressed, and largely unacknowledged—that had assailed him for months rising high in his mind; that dull, deadening feeling had been growing increasingly weighty, dragging him down, until Miss Matcham had arrived to tempt him. "I would, in all honesty, consider it a favor were you to allow me to investigate this matter." Aside from all else, it would allow him

to continue to meet with Miss Matcham. "I was feeling rather jaded, but this"—he held up the papers—"is
challenging. At least for a gentleman like me. The satisfaction of finding an answer for you—and myself—
will be payment enough."

Lady Halstead arched her brows, considered him
for a long moment, but then nodded. "If that is
what you wish, then so be it." She glanced at Miss
Matcham.

Who met Montague's gaze, then dipped her head,
indicating the papers he still held. "That's a copy you
may take with you. Is there anything else you need?"

He held her gaze for an instant, quite surprised by
the tenor of the answers rolling through his mind.
Then he concentrated and frowned. "Actually, yes.
I would like the style and direction of her ladyship's
man-of-business . . . Runcorn. And also"—he looked
at Lady Halstead—"I will need a letter of authority
to act as your investigator—to ask questions on your
behalf and for those I ask such questions of to be autho-
rized to answer as if I were you."

Lady Halstead nodded. "I can imagine that will be
necessary. Do you know the proper form of such an
authority?"

"Indeed. If you like, I can dictate it for you." He
glanced at Miss Matcham, then looked back at Lady

Halstead. "And if at all possible, ma'am, I would prefer the entire letter be in your hand. It's much less easy to question such a document."

"Of course." Lady Halstead looked at Miss Matcham. "Violet, dear, would you fetch my writing desk?"

With a nod, Miss Matcham rose and left the room.

Montague watched her go. *Violet.* The name suited her.

"Now," Lady Halstead said, "Runcorn's address is . . ."

Setting the papers on his knee, Montague pulled out his notebook and quickly jotted down the address.

Twenty minutes later, the required letter of authority in his pocket, along with the copy of the bank account statement, Montague took his leave of Lady Halstead. Violet Matcham walked him to the front door.

Opening it, she met his gaze. "Thank you. You might not have been able to see it, but she's already much relieved and more settled—she's been in a fret ever since she noticed the irregularity in her account a week ago."

Montague held her gaze and considered various responses—all of them the truth—but, in the end, settled for a brief bow and "I'm happy to know I've already been of some service, however small." He paused, then, his eyes still on hers, added, "I will get to the bottom of this. If her ladyship starts to grow anxious, please do assure her of that."

Violet found it difficult to draw her eyes from his, but, lips curving at her own susceptibility, and because he was as he was, she dipped her head and murmured, "Again, thank you. We'll wait to hear from you in due course."

Montague inclined his head, stepped over the threshold, crossed the porch, and went down the steps.

She watched him stride away and realized she felt lighter—as if he'd lifted a burden she hadn't been aware she'd carried on her shoulders. He really was something of a white knight; he'd answered her summons, had ridden in, and had commenced the process of alleviating the trouble besetting Lady Halstead and, therefore, her, too.

No doubt that was why he left her feeling giddy.

Smiling again at her unexpected susceptibility, she closed the door and returned to Lady Halstead.

That evening, Lady Halstead hosted a dinner for her family. As she no longer had the strength to visit their homes, she invited them to dine in Lowndes Street once a month, and they all came.

Every time.

During her first months with Lady Halstead, Violet had been somewhat surprised that even her ladyship's three adult grandchildren invariably attended and stayed for the entire evening, but as the months had rolled past, she had realized that among the Halstead children, sibling rivalry had reached astonishing heights; even though said grandchildren might wish to be elsewhere, they had to obey their parents' commands and show all due observance to their grandmother's dignity.

As usual, Violet sat at the table on Lady Halstead's left, ready to lend assistance if required. The Halstead children, all of whom were also very conscious of *their* dignity, tolerated her presence because Lady Halstead insisted on it, and, as Violet's birth was as good as, if not better than, their own, they had no viable excuse to exclude her.

They did, however, ignore her, which suited Violet. She was immensely grateful not to have to interact with "The Brood" as she, Tilly, and Cook privately termed them. Instead, she kept her lips shut and observed; as an only child, she found the tensions and constant sniping between members of The Brood curious and fascinating in a horrifying sort of way.

More than once, she'd retired to her room after a Halstead family dinner giving thanks that she had never had brothers or sisters; then again, she doubted most families behaved like the Halsteads. They seemed a law unto themselves.

Tonight, the conversation had ranged from the importance of the bills currently before Parliament, to the Irish Question and the weightiness of the relevant deliberations taking place inside the Home Office. The former topic was espoused by Cynthia, only daughter and second-born of the Halstead children, in order to call attention to her husband, the Honorable Wallace Camberly, Member of Parliament, and underscore his importance and, by extension, hers.

A severe-looking matron in an azure satin gown, Cynthia sat on Lady Halstead's right, opposite Violet. Cynthia's features were hard, her brown eyes like onyx. Constant bad temper had left her lips pinched and thin; her most frequent expressions were of disapproval and disdain. Very little in life, it seemed, found favor with Cynthia. If blind ambition had a face, it was hers. "Of course," she declared, "the coronation will soon take precedence over all else. The parliamentary committee to oversee it will shortly be named."

Seated down the table on the opposite side, Constance Halstead, wife of Mortimer, who was her ladyship's firstborn, reached for her wineglass. A tall, large-boned lady with a buxom figure and round features, Constance had an unfortunate fondness for frills and furbelows, and a voice that, regardless of the company, was always pitched too loud. "I daresay," she stated. "But, of course, it will fall to the Home Office to oversee all the details of the day. Mortimer"—Constance glanced at her husband, seated at the head of the table—"will no doubt be heavily involved."

Violet, too, glanced at Mortimer. Of average height and build, Mortimer's adherence to rigid correctness in every aspect of his dress only served to make him unmemorable, easily overlooked in a crowd. His face, too, lacked distinction, his features held under such absolute control that his expression was usually bland, if not blank. Mortimer had been addressing the excellent roast beef, but now he looked up, his pale eyes going to Cynthia, his expression a stone-faced challenge as he said, "Indeed. There will be a great deal to be organized, and the Home Office will be in charge. There have already been preliminary discussions, although I am not at liberty to divulge any details."

All he got out of Cynthia was a smirk, effectively communicating her belief that Mortimer could not reveal any details because he didn't know any, not actually being involved at all.

Mortimer's choler started to rise, but before he could respond to Cynthia, Maurice Halstead, second son and social black sheep—rake, roué, gambler, woman-izer, and general profligate—drawled, "So it'll be you who'll be consulted as to how many frills will be on Alexandrina's coronation gown? Oh, no, wait—she's to be called Victoria, isn't she?"

Mortimer narrowed his eyes on Maurice. "The coronation gown will be decided by the Palace, as is proper, and, yes, as even you should have heard, the young queen has declared she will be Victoria."

The man seated next to Constance stirred. "What's she got against the name Alexandrina, then?" William Halstead's words were fractionally slurred.

If Maurice was the social black sheep, William was the family's pariah. Violet was certain he attended Lady Halstead's dinners in order to get at least one good meal a month, but even more because he knew his presence severely disturbed his brothers and sister, and their spouses, all of whom viewed William much as they would a cockroach, one they could sadly not squash.

The youngest of the Halstead children, William was always the most soberly dressed, in a plain black suit that was only just passable as suitable attire for a gentry dining table.

"Actually"—Wallace Camberly spoke for what Violet thought was the first time since they'd sat at the table—"I understand the boot's on the other foot, so to speak, and it was more that she favors the name Victoria over all others."

The reasonable and, coming from Camberly, most likely informed comment defused that topic, effectively ending it.

Seated beside Cynthia, Wallace Camberly was, Violet judged, even more ambitious than the lady he'd taken to wife. However, unlike Cynthia, he had no stake in the Halstead family's internecine battles and largely remained aloof, commenting only when some subject interested him. As usual, he was quietly but fashionably dressed, as befitted his station. Violet knew him to be cold and utterly ruthless in pursuit of his goals, but he assiduously played by the rules as he perceived them—because that served him best in the long run, and if something did not benefit him, he didn't waste time or energy on the matter.

The Halstead family sniping did nothing for him, so he ignored it.

Wallace's lead was largely followed by his son, Walter Camberly, seated opposite, between Violet and William. Although already twenty-seven years old, Walter had yet to settle on any occupation; he drifted through life, apparently aimlessly. Violet wasn't sure how Walter filled his days, but as Cynthia ruled that roost with an iron fist, Violet doubted that Walter derived much joy from his outwardly unfettered existence.

Like Violet, Walter kept his head down and let the conversational volleys fly past. The others of the younger generation—Mortimer and Constance's children, Hayden, presently twenty-three years old, and his sister, Caroline, just twenty—likewise endured, rather than enjoyed, these evenings. They rarely made a comment of any sort. As far as Violet knew, the younger Halsteads were ordinary, unremarkable young people; if she had to guess, she would have said they found the Halstead dinners utterly boring but were too polite, and too reliant on their parents' goodwill, to do anything but attend and remain silent. They spoke when spoken to but contributed little.

Then again, not attracting the attention of any of their Halstead elders was undeniably wise.

Mortimer fastidiously patted his lips with his napkin and again made a bid to seize the stage. "I believe we will be advising that the new queen meet with the Irish representatives at some point—I may have to travel to Ireland as part of the delegation."

"Indeed?" Cynthia reached for the sauceboat. "Who knows? They may make you a permanent secretary over there." She glanced at Constance. "My dear, you will have my sincerest sympathy if you are forced to relocate to Ireland."

Mortimer's face mottled. "Don't be absurd! I'm held in far too high esteem, my opinions too highly valued for the Home Secretary to even contemplate burying me in Ireland." Mortimer halted, belatedly realizing he'd risen to Cynthia's bait. His gaze locked on his sister, lips compressing, he drew in a breath and held it for a second, as if pulling back from the brink of what, from experience, Violet knew could be a rapid descent into a cutting exchange of barbed insults. As the fraught moment passed, Mortimer shifted his pale gaze from Cynthia to Lady Halstead.

As usual, Lady Halstead remained unmoved by the vicious, almost violent undercurrents swirling about her table as she steadily sawed and ate her roast beef.

With a certain deliberation, Mortimer set aside his napkin. "How are you, Mother? I do hope the exertion of having us all to dine isn't too draining."

Lady Halstead's brows faintly arched as she glanced up the table. "I'm well enough—as well as can be expected at my age. Thank you for asking, Mortimer."

Cynthia immediately leapt in with a solicitous comment, one Constance then felt compelled to top. Not to be outdone, Maurice noted that Lady Halstead was looking a touch paler, but otherwise seemed to be "up to snuff." For several minutes, Lady Halstead had to exert herself to fend off her children's patently insincere interest.

Mortimer sought to end the discussion by stating, "I daresay, Mama, that you have many long years ahead of you yet."

"Perhaps," William said, now slouching in his chair, his hands sunk in his pockets. "But in any case, I hope you've got your affairs in order." His dark gaze swept his siblings. "Heaven help us if there's any question over the estate once you're gone."

Violet fully sympathized with the comment, but, of course, Mortimer, Cynthia, Constance, and even Maurice took it badly. The resulting furor broke over William's head and looked set to last for quite some time—

Lady Halstead set down her cutlery and clapped her hands sharply. "Quiet! Oh, do be *quiet*." As the voices faded, she picked up her cutlery again and returned her attention to her plate. "If you must know, I've asked Runcorn—the young man who has taken over from his father—to review my affairs and those of the estate and ensure that all is in order." She glanced up briefly, her gaze bleakly severe. "Although I have no intention of dying just yet, rest assured that when I do, there will be no uncertainty concerning the estate."

Silence held the table for a moment, then quiet mutterings rose, all to do with "young Runcorn" and whether he was up to the mark.

Violet glanced at Lady Halstead, then followed her lead in ignoring the rumblings.

As Tilly came in to clear the table prior to laying out the desserts, Violet wondered, as she had many times over the past eight years, how it came to be that a lady as kind and gentle as Lady Halstead had ended with a family like this, in which all the members were selfish and self-serving, albeit to variable degrees.

"Damn it!" He peered at the reflection in the round shaving mirror. With a vicious jerk of his wrist, he plucked the stray hair from his chin, then half straightened, turning his face from side to side, confirming that all was as he wished it to be.

Beyond his shoulders, the paneling of his dressing room was barely lit by the single lamp he'd brought in. He found the gloom comforting. This was his most private place, the place where he made his plans, refined and adjusted them.

In the mirror, he met his eyes. "She isn't even close to dying. Here I've been patiently waiting for her to fade and pass on, and instead she's rattling on . . . and now, damn it all, she's got this young blighter looking into the estate's finances."

Straightening fully, he forced himself to think through this new, unexpected, and unsettling development. "Will he find it? That's the question."

After a minute, he went on, "If he does . . ."

Several moments later, he shook his head. "Even if he doesn't realize, *she* will. He'll bring it to her attention in some way, even if only by *not* including it on some list. And once she realizes, she'll start asking questions—I know she will. She won't simply let it rest."

His escalating tension rendered the last words sharp enough to cut.

As the sound faded, he continued following his thoughts.

The pervasive silence of the night was broken only by the distant ticking of a clock.

Eventually, he drew himself up and, in the mirror, looked himself in the eye. "I can't afford to have it come to light—not now, not ever. So I'll have to take care of it. I won't be able to breathe easily again until I'm safe. Obviously, there are others I'll have to silence, too, but . . . one step at a time."

That had been his private motto for as long as he could recall; thus far it had served him well.

Chapter 2

Montague hadn't previously realized how satisfying bringing relief to those who found financial matters overwhelming could actually be. It was, he now saw, a facet of his professional activities that he had failed to appreciate but should acknowledge and, indeed, take more pride in.

After leaving the house in Lowndes Street, the satisfaction of having in some small part allayed Lady Halstead's immediate anxiety had stayed with him through the rest of the day and the routinely uneventful evening that had followed, and had fired him to set out first thing that morning to consult with Lady Halstead's man-of-business.

While her ladyship appeared to have no suspicions of Runcorn, Montague would make up his own mind.

Had the matter been one of embezzlement, he would have been far more skeptical, not to say distrustful, but as he strode along the pavement, he was more curious than concerned.

An entire day and evening of allowing Lady Halstead's "irregularities" to percolate in the deepest recesses of his brain had still not brought forth any possible solution. Far from being discouraged, he was even more enthused; it had been a long time since anything financial had managed to surprise him, much less intrigue him to this degree.

He almost felt like a new man as he swung around the corner from Broad Street into Winchester Street. Runcorn's offices were some way along, on the ground floor of a building near the elbow where Winchester Street turned north. There was a public house across the road, in the opposite corner of the bend, but the office of Runcorn and Son was flanked by a small printer on one side and a tobacconist's on the other.

The area was not as heavily dominated by businesses connected with finance as those streets and alleys close by the Bank of England, where Montague and his peers hung their plaques, yet Winchester Street was only a few blocks from that more established sector, and Runcorn's office was a decent set of premises for a minor firm.

Pausing before the door, Montague studied the faded lettering above the single broad window giving onto the pavement, then looked through the glass in the door itself, unsurprised to see lamps burning inside. The window allowed some light to penetrate, but not enough for a business that relied on reading figures upon figures.

Opening the door, he went in. Pausing to shut the door, he surveyed the interior, more out of professional curiosity than anything else. Although poky, the office was very recognizable, at least to him; file boxes were piled high along the shelving occupying every square foot of wall, and formed a man-high stack in one corner. Papers were spread over the narrow desk behind which a clerk labored; the middle-aged man had looked up as Montague entered.

Soberly attired in the proper manner for a clerk, the man rose and came forward. "Can I help you, sir?"

Already reaching into his inner pocket, Montague withdrew his card case, extracted a card, and handed it to the clerk. "If Mr. Runcorn could spare me a few minutes of his time, I would like to consult him on the matter of the Halstead estate."

The clerk read the script on the card and his eyes widened. "Yes, of course, sir." He waved to a pair of chairs set before the window. "Please take a seat,

Mr. Montague, and I'll inform Mr. Runcorn of your arrival."

Montague inclined his head and obligingly sat. He had no doubt Runcorn would see him. Even if the younger man had not been long enough in the business to recognize his name, the clerk certainly had and would duly inform his master.

The clerk tapped on an inner door, then entered, shutting the door behind him.

A moment later, the door opened again, and a man of some twenty-eight or so summers stood for a moment in the doorway, then came swiftly forward, Montague's card in his hand.

Montague rose as he approached.

"Sir!" Runcorn Junior halted before him, his round face alight with childlike pleasure. He met Montague's eyes, his own alive with an equal mixture of delight and conjecture, then he drew breath, reined in his excitement, and inclined his head. "It's an honor, Mr. Montague, to welcome you to Runcorn and Son. How may we assist you?"

Montague smiled approvingly. "I have a matter to do with the Halstead estate that I would like to discuss with you. If you have the time?"

Runcorn stepped back and waved to his office. "Of course."

He ushered Montague into the office, and into a chair before the large and well-used desk. As Runcorn rounded it, making for his own chair, he offered, "The office was my father's before me, of course. I'm the son."

Montague found the young man's enthusiasm infectious. "I had heard as much." When Runcorn looked his question, Montague added, "From Lady Halstead." Reaching into his pocket, he withdrew her letter of authority. "Before we proceed, you will need to read this."

Sobering, Runcorn took the letter, unfolded it, read it, then, slowly refolding the sheet, he looked across the desk at Montague with a faint, puzzled frown.

Montague had no difficulty reading the thoughts passing through Runcorn's head, not with such an open, expressive face; even the vague possibility of a suspicion he'd harbored that Runcorn might in some way be involved in the irregularities was rapidly fading. "Permit me to assure you that I am not here to poach your client, Mr. Runcorn." Holding out his hand for the letter, when Runcorn surrendered it, Montague stowed it in his pocket once again.

"Then I admit I'm confused, sir." Runcorn regarded him steadily. "Why are you here?"

"Lady Halstead requires . . . shall we say 'reassurance'? . . . that whatever explanation you find for the irregularities in her bank account is the correct one. That is my focus and that alone. I will also state that I have no financial interest in this matter—I have agreed to provide my oversight purely out of professional curiosity." Montague held Runcorn's gaze. "I am quite intrigued, Mr. Runcorn, as to what the explanation for the unusual payments into her ladyship's bank account might be."

A moment passed, then Runcorn blinked and, as if assuring himself, said, "She wants reassurance . . . well, I can understand that. I haven't been in this business for all that long, and . . ." After a second, he met Montague's eyes. "To be candid, sir, I would greatly appreciate your guidance in this matter. I had thought the payments must be due to some old, long-forgotten investment, but they're not—or, at least, that doesn't appear to be the case."

"No." Montague hesitated, then added, "In fact, that's what sparked my interest in this matter. I've been in this business for a very long time, yet I do not recognize the style of these payments. They don't match any pattern I've seen before."

"Exactly!" Runcorn held up his hands in a helpless gesture. "Pringle—he's my clerk—and I have been wracking our brains trying to think of what they might be arising from, but as yet we've found no clue. And as the bank has noted the payments as cash deposits, it's unlikely they'll be able to shed light on the source, and"—Runcorn looked uncomfortable—"I didn't think it wise to raise the issue with the bank at this time—not without Lady Halstead's explicit permission, and not until we've eliminated all the more likely investment sources."

Meeting Runcorn's gaze, Montague nodded approvingly. "Indeed. We should only involve the bank once we've exhausted all other avenues of inquiry. No need to air our questions more widely than necessary."

"So we thought." Runcorn looked reassured. "Consequently, pursuing the angle that the payments relate to some forgotten investment, we've pulled the complete Halstead file—it goes back a good thirty years—and we're combing through it page by page, but as yet we've had no luck."

Montague considered, then nodded again. "At present, that's the first question you must answer—regardless of appearances, are these payments in some way linked to some past investment? You are, indeed, taking the right tack." He smiled at Runcorn's expression of relief, which was almost immediately tempered by the realization of just what a huge undertaking lay before him. "Indeed," Montague confirmed. "Learning the answer will take time and effort. However, as to my own approach, at this point I would be grateful if you would provide me with a copy of the statements of the bank account in question, going back to when these odd payments first appeared. Lady Halstead gave me her copy of the most recent statements, but I will need the earlier statements as well. In addition, I would like a list of all investments of any type, whether believed to be current or not, and all loans and deposits into interest-bearing securities."

Runcorn was nodding; Lady Halstead's letter gave Montague the authority to request such details and Runcorn permission to provide them. "We can give you a copy of the bank statements today—Pringle will have a spare. Likewise for the currently held investments, those that are presently paying income—we've been searching through those ourselves. But a listing of the wider investments—that will take a few days to compile." He met Montague's eyes. "To be sure we have the entire picture, all nearly thirty years' worth of it."

"That will be entirely satisfactory." Montague smiled and rose. "I'm well aware that to survive, you must service your other clients as well."

"Indeed." Rising and coming around the desk to open the door, Runcorn grimaced. "It's something of a juggling act at the moment, what with the Halstead review proving so much more time-consuming than anyone would have expected."

Montague allowed himself to be ushered out and introduced to Pringle, who, on receiving Runcorn's instructions, proved to be meticulously organized. He produced the required copies of the bank statements and the list of currently paying investments.

Pringle eyed a foot-high stack of papers on his desk. "As for the complete list of investments, that might take a few days."

Montague nodded. "That's entirely acceptable. It's critically important in a case like this that the list be complete and accurate with respect to every detail. If that takes a few days more, so be it. An inaccurate list will get us nowhere."

Pringle bowed. "Of course, sir. I'll give it my best attention."

Given what he had already noted of Pringle's meticulousness, Montague had no doubt that that would prove more than adequate, and said so.

Leaving Pringle and his master both preening, he exited the office of Runcorn and Son and, with a spring in his step, set out to embark on his own researches.

Montague didn't get a chance to return to the Halstead puzzle until late in the afternoon. On his return to his office, he'd been claimed by a succession of clients, interspersed with presentations from several different firms seeking capital.

Investment was the blood and bone of his business, so he'd had to put Lady Halstead and her mysterious payments aside.

Finally, as the light was fading from the sky beyond his window, he drew the thin file containing her ladyship's bank statements and list of investments to the center of his blotter and opened it.

Two hours later, when Slocum tapped on his door to bid him good night, he'd reached the end of the laborious process of matching payments to investments, and found himself in complete agreement with Lady Halstead. Something extremely odd was going on with her bank account.

After farewelling Slocum, Montague sat back in his chair and stared at the papers spread out on the desk. Fingernail tapping on the chair arm, he finally let the explanation—the one possibility he hadn't discounted—form in his brain.

"Concealment of funds." He frowned. "But by whom, and why?"

In financial terms, concealment was the opposite of embezzlement but was almost always equally illegal in that money that needed to be concealed almost certainly had some element of illegality attached to it.

"So in pursuing the matter of these payments, I'm investigating what might reasonably be supposed to be the fruits of some crime."

Should he involve the authorities?

He considered—in particular what he might report—and grimaced. "I can't yet be certain that there is any crime—I certainly don't have proof of one."

And involving the police wouldn't, he suspected, endear him to Lady Halstead and Miss Matcham. Not that such a consideration would stop him, but . . .

He tapped his finger more decisively. "If I had proof of a crime, my way would be clear, but until I do, the possibility exists that there's some innocent explanation behind this."

Scanning the documents splayed across his desk, he sifted through the possibilities of what he might do next. Tracing the payments, if that proved feasible, appeared to be the most direct route forward.

He had often assisted others with their investigations when said investigations had drifted into financial waters. This, however, was the first time he had initiated such an investigation himself rather than contributing to someone else's undertaking. Courtesy of those previous, supporting roles, he now had connections, acquaintances who knew a great deal more about investigating than he did, who, he didn't doubt, would be happy to assist him should he ask for their help.

"But at present this is an entirely financial matter, and when it comes to investigating finances . . ." He was the best man for the job. That was why, when it came to anything involving money, those others turned to him.

Huffing out a breath, he sat up and regathered all the documents. As he returned them to the Halstead file, he recalled his earlier restlessness, his wish for some new and more exciting project; apparently Fate had been listening.

Be careful what you wish for.

Even though she'd died when he'd been ten years old, he could still remember his mother telling him that.

On the other hand, his niggling inner voice—the voice of dissatisfaction—had been silent for the past few days, a definite improvement.

Leaving the Halstead file on his desk, he rose and turned down the lamp, then, by the light thrown through the windows from the flares in Chapel Court, he made his way through the outer office. As he reached for the doorknob, the atmosphere—the anticipation—that filled that particular moment when the others in the office left for the day replayed in his mind.

Something he observed in others, not something he experienced.

He felt no happy eagerness as he opened the door, stepped through and locked it, then turned and ascended the stairs to the next floor.

He had bought the building in Chapel Court, off Bartholomew Lane, behind the Bank of England, over ten years ago, and had converted the floor above his office and the offices to either side into a comfortable apartment. The proximity to his office suited him; if he thought of some question during the evening or night, it took only a minute to check a file, or make a note at his desk. And this section of the City, although humming with activity during the day, grew quiet at night. It wasn't deserted by any means—what part of London was?—but the denizens who lived in the area were by nature a sober, reserved lot.

Fishing his key out of his waistcoat pocket, he paused on the upper landing to unlock and open his front door. The apartment was spacious, comprising a small foyer giving onto a long sitting room, with a dining room beyond, a small study he used as a library, and a master suite including a large bedroom, twin dressing rooms, and a bathroom with the latest accoutrements. The apartment also contained a large kitchen and separate staff quarters, which were the domain of his housekeeper, Mrs. Trewick, and her husband, Trewick, who acted as general manservant. The middle-aged couple had been with Montague for nearly twenty years and knew his habits and requirements to a T.

He walked into the sitting room, his footsteps faintly echoing.

"Dinner's ready and waiting, sir!" Mrs. Trewick sang from the kitchen. "Just take your seat at the table and Trewick will bring it out."

Montague smiled and did as he was bid. He exchanged the usual comments with Trewick as the man served the three courses of succulent and substantial fare; at the completion of the meal, as he usually did, Montague sent his compliments to Mrs. Trewick, which, as it always did, pleased Trewick no end.

In pleasant accord, he and his staff parted for the night, the pair to retreat to their quarters while he ambled into the study, then, book in hand, wandered into the sitting room, where the fire Trewick had stoked blazed, eradicating the chill of the evening.

Sinking into his favorite of the pair of armchairs angled before the fire, Montague reached for the small tantalus that sat on the side table. He poured himself a small glass of whisky, a drop he'd grown partial to since taking over the Earl of Glencrae's accounts, then sat back and sipped.

For several moments, he simply sat, book closed in his lap, glass poised in one hand, and stared into the flames.

And heard again in his mind the contrast in sound between when his staff left the office for their homes, and when he did.

When his staff left, their expectations of pleasure, of simple joy, and their confidence in finding those things when they returned to their hearths, homes, and loved ones rang in their voices. When he left, all was silent, even within him.

Because he didn't have anyone, no one dear to him, so he only had a house, not a home.

That, he knew, was the critical difference, and while it hadn't previously bothered him—not over the long years during which he had striven to build his firm to its present preeminence—the silence, the emptiness of his house, the loneliness, all reached him now.

He'd achieved his goals, and more, but the triumph seemed hollow.

After a moment, his gaze drifted, coming to rest on the empty armchair opposite. Unbidden, his mind supplied an image of Violet Matcham sitting there, the firelight glinting in her dark hair, her head tilted with that subtle grace that was peculiarly hers, a gentle smile curving her lips, lighting her blue eyes.

Montague considered the image for several minutes, then shook his head, dismissed the dream, opened his book, and settled to read.

Across London, in Albemarle Street in Mayfair, Penelope Adair sat at the foot of her dinner table and exchanged a meaningful look with her friend, Griselda Stokes, then both ladies turned their eyes upon the two gentlemen sharing the table with them.

"There must be *some* interesting case we can assist you with," Penelope declared.

Barnaby Adair, seated at the head of the table, glanced at Basil Stokes, friend and colleague, then Barnaby straightened, negligently waved, and nonchalantly said, "There really isn't much by way of 'crimes-to-investigate' plaguing the ton and Scotland Yard at this particular time."

Aware of the oblique qualifications built into that statement, Penelope regarded her spouse through narrowing eyes. "It needn't be anything expressly to do with the ton—you aren't about to tell me that there aren't any crimes to investigate in London at all, are you?"

"Hardly!" The spontaneous reply came from Stokes, lounging in his chair. He immediately recovered and stated, "However, Barnaby's correct in that there are no drawing room dramas, so to speak, presently unsolved."

"The Crimmins affair was the last," Barnaby said. "But since then—over the summer and into the autumn—all has been quiet in Mayfair."

"I believe," Griselda said, her soft voice a contrast to the bolder, more confident tones of the others; of the four of them, she spoke the least, but when she did, the others listened, as they did now, "that what Penelope meant to imply was that the insights she and I can offer, and the investigative skills we possess, would almost certainly be of value in investigations over a wider social arena."

Penelope nodded. "Well said." Shifting her gaze to their husbands, she added, "Dealing with the infants—with Oliver and Megan—absorbed us entirely for the first months, but now that the pair have grown to the point of no longer requiring our attention hour by hour, both Griselda and I need"—she airily waved—"something to engage us, to challenge us, mentally at least, and provide greater stimulation of the cerebral sort."

Stokes frowned, rather blackly. "What do other ladies with small children do for 'cerebral stimulation'?"

Penelope's nose tipped upward. "Other ladies are not us."

"Indubitably," Barnaby muttered, quietly enough that only Stokes would hear.

Penelope still narrowed her eyes at him. After a moment, she said, "Helping to protect Henrietta when she had to go with that blackguard Affry in order to find James reminded us, Griselda and me, of what we were missing—of what we most enjoyed doing other than being with our children."

"And," Griselda murmured, "you should remember that us assisting you, even in the minor way we do, does help us understand what you, both of you, are absorbed with, and why the pair of you are so devoted to apprehending villains, be they lord or servant."

Silence fell as both men considered their wives, then Stokes heaved a sigh and straightened from his slouch. "The fact is that there truly is no investigation currently underway in which we might benefit from your help."

Penelope regarded him, her dark brown gaze, as always, unforgivingly direct. "Very well, but if one should arise, you will tell us, won't you?"

A fractional hesitation ensued, then both men heaved tiny sighs.

Stokes merely tipped his head in resignation.

Barnaby met Penelope's gaze and said, "When the next case in which the pair of you might be able to assist us arises, we—all four of us—will discuss the possibilities then."

"Is there truly no case we might *possibly* help with?" Penelope trailed across their bedroom to the window overlooking the side garden. She and Barnaby had lived in this house for eighteen months now, and she truly considered it her home. Hers. Just as he was.

Reaching the window, she turned and watched him walk slowly across the room to her. He still moved with the same predatory grace he had always possessed; the sight of him still brought a smile to her heart, even if sometimes, as now, she strove to keep the expression from her lips.

He halted before her, frowning slightly as he studied her uptilted face. "There truly is nothing. Stokes has been assisting with those murders about the docks—and, trust me, none of those are in any way linked with endeavors you and Griselda know anything about. And as you already know, because of the dearth in interesting crimes, I've been working with my father on his various political machinations." Barnaby's lips twisted in a reluctantly rueful smile. "And although I would love to have you help me with that, you know you're hopeless with political machinations—you're so direct you scare the marks away."

Penelope waved dismissively. "Politicking is such a waste of time."

"I rest my case." Barnaby reached for her, sliding his hands around her narrow waist and drawing her to him.

She came readily. After more than eighteen months of marriage, the magic was still there—the delicious jolt to the senses, the resulting rapid rise of desire.

Of a hunger that, through growing accustomed to being sated, had become even more potent.

Sinking against him, spreading her hands on his chest, she looked into his face. And the magic—the sudden focus, the heightening of tension as anticipation sparked, the sharpening of their senses as their intentions aligned—gripped. As he spread his hands over her silk-clad back, she tilted her head, searched his eyes. "You're going to try to distract me, aren't you?"

His lips quirked. "It had crossed my mind." Lowering his head, he brushed his lips over hers, lingered just long enough to hear her breath catch, to sense her hunger leap to meet his, then murmured, "Are you going to let me?"

She pushed her hands up over his shoulders, wound her arms about his neck. "By all means—you have my permission to try."

Just don't expect to succeed. Barnaby heard the words she didn't say—the challenge she didn't utter—but for his own peace of mind, he had to try.

He gave it his best shot.

Drawing her into a heated exchange, into a heated melding of their mouths, an increasingly ravenous duel of lips and tongues that swelled and grew to consume them both, he orchestrated the moments, with consummate skill drew each fragile instant out, until they were both panting and yearning, hungry and desperate.

Clothes were shed, but by his dictate. Wanton and delighted, she held to her permissive stance and let him lead, let him manage the reins as he would and devote himself—to the top of his bent—to his aim of distracting her.

Utterly. Completely.

In this world, and on that other plane.

His hands roved her body and made her arch and moan.

He allowed her—nay, encouraged her, knowing the exercise to be enthralling to her—to explore his body and fill her senses with him, and she seized the chance and immersed herself in their passion.

Together they pushed and strove to extend the long moments of worship, of reverence and delight, of pleasure and fraught joy, but the escalating beat of passionate need could not be forever denied.

They came together in a rush of fire and heat, the sensual cataclysm of bodies and souls so familiar, so gloriously reliable yet never to be taken for granted.

Joined and urgent, now desperate in their need, together they rode, together they climbed, together they reached the pinnacle's peak where ecstasy found them, wracked and bound them, then flung them into the void . . . to where love lay waiting to wrap them in bliss, and cushion them, cocoon them, as they spiraled back to earth.

To the haven of each other's arms, to the comforting sound of each other's ragged breaths, of each other's thudding hearts.

To the soul-easing closeness of their intimate embrace.

Later, when they'd disengaged and settled in the bed, and Penelope snuggled deeper into his arms, Barnaby brushed a kiss to her temple. "I promise to tell you when next Stokes and I have some case you and Griselda can help with."

He felt Penelope's lips curve against his skin. Blindly, she patted his chest. "Thank you."

Her limbs lost what little tension they'd regained; he listened as she sank into sated slumber.

Somewhere amid the glory, reality had broken through and he'd realized that he and Stokes had no option but to find a solution to their ladies' need—to re-involve them in suitable investigations as and when such investigations arose.

It was that, or have them striking out on their own—and he didn't need to think to know what he thought of that. The sudden lurching of his heart at the mere idea provided all the incentive he needed.

So he would do as he'd promised.

But he didn't have to like it.

Chapter 3

Violet walked into the kitchen the next morning to find Tilly already busy setting out Lady
Halstead's breakfast tray. Violet smiled. "Good morning." Scanning the tray, she added, "Nearly ready?"

She routinely accompanied Tilly upstairs to wake
Lady Halstead and hold the door, then help her ladyship sit up in bed.

"A good morning to you, too," Tilly sang back.
"And yes, almost there. Just the toast—ah, thank you,
Cook, dear."

Tilly was a tallish, raw-boned, middle-aged woman,
her brown-gray hair pulled back in a neat bun, her
large hands capable as they set the two slices of toast
into the toast rack, then grasped the tray's handles.
Tilly hefted the tray. Perennially cheerful, she'd been

with Lady Halstead for decades, far longer than Violet or Cook. Looking at Violet, Tilly beamed. "Lead the way."

Exchanging a quick smile and a good morning with Cook—a short, rotund, older woman with corkscrew red curls bound back with a white scarf—Violet held open the kitchen door, waved Tilly through, then followed and, as directed, took the lead through the hallway and up the stairs.

Tilly trudged heavily but happily at her heels. "Hope her ladyship slept a trifle better last night."

"Indeed. I'm hoping that Mr. Montague will return soon and set her mind at rest. She's still fretting over those odd payments." Violet didn't hesitate over mentioning the payments to Tilly; Lady Halstead herself had shared the information with her longtime maid.

Reaching the first floor, Violet went along the corridor to Lady Halstead's door. She tapped. "Lady Halstead?" No answer came, but that wasn't uncommon. Despite her sometimes disturbed slumber, Lady Halstead adhered to a rigid regimen and expected to be woken and supplied with her breakfast tray at eight o'clock sharp. Sharing a resigned look with Tilly—if it had been left to them, they would have let the old lady sleep—Violet opened the door and went in.

As usual, the room was drenched in gloomy shadow; Violet crossed to the window to draw back the heavy curtains.

Tilly followed Violet over the threshold but halted just inside the door, waiting patiently until she could better see.

Violet smoothly drew one curtain, then the other, wide and turned to the bed. "Good morning, your ladyship."

Violet halted, not quite sure what she was seeing.

Tilly, taller and closer to the bed, had a clearer view. "Oh, my God!"

A sharp rattle of crockery broke the silence as Tilly shook and the cup on the tray rattled. "Oh, my God. *Oh, my God.*" In a fluster, Tilly swung around, saw the tallboy, and rushed to set the tray down upon it. Then she whirled and hurried to the bed—just as Violet did the same on the other side.

Stunned, shocked, barely able to breathe, Violet looked down at Lady Halstead. The old lady's eyes were closed, but her mouth was open, her jaws wide, as if she'd been shouting. Or screaming.

Her arms, Violet saw, were oddly splayed, and her hands lay lax on the covers, gnarled fingers crooked, as if she'd been clutching, seizing. Her legs, too, weak though they'd been, had churned beneath the sheets.

That Lady Halstead was dead Violet did not doubt. But her ladyship hadn't died peacefully.

Tilly put Violet's thoughts into words. "I knew she'd go, and probably soon, but I didn't think she'd go like this."

Violet forced herself to look, to see what was before her. "Tilly—this isn't how she should look, is it? Not if she went quietly in her sleep."

Tilly audibly gulped. Her eyes locked on her mistress's face, she murmured, "You're thinking the same as I am. She was murdered, wasn't she?"

"Look at the top pillow. No—don't touch. But see how it's been stuffed under her head? That's why her head is at that odd angle. But she never sleeps with that many pillows—she wouldn't have put it there herself." Violet glanced at the chair by the bed. "When I left her last night, that pillow was on the chair."

"We have to call the doctor." Tilly wrapped her arms tightly about herself. "That's what you're supposed to do with a death these days."

Violet's wits were whirling, but she knew well enough how matters would proceed. "If we just call the doctor"—looking up, she met Tilly's wide eyes—"he'll say she was old, that she died in her sleep, because he'll know the family will be furious if he declares this a murder."

Tilly blinked, then her jaw firmed and she nodded. "Aye, that he will, weak weasel that he is. And none of the family will care, will they?"

"No, they won't. They won't bother about getting justice for Lady Halstead—won't care about finding her murderer. All they'll care about is the will and the estate."

"Getting their share of it—you don't need to tell me. She's known for years they've just been waiting for her to die."

"Exactly. They'd seemed to be waiting patiently enough, but now . . ." Violet looked down at the gentle old lady she'd come to love. "We can't let her murderer get away." She glanced at Tilly. "I don't think I could live with myself if I . . . just let this be swept under the carpet."

"Nor me." Tilly paused, then asked, "So what do we do? Send a boy for the police? Chances are they'll just have us send for the doctor anyway, and he'll say what you said, and it'll all come to nothing."

Violet did not know where her certainty sprang from, did not know on what it was based, but she had no doubt whatever about her tack. "We send for Mr. Montague. Lady Halstead gave him a letter of authority—it's reasonable for us to consult him over this. We're only females, after all, and our sex is known to panic." She looked at Tilly. "So we're in a panic and we don't know what to do—so we'll summon Mr. Montague, because we know that her ladyship only very recently put her faith, and her trust, in him."

Tilly blinked, then slowly nodded. "But will he know what's best to do next?"

"Yes." Violet thought of the solid assurance with which Montague moved through the world. "I'm sure of it."

Tilly nodded more decisively. "Right, then—you write a note, and I'll go and fetch a boy to take it." Tilly glanced at her dead mistress, reached out, gently stroked the back of one crooked hand, then, jaw tightening, raised her head, turned, and headed for the door.

Her gaze on Lady Halstead, Violet slowly straightened, then, more slowly, more lingeringly, mimicked Tilly's loving gesture, then followed the maid from the room.

Violet wrote the note in the sitting room, and was still sitting there in a daze when Montague arrived.

Rising to answer the door, she glanced at the clock on the mantelpiece. It was barely nine o'clock; he must have raced to have got there so quickly.

Opening the front door, she registered the concern vivid in his face.

"What's happened?" His gaze raced over her features, returning to her eyes. "Are you all right?"

"Lady Halstead is dead." Violet heard her voice say the words, intonation flat, and she finally accepted it as real.

"Dead?" Montague's features registered his shock. "But . . ." He searched her face, her eyes. "Did she die peacefully?"

Violet drew herself up, drew breath, and said, "I—we, Tilly and I—don't think so." She stepped back. "Please, come in."

Stepping over the threshold, Montague felt an unexpected urge to take her in his arms, to comfort her. She was pale, her expression, judging from their previous encounters, uncharacteristically closed in.

Brittle. Fragile. In need of help.

His help.

He bludgeoned his brain into functioning. "Who else have you notified?"

Turning from closing the door, she met his eyes. "No one—not yet. We know we're supposed to notify the doctor, and I'm sure he will immediately send word to her family, but . . ." She paused, then, raising her head, went on, "He—Doctor Milborne—will be more interested in serving the interests of the family, the interests of the living rather than the dead."

Montague nodded curtly. "Yes. I see." He glanced at the stairs. "Where is she?"

"In her bed upstairs." Violet waved him on, following as he strode for the staircase. "She went to bed last night as usual. Nothing seemed amiss, nothing at all. Tilly and I went to wake her this morning, as we always do, taking up her breakfast tray and . . . we found her."

Reaching the head of the stairs, Montague halted. "Tilly?"

"Lady Halstead's maid—Tilly has been with her ladyship for more than twenty years."

When he nodded and glanced around, Violet indicated a door along the corridor. "In there."

Suppressing the impulse to ask why she thought Lady Halstead's death was suspicious—was murder, even if she hadn't used the word—Montague strode for the door. "Did anyone—you, or Tilly, or anyone else—move anything?"

"No. Other than opening the curtains and placing the tray on the tallboy, we haven't moved or changed a thing." Violet paused, then added as he opened the door, "It's painfully obvious she's dead."

Montague walked into the room and saw what she meant. He halted a yard from the foot of the bed and surveyed the scene. A bare minute passed, then he said, "I concur. This was not a natural"—*much less peaceful*—"death."

Violet had halted nearer the door. In a small voice, she asked, "So what should we do?" When he turned to face her, she nodded toward the old lady lying in the bed. "For her." Meeting his eyes, voice strengthening, she stated, "We—Tilly, Cook, and I—want to see justice done. We want to see her murderer caught and held to account. She was a gentle old lady. She never harmed a soul. She might have been old, might even have been dying, but she didn't deserve to die like this."

Looking into her eyes, seeing the resolve behind the soft blue, he stated, "In that case, while we must at some point call for her doctor, we should first summon the police."

As matters transpired, Doctor Milborne arrived first.

After leaving Lady Halstead's room, Montague had gone downstairs with Violet. In the kitchen, he had consulted with her, Tilly, and Cook, then he'd written an urgent note to Inspector Basil Stokes at Scotland Yard, sending it off via a local boy Tilly and Cook often engaged to run errands. Montague had assisted Stokes in several cases over recent years; he'd felt confident Stokes would return the favor.

They had then waited for as long as they'd dared—for as long as they would reasonably be able to explain—before dispatching a summons penned by Violet to the doctor. That note had been sent via the first boy's brother at eleven o'clock.

The doctor knocked on the door half an hour later.

Subdued and somber, Violet greeted the man, saying only that she and Tilly believed that Lady Halstead had died during the night.

Standing behind Violet in the shadows of the front hall, Montague assessed the doctor; he was in his late thirties and, from the cut of his coat, appeared to be prospering.

Milborne assumed a suitably grave mien. "Of course, we knew this day would come. Nevertheless, you have my condolences, Miss Matcham. You must be overwrought."

"As to that, sir . . ." Violet paused to draw in a breath that wasn't entirely steady. Pressing her hands together, she tipped her head toward the stairs. "We believe we need you to view the body and give your opinion as to how her ladyship died."

"Indeed, indeed." Milborne glanced at the stairs. "In her room, is she?" He headed for the stairs. "I know the way."

Violet and Montague ignored the implied dismissal and followed Milborne up the stairs; they were at his heels when he walked into the bedroom.

Milborne checked at the sight of Lady Halstead's body, but then recovered and, rather more slowly, continued to the side of the bed.

Thinking, Montague decided; Milborne was thinking hard about how best to handle the situation—about which avenue promised the greatest benefit to him.

Milborne looked down at her ladyship's face, jaw hinged wide, mouth agape, then he reached for her wrist and made a show of checking for a pulse there, and then at the side of the old lady's neck. Then he raised her lids, first one, then the other, but he only gave a cursory glance at the staring eyes thus revealed.

He was going through the motions.

Violet felt certain her and Tilly's assumptions about the doctor were correct; he would do what was best for the family.

Sure enough, after that most superficial of examinations, he sighed and turned to face her. "It seems her heart gave out. To be expected, at her age."

Especially if someone held a pillow over her face while she screamed and screamed. Violet dragged in a breath. Wrapping her arms about her, she swallowed the words and glanced at Montague. They'd agreed it would be unwise to try to force their opinions or conclusions on Milborne, but . . .

Montague met her gaze, almost imperceptibly nodded in support. Then he looked at Milborne. "Am I to take it you intend to declare this a natural death?"

Milborne blinked, shifting his attention to Montague. "Well, in the circumstances . . ." Then he frowned. "I'm sorry—you are?"

"Heathcote Montague, of Montague and Son, in the City." Montague said nothing more; they needed to delay Milborne, to keep him from issuing a death certificate declaring the death natural, until help, in the form of Stokes, arrived. Stokes would take one look at this scene and know there was nothing natural about the manner of Lady Halstead's passing.

Milborne's frown grew more puzzled. "I'm unclear as to what your interest in Lady Halstead's demise might be."

"Her ladyship recently engaged me as a financial consultant with wide-ranging authority to delve into all matters concerning her situation." Montague let Milborne puzzle over that for a moment, then, when the man was clearly searching for the correct words with which to frame his next question, added, "Given the circumstances surrounding the initiation of my consultancy, and given the scope of the formal letter of authority Lady Halstead enacted, I believe her demise most definitely falls within my purview."

Milborne blinked, now clearly uneasy. "I . . . see."

Meaning he no longer had any idea of what was going on, or which way he should bend. Milborne glanced again at the bed, at the frail body lying in it.

A heavy knock sounded on the front door.

Montague looked at Violet.

"Tilly will get it," she said.

That Tilly had, indeed, opened the front door was immediately apparent as a rumble of male voices in the hall downstairs reached them.

Several male voices. Stokes had brought others—at least two others—with him.

Straining his ears, Montague caught an inflection, a certain deep drawl, one rather more sophisticated than Stokes's raspy growl, and wondered . . . suddenly hoped.

Sure enough, when, a bare minute later, Stokes walked into the room, the tall, elegant figure of Barnaby Adair appeared behind him.

If knowing Stokes had arrived had brought relief, Adair's coming with him meant salvation was assured.

Violet watched the large, dark-haired, and dark-featured man pause just inside the doorway, his open greatcoat hanging from broad shoulders, his eyes—slate gray and oddly piercing—taking in the entire bedroom and all in it in one single, comprehensive glance. That glance ended on Montague, and the man inclined his head.

"Montague."

Montague nodded back. "Inspector Stokes." With one hand, Montague indicated Violet. "This is Miss Matcham, the late Lady Halstead's companion of many years. And this"—Montague turned to the doctor—"is Doctor Milborne, who, I understand, has been overseeing her ladyship's health for several years."

"Ah—yes, about five years . . ." Milborne looked confused; he glanced from Stokes to Montague. "Did you say 'Inspector'?"

"Yes—he was referring to me." The dark-haired man—Stokes—moved toward the bed. "Inspector Basil Stokes of Scotland Yard. We"—Stokes glanced back at his companion, who had curly blond hair, was most definitely a gentleman by his dress, and was lingering in the doorway—"have reason to wish to satisfy ourselves as to the nature of her ladyship's death." The slate gray gaze returned to pin Milborne. "So, Doctor, what say you? Is this a natural death, or something the Yard needs to be aware of?"

"Ah . . ." Milborne was out of his depth and floundering; he patently did not know which way to leap. "I . . . ah, had thought it might be, *could* be, purely the result of old age. I mean, although she appears to have struggled, well, she might have been gasping her last, as it were, and—"

"Were her eyes closed, her lids lowered, when she was found?"

The question, uttered in an urbane voice that instantly commanded attention—and respect—came from the tall, blond man who had accompanied Stokes. Strolling into the room, he politely inclined his head to Violet, nodded briefly—as to a friend—to Montague, then glanced at Milborne, before halting by the bed and looking down at Lady Halstead's face.

After an instant, the man glanced up at Milborne, then at Violet. "The Honorable Barnaby Adair. I'm a consultant to the Yard, and often work with Stokes. Especially"—his distinctly blue gaze returned to Lady Halstead's face—"in cases involving members of society."

It took Milborne another moment to digest that, then some of his tension left him. "In that case—"

Violet spoke over him. "Her eyes were shut—the lids lowered—when we found her." At Adair's cocked brow, she elaborated, "Tilly, her ladyship's maid, and I came up to wake her as we usually did, and found her." Violet nodded at the bed. "Just like that. We didn't move her at all."

"Excellent." Adair crouched and looked at Lady Halstead's face from close quarters, then angled a glance at Milborne. "Any bleeding in the eyes?"

Milborne shifted. "A little. But she's old, and—" He broke off, then bent, raised one of the lids, and looked again. When he straightened, one could see that he'd paled. "Yes. There's unnatural bleeding in the eyes."

"Hmm." Adair slowly straightened. "That's usually a sign of suffocation, isn't it?"

Milborne's lips tightened, but he nodded. "Yes."

Adair glanced at Violet. "Was there anything else in the room when you found her—or anything you've noticed that's missing?"

Violet stepped forward and looked at Lady Halstead. "The only thing that's wrong, that's out of place, is that pillow. The one that's been pushed under her head. Her ladyship never slept with that many pillows, but that one was left on that chair by the bed"—she nodded at the armchair—"because she needed it behind her when she sat up."

"So," Adair all but purred, "when you and her lady-ship's maid arrived with her breakfast tray, had it been a normal morning, you would have found Lady Halstead lying asleep on one less pillow, and the pillow presently beneath her head would have been waiting on the chair for you to place at her back when she sat up." Adair slanted a quietly encouraging look at Violet. "Is that correct, Miss Matcham?"

Meeting his eyes, Violet raised her chin and nodded. "That's precisely correct, Mr. Adair."

Adair glanced at Stokes. "I believe that settles it." He looked at Milborne. "So, Doctor, what's your verdict?"

Milborne looked grim but dutifully intoned, "Death by suffocation by persons unknown."

Violet glanced at Stokes and saw him smile a positively sharklike smile.

"Murder, then," Stokes said.

Milborne grimaced. "As you will have it so, but I warn you the family aren't going to like it."

Stokes's face darkened and his response came in a dark growl. "*I* don't like it and I'm not even related. But I'm sure you're not saying that the Halsteads are the sort of family who would happily sweep murder under the carpet in order to avoid a little inconvenience?"

Milborne shifted and reached for his black bag. "No. Of course not." Lifting the bag, he moved to pass around Stokes. "If you have no further need of me, I'll go downstairs and write the certificate, then take my leave."

Stokes watched him go. As Milborne passed through the doorway, Stokes narrowed his eyes and raised his voice. "Just make sure you send the certificate to the Yard."

"Right, then." Basil Stokes sank into a chair midway down one side of the dining table in Lady Halstead's Lowndes Street house. Barnaby drew out the chair to his left as Montague, having seen Miss Violet Matcham to the chair opposite Stokes, settled into the chair opposite Barnaby.

Stokes regarded Violet Matcham with no expression but with a degree of sympathy. He was not a naturally empathetic man, yet it required little insight to comprehend that Miss Matcham had been sincerely fond of her late employer. Her eyes were red-rimmed, and the tip of her nose was a trifle pink, but she was making every effort to remain calm and composed. Something Stokes appreciated.

Once the doctor had quit the scene, Stokes had sent one of the constables he'd brought with him back to the Yard to summon their medical man to take charge of the body. He'd left the other constable on guard in the room, watching over the deceased and any evidence yet to come to light.

Stokes and Barnaby had accompanied Miss Matcham and Montague downstairs to the kitchen, and there had met the other two members of the small household—her ladyship's maid and the cook. Both had exhibited a mixture of alarm and resolution; if Stokes was any judge—and he was—the alarm was caused more by the unexpected necessity of having anything to do with a crime and the police, while the resolution stemmed from the same devotion that was keeping Violet Matcham's spine poker straight.

They'd all liked the old lady and wanted her murderer caught.

None of the three women showed even the vaguest sign of guilt, nor even any hint of an uneasy conscience.

Which suited Stokes; he was quite happy to cross them off his list of suspects. Although he would interview each of them, his focus would be on learning everything they knew that might be relevant.

Leaning forward, resting his forearms on the polished mahogany, he took a moment to order his thoughts, then fixed his gaze on Miss Matcham's face. "I understand you've been with her ladyship for several years."

She nodded. "Yes. Eight years this August."

"And before?"

"I was companion to Lady Ogilvie in Bath. I was with her for five years—from soon after my father died."

"And your father was?"

"The Reverend Edward Matcham of Woodborough— it's in the Vale of Pewsey." She hesitated, then added, "My mother had died several years previously, and I was left to find my way."

Stokes appreciated her candor. "Thank you. With regard to her ladyship's murder, the first question I must ask is whether you have any reason to suppose that anyone—anyone at all—might have wished the old lady dead."

Violet hesitated, very aware of the two shrewd gazes trained on her—Stokes's slate gray, hard and uncompromising, and Adair's quietly observant blue—then she lifted her chin and firmly stated, "I have no reason to suspect that anyone bore her ladyship any degree of animosity. I'm not aware of any direct quarrel, recent or otherwise, much less any clash of the sort that might lead to murder. However"—she glanced at Montague, seated alongside her—"as Mr. Montague can explain in greater detail than I, Lady Halstead had become . . . concerned over a matter of unidentified payments into her bank account." Returning her gaze to Stokes's dark-featured face, she went on, "Over the past week, her ladyship had grown increasingly intent on learning what those payments were about—where they came from, who the money really belonged to, and why whoever it was was using her account."

Stokes looked at Montague. "That's the reason her ladyship gave you that letter?" Montague had already shown him the letter of authority Lady Halstead had written and signed; Stokes would lay odds Montague himself had dictated it—the letter gave him virtually unlimited authority to involve himself in Lady Halstead's affairs. It was one reason why Montague was sitting at the table now; even had Stokes wished to exclude him, he wouldn't have been able to. As it happened, given it had been Montague who had summoned him, and Stokes already knew the man, knew his caliber, Stokes was very happy to have him present—another pair of observant eyes and ears to call on.

Montague nodded. "I needed the scope so I could freely investigate this matter of the odd payments into her account."

Montague opened his mouth to continue, but Stokes held up a staying hand. "One moment." Looking at Violet Matcham, he said, "I know what you're going to tell me, but I have to ask. No tensions between yourself and her ladyship, or between her ladyship and her maid or cook?"

The look he got was predictably frosty. "No." After a heartbeat's pause, Miss Matcham added, "This was a very peaceful and contented household." The past tense made it sound like a eulogy.

Stokes nodded and looked at Montague. "Tell me about these odd payments."

Montague did, in concise and strictly chronological fashion, commencing from the moment he'd been approached by Violet Matcham on behalf of Lady Halstead. Stokes questioned how that had come about—how Lady Halstead had chosen Montague, someone she hadn't previously dealt with. Consequently, they—Stokes, Adair, and Montague, too—learned of the enterprising notion the old lady had had of asking the question of *The Times*'s columnist.

Montague stared at the lady seated beside him. "So it was you who sent that question to *The Times*?"

"On behalf of Lady Halstead." Miss Matcham colored. "I do apologize for any embarrassment or inconvenience the article might have caused, but it was the only way we could think of to quickly and reliably learn who would be best to approach over those odd payments." She looked at Stokes. "Lady Halstead had grown seriously agitated and was in dire need of reassurance, and because of young Mr. Runcorn's age, and therefore his inexperience, she didn't feel able to place her faith in his findings alone."

Montague had explained about Runcorn, of Runcorn and Son, her ladyship's man-of-business.

Barnaby nodded. "I can understand that." He met Stokes's eye. "Old ladies can get distinctly querulous."

Having met the old ladies to whom Barnaby was alluding, Stokes suppressed a snort and returned his gaze across the table. "So it's possible that her ladyship was murdered because of her sudden and, by all accounts quite dogged, interest in these odd payments." He looked from Miss Matcham to Montague. "So who knew about her ladyship's concerns? Who had she told about the payments?"

Violet Matcham frowned. "Me. Tilly. And I suspect Cook would have heard me and Tilly talking."

"In my office," Montague said, "only I know the reason for Lady Halstead consulting me. I haven't confided in anyone else. Runcorn, of course, knows, and so does his clerk, Pringle, but there's only the two of them there." Montague frowned, clearly checking his memory, then stated, "I can't think of anyone else who would know. I haven't yet inquired directly of the bank, and Runcorn had done no more than ask for the statements, which is nothing out of the ordinary and shouldn't have occasioned any alarm."

Stokes met Montague's gaze. "Are you sure Runcorn himself isn't responsible?"

Montague returned his regard. "Professionally, that's not a question I would prefer to answer, but if you insist that I reply yea or nay, then I would have to give it as my opinion that Runcorn is as honest as the day is long."

Violet Matcham nodded. "That would be my reading of him, too. He was quite sure, to begin with, that the payments must have come from some investment."

Stokes grimaced. "If her ladyship's interest in these odd payments is the motive behind her murder, that doesn't leave us with many possible suspects."

Violet Matcham's expression blanked, then her eyes widened. "No, wait—all the Halsteads knew."

Barnaby straightened. "Her ladyship's family?"

"They were here for dinner—that's a regular monthly event." Violet paused, then said, "But I have to qualify—Lady Halstead didn't mention, not in any way, the odd payments, but she did say that she was having her affairs and those of the estate put in order so that when she eventually died, there would be no questions concerning the estate."

A second passed, then Barnaby asked, "I take it that Lady Halstead's will, such as it might be, will essentially bring her life-tenancy of Sir Hugo's estate to a close and allow execution of the provisions already stipulated in Sir Hugo's will?"

Violet glanced at Montague. "That is my understanding."

Montague arched his brows. "I would be exceedingly surprised if that wasn't the case. From all that I've seen and been given to understand, Lady Halstead had little real wealth of her own. As one might expect, the majority of the funds and all property belong to the estate, the disposal of which will be governed by her husband's will."

"So," Barnaby concluded, "her will can't hold any surprises, at least not with respect to the estate. Even if she'd changed her will, she can't affect anything that matters."

"I'd gathered," Violet said, "that the estate is to be divided equally between the four children."

Stokes grimaced. "So there's unlikely to be any motive arising out of the will—at least, not directly. However, if the person responsible for these odd payments heard that the estate's affairs were going to be reviewed, it's possible—depending on just what those payments are—that they might have felt, for some reason, that it was better for Lady Halstead to die now, before any investigation could get properly underway."

"I should point out," Montague said, "that having studied these payments as far as I've thus far been able, my conclusion at this point is that they're being made in order to conceal funds—and as we all know, the principal reason for concealing funds is that they derive from some illegal activity."

Stokes was nodding. "So the villain, hearing that the payments are likely to be uncovered—" Breaking off, he looked at Violet. "Neither Lady Halstead nor you mentioned the payments to the family?"

When Violet shook her head, Stokes continued, "So there was no reason for the villain to realize that the existence of the payments had already been uncovered. With that in mind, learning that her ladyship was about to order a presumably extensive review of her affairs and those of the estate, the villain—wishing to conceal the evidence of his illegal activities—therefore had a strong motive to murder her ladyship."

They all thought that through; no one disagreed.

"And," Barnaby said, "if the villain is a member of the family—and we should remember that a murder of this sort usually is committed by a family member—that also explains something else that's been bothering me." He glanced around the table, meeting the others' eyes. "How did the murderer get into the house? Is there any evidence of a break-in, of a door or window being forced?"

Violet blinked. "Not that I know of." She glanced at Stokes, who was already getting to his feet.

"I'll have my constable take a look around the house, have him check all the windows and doors. And while he's doing that"—Stokes caught Violet's gaze—"you can tell us all about the Halsteads."

Chapter 4

At two o'clock that afternoon, along with Stokes and Adair, Montague took one of the four chairs arranged about the head of the dining table in the Lowndes Street house. Violet, who he had ushered into the room and seated in the chair alongside him, had described the family in detail, guided by questions from Adair, Stokes, and himself.

All three of them had instantly realized the difficulty they would face, the care they would have to exercise in interrogating and investigating a family that included a Member of Parliament and a high-ranking Home Office official, as well as both men's wives. Such men were wont to stand on their dignity and consider themselves above such things as police interrogations, and their wives would almost certainly support them in such a stance.

Consequently, Stokes, Adair, and Montague, aided by Violet's insights, had discussed their best approach and had settled on an exploratory, relatively gentle, first foray.

After learning the structure of the family and confirming that all had been present at the recent dinner, and provided by Violet with a list of names and directions, Stokes had dispatched messages to each family member, stating only that a tragedy had occurred at the Lowndes Street house and Scotland Yard requested their attendance at the house at two o'clock.

When Montague and Violet, followed by Stokes and Adair, had entered the dining room, all of those summoned had already been seated about the table. As Lady Halstead's family took note of Violet's appearance and their hushed whispers died, and they looked—puzzledly, expectantly, and with dawning suspicion—at Stokes, Adair, and himself, Montague found putting names to faces not at all difficult.

Stokes was no doubt discovering the same as he allowed his gaze to sweep the group.

If Montague's assumptions were correct, Wallace Camberly sat to the left nearest the head of the table, with Mortimer Halstead opposite. Both men were middle-aged, but while Camberly bore his years with hawkish grace, Mortimer wore the faintly harried air and quick-to-frown mien favored by many upper-level civil servants who considered their work—and therefore themselves—of supreme importance. Camberly was dressed to project an image of conservative elegance eminently appropriate to a Member of Parliament, while Mortimer Halstead appeared fussily, rigidly correct, the cut of his dark coat lacking the flair that distinguished Camberly's.

Next to each man sat his wife—Cynthia Camberly, née Halstead, alongside Wallace, and Constance Halstead beside Mortimer. Both women were handsome enough, the former more slender than the latter. Both were fashionably turned out, but neither radiated any warmth; their expressions appeared carefully controlled.

Next to Cynthia sat her son, Walter. An idle gentleman, according to Violet twenty-seven years old, Walter Camberly kept his chin sunk in his overblown cravat and otherwise watched and observed the rest of his family in silence. Opposite Walter sat his cousin Hayden Halstead, Mortimer's son, an unremarkable gentleman of twenty-three summers, and beside Hayden sat his equally unremarkable sister, Caroline, just twenty.

Completing the company about the table were Maurice Halstead, who lounged elegantly in the chair beyond his nephew Walter, and William Halstead, who had slumped in the chair at the end of the table with a black look and a faintly curling lip, not-so-subtly distancing himself from his siblings and their children.

As he settled on the chair, Montague found it difficult to imagine any of the three of the younger generation— Walter, Hayden, or Caroline—as their grandmother's murderer; to his eyes, they lacked the requisite gumption. Their elders, however, were a different matter.

And as the constable who had carefully searched the house for signs of how and where the murderer had entered had reported no evidence of any door being forced or window latch being broken or tampered with, the suspicion that it was one of those seated about the table who had held a pillow over Lady Halstead's face had gained considerable weight.

The last to take his seat, Stokes finally did, then baldly stated, "I am Inspector Stokes of Scotland Yard. I regret to inform you that Lady Halstead was found dead this morning." Stokes paused to let the inevitable exclamations roll through the room.

It was instructive to watch the reactions; the initial expressions of shock, of surprise, were all but immediately superseded by expressions of calculation, of speculation and consideration of what Lady Halstead's death might mean for each individual. Although he watched closely, Montague detected no suggestion of sorrow, even of simple sadness; Violet had warned them that the family were a self-centered lot, but even so, he hadn't expected such a comprehensively detached response.

Across Stokes, Montague briefly met Adair's blue eyes and saw the same realization—and the same instinctive disapprobation—reflected there. Then Barnaby looked back at the assembled company, and Montague did, too. If they were correct in their reasoning, then at least one person seated at the table had already known Lady Halstead was dead. Yet given the singular lack of finer feelings on display, search though he did, Montague couldn't say one member of the family was less affected by the news than any other.

Wallace Camberly shifted restlessly. After sharing a glance with his wife, Camberly looked at Stokes and somewhat peevishly remarked, "While that is, indeed, a tragedy, Inspector, I fail to see what interest Scotland Yard might have in this matter."

"As to that, sir, permit me to inform you"—with his head, Stokes indicated all those about the table—"and the rest of those gathered here that Lady Halstead did not die peacefully. She was murdered."

Once again exclamations of shock and surprise rang out, but, as before, it was impossible to label one person's response less convincing than the others. The reactions of all the family members lacked emotional depth; although all seemed genuinely surprised, even shocked, by the news, they displayed no strong emotional link to Lady Halstead. Instead, their thoughts turned immediately to themselves—leaving no simple way to distinguish a murderer who had acted out of self-interest from the rest of the group.

That somewhat shocking superficiality of emotional connection with her ladyship was borne out by the next exchange.

"How did she die?" Constance Halstead asked, her tone making it clear that the question was prompted by curiosity, plus, perhaps, a realization that someone should ask.

Her query, however, was drowned out by her husband's clipped and rather pompous observation, "Be that as it may, Inspector, I am unclear as to who these other gentlemen are, and what their interest in what is plainly a private family tragedy might be."

Stokes looked first at Mrs. Halstead. "Her ladyship was smothered. A pillow was placed over her face while she slept, and held there until she died. Although frail, she struggled, but to no avail."

Montague saw nothing beyond expressions of detached distaste pass across the family's faces at that news.

Shifting his gaze to Mortimer, Stokes smoothly continued, "And as for my colleagues, this"—he gestured to Adair on his right—"is the Honorable Mr. Barnaby Adair, consultant investigator to Scotland Yard." Stokes indicated Montague on his left. "And this is Mr. Montague, of Montague and Son, whom Lady Halstead recently consulted. Mr. Montague holds a letter of authority from Lady Halstead giving him far-reaching powers with regard to her ladyship's financial affairs. I have viewed that letter and found it to be genuine and comprehensive. Consequently, in this matter, Mr. Montague will be an observer, in effect nominated by Lady Halstead herself."

That news caused puzzlement and minor consternation as the family decided how they should react. Noting the assessing glances thrown his way, Montague felt certain that had Stokes not confirmed his good standing, his presence would have been challenged.

William Halstead, slouching deeper in his chair, his hands in his pockets, his dark eyes, his entire expression, cynically dour, drawled, "It seems Mama was more farsighted than any of us knew."

Violet had described William as the family's pariah; his appearance suggested he relished the position. His dark suit had once been of good quality, but it was now irretrievably creased and showed patches shiny with

wear; his jaw was shaven, but roughly, his eyes somewhat sunken, his lips appearing more likely to twist in
a sneer than lift in a smile.

Viewed against the strictly conservative façade the
rest of the family clearly took pains to project, William
stood out. Stood alone.

The heads of all the rest of his family had swung
William's way, but after an instant of observing him,
all returned to looking at each other, then, almost as
one, they looked at Stokes, Adair, and Montague.
Experienced at assessing clients' reactions, Montague
understood that the consensus was that the family
had more pressing matters to contend with than his
presence.

Cynthia, Lady Halstead's second child and only
daughter, fixed her gaze on Stokes and rather chillingly
inquired, "Are you *certain*, Inspector, that my mother
was murdered? Could she not merely have died by
some"—Cynthia waved—"misadventure?"

"She was old and frail, after all," Constance
Halstead put in. "Are you certain she didn't simply
stop breathing?"

As expected, the family would much rather her
ladyship's death wasn't declared a murder.

"Both Lady Halstead's doctor, who was summoned
to attend, and the police surgeon concur." Stokes

paused, then definitively stated, "There is no doubt whatever that her ladyship was murdered."

Cynthia's pinching lips testified to her irritation, but she said nothing more.

Constance grimaced and sat back.

"That being the case, Inspector, what progress has been made in apprehending the villain?" The question came from Maurice Halstead, according to Violet and all appearances the black-sheep-cum-rake-cum-roué of the family.

Maurice's question, unsurprisingly, focused the attention of the rest of the family. They all looked to Stokes with varying degrees of haughty demand.

Stokes's expression remained stoically uninformative. "Our investigations have only just begun. I called you here as a formal courtesy, to ensure you learned of the murder firsthand. We will be pursuing several avenues, and will speak with you all in due course." Stokes had decided to postpone asking for alibis, explaining that he would rather each family member had a chance to concoct one, as a fabricated alibi, which the police usually found relatively easy to break, was a surer indication of guilt than the absence of an alibi.

"But you must have some idea," Maurice pressed. "You said you had 'avenues' to follow." His gaze shifted to rest heavily—meaningfully—on Violet. "It seems somewhat far-fetched to imagine some blackguard just happened to choose this house to break into and kill an old lady, apparently for no reason."

Stokes showed his teeth. "Indeed. But equally, at present, we have no reason to suspect any particular person—nor to discount anyone, either." He sent a raking gaze around the table. "My immediate question for everyone here is whether you know of or in any way suspect anyone of bearing ill will toward Lady Halstead. For any reason whatever."

Silence ensued, then the Halsteads and Camberlys looked at each other; brows rose, but no one spoke.

Stokes nodded. "Very well. I will take that as a negative—that none of you know of any reason to suspect anyone of Lady Halstead's murder."

A fussy, civil-service frown had appeared on Mortimer's face as he, too, now stared at Violet. "As you are investigating everyone, am I to take it that that includes females—for instance the three females who live in this house, all of whom could easily have entered my mother's room, and any of whom might have had some reason, a reason known only to them, to wish my mother dead? My mother was weak and frail. It wouldn't have taken much strength to overcome her."

Stokes had warned Violet that such an accusation might well be made, and he had assured her that he, Adair, and Montague considered it without foundation. Despite the warning, she still felt the instinctive urge to violently rebut the notion, to defend not just herself but Tilly and Cook, too, against the scurrilous slur, but remembering Stokes's caution against doing so, she literally bit her tongue and remained mute.

She did, however, hold Mortimer's gaze unflinchingly, returning his suspicion with silent defiance.

Mortimer looked away first, glancing questioningly at Stokes.

Who had watched the exchange with unrelenting patience. "I am discounting no one. That includes everyone about this table, and anyone else who has had contact with her ladyship." His expression mild, Stokes glanced to his left. "That even includes Mr. Montague, although considering his position in the City and his significant reputation, I cannot imagine I will have any difficulty confirming his alibi."

Gravely sober, Montague inclined his head.

Turning back to the gathering, Stokes swept the faces with his steely gaze, then, his expression and tone growing harder, said, "Unless we gain some early indication of the murderer's identity, you may expect to be interviewed at some point within the next few days. It would be helpful if you made a note of where you were throughout last night, and who, if anyone, can confirm your presence there."

Easing back his chair, Stokes stood. "That will be all for now." He inclined his head to Mortimer Halstead, then to Wallace Camberly. "We will, of course, inform the family once we have the murderer in custody."

Barnaby, Montague, and Violet also rose.

Cynthia Halstead looked at Stokes. "One moment, Inspector. When may we view the body and make arrangements for the funeral?"

"Her ladyship's body is presently at the morgue. I believe it will be released for burial the day after tomorrow, but you may send your undertaker there. He will know how to inquire."

Cynthia's face blanked. "That's thoroughly inconvenient."

Unmoved, Stokes responded, "That's the way things are done."

Cynthia sniffed and desisted.

"What about her things?" Constance Halstead asked. When Stokes looked at her, she waved. "In her room, in the sitting room, elsewhere in the house."

"This house is a crime scene, Mrs. Halstead—no one will be permitted to remove anything from it until I give my permission, which I anticipate will be in a day or two. I will advise the family when they are free to come and go. Until such time, access to the house will be restricted."

Constance pulled a face, and with a glance at her sister-in-law, mimicked her. "*Exceedingly* inconvenient."

Cynthia huffed, then beneath her breath, but not quite softly enough, said, "At least let's get Mama buried first."

Constance colored. She drew in a huge breath, her bosom swelling dramatically. "The funeral—"

"Will be held at St. Peter's, of course." Cynthia's tone had turned brittle.

"I would have thought St. George's would be more appropriate," Mortimer observed.

"Nonsense!" Cynthia sat bolt upright. "St. Peter's is where Mama attended. It's been the family's church for decades, and just because you chose to move away—"

Violet turned and led the way to the door. Montague followed, and Stokes and Adair fell in behind. She paused before the door, allowing Montague to reach around her and open it. Stepping into the long front hall, she walked toward the front of the house.

Montague joined her, pacing alongside. "Is it always like that?" He tipped his head toward the dining room. "Them at each other's throats, even about something like their mother's funeral."

"Always." Halting before the sitting room door, Violet glanced back. Adair had followed close behind Montague, but Stokes had paused to instruct his constable—no doubt ensuring that the family obeyed his edict against removing items from the house. She looked at Montague, then Adair. "They are worse than squabbling infants. I doubt Lady Halstead's passing will change anything—as far as I ever saw, their sniping wasn't dependent on her presence but is simply their established way with each other, regardless of the subject."

"Delightful people," Adair murmured. "I suspect Stokes will want a short conference." Adair indicated the sitting room door. "Can we speak privately in there?"

Violet nodded, opened the door, and led the way in.

She and Montague took the chintz-covered sofa, while Adair claimed one of the pair of armchairs facing them.

They'd just settled when Stokes walked through the door they'd left open. Shutting it, he said, "Camberly has excused himself—apparently there's a parliamentary session he needs to attend—and William simply upped and left without a word. The rest are still hard at it, arguing the merits of this burial ground versus that." Crossing the room, Stokes shook his head. "I've seen some difficult families in my time, but these people take the cake."

Dropping into the second armchair, Stokes studied Violet. "From your lack of surprise, I take it such behavior is the norm for them."

She nodded. "For the Halstead brood, that performance was entirely unremarkable."

"I must say," Adair drawled, "that I appreciated the nice touch of splitting your announcement—first stating that her ladyship was dead, and then subsequently mentioning that she was murdered. That gave us two chances to catch the murderer out, to see if he failed to react appropriately, but I, for one, saw nothing that would distinguish one from the other."

He glanced at Violet and Montague. "Did either of you notice anything?"

Violet shook her head.

Montague grimaced. "What I did notice was that none of them appeared to care that her ladyship was dead—their attitude seemed to be that she was old, and she'd died, and that was that. But as for her being murdered, I got the impression the family as a whole viewed that as a great nuisance."

"Sadly, that's true." Violet fought to maintain a suitably detached distance, tried hard not to think of Lady Halstead, not to dwell on the fact that she'd been

killed, murdered, most likely by one of her poison-
ous brood. Remembering all the calm, gentle hours
she'd spent with the old lady, who had rarely had even
a grumpy word to say, much less any sharpness or ill
temper, made it difficult to maintain her composure
and not give in to the sweeping sadness.

"Tell me," Stokes said, and, glancing up, Violet saw
he was regarding her. "In all the time you've been
with Lady Halstead, have you ever heard of any argument between her ladyship and one of her children or
grandchildren?"

She cast her mind back over the years but, in the
end, shook her head. "No." She hesitated, then said,
"But you shouldn't be surprised by that. As far as possible, Lady Halstead kept them—her family—at a certain distance. For instance, I joined this household after
Sir Hugo died, but none of the family was involved in
hiring me. Normally, family members—daughters,
daughters-in-law, even sons—take care to be there
to vet whoever an older female relative takes on as a
companion." She shifted, then added, "I've only been
interviewed for two positions—the one here with
Lady Halstead, and my previous position with Lady
Ogilvie—but with Lady Ogilvie, both her daughters
were present, and from all I've heard that's the norm."

Montague was nodding, as were Stokes and Barnaby.

"To your knowledge, were any of the Halstead children ever involved in any of her ladyship's financial decisions?" Montague asked.

"No. And I'm quite certain of that," Violet replied. "Lady Halstead once made a comment about feeling much happier making her own decisions, and I know she rebuffed Mortimer, and also Maurice—both independently offered to assist her with managing her fortune, but she declared Sir Hugo had taken care of it all, and she was quite happy with the way things were."

"Hmm." Adair had a faraway look in his eyes, as if he was replaying the moments around the dining table. "One thing I noticed—and perhaps, Miss Matcham, you might confirm—but the impression I received is that the animosity, as witnessed by the tensions and tart comments flung across and down that table, lies primarily between Lady Halstead's children, with supporting contributions from the two spouses." Meeting Violet's gaze, Adair arched his brows. "Was it always like that—them against each other—or was the animosity sometimes directed at Lady Halstead?"

"No," Violet said. "Their sniping was never directed at her. It always amazed me that, during the dinners, her ladyship paid the strife no attention at all. She would eat and ignore them—unless they became too noisy. Then she would insist they ended it, but . . . no. Even at such times, their viciousness was never directed at her."

Barnaby sighed and shifted his gaze to Stokes. "So out of that interlude, while we've established that the Halsteads are a highly unpleasant lot, overall we've got not one decent whiff of the murderer."

Stokes inclined his head. "Maybe so, but what we did gain was confirmation that, regardless of their behavior toward each other, there is no suggestion of any personal motive—no hint that any of her ladyship's family held a grudge against her, no evidence of arguments or disagreements between her and any of her children."

Nodding, Montague picked up the train of thought. "And as we have reason to believe that the murderer is a family member, not just because of the apparent ease of entry to the house but also the timing of the murder so soon after her ladyship's announcement that she intended to have her affairs looked into—"

"*And*"—Barnaby sat straighter—"as we also have every reason to believe that there is something illegal behind these payments into her ladyship's account, we're left with that, and only that, as a strong motive." He looked at Stokes. "It's money, simply money, behind this."

Gravely, Stokes nodded. "What we've established is that there is no suggestion of any other motive—no personal animosity, nothing about her will. It's those payments, whatever they are. Keeping them hidden is the motive behind Lady Halstead's murder, that and nothing else." He glanced at Montague, then Violet, then Barnaby. "Until and unless we get information to the contrary, I suggest we should proceed on that understanding."

Their small meeting broke up shortly afterward, with the three men making arrangements to meet the following morning at Montague's office to examine the evidence he'd already assembled regarding the odd payments they all believed were behind Lady Halstead's murder.

Violet accompanied the men into the front hall. She had felt not just accepted and appreciated but also reassured to have been included in the discussions thus far. Everything had happened so rapidly—the discovery of Lady Halstead's body, the summoning of help, calming Tilly and Cook, coping with the doctor, and then the police, much less all the rest—that she hadn't yet had time to grieve, to come to grips with her own roiling emotions. But of one thing she was instinctively sure: She wanted to help. She *needed* to do whatever she could to help catch the murderer and win justice for Lady Halstead. The violence of her feelings was unexpected and unsettling; she was relieved the three men seemed to understand without her having to explain.

On his way out of the front door, Stokes paused to tell her, "I've left a constable on guard inside the house, and there's another outside—he's out of sight, but he's keeping an eye on the place." Stokes hesitated, then added, "I meant to go into the kitchen and assure the maid and the cook that neither of them are suspects, not in our eyes. Perhaps you could tell them?"

Violet nodded. "Of course."

Stokes left; with an encouraging look and a salute, Adair followed him down the steps. Realizing Montague had hung back in the hall, Violet closed the door and turned. Gently smiled.

With a brief, answering smile, Montague went forward. Greatly daring, he reached for one of Violet's hands, lightly held it. "This has all happened very quickly."

He wasn't simply speaking of Lady Halstead's death and the consequent happenings of the tumultuous day; he was still coming to grips with his feelings for Violet, with the intensity of his reaction to her being within the orbit of a murderer, and to the implicit, if nebulous, threat hovering over her. He looked into her eyes, studied her expression. "This was the first time you've met Stokes and Adair—I wanted to reassure you that you may have every confidence in them. The investigation couldn't be in better hands. They will work tirelessly to bring Lady Halstead's murderer to justice." He held her soft blue gaze. "I know that's important to you. I understand why. It's much the same compulsion I experience when one of my clients is harmed, but, I imagine, you feel the need even more keenly, as clearly you were close to Lady Halstead."

Violet felt her smile go awry. "She was a dear and didn't deserve to be murdered."

"No. But"—Montague inclined his head in a gesture that was a vow—"I, too, have an interest in this now, and with the four of us devoted to the cause, her ladyship will not go unavenged." He held her gaze for a moment more, then bowed briefly and released her hand.

Violet turned to open the door. "Thank you for all your help today. I'm more grateful than I can say."

Pausing in the doorway, he met her gaze again, then dipped his head. "I'll call when we have further news."

She inclined her head and watched him go down the steps and out of the gate. Lingering in the doorway, she let her gaze follow him as he strode down the pavement, broad shoulders square, head held high, solid, masculine confidence in every powerful line.

When he rounded the corner and disappeared from her sight, Violet sighed, then, feeling the tug of the sadness waiting within, she closed the door and turned away, sternly telling herself that this was neither an appropriate nor useful time to discover she still possessed the ability to dream.

After quitting the Lowndes Street house, Barnaby and Stokes hailed a hackney, and after a brief discussion elected to journey to Stokes's house in Greenbury Street, in St. John's Wood, there to mull over their impressions and observations in peace and comfort.

Through the rocking, rattling trip they kept their private counsels, allowing their minds to freely pick over the accumulated observations, searching for fresh insights to share once they'd gained the quiet of Stokes's sitting room. But on arriving in Greenbury Street and entering Stokes's neat abode, they discovered their wives already in possession.

Both ladies were sitting on the floor, their skirts puffed about them, playing with young Oliver and the slightly younger Megan. Both babies were rolling on their backs, alert and chortling as they batted at toys their mothers dangled over them.

The sight brought Stokes and Barnaby to a halt in the doorway.

Barnaby felt as if something—some power—had punched him in the chest. He knew from the sudden stillness, the complete and utter absorption of the man beside him, that Stokes felt the same.

Penelope and Griselda had heard their footsteps—had seen them enter and had taken the moment of their stillness to study their faces and appreciate their reaction.

Then Penelope smiled and, with a flick of her wrist, sent the toy with which she'd been distracting Oliver flying at Barnaby's chest.

Reflexively, he caught it. Spell broken, he glanced at her, met her dark, too-observant eyes.

Her smile deepened, edged with intent. "The investigators return—and clearly with some case afoot." She waved to include the children. "So come and join us—and tell us all."

Griselda, also smiling, nodded. "Indeed." She threw the toy she'd been jiggling to Stokes. "Come and take over." She started to get up. "I'll have Mindy bring in the tea tray, and meanwhile you can sit, stretch your legs, and share the news about your latest case."

They know us far too well. Resigning himself to the inevitable, Stokes helped his wife to her feet, lightly kissed her cheek, then let her go to the kitchen to arrange for the tea tray. Crouching, he looked into the smiling, laughing blue eyes of his tiny daughter—and promptly fell under her spell again.

Grinning and dutifully jiggling the toy over her, he didn't feel so bad—quite so silly—when at the edge of his vision he saw Barnaby sprawling on the floor next to his rolling bundle of a son.

Penelope rose, looked down at them for a moment, then, apparently satisfied that they knew what they were doing, went to the sofa and sat. She said nothing, merely watched over them; Stokes got the impression she was overseeing to make sure he and Barnaby did nothing wrong.

Twenty minutes later, with the now drowsy children handed over to Gloria, Megan's nursemaid, and carted off to the nursery, with the tea poured and slices of pound cake passed around, the four of them settled into the comfort of the well-padded chairs and, finally, with the air of one who had waited patiently and was now due all she wished, Penelope said, "So, gentlemen, what's your new case?"

Stokes glanced at Barnaby; they'd been colleagues and friends for long enough now that he had little doubt about the thoughts, the considerations, rolling through Barnaby's mind. It still surprised him, the easy rapport they shared—the son of an earl and the son of a merchant, albeit a merchant's son with a better-than-average education. As for the friendship, real and true, that had formed between their wives, that was an even greater wonder—an ex-East-Ender-milliner-shopkeeper-cum-police inspector's wife rubbing shoulders with the wife of the son of an earl, herself the daughter of a viscount and connected by marriage to several of the most powerful noble families in the land.

Yet there they all were, sipping tea and munching pound cake in his small but comfortable sitting room. And in the past, before their foray into motherhood, their wives had, indeed, been of significant help in several of their cases. He and Barnaby had both hoped that the advent of Oliver and Megan would permanently distract Penelope and Griselda from their earlier interest, but as that patently wasn't to be, then the Halstead case was, perhaps, a gift horse he and Barnaby shouldn't try to turn away.

A murder where the motive was solidly and simply financial transactions held far less risk of any danger.

Meeting Stokes's gaze, Barnaby all but imperceptibly nodded—an encouragement to go ahead, to take the lead, with his blessing.

Stokes shifted his gaze to Penelope's eager face. "It's a matter of murder." When she and Griselda only looked more interested, he went on, "This morning, a Lady Halstead, who lived in Lowndes Street, was found dead by her staff . . ." In his usual, bare-bones, policeman's language, he described all that had happened that day.

Predictably, Penelope asked questions, and Griselda posed a few, too. Both focused on the people, insisting that Stokes, and Barnaby, too, report what they'd sensed, as well as what they'd seen and heard, of all those involved.

Stokes had forgotten that, unlike him and Barnaby, their wives tended to concentrate on people, their foibles and emotions first, and secondarily on facts and actions.

Penelope knew Montague; she gave Griselda a quick verbal sketch, ending with, "He's utterly reliable and trustworthy. A real rock, the sort one can always rely on to behave . . . in the way that will best serve justice." Penelope glanced at Stokes. "Montague's amazingly astute about everything to do with money and finances, and his ability to get information on those subjects is nothing short of astounding."

Stokes snorted. "I've heard tales enough of the information he can get. If it comes to that in this case, I won't be asking questions about how or where he gets his facts."

Penelope grinned. "Precisely." She turned back to Griselda. "But the point I find most interesting is not that the companion, Violet Matcham, sent for

Montague—the poor woman clearly had the family to rights and must have been desperate for a way to see her late mistress's death properly investigated, so sending for Montague makes perfect sense—but that Montague dropped all his usual work and came. Now *that* I find quite fascinating."

Barnaby eyed the light in his wife's dark eyes and decided he wasn't going to comment. Instead, he steered the conversation on. "We were in Smithfield when Montague's message reached us, so by the time we got to Lowndes Street, the doctor had already arrived." Going over all that had occurred and, in catering to Penelope's and Griselda's particular bent, having to describe the people and their reactions proved an excellent exercise in reviewing what they had actually seen, what they actually knew.

Unsurprisingly, the description of the family gathering consumed many long minutes as their wives extracted every last little detail Barnaby and Stokes had noticed about the Halsteads and Camberlys.

Penelope fixed Barnaby with a direct look. "Your father would know about Camberly. And your mother might know more about Mrs. Camberly and the son."

Barnaby nodded. "I'll ask."

"We're due there for dinner tonight, which will be the perfect opportunity." Penelope looked at Griselda.

"What do you make of the family? They seem . . . well, not quite right to me. They're destructive rather than supportive."

Her gaze abstracted, Griselda nodded. "But what makes them like that, what drives them . . ." She focused on Penelope. "Do you think it might have something to do with their ages?"

Barnaby straightened; he glanced at Stokes and saw his friend blink, then pay greater attention, too.

Frowning slightly, Penelope was slowly nodding. "I see your point—and, yes, that might well be it."

When neither said anything more but just sat there cogitating deeply, Barnaby prompted, " 'It' what?" When Penelope glanced up, he caught her eye. "What are you two thinking?"

"Well," Penelope said, "it's the sort of thing that can sometimes happen when two siblings are born close—a year or less apart. From what Miss Matcham told you, Mortimer is the eldest, but Cynthia is less than a year younger. People assume that children close in age will support each other and share a deeper bond, but it can also go the other way. Especially if the second child has a stronger, or even equally strong, character. Then you have competition, a battle for supremacy." She glanced at Stokes, then back at Barnaby. "Is that what was happening across that table? Was it competitiveness? One-upmanship? That sort of thing?"

His gaze on her face, Barnaby nodded decisively. "That's exactly what it was."

"And if that's so," Griselda said, catching Penelope's gaze, "that makes Maurice and William more understandable, too." She glanced at Barnaby, then Stokes. "Imagine what it must have been like when all of them were children. Mortimer and Cynthia are fighting for dominance, most likely portraying themselves as the most perfect, the most successful, to gain the most praise and status. Maurice can't compete, so, in a bid for attention, and even perhaps rebelling against his older siblings, he goes the other way. Because Mortimer and Cynthia are fighting over the perfectly correct end of social behavior, Maurice goes to the other extreme and becomes a black sheep."

"But"—Penelope held up a finger—"Maurice can go to the other extreme while still remaining within the social pale. But when William came along, he had nowhere to go—no way to distinguish himself within the social pale because both the perfect end and the imperfect end had already been claimed."

Barnaby was nodding. "So William stepped beyond the pale and out of society altogether."

"Exactly!" Penelope looked at Stokes. "So that's why those four are as they are, and if you bear that in mind, you'll have a much better chance of predicting their behavior and understanding the reasons behind what they say and do."

Stokes digested that, then said, "One thing—you say that the characters the Halstead children have grown into came about because they were, each of them, seeking attention." When Griselda and Penelope nodded, Stokes asked, "From whom?"

Penelope looked at Griselda, then Griselda turned to Stokes. "Most likely from their parents."

All four of them paused to consider, then Barnaby mused, "According to Violet—Miss Matcham—both Lady Halstead and her husband were nice people. Which suggests this is one of those strange instances where perfectly decent parents raise a brood of much less acceptable children."

Stokes humphed. "It happens."

After a moment, Penelope sat back and asked, "So what are you planning to do next?"

Stokes exchanged a glance with Barnaby and saw in his friend's expression the same acceptance he felt. Their ladies' insights were proving useful, even potentially invaluable, and, really, with this case, there was no reason they couldn't assist. He looked back at the pair seated on the sofa. "Our next move is to examine all the information Montague has thus far assembled about these mysterious payments, and then, I suspect, while he pursues them as only he can, we"—he inclined his head toward Barnaby—"will continue investigating the murder itself."

"And the family," Barnaby added.

"Hmm." Penelope frowned into space. "You need to find out how the murderer got in."

Barnaby grimaced. "To be thorough, we should search Lady Halstead's papers in general to see if there's any document that might shed light on either the payments or some other issue as yet unknown to us that might have been behind this."

"Regarding the payments, you might see if there's anything known about any member of the family being involved in anything nefarious," Griselda suggested.

Stokes grunted and set down his cake plate. "Regardless, after what we've discussed, I feel a need to interview the family again, but before we do"—he met Barnaby's eyes—"we need more details about these peculiar payments."

Barnaby pulled a face but nodded. "Much as I would like to press them harder, with the caliber of people involved, I suspect you have that right."

Chapter 5

The rest of the copies of Lady Halstead's financial documents that Montague had requested from Runcorn arrived just in time for Slocum to receive them before closing up for the day.

When Slocum carried the pile into his office, Montague was already tidying away the ducal accounts he'd been working through. There was nothing amiss in those ledgers; they could wait.

"Thank you, Slocum." Taking the stack of documents, which was several inches thick, Montague placed the pile on his blotter, then looked at his senior clerk. "It was lucky that I didn't have any meetings scheduled earlier today." He'd arrived back in time for a late afternoon consultation with one of his newer clients. "Given that unraveling Lady Halstead's accounts has taken such a drastic and serious turn, I might well have to absent myself with little notice over the next several days. What meetings have we scheduled? Are there any we should reschedule?"

"Let me get the book." Slocum went out to his desk and returned with his heavy office diary. "Well, you're in luck. Over the next week or so, you've only got meetings with second-tier clients, so Gibbons and Foster could deal with those." Slocum looked up, brows arching. "I'll word them up in the morning, if you like?"

"Who are the clients?" Montague listened as Slocum listed the names. He considered, then nodded. "You can inform Gibbons and Foster they'll be taking those meetings. If I'm here, I'll attend, but as an observer. Gibbons and Foster can handle those meetings regardless—Gibbons to lead, Foster to support." Frederick Gibbons was a sound man who had been with Montague and Son for years, and Phillip Foster, although much less experienced, was shaping up nicely. "It'll be good experience for them both."

"I agree." Slocum was scribbling notes in the big diary. "Never fear—between us we'll take care of business." Raising his head, Slocum glanced at the pile of papers on the blotter. "Looks like you'll have your hands full combing through those."

"Indeed." Montague eyed the pile and couldn't wait to plunge in. He glanced at Slocum. "Anything else?"

"No—that's it." Slocum closed the diary and saluted. "The others have already gone, so I'll be off, too."

"Good night." Montague didn't even wait for Slocum to leave before picking up the first document and starting to read.

The next hour ticked by. Only when the lamp on his desk started flickering and he realized the oil had burned low did he look up and through the window, and realize that evening had well and truly fallen. A glance at the clock on the corner of his desk informed him that Mrs. Trewick would have his dinner ready and waiting upstairs; he tried not to inconvenience his housekeeper any more than was unavoidable.

He looked at the papers scattered over his desk. The compulsion to pursue the explanation for the odd payments that had appeared in Lady Halstead's account—which were possibly the motive behind her murder—was familiar to a point; in past cases, he'd often felt the call of professional duty, of a need to ensure that the laws were observed and justice was served in his chosen field.

This time, however, the impulse that drove him had a different feel, a sharper edge.

Violet Matcham was too close to the crime for his peace of mind.

He shied from looking too deeply at why that consideration should affect him so powerfully, yet he wasn't about to deny that it did. He needed to discover what in Lady Halstead's accounts was worth murdering to conceal, and only when he had, and only when the murderer had been caught, would he be content that he'd done all he could.

That he'd accomplished what now seemed so vital: Protecting Violet from the murderer.

Keeping Violet safe.

He stared at the papers for a moment more, then rose, gathered them up, and with them tucked under his arm, he headed for the door, for his waiting dinner and his study upstairs.

That evening, Violet took her dinner with Tilly and Cook at the table in the kitchen. It was cozy there, and the warmth was much appreciated; upstairs, the house seemed to have grown unnaturally cold.

Cook, wispy red curls escaping from the edges of her white cap, huddled in her chair and poked at her perfectly tasty stew. "What if he comes back?"

Violet glanced up. "The murderer?"

"Aye." Cook didn't look up; she stared at her plate. "Just waltzed in here and killed the mistress, didn't he? So what's to stop him doing the same and smothering one of us in our beds?"

Violet glanced at Tilly and saw a similar anxiety in the maid's eyes. "I . . . can't tell, of course." She looked at Cook. "Who can? But it does seem that there might be a reason behind her ladyship's murder—those payments she was so exercised about—and if that's true, then . . . well, I can't see any reason he would come back to kill any of us."

Tilly had lifted her glass of water. She took a sip, then, lowering the glass, cleared her throat and said, "Seems like, if he thought he had to kill her ladyship for a reason, and so far has got away with it, then the last place he'd think of coming back to would be here."

"Yes, indeed." Violet sat straighter. "And I've just remembered that the inspector told me that he'd left a man outside to keep an eye on the house. The constable inside has left, but for all we know, the man outside is still there."

"Aye, well—here's hoping he is." Cook pushed her half-full plate away. "And that the blackguard, whoever he is, is more worried about hiding his face than bothering with us three here. It's not as if we know anything."

"Exactly." Determined to steer talk away from the murder, and the murderer, Violet rose and lifted her plate. "I'll help clear."

It would keep her busy, keep her from dwelling on the fact that she wasn't spending that evening in the sitting room reading to Lady Halstead. That she and

Tilly wouldn't have to help her ladyship up the stairs, and help her get ready for bed.

The big bedroom upstairs lay empty; the police had come and taken the body away for further examination.

Violet didn't want to think about that. Once the dishes were done, she turned to Tilly. "Perhaps we can work on the mending."

Both she and Tilly were excellent needlewomen; Cook sat for a while, silently staring at their flying fingers, then she humphed and went off to her bedroom beyond the kitchen.

Violet heard the door shut. A minute later, she heard a heavy thud, as if Cook had moved some piece of furniture up against the door.

Violet exchanged a glance with Tilly, who shrugged. "Can't say as I blame her," Tilly said. "Quite a shock today's been."

Lips twisting, Violet returned her gaze to the seam she was repairing.

Eventually, the mending all done and the lamps in the kitchen doused, each holding a flickering candle, Violet climbed the stairs with Tilly. They parted on the first-floor landing, Tilly going along the corridor to the door to the staircase to the attic and her tiny dormer room. Violet drew breath, then walked down the corridor in the opposite direction, past the door to

Lady Halstead's room, and further, to the door to her own small bedroom.

Opening it, she went in. Shutting the door, she studied the panels for several moments. Eventually, she turned away; there was no reason to allow fear to rule her.

Montague had assured her that, together with Stokes and Adair, he would work to see Lady Halstead avenged—to catch and bring her murderer to justice. Placing trust and faith in the words of a man she barely knew would have seemed foolhardy a week ago; it didn't now. She believed him, had faith in his certainty.

Or was it that his faith fed her own?

Crossing to the chest of drawers, she set down the candlestick. Her thoughts continued to churn, freed, it seemed, by her finally being alone.

The fact that the villain was almost certainly one of Lady Halstead's children, or their spouses, or possibly one of her grandchildren, was only now fully crystalizing in Violet's mind. That conclusion hadn't been stated, not definitively, but the implication, the expectation, had colored the investigation thus far.

What to her was more damning was that it required near-impossible mental contortions to imagine that her ladyship's murderer *could* be anyone else; other than her family, Lady Halstead had lived reclusively, increasingly so over the last two years.

Making a mental note to remember to mention that to Montague—or Adair or Stokes—Violet reached up and started unpinning her hair.

After brushing out the thick tresses, she undressed and donned her nightgown, a slight frown on her face, her mind revisiting all she'd ever witnessed of Lady Halstead interacting with her brood. Was there a hint there, somewhere, of which one was to blame?

As she slipped between the sheets, looking inward, she was somewhat surprised to discover a strength, a determination, she hadn't known she possessed. Despite the shock, despite the fact she wasn't related to Lady Halstead in any way, she found a core of focused intention—she would see her ladyship's killer caught.

The realization, the acknowledgment and acceptance of her instinctive commitment, that it was made, that it was there, that it would not waver, didn't precisely soothe or calm her but rather gave her enough certainty, enough of a foundation on which to stand firm—and close her eyes.

To her surprise, sleep swiftly drew near. She must have been more exhausted than she'd realized.

As slumberous mists rolled into and through her mind, a face formed within them, strong and clear.

Behind him ranged two others, but they were less distinct.

Montague stood sharply etched in her mind's eye, the assurances he'd uttered in his deep, solid voice echoing in her mind, both comfort and anchor.

Lady Halstead's murderer would be caught. She would fight for that, and Montague would be by her side.

Stokes found Griselda standing beside Megan's crib and looking down at their baby daughter, the smile on his wife's face one he hadn't seen before Megan's birth.

A madonna-smile, one only a mother looking at her child could achieve.

The sight made his own lips curve, made his harsh features, the hard face he showed to most of the world, soften.

Sensing his approach, Griselda turned and smiled at him.

A slightly different smile, but one he treasured. It, too, was unique—that smile she reserved just for him.

Coming up beside her, he dipped his head and brushed his lips over hers, then looked down at their daughter.

Griselda leaned against him; he slid one arm around her, lightly held her.

A moment passed, then he murmured, "Do you really want to help with this investigation? Are you really interested?" Angling his head, he met her eyes. "Or are you simply following—supporting—Penelope?"

Lips twitching, Griselda studied his face. "She is something of a force of nature, I grant you, but"—she sighed—"I really do feel a need of a sort to . . . do something. To contribute in however small a way." Shifting to face him, her arms going around his waist as his settled about her, she tipped her head back and looked into his eyes. "I'm happy here, with you, with Megan. It's not that part of me that needs to be involved. I could, very easily, simply stay at home, keep busy with the shop, and be happy and content, but . . . I have to wonder if, years from now, I'll look back on that and . . . feel ashamed."

As if searching for the words to make him understand, her eyes locked with his, she paused, then went on, "I have . . . everything my heart could desire. I have a life that's not just good but wonderful. The future beckons, and there are no clouds on my horizon. You might say, in a sense, that it's a way of honoring that—all that I have, all my good fortune—a way of feeling that I deserve it, or perhaps that I've earned the right to such happiness, by doing what I can to . . . make the world about me a better place. By helping others." Her lips softened, lightly lifted. "By helping you, and Barnaby, too, to see justice done."

He tightened his arms about her, feeling her warmth, the inexpressible trust with which she sank against him, something that, now he'd found it, he never wanted to lose. "I can't claim not to understand, although I have to wonder if I've infected you with my calling."

She smiled. "More likely it's a reflection of the people we are—that I'm the right match for you precisely because we do have similar thoughts, wants, and ideals, similar ways of seeing the world."

His lips tightened, but he forced himself to ask, "So what do you think to do? Involving yourself in all my cases—"

"No—I don't want, or need, that." She searched his eyes. "I know that many, perhaps most, of your cases are petty to violent crimes perpetrated by established criminals. Neither I nor Penelope would have useful insights to offer in such cases. But in cases like your current one, there's considerable scope for us to help—as we did tonight."

"I can't, and won't, deny that. Your explanation of why that family might be as it is will be a real help." He paused, then nodded. "Very well. Let's see how this develops."

"And if there are areas in which we can assist, we will."

For a long moment they simply looked into each other's eyes. Then his lips lifted. "There's one area you might assist me with tonight."

Her smile deepened, then she stretched up, pressed her lips to his in a swift, challenging kiss, and murmured, "Lead on, Inspector."

Stokes laughed—softly, so as not to wake the baby. Swiftly stooping, he swept Griselda into his arms, surprising a shocked gasp, then a smothered peal of laughter from her as, leaving the door ajar so they would hear if Megan awoke, he carried Griselda out of the nursery and on into their bedroom down the hall.

He dropped her on their bed. She reached up and pulled him down.

And the warmth they'd found together flared and engulfed them.

They gloried in the heated moments, sharing and giving, relearning again, reminding themselves of the elemental wonder, the effervescent joy.

The sheer, unadulterated glory of physical intimacy.

Sharing again the ecstasy and the bliss, and, at the last, settling, sated and content, to sleep in each other's arms.

Stokes listened to Griselda's breathing slow.

Uncertainty hovered, of a sort he'd never encountered before. He felt as if he was embarking on a new and potentially dangerous personal journey, one heading into regions unknown. The implications of what he'd agreed to slid through his mind, flitting like dark shadows. Fears, silly and unfounded, but real nonetheless, that in agreeing to her involvement—not just in this case but in others to follow—he might have opened the door to some fundamental upheaval that would, somehow, threaten this—this splendor, this comfort, this signal joy.

This closeness.

Something he valued more than his life.

Yet he would give her the world were he able, and if she wanted, needed, this . . . then he would stand by her side and they would find a new framework, one that would incorporate all they both required, one built on the foundation they'd already laid.

He would try, as would she, and together they would make it work. Commitment wasn't something they lacked.

Somewhat reassured, he let sleep have at him.

As he started to sink, the sight of Griselda's face smiling her madonna-smile filled his mind. That smile carried such a wealth, such a depth, of love, one no other relationship could evoke. No wonder the link between mother and child was held sacred.

So what had happened with the Halsteads?

The thought brought him awake, awake enough to clearly see that in that family's case, in at least one instance, possibly more, the mother-child link had been broken.

He—they—were investigating a matricide.

So how, or why, had the link broken?

Or had it never been strong in the first place?

He toyed with the questions, accepted that they hinted at avenues he should explore.

Closing his eyes again, he let his lips quirk. Griselda had been more help than she knew.

As sleep finally claimed him, his last conscious thought was a prayer that nothing ever damaged that precious link between Griselda and their children.

"Your father described Wallace Camberly as a *careful* politician." Clad in shimmering blue silk, Penelope led the way into the master bedroom of the Albemarle Street house. Jewels winked about her throat and dangled from her ears as she swept across the room to set her silver evening reticule on her dressing table.

Barnaby followed her into the room. They'd just returned from a formal dinner at his parents' London house. After crossing the threshold and being greeted by Mostyn, their first stop had been the nursery, but Oliver was sleeping peacefully and they'd left him to his dreams. "What did the pater mean by 'careful'—did he say?"

"I asked." Penelope set to work easing the earrings from her lobes. "He—your father—said that Camberly holds his seat by a good margin and is careful to do nothing to risk that safety. Contrarily, your father also said Camberly was ruthlessly ambitious, but that said ambition was tempered by the aforementioned caution."

Shrugging off his evening coat, Barnaby grinned. "You're starting to sound like a politician yourself."

"Indeed—I blame it on the company." Setting down her earrings, she glanced at him. "Did you learn anything more about Camberly?"

"Only that he's expected to advance through the ranks, but not in spectacular fashion." Barnaby started unwinding his cravat. "I got the impression he and his wife are being watched and assessed with a view to future advancement, possibly into the Ministry." Glancing across the room, he saw Penelope lay aside her necklace, then reach up to start unpinning her hair. "I didn't encounter anyone with links to the Home Office. Did you?"

"No, so in the end I fell back on your father again. It took him some time to place Mortimer Halstead. It seems Mortimer holds his position more by seniority than talent. Your father's term was a plodder, one not expected to rise beyond his present position of assistant to some undersecretary." Her hair loose, Penelope crossed to stand before Barnaby, presenting him with her back. "If you please . . . ?"

Setting the long ribbon of his cravat on the top of the tallboy, Barnaby grinned and obligingly set his fingers to the row of tiny blue bead buttons marching down the back of her evening gown. One of the duties of a husband he rather enjoyed; given the nature of Penelope's gowns, it often felt like unwrapping a present.

But as he worked down the long line, his smile faded.

After a moment, he glanced at the section of her profile he could see. "You enjoyed it, didn't you? Ferreting out what you could about our suspects."

She nodded. "Yes, I did. It made an evening embarked on out of duty—out of helping your mother with her numbers—into something much more engaging. Into an evening with purpose."

Reaching the end of the line of buttons, he set his hands to her sides, slid his palms over and around, easing her back against him.

Obligingly, she sank back, her shoulders across his chest, her head coming to rest in the hollow below his shoulder, her curvaceous derriere against his thighs.

For a moment, he simply held her, savoring the sense of how well she fitted, how well they suited.

Then he found the words and the courage to say, "I'm not all that sure how I feel about this. About you involving yourself in investigations again."

He'd hoped that Oliver's birth would put an end to her engaging in potentially dangerous endeavors, yet even as he'd hoped, some part of him had known it was unlikely, had known that her questing mind would need the stimulation he himself found in solving crimes. It was what had brought them together, and their natures hadn't changed with their baby's birth.

She didn't immediately respond, but neither did she stiffen in his arms. After a moment, she raised one hand and drew her gold-rimmed spectacles from her face. Then she tipped her head back and to the side so she could look into his face; at such close quarters she didn't need her glasses to study his features, to read his eyes. Several heartbeats passed while she did, then she said, "I wasn't sure about it, either."

Not knowing how to interpret that, he waited, and after a second's pause, she went on, "When Oliver was born, I wondered if he would fill my life to the exclusion of all else, certainly of things like investigating. But now . . . I think that that isn't how it goes. How life evolves."

She held his gaze. "I feel as if my life has expanded—as if there's more space to be filled, as if Oliver being born to us created a new field in our lives. I've realized that, at least for me, and I hope for you, too, life isn't fixed, static, of finite girth. But while over the months since his birth I've been absorbed with acclimating myself to the new arena that Oliver inhabits, I've neglected the other areas of my life. But they're still there, and I still need them to be. They're still a part of me, of who I am—a part of what makes me me, and they're aspects, facets, I still need in order to be me." She looked questioningly at him. "If that makes sense?"

He looked into her dark eyes. "I've followed so far—it's an interesting hypothesis."

"Yes, well." She waved her glasses. "Clearly, having Oliver has changed things for me, and for you, too, although to different degrees and possibly in different ways, and those changes flow through to how we manage in all other areas of our lives." She paused, then faced forward and settled against him once more. "I feel as if, overall, my life is a trifle out of balance, especially in the area of my other interests, which includes investigating. I need to find a new balance, so to speak, but exactly what that will be . . ." She glanced up and met his eyes again. "I think it's one of those things one can only determine by trial and error."

He held her gaze, then murmured, "So we try with this latest case?"

She turned within his hold, raising her arms and draping them about his shoulders, her small hands drifting to his nape. "We try. And if at first we don't exactly succeed perfectly, we adjust." Her eyes on his, she tilted her head. "Will you work with me to find our new balance?"

Looking into her face, he realized that, since embarking on this case, she'd been more engaged, somehow more alive in a way he hadn't known he'd missed until it had returned. His impulse, as always, was to give her anything, agree to anything that contributed to her happiness, her well-being, a compulsion tempered only by his protective instincts.

His protective instincts didn't like her being anywhere near anything dangerous—like investigations.

Balance.

She had it right.

He nodded. "So . . . trial, possible error, and subsequent adjustment."

She smiled, a brilliant smile shaded with understanding. "Thank you."

Stretching up, one hand gripping his nape, the other framing his face, she pressed her lips to his. Any doubt he possessed that she didn't understand, that she hadn't understood exactly what thoughts, what considerations and reservations had passed through his mind, was eradicated by that kiss.

That they were together in this, that they would face the challenge side by side, hand in hand, was underscored by all that followed.

Later, much later, when she snuggled deeper into his arms and they settled to sleep, he lifted her hand and pressed a kiss to her palm. "Together, we'll find our way."

"Well! That was much easier than I'd imagined." He felt slightly giddy—with relief, with satisfaction, with the fading remnants of the illicit thrill of the act; his hand shook as he lit the wick of the lamp in his dressing room.

Once the flame had steadied, he replaced the glass, then looked down at his clothes, examining them carefully in the golden light. It was after midnight; all about him was silent and still. Only he stirred in this time between one day and the next.

Satisfied there were no telltale signs, he set about shedding his clothes.

Along with his conscience.

"There was no help for it, really, not once the old girl had started the ball rolling. I could hardly let it go on. If she'd just let things be, but no—she had to do the right thing and get her affairs in order . . . *bah!*"

Donning his nightshirt, he checked his face in his shaving mirror, as he did every night.

And as often happened when he did, doubts rose like phantoms in his mind. His eyes locked with those in his reflection, then he murmured, "If she'd spoken to her agent . . . she would have discussed doing so, wouldn't she?"

After a moment, his features contorted and he straightened. "Damn! I'm not safe yet."

Chapter 6

"There it is." Montague nodded across Winchester Street at the office of Runcorn and Son.

Beside him, Mrs. Adair—Penelope, as she'd insisted he call her—held up a gloved hand to screen her eyes. "Ah, yes. It looks decently prosperous." Lowering her hand, she scanned the street. "I haven't been in this area before. I'm always amazed by how immense London is."

Striding along on her other side, Adair grinned but said nothing. He, too, was surveying the street, taking note of the area and the office.

The pair had arrived at Montague's office for the meeting arranged the day before, bringing with them the news that Stokes had been summoned to a meeting on another case but hoped to join them within a few hours.

Adair had briefly explained his wife's interest in the case, and that Stokes was aware of her involvement. Having been exposed to ladies of Penelope Adair's ilk through his association with various noble families, Montague took her presence—and her interest—in his stride. He wasn't foolish enough to underestimate her abilities, and he could easily imagine several ways in which her insights might prove valuable. Consequently, he'd felt no reservations over sharing everything he'd thus far learned about Lady Halstead's accounts, investments, and estate with Penelope as well as Adair.

Although he'd spent hours combing through the copies of Lady Halstead's financial records, he had yet to find any hint of a legitimate source for the odd payments. However, as he'd told the others, Sir Hugo Halstead had had his finger in a great many pies, and tracking, accounting for, and excluding every last possible avenue that might explain the odd payments was going to take considerable time.

The payments didn't follow any recognizable pattern, but that didn't mean some peculiar investment hadn't been structured to pay out in such a fashion. Until they excluded such a source—and that could only be done by exhaustive searching and analysis—that the payments were legitimate had to remain a possibility.

Against that, as Penelope had noted, stood the fact that her ladyship had been murdered all but coincident with her announcement that she was looking into her financial affairs.

Or rather, having them looked into.

They'd concluded that consulting with Runcorn as to whether he had a complete listing of the Halsteads' investments, past as well as present, would be a helpful next step. Adair and Penelope had also been keen to meet the young man-of-business, in their eyes another player in the drama.

Crossing Winchester Street, they reached the door of Runcorn and Son. Opening the door, Montague stood back while Penelope and Adair entered, then Montague followed.

Only to walk into consternation.

An ashen-looking Pringle came hurrying up, waving his hands. "No, no—I'm sorry, ma'am, but the office is closed."

Penelope blinked, then looked past the slight man at the two constables hovering about an inner door. "Why?"

Her question threw Pringle into an even greater fluster. "Ah . . ." Wringing his hands, he looked past Penelope to Adair, then further . . . and recognized Montague. "Oh, sir! Such a thing! It's Mr. Runcorn, sir—he's dead."

"Dead?" All three of them echoed the word.

Adair threw Montague a glance.

"How?" Montague asked, moving forward to face Pringle.

"I'm . . . not sure." Pringle looked unsteady on his feet. "If I had to guess, I'd say he was knocked on the head and strangled. Oh, my!"

"Here." Penelope took Pringle's arm and gently steered him to a chair—the one behind his raised desk, as it happened. "Sit and compose yourself." She glanced around the small office. "Is there somewhere I could make you some tea?"

Pringle babbled his gratitude and pointed out the small door that led to a cramped service area. Penelope patted his arm and headed that way.

Montague studied Pringle's face; if anything, the man had paled even more. He gentled his voice. "When did it happen, do you know?"

Pringle gulped. "I left him here as I usually do, about seven o'clock last night. He was still searching through Lady Halstead's file—he had all the documents spread out on his desk." Pringle looked toward the inner office. "They're still there. I saw them when I went in this morning . . . and found him." His voice broke. "Lying on the floor behind his desk . . . dead." Pringle looked at Montague. "I knew he was dead right away."

"Why did you go into the office?" Barnaby quietly asked. "Did something alert you?"

"No, no." Pringle shook his head. "I went in to return the originals of the documents I'd copied for Mr. Montague. I finished the copies late yesterday afternoon and hadn't yet returned the originals to the Halstead box. Mr. Runcorn had the box with him and was up to his eyeballs, so to speak, so rather than disturb him, I left the documents I had in my desk. If he'd wanted them, he knew I had them and where they would be. So this morning I thought he'd be finished with the box, and I went in with the documents to put them away . . ." He swallowed. "And that's when I found him."

"How very distressing." Penelope arrived with a mug of strong tea. "Here—drink this, and try not to think about anything for a while."

"Thank you, ma'am." Pringle accepted the cup, wrapping his thin hands around it. "You're very kind."

Barnaby waited for Pringle to take a sip of the tea—highly sugared, he had not a doubt; Penelope knew what was needed—then he asked, still speaking in a gentle tone, "After you found Mr. Runcorn, what did you do?"

Pringle sighed. "Didn't know what to do, did I? I panicked, dropped the documents on his desk, and rushed out into the street—and there were the two constables on their beat. I dragged them in and showed them." Without glancing at the inner office, he nodded that way. "They've been in there ever since. I think they've sent for help from their station." He sipped, then glanced at the clock. "It hasn't been that long. I didn't go into the office until after nine." He looked down. "I just thought he was in there working."

Barnaby glanced at Montague, then walked toward the inner office. The door was fully open, but before he reached the doorway, a burly constable hove into view.

"I'm sorry, sir, but you can't come in here. Murder most foul. We're waiting for the doctor and our sergeant—can't let anything be touched until they say."

"Indeed. I do hope you've touched as little as possible." Barnaby drew out a card case and flicked it open. "I'm a consultant to the Metropolitan Police and am presently working on a case with Inspector Stokes of Scotland Yard. The case concerns a client of Mr. Runcorn. She, too, was recently murdered. It's therefore highly likely that Runcorn's murder is linked to Stokes's case. That connection is why we"—with a wave, he indicated Penelope and Montague—"arrived to consult Mr. Runcorn." Handing the constable one of Stokes's cards, Barnaby added one of his own for good measure; there were times when being an "Honorable" could be helpful. "I strongly suggest you send some-one to summon Stokes immediately. He's presently at the Yard in a meeting." Imagining Stokes's response, Barnaby hid a wry smile. "I can assure you he'll want to be disturbed."

The constable frowned at the cards, then looked up at Barnaby and nodded. "Right. Thank you, sir. I'll send my partner right away."

Barnaby inclined his head and drifted back to rejoin the others. "Let's give them a few minutes to get them-selves organized."

A few minutes was all it took; the burly constable sent his young, gangly partner off with orders to take a hackney to Scotland Yard and report to Inspector Stokes with all speed.

When the door shut behind the younger man, Barnaby arched his brows at Penelope and Montague, then ambled back, the other two following, to the inner office.

The burly constable saw them coming and straight-ened. "Sir?"

Knowing that the police surgeon for the district, harassed individuals though they always were, was likely to arrive before Stokes, Barnaby thought it wise to push a little. "I wondered, Constable, if I might take a brief look. Our own investigations are pressing, and

as what happened here was almost certainly an outcome of the earlier murder, if I could view the body,
and even more the desk and the papers on it, we might
be able to move matters forward at a better pace."

From his expression, it was obvious the constable
wasn't sure he should agree but equally wasn't sure of
the wisdom of refusing.

In an understanding tone, Barnaby promised,
"I won't touch anything."

The constable glanced past him at Penelope and
Montague. "Just you?"

Penelope smiled reassuringly at the man. "We'll
wait in the doorway and just watch."

The constable considered, then glanced at Barnaby.
"All right, then. Just as long as you don't move anything. Worth me job, that would be."

Barnaby inclined his head and, sliding his hands into
his greatcoat pockets, moved into the room. The constable watched from his station to one side of the open
door. Penelope edged into the room, taking up position
on the other side of the doorway while Montague hovered on the threshold.

While Adair slowly paced around the desk, Montague
scanned the room, identifying what had changed since
his previous visit.

Adair noticed. "Anything different?"

"Aside from poor Runcorn being sprawled on the floor"—Montague could see an out-flung hand, the arm, and not much more; it appeared Runcorn had been pulled backward out of his chair—"there's a bookend missing off that shelf." He pointed to a shelf behind the desk, midway up the wall; the empty space was obvious once pointed out. "I think it was a horse's head. And"—he surveyed the documents scattered over the desk; other than the stack that Pringle must have left, obviously dropped on one corner, the entire surface of the desk was awash in a ruffled tide of paper—"that mess isn't normal. Last time I was here, he had documents on the desk, but most were in stacks. That looks like someone searched through all the stacks, one after the other, without setting the documents back as they went. Runcorn would never have done that."

"Hmm." Adair had halted on the other side of the desk, looking down at the body lying stretched upon the floor. "Constable . . . I'm sorry, what was your name?"

"Watkins, sir."

"Constable Watkins, did you or your colleague move the body at all?"

"No, sir. Just checked his pulse at his wrist and neck—which, of course, there wasn't any."

"Good." Adair glanced at Penelope. "Check with Pringle, will you?"

With a nod, Penelope went, slipping past Montague.

She returned less than a minute later. "He said he didn't touch the body at all."

Looking down, Adair grimaced. "Understandable." Hitching up his trousers, he crouched, then bent lower until all Montague could see were the blond curls on the back of his head. "Very well. I can see the bookend—it's lying off to one side. We won't know for certain until the doctor examines him, but I'd wager he was hit on the back of the head with the bookend—it looks more than heavy enough—and then . . ." His voice hardened. "The murderer, whoever he was, and I think we can be sure it was a he, looped a length of cord of some sort . . ."

Adair's head and shoulders swiveled as he looked about, searching the floor. "And there it is. Rather sloppy of our murderer to leave it, but what looks like a length of silky curtain cord—the sort used to loop back curtains—is lying half under the desk."

Rising, his hands still sunk in his pockets, Adair bent over the desk, head tilting this way and that as he scanned the documents rumpled and shuffled and flung in disarray upon it. "As far as I can make out, all of these relate to the Halstead estate. There's nothing obvious, like a piece torn away, or a blot where something may have been copied." Bending, he peered at the underside of the rocking blotter. "And nothing that looks recent on the blotter."

"The most likely outcome"—Montague waved—"of all this would be something taken—a letter, an account, a statement—a record of some sort removed."

Straightening, Adair grimaced. "Which will be very hard to identify."

Montague nodded. He glanced at Watkins, then looked back at Adair. "When the police are satisfied here, my staff might be able to pinpoint some gap in the records, perhaps with Pringle's help. We can at least look."

Adair nodded; his gaze had returned to the body. "I think the blow to his head was powerful enough to render him unconscious. I can't see any evidence that he struggled, that he fought."

The weight of the silence that followed suggested that none of them found any great solace in that fact.

Adair was on his way back to the door, and the others were moving back into the outer office, when a dark-suited individual carrying a black bag came through the street door. A sharp, shrewd gaze from very weary eyes found Watkins. "Constable?"

Watkins waved the doctor to the inner office. "He's in here, and no, no one's touched him."

The doctor briefly nodded to Adair, Penelope, and Montague, then strode past and into the inner office.

Montague returned to stand by Pringle at his desk. "The Halstead file—did you notice the documents on Mr. Runcorn's desk?"

Pringle, whose color had improved, nodded. "Aye— looked like the lot had been thoroughly searched."

"Any chance of you being able to tell if anything's been taken?" Montague asked as Adair and Penelope joined them.

Pringle's brows rose as he considered. "Well, I had the most important records with me, in my drawer, so we know he didn't get any of them."

"You're sure they weren't searched?" Barnaby asked.

"Aye. I'd left them in a nice neat stack in my drawer there"—Pringle looked down at the second drawer on the right side of his desk—"and set my ink-bottle and capped nibs on the top of them, as I usually do. When I opened the drawer this morning to get the stack out, the ink-bottle and nibs were exactly as I'd left them."

"Good," Barnaby said. "So we know those records, at least, are intact. What about the rest of the Halstead documents, the ones Runcorn was looking through?"

"As to that," Pringle said, his thin chest swelling a trifle, "we have our own system of numbering."

He glanced toward the inner office. "If the police let me at them, I can re-sort the file, check by the numbers if any pages are missing. If any are, there's a master list of numbers—it was in the file with all the rest in Mr. Runcorn's office, but unless he knew what the numbers and our notations meant, I can't see any reason any murderer would have taken the list." Pringle's voice had grown stronger. He straightened, meeting Barnaby's gaze. "I can at least do that if it will help catch whoever did for Mr. Runcorn. Young he might have been, but he was a good man."

Barnaby nodded. "I'll do what I can to make sure you get a chance to check the documents."

On the words, the door swung open and Stokes strode in. He came straight to them. "What's happened?"

Barnaby told him what they knew, and what they'd deduced, in a rapid-fire report.

Stokes took it all in without a word, his face giving nothing away. When Penelope introduced Pringle and explained his role, Stokes inclined his head, his gray gaze absorbing every little detail about Runcorn's clerk.

"So," Barnaby concluded, "other than having the police surgeon verify our deductions about how Runcorn was killed, the two most important clues we have are that length of silk cord and the documents."

He nodded to Pringle. "Pringle here will re-sort and tell us if anything's been taken."

Stokes nodded. "Good. Let me handle it." Stepping past them, he walked with a powerful, prowling stride to the inner office.

The deep growl of Stokes's voice reached them, but Barnaby couldn't hear exactly what was said. In less than five minutes, however, Stokes walked out of the office, a foot-high pile of papers filling his arms, an envelope balanced atop them.

Stokes handed the documents to Pringle. "That's everything that was on Runcorn's desk. Scotland Yard have officially seized them as part of the investigation, and I'm now handing them to you to sort for us. Just so we're clear, the papers are for the moment the property of the police, and not to be handed to anyone without my express authority."

"Indeed, sir." Pringle accepted the documents.

Stokes lifted the envelope from the top of the stack, held it up to Barnaby, then slid the envelope into his pocket. "The cord. Interesting find."

"We can only hope it'll prove useful," Barnaby said.

Settling the roughly stacked documents on his desk, Pringle turned to Montague. "Sir—I'm not sure what to do." He waved at the office. "There was no other partner, just Mr. Runcorn, and while I can manage the documents well enough, I can't handle the clients, and some will surely turn up soon."

Montague thought, then nodded. "Indeed." Reaching into his pocket, he pulled out a card. "I suggest you place a note in the window, stating that the office is closed and will remain so for the foreseeable future, but that clients of Mr. Runcorn can seek information at this address." He handed Pringle his card. "Then take the Halstead papers, and . . ." Drawing a sheet of fresh paper from the pigeonhole along the top of Pringle's desk, he drew out a pencil and wrote rapidly. "Take this letter to my office and give it to Mr. Slocum, my head clerk. He'll find a desk for you. Your first task must be to re-sort the Halstead file and determine if any pages have been taken, and if so, which. If any of Mr. Runcorn's clients appear, my junior assistant, a Mr. Phillip Foster, will assist you in dealing with them." Reaching the end of his missive, Montague signed the letter, then tucked away his pencil, folded the sheet, and handed it to Pringle. "That will take care of business, as it were, for the moment. We can work out what's to be done once this matter of murder is behind us."

Pringle met his gaze, then bowed. "Thank you, sir." Tucking away the letter, he looked at the mammoth task represented by the pile of papers on his desk. "I'll get on to this straightaway."

"Before you do," Stokes said, "I need to ask you a few questions."

Pringle nodded; straightening, he waited.

Stokes glanced at the others. "I've already sent constables to canvass the neighborhood, asking if anyone noticed anything." Returning his gaze to Pringle, he said, "So first, I want you to think back to when you last saw Mr. Runcorn alive." When Pringle nodded, Stokes asked, "When was that?"

"Yesterday evening, about seven o'clock. I went into his office to let him know I was leaving. He was still working through the Halstead file."

"Was it normal for him to be working so late?"

Pringle nodded. "Often worked late, he did. Like I said, he was the only partner in the firm, so he had to handle everything I couldn't."

"Did he ever meet with clients late, after you'd left?"

Pringle wrinkled his nose. "Sometimes, but not often. Far as I know, he had no meetings arranged for last evening. If he'd had, the meeting would have been entered in the book, which I always check every morning so I can make sure he has the relevant file before I leave."

"So we can be quite sure that whoever saw him last night—the murderer—did not have an appointment." Stokes nodded rather grimly. "Was your master likely to have let anyone in who he didn't know? Not just into the main office, but into his own office. It seems fairly clear that whoever was there with him, your master was relaxed enough to be sitting in his chair, with the murderer beside him, possibly looking over the papers, when he was attacked."

Pringle paused, then shook his head. "I don't know what I can say, Inspector. I never knew him to entertain any friends here. Only clients."

Or, Stokes thought, *clients' relatives.*

"When you left," Barnaby asked, "did you see anyone at all? Did you pass anyone? Notice anyone, even if they're people you might expect to see?"

Pringle blinked, clearly thinking back. "There was the usual crowd going in and out of the public house across the street, but I didn't go that way. I walked down the street toward Broad Street and . . ." Pringle paused, staring into space, then more softly said, "There *was* a man I hadn't seen before, standing under the overhang of the tobacconist's next door. He was staring at the window, although, now I think of it, as the store was shut, I don't know what he could have been looking at—Samuel, the tobacconist, always puts his wares away every night and leaves the shelves empty. But as for the man, I walked past him, but he had on a cloak and a broad-brimmed hat. The hat was tipped down, so I didn't see much of his face."

Stokes felt a familiar thrill go through him. "How tall was he?"

"Not that much taller than me," Pringle said. "Maybe an inch or two, no more than that."

"Medium to tall then. Did you see what color hair he had?"

Pringle squinted. "Not clearly, but it was at least brown. It wasn't blond." His gaze went to Barnaby's curls. "Definitely not fair."

Stokes drew breath, and asked, "What about his face? Did you see it well enough to recognize him?" It was a long shot, but . . . stranger things had happened.

But Pringle visibly deflated. "No." His lips twisted in a grimace. "I'm sorry, Inspector, but I only caught a glimpse of his profile. All I can tell you is that he was clean shaven but had side-whiskers." Pringle drew phantom whiskers on his own cheeks. "And his cheeks weren't . . ." He looked at Stokes, then Barnaby. "Like yours—they were rounder."

Stokes nodded. "Thank you. You might not be able to identify him, but that's still very helpful."

"I have a question." Penelope's softer, yet still commanding, voice was such a contrast that it focused all attention. They all looked at her, but she was studying Pringle. Capturing his gaze, she tilted her head and smiled encouragingly. "You see clients all the time.

You're used to dealing with lots of different sorts of people. You will know the answer to my question. When I put my question to you, I want you to think of the man you saw and answer immediately—the first answer that pops into your mind. All right?"

Pringle looked a touch uneasy but nodded.

"The man you saw outside the tobacconist's—was he an aristocrat, a gentleman, a merchant, or a working man?"

Pringle answered without hesitation. "A gentleman." Then he blinked and looked surprised, but he didn't retract the answer.

Penelope beamed. "Thank you."

"Indeed," Stokes said. "Thank you, Mr. Pringle, you've been of considerable help." He nodded at the Halstead papers. "If you wish to put up that notice and take yourself off to Mr. Montague's office, you're free to leave."

Pringle half-bowed. "Thank you, Inspector. Ma'am. Sirs."

Turning to his desk, he started neatening the papers, then searching for string to tie them up.

Stokes beckoned the other three closer to the door, but before he spoke, someone tapped on the glass.

Stokes turned to see the constables he'd sent to ask questions around the neighborhood in a loose group on the pavement, clearly waiting to report. "One moment," he said to the other three. Opening the door, he beckoned the sergeant in charge inside. "Well, Phipps? Anything?"

"Bits and pieces, sir. Other than those at the pub, there weren't that many people out and about. Dinnertime for many, so most were indoors. That said . . ." Portentously, the sergeant flicked open his notebook. "We've several people, most from the pub, but also a match-seller who has her spot just on the corner, who saw a gent going into this office, and then leaving again about half an hour later. Time seems right—all say it was after seven when he went in, and somewhere after the half hour when he left, and they can hear the bells easy from here."

"What description did they give?" Stokes asked.

"Nothing definitive. No one who says they'd recognize the blighter." Phipps proceeded to recite the descriptions given by five different people.

The descriptions matched Pringles's in every degree.

"So," Stokes said, "we have a gentleman—they're all clear on that—clean shaven, but with shortish side-whiskers and rounded cheeks. Not tall, but a little above average height. Brown to dark hair."

"That sums it up, sir." Phipps closed his notebook.

"One question, Sergeant." Again all eyes swung to Penelope. "These people who saw the man—did any of them mention the man giving any indication that he'd noticed them?"

Phipps shook his head. "No one mentioned him noticing them, ma'am. All said he strode along, eyes forward. The match-seller did say that she was certain he hadn't even seen her—marched right on by, his cloak swinging, as if he hadn't registered her at all."

Penelope smiled and inclined her head. "Thank you, Sergeant."

Phipps looked to Stokes, who nodded a dismissal.

As the door swung shut behind the sergeant, Stokes lowered his voice and said, "So we have a description that, from memory, *could* fit any of the Halstead males." He paused, then allowed, "I'm not sure if it fits all of them, but certainly some of them. More than one."

"I think," Barnaby said, also lowering his voice in deference to Pringle, who was putting on his heavy coat and getting ready to leave, "that, all the evidence considered, it's safe to assume that both Lady Halstead and Runcorn were murdered because of those irregularities in Lady Halstead's account."

Montague started to nod, then froze. He blinked, then whirled. "Pringle—one thing."

Caught in the act of hefting the bound pile of papers into his arms, the clerk looked across. "Yes, Mr. Montague?"

No one had mentioned Lady Halstead's death in Pringle's hearing. Montague asked, "Were Runcorn and Son notified of Lady Halstead's death? Of her murder?"

Pringle's face told the tale. "*Murder?*" His eyes goggled. "Her ladyship, too?"

If Runcorn hadn't known, then . . . Montague swung around. "Good God! The money!" He strode for the door.

The others stared for a second, then recovered and piled out of the door on his heels.

They quickly caught up, even Penelope, holding up her skirts so she could hurry along. It was she who demanded, "What about the money?"

Montague didn't slow but forced himself to order his thoughts. "If we're right about the payments being the motive for the murders, then the money is the murderer's. Now that Lady Halstead is dead, sometime soon her account will be closed—normally Runcorn would have been advised of the death and would have handled it—and the money will be bound over—"

"—and the murderer will lose it." Penelope went on, "So he has to get it out of the account as soon as he can."

"And," Stokes grimly concluded, "if he hasn't already done so, we have a chance to set up a watch and catch him when he comes for it."

"Which bank holds the account?" Adair asked, taking Penelope's arm as they neared the busier thoroughfare of Broad Street.

Montague rarely forgot such details. "Grimshaws in Threadneedle Street."

Threadneedle Street wasn't far; there was no sense taking a hackney. This was Montague's territory; he led the way past the Excise Office and down a narrower street, then they were on Threadneedle Street and the bank was just ahead of them.

"Do you have that letter of authority?" Stokes asked.

Montague patted his top pocket.

"Good," Stokes growled. "You lead, and I'll hang back. Let's not alert anyone to the murder unless we have to."

Montague nodded, opened the door to the bank, and led the way inside.

His card ensured that his request to see the manager was instantly granted; few working in that square mile of the City did not recognize his name, did not know of his reputation.

The letter of authority from Lady Halstead was duly produced and examined, then the manager called in the clerk of accounts, who quickly produced Lady Halstead's register.

The manager looked at it, then blinked and somewhat carefully turned it around so Montague could see the entries for himself.

"Ah-hem." The manager cleared his throat. "It appears, Mr. Montague, that Lady Halstead closed that account this morning, a little over an hour ago."

His face setting, Montague looked at the figure. "It was withdrawn in cash?"

He glanced up at the clerk, who nodded. "Indeed, sir. I was consulted, of course, but everything seemed in order . . ."

Montague grimaced, then glanced at the manager. "With your permission . . ." He looked at the clerk. "If you could ask the two gentlemen and the lady waiting just outside to join us, I believe you both need to be informed of some recent developments."

The manager's eyes widened, but he nodded to the clerk, who went to the door and admitted Stokes, Adair, and Penelope.

The manager and Montague stood. Montague performed the introductions, then, when chairs had been found and all but the clerk were seated, Stokes informed the manager, "I regret to inform you that Lady Halstead was murdered, sometime during the night two nights ago." He shifted his gaze to the clerk. "We believe that the money in her ladyship's account with this bank is a large part of the reason she was killed. I must therefore ask who withdrew the money, and what form of authority they presented to you to be able to do so."

At a curt nod from the manager, the clerk cleared his throat. "The money was withdrawn by a lady—because of the amount, I was summoned and attended to her myself."

"Please describe her," Stokes said.

The clerk hesitated, then said, "She was of average height, neither fat nor thin, but as to her face, she was wearing a hat with a fine veil. I could see her face, but not clearly."

"What color was her hair?" Penelope asked.

"Brown—not dark." The clerk's gaze had risen to Penelope's lustrous locks. "More a mid-brown. Ordinary brown."

"And," Penelope continued, "how old would you say this lady was?"

The clerk clearly thought back, then wiggled his head. "Not old—not middle-aged. But she wasn't a young lady, either."

"Lady." Penelope arched a brow. "Why did you think she was a lady?"

"Well, she was well dressed and well spoken, ma'am. Easy to deal with and . . . well, confident, if you know what I mean."

Penelope nodded. "Thank you." She sat back.

"Do you have the withdrawal authority?" Montague asked. "I would like to examine it."

The clerk exchanged a look with the manager, then, receiving another terse nod, reached for the ledger still lying open before Montague and turned the page, revealing a handwritten letter. "This only happened an hour or so ago, so I haven't had a chance to put it in the file."

Montague nodded as he picked up the letter. He read it, then handed it to Stokes, seated beside him. "It's supposedly from Lady Halstead, authorizing the withdrawal, the bearer of the letter to be given the full sum of the monies in the account."

While Stokes scanned the letter, Montague again took out the letter of authority Lady Halstead had written for him. When Stokes reached the end of the withdrawal authority, Montague held out his letter. Stokes took it and held the two side by side.

Montague leaned closer; Penelope, on Stokes's other side, did the same. All three of them looked from one letter to the other, comparing.

Eventually, Stokes sighed. Handing Montague back his letter, Stokes lowered the withdrawal authority and, across the bank manager's desk, met the man's eyes. "I'll be keeping this, and I'll also have to take the ledger. Both are now evidence of a crime."

The manager looked a trifle ill. "The letter?"

"Is a forgery," Penelope said. "But a very, very good one. Without having, as we have, a letter known to have been written by Lady Halstead to compare, I seriously doubt anyone could have spotted it."

"I don't believe there will be any repercussions with respect to the bank or its employees," Montague said. He glanced at Stokes.

Stokes nodded. He slipped the withdrawal authority back into the ledger, then closed the book, picked it up, and rose. "Thank you for your cooperation. We'll see ourselves out."

They halted on the pavement outside the bank and looked at each other.

"What now?" Montague asked.

"Now . . ." Stokes glanced at Adair, then Penelope, then looked back at Montague. "If you all have the time, I believe we should take an hour or so to revisit everything we've seen, heard, and learned this morning."

Penelope nodded decisively. "If we don't, something vital might slip past us." She looked at Stokes. "Speaking of which, might I suggest that we adjourn to Greenbury Street?" She glanced at Montague. "Stokes's house. Griselda will be there, and as she's the only one of us who hasn't been through all the events of the morning, she's the only one of us who is likely to have a truly detached view." Penelope looked at all three men's faces. "I vote we go to Greenbury Street and tell Griselda all."

Stokes met Adair's eyes, then sighed and nodded. "Very well. Greenbury Street it is."

They took two hackneys and arrived in Greenbury Street as Griselda was pushing Megan's perambulator up the front path, having just returned from taking her daughter for an airing in the nearby park.

Griselda was delighted to see them. Grinning, Penelope touched cheeks, then bent to coo at Megan, who waved her chubby fists and chortled in reply. Barnaby greeted Griselda, then joined Penelope in admiring Megan.

Stokes kissed his wife's cheek, then considered the sight of his friends paying their dues to his daughter with a proud, paternal air.

Montague hung back, watching the interaction between the two couples, noting the warmth and the strong friendship so openly on display. Then Stokes turned to him and drew him forward, introducing him to Mrs. Stokes—Griselda, as she, like Penelope, insisted he call her—and then to the small girl-child, who looked up at him with wide, curious eyes.

"Careful," Stokes murmured. "They wind you about their tiny fingers with looks like that."

Montague realized he was grinning in the same faintly besotted way Stokes was.

Somewhat to his surprise, Montague found himself swept up in the camaraderie, in the wave of relaxed enthusiasm that carried them all inside to settle in a neat sitting room. They sank onto chairs and the sofa. After handing little Megan into her nurse's care, Griselda joined them.

Settling on the sofa alongside Penelope, Griselda commanded, "So! Tell me all."

They proceeded to do so, and in the telling consolidated and refined their collective understanding.

By unvoiced agreement, they held to the facts as they knew them until they'd told the story to the end, to the moment when they'd left the bank, the forged letter of withdrawal in Stokes's keeping.

Only then did they turn their minds to the questions those facts raised, to speculation, to the possibilities.

"The woman who presented the letter of withdrawal," Stokes murmured. "Where did she get it? And what does that tell us about who she is?"

Penelope straightened; as if taking up the challenge, she replied, "The letter is such a good forgery that it could only have been created by someone familiar with Lady Halstead's hand."

"Or someone with access to letters her ladyship wrote," Adair put in.

Penelope inclined her head. "True. Which puts the companion, Miss Matcham, at the top of the list of possible suspects." She held up her hand. "However, I have severe doubts that it was in fact her."

"Why?" Stokes asked, before Montague could.

"Well, I haven't yet met Miss Matcham, so I can only go by what you've said of her, but it strikes me that, if she was behind the withdrawal of the money, she's intelligent enough to ensure no one would associate the withdrawal with her. The letter gave the money to 'The Bearer,' not to any named individual, so she could have dressed however she wished. She could have enlisted male assistance. Or—and this is what I would have done—she could have pretended to be male. It's not that hard, especially for only a short time, with only a bank clerk to fool." Penelope frowned. "Regardless, I have a strong suspicion that we're intended to think it is Miss Matcham, to leap to that as the obvious conclusion—which, of course, means it's untrue."

"There's also the fact," Montague said, "that Miss Matcham was, and still is, sincerely devoted to Lady Halstead. I really cannot see her condoning, much less doing, something that is, in effect, stealing from her late employer."

"And," Stokes said, "the same can be said of the maid, Tilly Westcott. At a pinch, she could have been the woman who presented the letter at the bank, but she, too, is devoted to her ladyship." He looked at Montague. "I take it there's no suggestion that Lady Halstead was in arrears with their wages?"

Montague took a second to bring the appropriate payments to mind, then shook his head. "No. We're in the middle of a quarter, and all the staff were paid as expected to this point."

"Right, then." Stokes stretched out his legs and crossed his ankles. "I believe we can discount the notion that either Miss Matcham or Miss Westcott was the woman behind the veil—"

"But we should perhaps accept that someone intended us to suspect them." Adair glanced about the company. "Because whoever wrote the forged letter was almost certainly a family member."

"Indeed." Stokes nodded. "And what's more, I'll lay odds the family will want to use the vague but suggestive description of the mystery woman to point the finger at Miss Matcham, or if not her, the maid."

"They've already tried that once," Montague reminded the gathering.

"And I'm quite sure they'll do it again," Penelope said, "if only because it's easier than accepting the alternative—that the murderer is one of them."

"Which," Stokes said, "brings us neatly back to the murderer, the gentleman seen by several people entering and later leaving Runcorn's office. The description would fit, and certainly suggests one of the Halstead men, but which one?"

Stokes, Adair, and Montague exchanged glances.

Viewing their uncertainty, Penelope helpfully recited the description, concluding, "Neither Griselda nor I have seen the Halstead gentlemen, but surely those side-whiskers give you some clue."

Barnaby grimaced. "So one might think, but, sadly, that isn't the case. They all have them, more or less to the same degree." He hesitated, then continued, "For me, at least, that description doesn't distinguish between the five males of Halstead blood—Mortimer, his son Hayden, Maurice, William, and Cynthia's son Walter." He glanced at the others. "In fact, if I encountered any of the Halstead men in the street at night, in poor light, I seriously doubt I would be able to tell one from the other. In good light, they are easy to distinguish, but in shadows . . ." Barnaby looked at Stokes. "Similar build, similar height, similar coloring, with key features, including the round cheeks, all similar, too. Even their dress is not wildly dissimilar."

Stokes slowly nodded. "It's their eyes that are different—Hayden's and Walter's, and also Maurice's, are all lighter—and there's also a slight difference in the set of their lips, and possibly the prominence, although not the shape, of their noses. But unless you can see all those details"—he tipped his head to Barnaby—"I agree. Telling those five apart isn't easy."

They pondered that fact, and its implications, in silence.

Griselda broke it; slapping her palms on her thighs, she rose. "No, don't get up. I'm going to organize some sandwiches for luncheon. You could all do with some food to fuel all this cogitating."

"I'll help." Penelope rose, too.

When the ladies had disappeared deeper into the house, Stokes looked at Barnaby and Montague. "We need to very carefully think through how we're to press forward with this. Especially with the complication of Camberly's position—even if he isn't a suspect, his son is—and we've also got Mortimer Halstead to contend with. My reading of him is that he will prove difficult over one of the family's being our prime suspect."

"Oh, yes." Barnaby nodded. "He's exactly that sort. And given the astounding lack of loyalty to

Lady Halstead—or rather their devotion to their own interests over seeking justice for her, which they've already amply demonstrated—dealing with this family while ferreting out the murderer in their midst is not going to be a simple matter."

Montague sighed. "One assumes that, in investigating a crime of any sort, those involved who are not the criminal will hold justice being served to have the highest priority, but, sadly, that's often not the case."

A disaffected silence fell. It was broken by Penelope, who appeared in the open doorway to announce, "If you will come to the dining room, gentlemen, luncheon awaits."

The three men rose and followed Penelope into the dining room, where they took seats about the oval table. They passed around platters of sandwiches and cold meats. A young maid poured ale for the gentlemen and lemonade for the ladies.

While they ate, they exchanged only the most minor comments.

Stokes waited until the sandwiches were gone and, replete, they sat back, the men sipping their ale, before returning to what he saw as his dilemma. "We have to investigate the Halstead family, thoroughly and exhaustively. Whoever this murderer is—and I think we all agree that it's one of the five males, with only

Camberly thus far excluded—he isn't stupid. He acted swiftly to, as he saw it, put a stop to Lady Halstead looking into her affairs, presumably because he knew she would notice the odd payments. He wasn't to know she already had. And then, just to ensure the matter went no further, he eliminated Runcorn—again, in his eyes, the only other person who might have been in a position to raise a question about those odd payments. The murderer wasn't to know—and still doesn't know—that Montague already knows about the payments."

"Hmm." Sitting forward, her elbows on the table, Penelope narrowed her eyes on Montague. "If all was as the murderer believes, and you didn't know about those odd payments, how would this situation—her ladyship's death, followed by Runcorn's, followed by the withdrawal of the money by some mysterious lady apparently with her ladyship's approval—be expected to play out?"

Montague took a moment to think before saying, "If I didn't know that there was anything odd about those payments . . . with both her ladyship and Runcorn removed, as well as the money, then barring the theft of the extra funds from the account this morning, everything should balance up nicely enough, at least as far as a cursory examination of the estate's books would go. If we *didn't* know about all the rest, this morning's theft would be put down as a regrettable loss, and there would, therefore, be no reason the estate wouldn't simply pass through probate without further question."

"So no further ripples or ructions from the murderer's point of view." Penelope nodded. "So at this point, he should be satisfied that he's done all that's necessary to obliterate his tracks."

"But," Stokes said, "he might see Montague as a threat." Slate gray eyes met Montague's gaze. "He might come after you."

Montague arched his brows, then raised a shoulder. "I can't see why he would—at least not over what we've let fall to this point. All he knows regarding me is that Lady Halstead recently gave me a letter of authority to oversee her financial affairs. He doesn't know she specifically engaged me to look into the odd payments. He also doesn't know that I have all the Halstead papers and am analyzing them for the police. If we don't mention those things, there's no reason for him to believe I or my office pose any active threat. For all he knows, my involvement in this is, and will remain, purely superficial."

Stokes's lips slowly stretched in a predatory smile. "Which brings me back to the question of how to deal with the Halsteads." He glanced around the table.

"Given we believe the murderer is one of them, I intend to tell them as little as possible."

"Hear, hear," Barnaby said. "As Montague just illustrated, the less they know, the better."

Stokes faintly grimaced. "In addition to that, however, at this juncture I think it will be best if Miss Matcham and Miss Westcott are also not informed of our progress. Even though we believe they're entirely innocent, they are nevertheless suspects, at least in the family's eyes, and"—he raised his shoulders in a slight shrug—"like it or not, we need to treat them as such."

Penelope didn't share that view and said so. Somewhat tartly.

Even though neither lady had yet met Violet Matcham or Tilly Westcott, Griselda agreed. "For all you know, they might be in danger, and not telling them of your findings might fail to put them on guard."

Montague cleared his throat. "As to that, I believe Miss Matcham's intelligence is such that she is already well aware that the murderer is most likely a family member. That being so, I can't see that telling her of Runcorn's murder at this point will serve any purpose other than to add to her distress." He met Stokes's gaze. "She met Runcorn recently, several times, when he called upon Lady Halstead."

Stokes nodded. "So it's agreed—we do our best to investigate the family while keeping our findings close to our collective chest."

The men all agreed; the ladies abstained but didn't argue.

"Right, then." Stokes set down his empty ale mug. "I need to return to Runcorn's office and finalize things there. And while I'm doing that, I'll have the constables go around again and ask for any sightings of a veiled lady." He met Adair's, then Montague's, gazes. "Just to ensure our mysterious lady hasn't played a larger role in this drama."

Adair nodded. "And I rather think I should return to Grimshaws Bank and see if anyone noticed which way the lady went. You never know—that might give us some clues."

"While you're there," Montague said, eyes narrowing in thought, "you might ask to speak with the head clerk again and inquire as to how the payments were made. It's a very long shot, especially with deposits made in cash, but one never knows— the tellers might recall." He met Adair's eyes and shrugged. "It's worth asking. And if the head clerk doesn't recall your connection to this matter"—he pulled out a card and handed it to Adair—"feel free to use my name."

Adair took the card, raised it in salute. "I will. It's a good point."

"And I," Montague stated, "will continue to seek information in my usual sphere. Those payments are puzzling. If I can't get to the bottom of them by analyzing the Halstead accounts, I might call in a few favors and see if any of my colleagues have any suggestions." He looked at Stokes. "All with the utmost discretion, of course."

Stokes nodded and pushed back his chair. "So we all have things to do."

Adair rose, too. "Matters to pursue, avenues to follow."

Montague hid a smile and got to his feet. With compliments and thanks to Griselda, and a bow to Penelope, he followed Stokes and Adair through the house, out of the front door, and out through the gate.

Stokes paused on the pavement, met Adair's, then Montague's, eyes. "I suggest we meet again at your office in the City later this afternoon and pool what we've learned. We'll need to see the family again, clearly, but I would like to have as much information as possible before we call them together again."

Adair nodded. So did Montague. With salutes, the trio parted and went their separate ways.

Penelope stood at the front window of the sitting room and, with Griselda beside her, watched the three men stride away. "Off they go, busily investigating. What odds will you give me that they plan to meet later—just the three of them—to compare notes?"

Griselda snorted. "That's no wager—it's a certainty." Arms crossed beneath her bosom, she nodded toward the pavement. "That's what that little gathering was about—setting a time and place."

"I suppose," Penelope said, head tilting as she considered, "in the circumstances, the violence of murder can only be expected to make them more protective."

"Not that they weren't protective enough to begin with, but I take your point." Griselda glanced at Penelope. "Matters have changed, and adequate adjustments have yet to be made."

"Indeed." Penelope nodded. "So they've headed off, and we know what they're doing. What does that leave us to do?" After a second, she answered her own question. "I rather think we should see what we can learn about the Halstead family from a social perspective. The Halsteads, and the Camberlys, too."

"Oh," Griselda said, her voice rising with interest and subtle excitement, "I know just where to start." She met Penelope's eyes, read her speculative, questioning gaze, and smiled. "Just let me have a word to Gloria and make sure Megan's settled, then I'll grab my bonnet and show you."

"Show me what?" Penelope asked.

Griselda grinned. "The other side of fashionable shopping."

Penelope looked intrigued. She waved Griselda on, then followed on her heels. "I'll get my coat and bonnet on and meet you at the door."

Chapter 7

Stokes spent an hour and a half at Runcorn's offices, finalizing details and overseeing the securing of the premises. "Just as a precaution," he said to the local sergeant, "I want two men watching the place at all times, but there's no need for them to make themselves visible. One can be inside, the other keeping an eye on the door and the street from the pub across the way."

The sergeant arched his brows. "Think he'll come back?"

"I think it's a possibility." Stokes looked up as the three constables he'd sent to ask around as to any veiled lady sighted in the area over the last days returned.

They saluted. At Stokes's questioning look, the more senior shook his head. "No luck, sir. We've asked up and down both legs of Winchester Street, even managed to catch that match-seller again—she's an observant one—but no one's seen any veiled lady loitering about."

Stokes nodded. "It was a long shot, but one we had to rule out. Good work."

Two minutes later, he left the sergeant and the constables to organize the details of the watch and headed back to Scotland Yard.

Barnaby elected to question the bank staff first, before the head clerk had a chance to forget him. He produced Montague's card anyway, judging that Montague's reputation had more weight in this sphere than his own.

"Mr. Montague suggested that some of your tellers might recall the means by which recent cash deposits into Lady Halstead's account were presented." He took care to affect a hopeful expression. "Any help you or the staff can give us would be much appreciated."

"Hmm." The head clerk, a somewhat officious, self-important little man, pursed his lips, but then nodded. "While I can't promise anything—this is a busy branch with many accounts—if you will give me a few minutes, I'll see what I can learn."

Barnaby inclined his head and drifted to where a row of chairs stood against one wall. Sitting in one, he watched as the clerk returned to his desk, flipped through a stack of papers, and withdrew one—presumably another bank record of some sort. After perusing the document, the head clerk took it with him. He scanned the four tellers at their stations, then made his way to one particular teller, an older man at the last window along the counter.

The clerk waited until the teller finished with the customer before him, then stepped in and, showing the teller the back record, pointed to it and asked a question. The two men exchanged words, then the teller nodded.

Barnaby fought the urge to rise and go and see, to question the teller directly . . . he would need to speak to the man directly, regardless of what the head clerk thought or said.

Luckily, the head clerk looked over and beckoned.

When Barnaby came to the counter, the head clerk smiled with arrogant satisfaction. "Mr. Wadsworth recalls receiving the last cash deposit into Lady Halstead's account clearly, and believes it was presented in the same manner as the previous cash deposits over the last year or so."

Barnaby inclined his head to the clerk. "Excellent." He looked at the teller. "Can you remember who paid in the money?"

"Indeed, sir," Wadsworth said. "I and my colleagues noted it especially, as it seemed . . . well, out of character for what one might imagine for a lady of Lady Halstead's standing."

Puzzled, Barnaby asked, "Out of character in what way?"

The teller glanced at the head clerk, as if confirming he was permitted to speak. When the clerk nodded, Wadsworth returned his gaze to Barnaby. "It was a courier service, sir. Always a different person, but they have a valid deposit slip, all properly signed, so we have to accept the cash."

Barnaby hesitated; the news wasn't at all what he'd anticipated, but . . . perhaps he should have. "A courier service—by that you mean the sort of service that criminals use for . . . shall we say, suspect payments?"

Wadsworth nodded. "Exactly that sort of service, sir. We tellers get to recognize the couriers, and we certainly recognize their sort. It's really rather obvious, of course, because they aren't the sort of person one would imagine having the amount of cash they're handing over the counter."

Barnaby nodded. "Thank you both. I'll take this information back to Mr. Montague and Inspector Stokes." He met both men's eyes and lowered his voice.

"I'm sure I don't need to mention that this information is highly sensitive and needs to be kept under your hat."

"Of course not, sir," Wadsworth said.

The head clerk drew himself up. "We at Grimshaws Bank pride ourselves on our discretion."

Hiding a smile, Barnaby inclined his head. "Again, thank you. I bid you gentlemen a good day."

With polite nods all around, Barnaby left the counter and, suppressing the spring in his step, strode out to the pavement. "One matter accomplished." He looked about. "Now for the second."

He spent the next hour in fruitless ambling along the streets surrounding the bank, asking any of those who were, for whatever reason, fixtures along the way if they had sighted the veiled lady earlier that morning. He'd almost given up hope—had almost accepted that one success a day was as much as he could expect—when he saw a boy of ten or so years wielding a broom at the corner of a lane just around the bend in Bishopsgate.

Strolling up to the lad, hands sunk in his greatcoat pockets, he used the line of patter he'd developed over the past hour. "I was supposed to meet my sister here this morning, and, of course, I slept in. She was supposed to go to the bank back there and meet me outside, but now I don't know if she came and left, or if she hasn't shown at all. She's a lady, and she would

196 • STEPHANIE LAURENS

have been wearing a veil—she usually does when she travels here."

"Yeah?" The boy eyed him. "So what does she look like, this sister of yourn? Other than being female and wearing a veil?"

Barnaby rattled off the general description—brown hair, middle height, about Barnaby's own age.

He could barely believe it when the boy nodded. "You saw her?" he asked in response to the boy's nod.

"Aye." The boy pointed along the street. "She came walking up from Threadneedle Street, and I'm sorry to have to tell you this, guv, but a gentleman was waiting for her in a coach pulled up to the curb just along there."

"A gentleman?" Swallowing his leaping excitement, Barnaby adopted a resigned air. "I expect that must have been my cousin. Did you see him?"

"Not well—he stayed in the carriage. Just opened the door and gave the lady his hand to help her inside." The boy looked at Barnaby questioningly.

Barnaby sighed, pulled out a half crown, and held it up. "So what did he look like?"

"Gentleman—couldn't say how tall 'cause he was sitting down." Like a magpie's, the boy's eyes had fixed on the shiny coin. "He didn't have a beard but those side bits as is common now, and his face was roundish, and he had brown hair." The boy looked at Barnaby as if to ask if that was enough.

"One last thing—how old was this gent?"

The boy blinked. "Thought he was your cousin—don't you know how old he is?"

"I have several cousins. I'm trying to decide which one it was."

"Oh." The boy hesitated, then screwed up his face. "Can't be sure, can I? I didn't see him clearly, but . . . the same age as the lady?"

His tone made it clear that his estimation was pure guess. Nevertheless, Barnaby handed over the coin. "Good enough."

The boy had told him enough to be sure that the veiled lady was working with—or perhaps for—one of the five Halstead males.

Barnaby turned to leave, then halted, hunted in his pocket, and pulled out a sovereign. He swung back to the lad, who had pocketed the half crown. "Here!" When the boy looked up, Barnaby tossed him the sovereign.

Swift as a hawk, the boy plucked the coin from the air. The dawning wonderment in his face as he turned it between his fingers and realized his good fortune made Barnaby grin.

When the boy glanced up, Barnaby jauntily saluted him. "That's for being observant. Put it to good use."

He left the boy staring at the wealth in his palm. Feeling thoroughly pleased, Barnaby strode down the street toward Montague's office.

After returning to Chapel Court and his office, Montague's first act was to check on Pringle. Seated at the desk Slocum had cleared and assigned to him, Pringle was steadily working his way through the accumulated Halstead financial records.

"They go back nearly thirty years." Pringle held up one account. "Sir Hugo dealt with young Mr. Runcorn's father, who had the business before him. I can't tell whether it was the villain who did it, or the constables when they gathered them up, but the papers are in a right jumble."

"So you can't yet say if anything's missing?" Montague asked.

Pringle shook his head. "Not until I get everything in order again."

Leaving him to it, suppressing his impatience to get on and do—to analyze the accounts and find the murderer and so ensure Violet Matcham was safe—Montague spoke with Gibbons and Foster, reviewing their on-going work with the firm's clients, then he confirmed the arrangements to have the pair take over all scheduled meetings for the next several days. His own slate thus cleared, he retreated to his office and settled behind his desk.

The papers Pringle had copied and sent to him sat in a thick sheaf to one side. They beckoned, but Montague resisted. There was one other effort he could and should make, an avenue he could pursue to directly identify the odd payments. Returning to his copy of Lady Halstead's bank statement—the document that had given rise to the intrigue of money and murder—he made a neat list of all the odd deposits stretching back over the last fourteen months.

List completed, he studied it, then called in Slocum and dictated four letters.

Each letter was a separate request, reminding the recipient, each of them one of his peers, of a past favor done for them by Montague or his firm, before describing the pattern of deposits into the Halstead account and asking whether the recipient was aware of any similar deposits made into their clients' bank accounts, and, if so, if they had identified the source and the purpose behind said deposits.

Within the circle of select men-of-business to which all those he'd elected to contact belonged, absolute discretion was assured.

As Slocum retreated to dispatch the letters, Montague stared at the list of deposits, then grimaced.

"Who knows? Perhaps this *is* a more widespread occurrence, something that's happening to others as well." Alternatively, one of his peers might have some insight into possible sources of such not-quite-regular mystery deposits.

Inwardly sighing, he turned to the Halstead records, the pile comprised of the papers Runcorn had initially given him, as well as those documents Pringle had subsequently copied and sent; lifting the inches-thick pile, he placed it squarely on the center of his wide blotter. Leaning back in his chair, he considered the stack.

Could Runcorn have been a party to whatever scheme the murderer had been running?

In his mind, Montague returned to his meeting with the younger man-of-business, studied again his fresh, open face, reviewed again his eager expression, his patent wish to please . . . the touch of awe he'd accorded Montague.

Everything Montague had sensed about Runcorn had rung true; even in hindsight, he could see no reason to change his assessment of the honesty and trustworthiness of the younger man.

"So"—Montague refocused on the pile of papers— "Runcorn had no idea what was going on, but the murderer believed that when Runcorn reviewed the file to get Lady Halstead's affairs in order, he would discover something, enough to be alerted to whatever illegality the murderer was engaged in."

Getting a client's affairs in order involved, among other things, a complete listing of all assets, including all investments currently held, an estimate of their current capital worth, and an accounting of the income deriving from them, as well as a complete reconciliation of bank accounts and monies in the Funds and similar deposits. The last review of the Halsteads' affairs would most likely have been done ten years earlier, at the time of Sir Hugo's death.

Between them, Runcorn and Pringle had extracted, copied, and had delivered to Montague all the papers necessary for him to perform such a review, essentially to get both the Halstead estate's affairs, as well as Lady Halstead's personal affairs, in order.

"Which means," Montague murmured, reaching out to check the numbers inscribed in Pringle's neat hand at the bottom left corner of each page, "that somewhere in this pile should lay some sign of what the murderer has killed twice to conceal."

Confirming via Pringle's notations that the pile was assembled earliest to most recent, Montague lifted the top sheet and started at the beginning.

The clock on his desk stolidly ticked on. Immersed in the documents though he was, checking and making notes on past and present investments, he found his gaze drawn, again and again, to the list of the odd, unaccounted-for deposits that he'd made earlier and had laid aside.

An hour passed. Then another fifteen minutes and he could stand it no longer.

Setting aside the larger pile along with his notes to that point, he picked up the list of deposits, studied it one more time, then rose and went to his door. Looking over the outer office, he called, "Gibbons?"

When Frederick Gibbons looked up, Montague waved the list. "If you would, I'd like your opinion."

Sometimes a fresh pair of eyes saw matters more clearly.

Gibbons promptly rose and followed Montague back into his office.

Returning to his chair, Montague waved Gibbons to a chair before the desk. He waited until Gibbons sat and leveled a curious look at him, before saying, "I want you to look over this list. It's a set of deposits made into a bank account—I've listed both the amounts and the dates on which each deposit was made. I'm trying to identify what the source of these payments might be."

With that, he extended the list.

Gibbons took it.

Montague watched as Gibbons scanned the amounts, noted the dates.

"It's not payments from an investment—not quite regular enough in the timing, and the amounts vary too much . . ." Gibbons glanced up. "These look like deposits from trade of some sort—from sales of something."

Montague blinked. He'd never dealt with trade accounts, but before he had joined Montague and Son, Gibbons had.

The list of figures he'd recently written flashed through his mind; reaching across the desk, he waved his hand for the list. "Give me that."

Gibbons handed it over. Setting the list before him, Montague picked up a pencil and went to work, jotting amounts and sums alongside each of the deposits.

Figures were his forte; all his mind had needed was the clue Gibbons had provided and he had the solution.

Gibbons leaned forward, angling his head to read the sums Montague was writing down the side of the list.

Reaching the end of the list and finishing the calculation to account for the last payment, Montague picked up the list, scanned it again, then handed it back to Gibbons. "What do you think?"

Gibbons looked through the deposits, his eye following the line of Montague's calculations. Reaching the

204 . STEPHANIE LAURENS

list's end, Gibbons nodded decisively. "That's it. Each deposit is the payment from sales of between five and nine items, with each item being worth two hundred and fifty pounds, minus an amount of between two and three percent." Gibbons glanced at Montague. "Were the deposits made by courier?"

"We don't yet know—someone is checking that now—but most courier services charge between two and three percent."

Gibbons was staring at the list again. "I'm trying to imagine what items one might sell at two hundred and fifty pounds each, and have such a level of consistent sales. Five minimum, month to month, reliable and regular."

Montague thought, too, then shook his head. "It might be lucrative, but it's almost certainly not legal."

Gibbons snorted and handed back the list. "If it were legal, I wouldn't mind getting into that trade myself. Nor would a host of others."

"Indeed." Taking back the list, Montague glanced at it again. "But this, it seems, is something someone has already killed twice to hide."

"In that case"—Gibbons pushed back his chair and rose—"count me out. Is there anything else?"

Montague smiled. "No. Thank you, Frederick—you've been a great help."

Gibbons grinned and saluted, then went back to his desk.

Montague studied the list and the notations he'd made. His smile turned grim. It was but a small break-through, but he felt they'd made headway. At least he'd have something to share with Stokes and Adair when they arrived later in the day.

As Penelope's carriage rocked around the corner into Dover Street, she was still shaking her head over the wealth of information she and Griselda had gath-ered thus far that afternoon. "I will never not notice a shopgirl again." When Griselda laughed, Penelope insisted, "No—it's true. Now that I know how much they remember of what one says and does, I'll be for-ever minding my p's and q's."

"I rather think the Halsteads are a special case," Griselda said. "Difficult behavior is always remembered."

She'd taken Penelope to visit a long row of shops in Kensington High Street, within easy walking distance of Lowndes Street, where Lady Halstead had lived; as it transpired, those were also the shops favored by Mrs. Wallace Camberly, who lived with her husband and son in Belgrave Square, and, even more impor-tantly, by their household staff. While Penelope had played the lady, examining items with a view to purchase, Griselda, in the role of lady's maid, had chatted with the shopgirls at each of the establishments.

"Yes, indeed, but behavior aside, the comments and information passed on by the Camberlys' staff were . . . well, amazing." Behind her spectacles, Penelope widened her eyes. "Amazingly detailed."

"It helped that the shop assistants still remembered Mortimer and his family from before they moved out of the area." Griselda glanced out of the window as the carriage slowed. "So what we heard wasn't simply bad-mouthing on the part of the Camberlys' staff but attitudes the shopgirls had had confirmed by the Halsteads' staff directly."

The carriage halted.

"Regardless"—Penelope sat up and eased toward the carriage door—"we've now got one quite definite view of the Halsteads and the Camberlys. Let's see what the grandes dames can add."

When the groom opened the door, Penelope let him hand her down to the pavement, waited until Griselda joined her, then spoke to the coachman. "We'll walk home, Phelps."

"Very good, ma'am."

With a salute, Phelps set the coach rolling again; Albemarle Street was only a block away.

Turning, Penelope led the way up the front steps of the house of her aunt-by-marriage, Horatia Cynster.

"Are you sure my presence won't be . . . well, awkward?" Griselda murmured. "I'm not the sort usually found swanning about ladies' drawing rooms."

Halting on the narrow porch, Penelope threw Griselda a reassuring glance "Don't worry. Horatia's at-home is such a regular event it goes like clockwork. By this time, the only ones left will be the Cynster ladies and perhaps Lady Osbaldestone. All of them have met Stokes at one time or another, and all of them know he's helped the family at numerous times. They know he helped Henrietta and James, and that was only recently." Lips lifting mischievously, Penelope turned and plied the knocker. "Trust me, if anything, they're going to be quite interested in meeting you."

Griselda shut her lips on a tart retort as the door swung open, held by a rather stiff-looking butler, who, on lowering his gaze to Penelope, immediately unbent enough to smile. "Mrs. Adair—a pleasure to see you again."

"Thank you, Grantley. Is her ladyship still receiving?"

"Not in general, but in your case I'm sure Lady Horatia will be delighted to have you join the ladies still here."

Leading the way into the front hall, Penelope inquired, "So it's the Cynster ladies, and who else?"

"Only Lady Osbaldestone, ma'am."

Penelope allowed Grantley to take her pelisse, then waved at Griselda. "This is Mrs. Stokes, Inspector Stokes's wife."

"Indeed." Grantley bowed. "Welcome, ma'am. May I take your coat?"

Griselda nodded. "Thank you." She mimicked Penelope's earlier stance, allowing the butler to help her out of her coat.

"The drawing room?" Penelope inquired.

"Indeed, ma'am." Grantley crossed to a door. "Allow me." Opening the door, he announced, "My lady—Mrs. Adair and Mrs. Stokes."

Penelope, of course, swept over the threshold; quashing a sudden attack of nerves, Griselda raised her chin and followed.

Only to have the doubts she'd harbored over being welcomed into such an august and exclusive social circle instantly banished. Five ladies were seated on the sofa and the armchairs arranged before the fireplace; they smiled warmly at Penelope, but the instant their gazes moved on to Griselda, their eyes lit and expressions of expectant delight bloomed across their fine features.

All of the ladies were older matrons, and one—
who, Griselda assumed, was the notorious Lady
Osbaldestone—was bordering on ancient.

One dark-haired lady, presumably their hostess,
Lady Horatia, rose to greet them. "Welcome, Penelope,
dear!" She pressed Penelope's fingers and they
touched cheeks. Immediately she released Penelope,
Lady Horatia's bright eyes fixed on Griselda. "And this
is Mrs. Stokes? Inspector Stokes's lady?"

"Yes, indeed." Penelope glanced at Griselda with a
smile that clearly said, *I told you so.* "Griselda, I'd like
you to meet . . ."

Griselda smiled, shyly touched fingers, and
exchanged greetings with Lady Horatia, Lady Louise
Cynster, Lady Celia Cynster, Helena, the Dowager
Duchess of St. Ives, and, finally, with Therese,
Lady Osbaldestone.

While Griselda was so engaged, Lady Horatia
instructed Grantley to set chairs for her new guests.
Once the introductions were over, and Penelope and
Griselda were seated and supplied with cups of nice,
strong tea and tiny, delicate tea cakes that Griselda
quite approved of, Lady Osbaldestone rapped the tip
of her cane on the floor—much as if calling a meeting to order. "So, my dears, how can we help you?"
Her ladyship's finely drawn brows arched over quite

terrifyingly piercing black eyes. "I presume that is why you are here?"

Transparently unrattled, Penelope nodded. "We—by which I mean Barnaby and Stokes, assisted by myself and Griselda, and also, in this case, Mr. Montague, who you all also know—are trying to unravel a puzzling case which we believe has led to two murders. The first victim was Lady Halstead, who lived in Lowndes Street, and the other was her man-of-business. Griselda and I have spent the last hour learning what we can about the Halsteads and the Camberlys, Lady Halstead's children and their families, from more general sources, and have now come to see if you can tell us more about both the Camberlys and the Halsteads from a social perspective."

Four of the five faces looked blank. Lady Celia said, "Exactly who are these people, dear?"

Penelope grimaced but answered, "Mortimer Halstead and his wife Constance—Mortimer holds some reasonably senior position at the Home Office—and they have two children, Hayden and Caroline. The Camberlys are Mr. and Mrs. Wallace Camberly—he's a Member of Parliament, and they live in Belgrave Square and have one child, a son, Walter."

Horatia, Celia, Louise, and Helena all exchanged looks. Lady Osbaldestone, meanwhile, was frowning in concentration, as if dredging the depths of her memories—memories that extended fathoms deep.

After glancing at Lady Osbaldestone, Helena met Penelope's eyes. "Sadly, we can't help—those people do not move in our circles. However, I suspect darling Caro would know at least something of them—she and Michael are still so very heavily involved in government circles."

"And," Celia said, "you might ask Heather, especially about the Camberlys. Now that Breckenridge—Brunswick, I should say—has acceded to the earldom and assumed his father's seat in the Lords, he's become much more heavily involved in politics."

"Indeed." Lady Osbaldestone nodded. "And now Michael Anstruther-Wetherby has his seat in the Commons, he would know something of Camberly, too." Lady Osbaldstone's black gaze settled on Penelope. "Of course, *I* used to move in both political as well as government circles, but that was long ago. I can't tell you anything about Mortimer Halstead or the Camberlys, but I remember Sir Hugo Halstead quite well, and I'm sorry to hear of his wife's death."

Penelope looked her interest. "You knew them?"

"Not to say knew, but he was in the Foreign Office, so of course I met him. He was considered a very sound man."

212 • STEPHANIE LAURENS

"Can you tell us more about him—about them?" Penelope asked.

Lady Osbaldestone faintly arched her brows. "He spent most of his active years in India—he was a large, quite jovial, agreeable gentleman who was one of those people others trusted on sight. You can imagine how helpful that was in dealing with the natives. He was seconded to the East India Company for many, many years, and also assisted the Office of the Governor-General. His wife—I've been trying to think of her name, and I think it was Agatha—was a quiet lady, but pleasant company and a good foil for him. She accompanied him on his postings and was by his side for most of his service. At the time of Sir Hugo's retirement, they were considered an exemplary couple who had made a very real contribution to King and Country." Lady Osbaldestone paused, frowning again. "The only comment I recall regarding the Halstead children was that they bred true for looks, but sadly not for character."

The front doorbell pealed, then feminine voices echoed in the hall. A minute later, the door opened and a youthful-looking matron of middle years led in a bevy of others. "Our apologies, Mama-in-law—we were delayed leaving Osterly Park. I will leave it to you to guess by whom."

Horatia laughed and accepted a kiss on her cheek, then signaled to Grantley to produce more chairs. "As it happens, my dears, you've arrived at precisely the right time. Penelope here, and Griselda—who is Inspector Stokes's wife—have presented us with a social query that we are unable to answer but on which several of you might have some insight to offer."

Griselda's head whirled as introductions were made; as had happened with the older ladies, the younger matrons showed no awareness of any great distinction between her class and theirs, at least not in this setting.

Grantley and two footmen ferried in more chairs and two fresh teapots, and finally everyone was seated and supplied with tea and cakes. Horatia fixed the newcomers with a commanding eye. "Mortimer Halstead and his wife, Constance—he holds a senior position with the Home Office—plus son, Hayden, and daughter, Caroline. Also Mr. Wallace Camberly, MP, and his wife, and their son, Walter. Whatever you know of these people, do share."

"Mrs. Camberly's name is Cynthia, and she was a Halstead—she's Mortimer's sister," Penelope explained. "And there's also a Maurice Halstead, who someone here might have heard of, and also a William, the youngest brother."

"Oh, I've heard of Maurice," the lady who had led the others in, Patience Cynster, said. She frowned. "But heavens, that was long ago, when I was first out in society. I was warned he was one to avoid."

Penelope nodded. "The description we have is of a rake, an ageing roué, definitely a gamester and general profligate, but he's thought to be harmless enough and can be charming."

"Yes, that's right," Louise put in. "I remember him in the sense of warning the twins away from him." She frowned. "But as I recall, he tended to hover on the outskirts of society, as it were."

Penelope nodded encouragingly. "That sounds right."

Several of the younger matrons had met the Camberlys, albeit only in passing. "My impression, for what it's worth," Honoria, Duchess of St. Ives, seated to Griselda's left, said, "is that they are both exceedingly ambitious. Camberly for himself, for his advancement, and his wife to assist him in securing that."

"And through that, securing her own advancement in the social ranks." The lady who spoke was the Caro who had been referred to earlier. She nodded at Penelope. "I've met the Camberlys several times, and there's no doubt that Camberly is pushy, but I would also say he's careful and intelligent enough not to overreach. He's building a solid reputation but is greedy for every little crumb of kudos and status he can legitimately garner to bolster his name. I expect he thinks to push for an undersecretary's post after the next election."

"What are they like as people?" Penelope asked.

Caro wrinkled her nose, took a sip of her tea, then, lowering the cup, said, "Not the sort of people you wish to claim as friends. Camberly is ruthless. Behind his easy smile and polished-to-a-gloss manners, he is utterly fixed on his goal, and one senses he would have no qualms over doing whatever he must to achieve it. His wife is equally ruthless, but in addition there's an element of pettiness and spite there . . ." Caro paused, then concluded, "I can't quite put my finger on what it actually is, but it's very much a case of her viewing everything through the prism of what it might mean for her. I've come across the son only once, and, as often happens with overbearing parents, he's something of a cypher and fades into the background."

Penelope looked hopeful. "And the Halsteads?"

Caro pulled a face. "I've only met them once, and that in passing at a major function, but I have heard whispers about them from others—the sort of gossipy comments that are always floating about within government departments. I can't vouch for their veracity, but if it

216 • STEPHANIE LAURENS

will help, and I suspect you have other sources to check what mine have related, then . . ." Caro drew breath and went on, "I've heard that Mortimer, and Constance, too, are also ambitious, but with less reason, and far less likelihood of it coming to anything. Mortimer Halstead is known as something of a mediocre man—a pedant who is not intelligent enough to respond to new or unexpected situations. He's considered sound in the general sense, but everyone, except presumably he and his wife, believe that he's reached his level of competence and did so long ago, and is unlikely to move further up the Home Office tree."

Shifting her gaze to Lady Osbaldestone, Caro said, "I have heard some wonder why he didn't follow in his father's footsteps into the Foreign Office, where the name would have counted for more, but it seems that Mortimer has absolutely no wish to ever leave these shores."

"Actually," Penelope said, setting her teacup on her saucer, "from the descriptions Barnaby and Stokes, and also Barnaby's father, have given us of the Halsteads and the Camberlys, which mesh with everything you've said, I hypothesized that for all four Halstead children, their characters and dispositions might be the result of overblown competitiveness between Mortimer and Cynthia, who are older and close in age, stemming perhaps from their childhood, and the consequent effects that might have had on Maurice, forcing him to take the position of black sheep to gain attention, which in turn made William—the youngest brother—step outside society altogether."

Lady Osbaldestone viewed Penelope with something approaching pride. "How very astute of you, my dear—for I've just remembered the only criticism I ever heard leveled at the Halsteads, mère and père, and that was, in fact, that their offspring had been allowed by the Halsteads to develop as a group in a quite unhealthy way. The specific criticism was that the potential of the Halsteads, the fruit of their union as it were, had been allowed to disintegrate, to decay and come to nothing, through lack of attention, indeed, put even more bluntly, through parental neglect.

"You see"—Lady Osbaldestone fixed her black gaze on Penelope's face—"while the Halsteads spent their productive years abroad, they left their children in England, in the care of nannies, governesses, and tutors at their country house, often for years at a time. For Sir Hugo, of course, had ambition, too, and his was all for his work, and Agatha supported him in that."

Arching her brows, Lady Osbaldestone glanced at the other ladies. "It should hardly surprise anyone that, under such circumstances, with no parental hand to guide them and what is most likely an inherited ambitious streak, then, as Penelope suggested, rather than bonding together, the two older children vied for attention, for dominance, forcing the younger two to find other ways to make their mark, to stake their claim."

Many heads nodded in agreement. "That sounds very right," Caro said. "That would account for exactly the impressions I've received from both Cynthia Camberly and Mortimer Halstead." Caro narrowed her eyes. "I've never met them together—as far as I know, I've never seen them in the same room—but I sensed in both of them that there was some deep drive to their desire to get ahead, that it was a *need* more than a wish."

Again there was a round of murmured agreement.

Penelope glanced at Griselda and arched her brows. "I'm so glad we came."

Griselda smiled, nodded, and finished her tea.

Soon after, Penelope rose, and she and Griselda took their leave.

Gaining the pavement, Penelope linked her arm in Griselda's and they set off strolling slowly along the street; turning right into Grafton Street, and then right into Albemarle Street was the fastest route to Penelope's house.

The afternoon was cool, soft gray clouds slowly drifting across the autumn sky, the sun already hidden by the buildings to the west. A light breeze threaded between the houses, flirting with the ribbons of Penelope's bonnet and teasing strands of Griselda's black hair free from her restrained topknot.

"Hmm," Penelope murmured as they slowly paced. "I truly want—even need—to involve myself in investigations again, to give myself that additional purpose, but, at the same time, I have absolutely no intention of neglecting Oliver and any other children we might be blessed with."

Griselda wasn't surprised to hear her friend's thoughts echo her own, yet her lips twisted in a wry smile as she admitted, "I was thinking the same, but, more, that it isn't just a matter of us taking time away from them to do our investigating but also that, when it comes to the situations those investigations lead us into, it's incumbent on us, our responsibility, as it were, to ensure we, ourselves, are never at risk." She glanced at Penelope and met her dark eyes. "Our children can't afford to lose us."

Penelope nodded, one of her curt, definite, forceful nods. "No, indeed. I agree, and that's the challenge—well, one aspect of the challenge—of us finding our way back into investigating and defining our roles with regard to the future. That's something we need to work on."

"And not just us," Griselda murmured.

Penelope laughed, then, sobering, tilted her head. "In fact, if we extrapolate from what Lady Osbaldestone said—and what has happened with the Halsteads should, indeed, stand as a salutary lesson—then it's not just us, you and me, who need to ensure that investigating doesn't pull us away from our darlings for too long. The time we need to devote to our children may be greater than what Barnaby and Stokes need to give them, but they do need to give them some part of their time."

"Some part of their life," Griselda said.

"Exactly." Penelope fell silent until they turned into Albemarle Street. Setting eyes on the door of her home, she said, "That's the responsibility one must accept in bringing a child into the world—that we, both parents, need to give that child a defined, and real, and uncontestable place in our lives."

Griselda echoed, "A defined, real, and uncontestable piece of our lives."

Chapter 8

"So," Stokes said, slouching in one of the chairs facing Montague's desk, "no one saw any woman who might have been our mysterious lady in the vicinity of Runcorn's office. I'm inclined to think that she may have been brought in, even hired, purely to withdraw the money from the bank." Stokes glanced at Barnaby, seated to his right. "Did you learn any more in Threadneedle Street?"

"As it happened," Barnaby said, "luck favored me, and in more ways than one. First, I can report that the payments in question were deposited using a courier service. The tellers who received them are experienced enough to recognize the signs, and have remembered because they thought it odd that couriers were making deposits into Lady Halstead's account."

Stokes grunted. "That increases the odds that this is something illegal and, what's more, being carried out by someone with a criminal connection."

Montague nodded. "That also fits with something I've discovered, but before we get to that"—he looked at Barnaby—"what else did you find?"

Barnaby grinned. "A young and observant street-sweeper, who remembers seeing our veiled lady come along the street from the bank to where a coach was waiting, drawn up by the curb. The door opened and the boy saw a gentleman inside the coach help the lady in."

"And could our observant tyke describe the gentleman?" Stokes asked.

"He saw enough to tell me that the gentleman in question didn't have a beard but sideburns, that his face was roundish, and he had brown hair. He couldn't tell me how tall he was, and wasn't sure about age."

Stokes looked grim. "It seems that every clue we uncover points to our villain being one of the Halsteads."

"True." Barnaby grimaced. "But that leaves us with five—Mortimer, Maurice, William, Walter, and Hayden—and thus far all five fit our bill."

"And," Stokes said, "we shouldn't at this point discount the possibility that two or more are in this together." He frowned. "If that proves so, it's going to make our job a lot more difficult."

"Hmm." Barnaby frowned, too. "If one did the first murder, and another the second . . ."

Stokes shook his head. "I don't even want to think about it."

After a moment, Barnaby looked at Montague. "You said you've discovered something?"

Montague, who had been following Stokes's and Barnaby's somewhat dismal line of thought, shook himself back to the present. Then smiled. "Yes, indeed." He lifted the list of payments with his annotations from his blotter. "We can thank my senior assistant, Gibbons, for the vital insight, but once he suggested that the payments looked like income from the sales of something, it was easy enough to work out." Reaching over the desk, Montague handed the sheet to Stokes, who held it so he and Barnaby both could view it.

After giving them a moment to scan his sums, Montague explained, "If one assumes that our villain is selling items each of which nets him two hundred and fifty pounds, and that he sells between five and nine such items every month, and that he then pays one of the courier services their customary two to three percent for the delivery into Lady Halstead's account"—leaning back, he concluded with some satisfaction—"then it's possible to account for each and all of those payments."

Barnaby glanced at him, then looked back at the list. "Fourteen different payments, and they all fit that pattern."

Stokes grunted. "I'm no expert with numbers, but even I would say that's conclusive." Looking at Montague, he waved the list. "Can I keep this?"

Montague nodded. "I've already made another copy."

Folding the paper, Stokes shifted to stow it in his coat pocket. "So at this point, we have a gentleman who appears to be one of the Halsteads, or Walter Camberly, who is selling, or causing to be sold, items valued at two hundred and fifty pounds each, and he sells five to nine such items a month on a regular basis. Given that he's sought to conceal his activities by using Lady Halstead's account to hide his cash, and also accepting that there aren't that many legal items one can sell for two hundred and fifty pounds at such a steady rate, then it's reasonable, I would say, for us to assume that whatever trade this gentleman is dabbling in is illegal."

"And that, presumably," Barnaby said, "is why he's sought to conceal the money. Which raises the interesting question of which of the Halstead males has most to lose from his illegal activities becoming known?"

Stokes considered, then said, "Correct me if I err, but for my money the answer to that question is Mortimer Halstead, tied neck and neck with Wallace Camberly—and given there's the possibility his son may be acting in conspiracy with Camberly, I believe we have to include him, too, even if he's not the actual murderer."

Barnaby nodded. "And after the two older men, I would list Hayden Halstead and Walter Camberly. Within their circles, both are sons of prominent men—if their involvement in some illicit scheme became known, it would cause a scandal."

Montague frowned. "What about Maurice Halstead, and the youngest brother, William?" When Barnaby glanced his way, Montague lifted one shoulder. "My impression of the pair is that neither would care all that much, not from the point of view of concealment. Were either of them the villain, they would be more worried about being caught and stopped by the authorities than about hiding their identity and avoiding scandal."

Barnaby thought, then slowly nodded. "I would have to agree. I can't see any reason why either Maurice or William would bother with using their mother's account, much less using couriers to do so. In fact, I can see at least two to three percent of earnings that would influence them not to do any such thing."

Stokes pulled a face. "It's tempting to speculate that William, at least, and likely Maurice, too, are more likely than any of the others to know how to contact the courier services, but you're right—they appear to have no pressing motive for doing so."

For several minutes, the three of them silently mulled over all they'd learned, then Stokes rose, and Barnaby followed. "I should get back to the Yard," Stokes said. He arched a brow at Barnaby.

"I want to have a word with the police surgeon, just to confirm there's no more he can tell us. I'll come up and see you if there is." Barnaby and Stokes both looked at Montague.

He noticed and, frowning, met their eyes. "There's one more thing I ought to do, just to be complete. The money taken from her ladyship's account has to go some-where." He glanced at the clock on his desk. "Although I doubt I'll get any answer until tomorrow, I will make discreet inquiries as to whether any of the Halsteads, or the Camberlys, made any large deposit into any of the accounts they have access to." He met Stokes's eyes and faintly smiled. "I would prefer that you didn't ask me how, but I can also arrange to be notified should such a deposit be made over the next week."

Stokes inclined his head. "As that would be useful to know, I'll refrain from asking you about your methods."

"Of course," Barnaby said, "it's unlikely there'll be any trace of it, not after he used her ladyship's account presumably to ensure the money never appeared in his, but"—saluting Montague, he turned for the door—"you're right. We do need to check, because when dealing with villains, you never do know when they'll slip up—"

"And then we'll have them." Stokes tipped a raised finger to Montague in farewell and followed Barnaby from the office.

Rising, Montague went to stand in the doorway to the outer office. Once Stokes and Barnaby had left, and Slocum, who had shown them to the door, shut it and headed back to his desk, Montague called, "Slocum? I have some letters to dictate."

After shutting up the office, Montague had intended to go upstairs, to his home, but the cool of a surprisingly pleasant evening drew him outside. The lamps were just being lit, but there was still enough light to comfortably stroll and enjoy the blanket of quiet that descended over the City now the bustling hordes who worked within it had streamed home to their dinners.

It was harder to use the pleasantness of the evening to excuse his hailing of a hackney and his consequent journey across town to Lowndes Street.

He understood Stokes's wish not to inform Violet of Runcorn's murder and the involvement of a lady who some might imagine to be Violet herself in the removal of funds from Lady Halstead's bank account. He even agreed with Stokes to some extent, but over the past hours, Penelope's and Griselda's words had tirelessly replayed in the back of his brain. Now . . . despite not wishing to further distress Violet, the notion of keeping her uninformed of what had occurred smacked too much of leaving her unnecessarily defenseless.

Some very determined part of him he didn't entirely recognize couldn't abide that.

The hackney pulled up outside the Halstead house. After paying off the driver, Montague opened the gate, walked up the path, and climbed the steps to the pillared front porch. Removing his hat, he knocked on the door.

And steadfastly refused to think of precisely what he was doing, and why.

Footsteps approached, then Violet—when had he stopped thinking of her as Miss Matcham?—opened the door. The instant she saw him her expression lightened. "Mr. Montague. Good evening." Stepping back, she waved him in. "Do come inside, sir. I take it you have news?"

Stepping over the threshold, he replied, "Of a sort." Now he was there, he had to think of all that he'd determinedly not thought of during the journey. "Ah . . . I hope I'm not interrupting your meal."

She smiled and reached for his hat. "No—Lady Halstead preferred to dine late, and we've . . ." Her voice faded and she blinked.

He handed her his hat. She took it and turned away to hang it on the hat-tree.

When she turned back, her face was solemn, but composed. She waved him to the sitting room. "Please, come in, and let's sit comfortably."

He inclined his head and stepped back to allow her to lead the way. She did and he followed her into the sitting room, the same room that Lady Halstead had received him in. In contrast to the more formal drawing room, it felt pervasively lived in; a small fire sent busy fingers of flame leaping up from the grate, chasing away the chill that had closed in with the fading of the light.

"So"—Violet sank into one of the chairs before the hearth—"what news, sir? Does Inspector Stokes have any suspicions as to who the murderer is?"

Sitting on the sofa facing the fire, Montague took in the angle of her chin, saw the tension in the fingers she clasped in her lap. "As to that . . ." He hesitated, then said, "I regret I must inform you that when I called at Mr. Runcorn's office this morning in company with Mr. Adair, we discovered poor Runcorn murdered."

One hand rose to her throat. Her face blanched; her eyes seemed to grow huge. After an instant in which she seemed to cease breathing altogether, she hauled in a swift breath and blindly—instinctively—reached out with one hand, as if seeking support. "My God—was it because of this business? Because of Lady Halstead's affairs?"

Montague didn't think but simply reached across and closed his hand about her fingers. They were icy; shifting forward on the sofa, his eyes on her face, he chafed her hand between both of his. When her horrified gaze focused on his face, he inclined his head gravely. "Sadly, it appears that way. Lady Halstead's papers were scattered over his desk—his clerk had left him working through the Halstead file, and we believe the documents had been searched."

Her face, her fine features, registered a depth of sadness he hadn't expected to see; he hadn't thought she'd known Runcorn that well.

"That poor young man. He was so . . . *eager* and keen to make a go of his firm—you could see that just by looking at his face. Oh!" She looked down, her other hand rising to her lips, the fingers of the hand he still clasped clutching lightly. "I'm sorry. Pray forgive me . . ." She briefly waved.

"There's nothing to forgive." His voice had lowered, softened, affected by her reaction, and more, drawn by it to acknowledge a sense of loss he hadn't yet allowed himself the time to feel.

Raising her head, blinking rapidly, she murmured, "It's bad enough to lose someone like Lady Halstead to a murderer, but when the victim is young, innocent, and had so much potential, so much to live for, the loss is even more tragic." She met his eyes; her lips twisted wryly. "I only met him three times, and briefly at that, but he seemed so earnest and . . . *true,* if you know what I mean."

As if only then realizing they were holding hands, she gently drew back her fingers; reluctantly he allowed them to slip free of his grasp. "I'm sorry," she said. "You must think me quite witless, being so affected by the death of someone I barely knew."

"No. Not at all. I think you quite"—*lovely, wonderful, glorious*—"admirably sympathetic." After a moment he added, gravely and sincerely, "Runcorn was a loss the world did not need."

Her gaze had drifted to the flames, but at that she met his eyes directly. "Exactly. You do understand."

He inclined his head.

She studied him for a moment, then prompted, "Is there anything more you can tell me? Are there any suspects in Runcorn's murder?"

Montague hesitated, then mentally decided: *Stokes be damned.* "There was a man—a gentleman . . ."

He told her about the Halstead-like male seen near Runcorn's office before and after the murder, then went on to relate all they'd done, all they'd discovered through the day. He told her of his discovery of the likely meaning of the odd payments into Lady Halstead's account; when he tried to heap praise on Gibbons, she seemed determined, while acknowledging Gibbons's input, to focus on his own contribution . . . enough to have him wonder if this was what it felt like to be seduced.

By her words and the thoughts behind them, by the admiration he saw shining in her fine eyes.

He was careful not to give any real details about the veiled woman who had conspired with the murderer to remove the suspect funds and more from Lady Halstead's account. But when he reached the end of his tale, Violet grew pensive, then proved that she was not at all lacking in intelligence. Meeting his eyes, she stated, "The family will try to say that it was me, that I was the woman who withdrew the money from Lady Halstead's account. And by that reasoning, I am also guilty of her murder, or was at least an accomplice."

There was something in her face, in the set of her chin, that warned him not to pretend he didn't think the same.

Resigned, he sighed and inclined his head. "Stokes, Adair, and I believe so. Either you, or, failing that, her ladyship's maid. However, I cannot sufficiently stress that none of us believe it, either of you or Tilly."

She straightened, incrementally drawing back, drawing away.

Spurred by an instinct, an impulse he had no name for, he reached across to take both her hands, one in each of his; she surrendered them with no resistance. He caught her eyes. "Violet—if I may call you that?"

She held his gaze for a moment, then, almost as if it was against her better judgment, fractionally nodded.

He drew breath and rushed on. "You must believe that none of us—those of us investigating this case—believe you or Tilly are in any way involved in these crimes. To us, it makes no sense to suspect you, but we realize that the family will attempt to point the finger at anyone rather than at one of their own, so . . ." He paused to draw breath, and something in him calmed, grew more certain. "Stokes knows what he's doing. He has standing, experience, and a great deal of discretion in what he consents to tell the family. A part of the reason he has not yet summoned them again, has not even as yet informed them of Runcorn's murder, much less the situation with her ladyship's account, is that he wishes to gather more facts and information before he does. The more knowledge we have of what occurred, the more obvious it will be that none of these crimes can be laid at your door."

Holding her gaze, he went on, his voice lowering. "You must believe me when I say we are all working to catch the murderer, and parallel to that, to exonerate you." It was suddenly very important that she did believe that. His eyes locked with hers, he murmured, "Trust me, Violet. Regardless of all else, I—we—will ensure that no harm comes to you."

Violet looked into eyes that overflowed with sincerity. With such rock-solid certainty that she couldn't deny what he asked of her—that she believe him. That she trust him.

She wasn't sure how he had managed in so short a time to figure so highly in her regard, yet somehow, at some level she could not question yet didn't understand, he had come to be her rock, the one person she could rely on.

"I do trust you." The words fell from her lips in a tone that instantly brought warmth to her cheeks. She cleared her throat, strengthened her voice to quickly add, "And Inspector Stokes and Mr. Adair. I . . . do have faith that you'll identify the murderer, or at least do your best—"

"We'll find him."

And there it was again—that unwavering certainty, the product, she sensed, of incorruptible devotion. From their earlier meetings, she'd recognized him as a cautious man who did not give his promises lightly, but when he did . . .

Looking into his eyes, meeting his certainty with the openness and directness she felt she owed him, she inclined her head. "Thank you."

His fingers tightened about hers and he drew breath as if to speak, but then the wind howled outside, and he fell silent. After a moment of studying her face, he lightly squeezed her fingers, then released them. Rising, he gave her his hand to help her to her feet.

When she straightened, her head barely reached his chin. Again their gazes met; again she sensed he debated his next action. Then he took a small step back. "I really must go—I've interrupted your evening for long enough."

She could have disabused him of any notion that she had tired of his company, but she suspected he lived some distance away, and from the sound of the wind the evening had turned vicious. "I'll see you to the door."

He followed her from the room and took his hat from her hand, but paused on the threshold. His gaze traveled her face before locking with hers for a last fleeting moment, then he inclined his head. "I will call again when we have news."

Stepping outside, he placed his hat on his head, settled and buttoned his coat, then went down the steps.

Violet pushed the door almost shut, blocking the chill wind, but she remained peering out. Watching him stride away.

Only when he had passed into the square and out of her sight did she close the door. She stood staring at the panels for several moments, wondering, reliving in her mind the past minutes, the swirling eddies of emotion he, his presence, had evoked, the currents that both of them—she would swear—had been aware of, had been sensitive to. She'd never felt the like, that strange mutual awareness.

The wind shrieked and broke the spell.

Abruptly shaking herself, she reached up and threw the heavy bolt at the top of the door, then bent to slide the lower bolt into place as well. She doubted they would have any further callers; the night had turned dark and ominous outside.

Glancing into the sitting room, she checked that the fire would safely burn down without further tending, then closed the door and walked down the narrow hall to the green baize door at the rear. Pushing through, she continued to the kitchen.

Since Lady Halstead's death—had it truly only been two nights ago?—the kitchen had become the hub of their small household. She, Tilly, and Cook gathered in the warmth, surrounded by the familiar smells of baking and roasting meats and vegetables, the better to hold the chill that had invaded the rest of the house at bay.

Truth be told, had it been at all possible, Violet would rather have slept in the kitchen than in her bedroom on the first floor, three doors from the room in which Lady Halstead had been killed.

Cook heard her footsteps and looked up, her ruddy face flushed as she ladled thick stew into three bowls. "There you are. Thought I'd have to send Tilly to fetch you. Who was it?"

"Mr. Montague." Violet slipped into a chair on one side of the table. Although she'd attended formal dinners at her ladyship's side, on all other occasions, she'd taken her meals in the kitchen with Tilly and Cook; the years had forged a strong bond between the three of them, one that stood them in good stead now.

"That special man-of-business her ladyship consulted?" Tilly was seated opposite Violet; she handed around the bowls as Cook filled them.

Violet nodded. "Yes, him."

"What did he want, then? You sat with him for over half an hour." Cook set her pot back on the stove, then took her seat at the table's head.

Violet took her first mouthful of the savory stew, waited until the others did the same, then swallowed and said, "He had news to impart."

Briefly, she told them of Runcorn's murder, and of the lady who had taken the money from Lady Halstead's account. She dwelled rather more on the sighting of a man who might have been one of the Halsteads near both Runcorn's office and the bank. As both Tilly and Cook were convinced that it was one of Lady Halstead's own family who had murdered her, they were very ready to focus on that aspect; neither saw the unwelcome possibility that Violet had—of either herself or Tilly being accused by the family of being involved in the crimes—and she saw no reason to point it out and cause Tilly and Cook more distress than the news of Runcorn's murder already had.

"Cor." Tilly shivered. "What happenings, to be sure." Across the table, she searched Violet's face. "But we're safe, aren't we? I mean, there's no reason to think this madman will come back here?"

Violet considered. "I can't see why he would. If this was about the money, then he's got what he wanted." She frowned, then shook her head. "It's all too complicated for me, but Mr. Montague and that Inspector Stokes and Mr. Adair are all working on catching the murderer."

"Aye, well." Cook scooped up another mouthful of stew. "I say we leave the a-hunting of the murderer to them. The three of us—we've got more pressing concerns." Cook looked at Tilly, then Violet. "We've been paid until quarter-day, but we'll have to find new posts, won't we, come the funeral and the family closing up this house?"

After a discussion with the police surgeon, during which he'd learned nothing of any significance that they hadn't already known, Barnaby joined Stokes in his office.

Stokes looked up as Barnaby entered. "Anything?"

Barnaby shook his head. "It was as we'd thought—the villain clouted Runcorn with the bookend, then strangled him with the curtain cord, pulling him up and out of his chair as he did."

Stokes grunted, then, sitting back, waved the note he'd been reading. "We've been summoned."

"Oh?" Barnaby dropped into his accustomed chair angled before Stokes's desk. "To where? For what? And by whom?"

"To Albemarle Street. To dinner. By your wife and mine."

"Ah." Barnaby nodded. "They want to pick our brains for every little fact we've managed to glean."

"That," Stokes conceded, consulting the note again, "but they also mention that they've had a wonderfully successful day learning more about the Halsteads and the Camberlys."

Barnaby widened his eyes. "Have they, indeed?" He blinked. "I wonder how." After a moment of pondering, he met Stokes's eyes. "Perhaps we'd better go and find out."

"My thoughts precisely." Stokes got to his feet and reached for his greatcoat. "I've nothing further to attend to, so . . ." He waved Barnaby out, then followed him into the corridor and shut the door.

They could have walked down The Mall and through Green Park, but that would have taken more than half an hour. Reaching the pavement, they hailed a hackney and, ten minutes later, reached Barnaby's front door.

Barnaby used his latchkey and led the way into his front hall. Mostyn, summoned by some mysterious alchemy, arrived to take their coats. "The ladies and the children are in the garden parlor, sir."

"Thank you, Mostyn." Barnaby led Stokes down the short corridor to the comfortable parlor that ran along one side of the rear half of the house.

Other than the library on the opposite side of the town house, the garden parlor was the room Penelope was most likely to be found in, especially when she had Oliver or others with her. One long side of the room and the wall at the far end were principally composed of windows and French doors; during the day, the room was awash with light. On chilly evenings, as now, the windows and glassed doors were covered by long curtains, and a large fire burned in the fireplace that occupied the center of the long inner wall. Well-padded damask-covered sofas and chairs were arranged around the room, and numerous lamps added their warm glow to the golden light thrown by the fire. Penelope's garden parlor was a perennially cozy and welcoming space.

The sight that met Barnaby's and Stokes's eyes as they walked in was one designed to warm the cockles of any man's heart. Both Penelope and Griselda were sitting on the floor in the space between the twin sofas, their skirts billowing about them. Both were laughing, their gazes, their entire attentions, fixed on the two infants who were rolling on a thick fur rug spread over the Aubusson carpet a safe distance from the grate and its screen.

Hearing their footsteps, both ladies looked up; seeing their husbands, they smiled.

Barnaby and Stokes halted, both drinking in the sight, then, as one, they smiled back and went forward to join their families.

To kiss their wives' proffered cheeks, then sink onto the floor and join in the game of interacting with and entertaining their children.

For the next twenty minutes, no mention was made of murder, money, or anything to do with the investigation.

But eventually the children grew sleepy. Getting to her feet, Penelope paused to look down at their small assembly with a certain satisfaction, then went to the bellpull and tugged.

The nursemaids—Oliver's Hettie and Megan's Gloria—had been waiting for the summons. Both arrived and carted their charges off to settle them in the nursery. Mostyn, who had also come in, gathered up the rug and the children's toys and followed, pausing only to say, "Dinner is waiting, ma'am. We can serve immediately if you wish."

"Thank you, Mostyn," Penelope said. "We'll go in."

Wrapped in the lingering warmth the children brought to them, the couples ambled toward the dining room, still sharing anecdotes of the children's days, of their latest fascinating exploits.

Only after they'd settled about the dining table and Mostyn had served the first course did the talk turn to matters criminal.

At their ladies' urging, Stokes, aided by Barnaby, reported on theirs and Montague's discoveries over that afternoon. Neither made any attempt to hold back; given Penelope had been present when they'd stumbled upon Runcorn's murder, any notion of keeping their ladies distanced from proceedings was, both accepted, futile.

As Barnaby and Stokes had come to expect, Penelope and Griselda had questions, some especially insightful and acute.

It was Penelope who focused on the grounds on which both the teller and the street-sweeper had labeled the woman who had removed the money from the bank a lady. After several minutes of discussion, they agreed that the judgment had been based on dress, deportment, and speech, all of which, as Griselda pointed out, could easily be assumed.

Subsequently, Penelope summarized, "So on the basis of the sightings near Runcorn's office, and the associated searching of the Halstead papers, we believe Runcorn's murderer to be one of the males of the Halstead bloodline. We're assuming he killed Runcorn and arranged for some female, who was to pass as a lady, to present a forged letter to the bank the following morning and thus remove all the funds from Lady Halstead's account." Dark eyes bright, she looked around the table. As heads nodded, she asked, "Is it possible that someone else killed Runcorn, and the Halstead male simply searched the papers left on Runcorn's desk?"

Stokes considered for only a moment before shaking his head. "Unlikely given the timing of the sightings of our Halstead male outside the office. He entered soon after Pringle had left. If his sole purpose for visiting Runcorn was to search the papers—or have Runcorn provide information from them—then he would have seen Runcorn alive and left while Runcorn was still alive, and the papers on Runcorn's desk wouldn't have been in such a mess."

"Hmm." Penelope nodded. "Yes, I will have to allow you that—which means that it was, indeed, our Halstead male who killed poor Runcorn."

Griselda frowned. "From your description of Runcorn's body, I take it that you don't believe he could have been killed by a woman, lady or not." When Stokes, Barnaby, and Penelope nodded, Griselda asked, "What about Lady Halstead? Could she have been killed by a woman?"

Stokes glanced at Barnaby. "Yes, she could have been. Her ladyship was ageing, frail, and physically weak. Any woman of average height and strength could have held the pillow over her ladyship's face long enough to do the deed."

"So," Griselda went on, "it's possible we're looking at two different murderers, whether acting in concert, as a conspiracy, or even possibly independently. We might be looking at a female and a Halstead male, or even two Halstead males, or a single Halstead male."

Several seconds ticked by, then Barnaby grimaced. "You're right that we can't tell if we're looking at one murderer or two, but I seriously doubt they acted independently. The correlation between Lady Halstead being murdered so soon after announcing she was having her affairs put in order, and then Runcorn, the person actively engaged in putting her ladyship's affairs in order, being murdered is simply too great." Barnaby met the others' eyes. "The motive for both murders is the same—to conceal those deposits. Subsequently, to prevent that money being absorbed into the estate, he, or they, removed it before we had a chance to put a watch on the bank and catch them."

Penelope nodded. "That's logically sound." After a moment, she went on, "From what Montague discovered, those deposits derive from some illegal trade, so we can assume that the drive to conceal the deposits is fueled by the fear of scandal. So by my reckoning, the one person in the family who isn't involved in the murders is Wallace Camberly. He couldn't have been the man seen near Runcorn's office, could he? And so . . ." Breaking off, she wrinkled her nose. "I've just seen the hole in that. The person fearing the scandal might be Wallace, but he or his wife or his son could have killed Lady Halstead, and his son could have killed Runcorn."

"Exactly." Glumly, Stokes grimaced. "If you entertain the possibility that there's more than one of them involved, then any member of the family, females as well as males, could be one of the murderers—a male or a female having killed Lady Halstead and any male having killed Runcorn."

"But"—Griselda held up a hand—"it's very much harder to see anyone other than a family member, even a female, being one of the murderers."

"Not unless there was evidence of some relationship between said female and one of the family's males," Penelope said. "And given what you've told us of the family's social attitudes, I seriously doubt any of the men would have stooped to dallying with Lady Halstead's staff, not even with Miss Matcham."

Barnaby snorted. "I'd put the boot on the other foot—I seriously doubt Miss Matcham would have stooped to having anything to do with any of the Halstead males."

Penelope frowned. "So where does that leave us?"

Stokes growled, "Wanting alibis from the lot of them for the nights of both murders." He stirred, sitting straighter as Mostyn reached around him to remove his plate. "I'll have to see them all again shortly and broach that topic, which will no doubt prove to be a minefield."

Mostyn had silently worked around them, pouring wine and serving and removing courses. As he unobtrusively set out the cheese platter and a fruit trifle, Barnaby glanced at Penelope. "In your note you said the pair of you had had a wonderful day learning more about the Halsteads and the Camberlys. So what did you learn? And from whom?"

"I fear what we learned was more by way of background information than directly relevant fact." Reaching to serve herself from the trifle, Penelope grinned. "Griselda can tell you about the first part, which was the most interesting, then I'll fill you in on the rest."

Griselda described their visit to the shops in Kensington High Street and related the gist of all they'd heard from the shop assistants. "In essence, the households of Mortimer Halstead and that of Cynthia Camberly, née Halstead, are engaged in a form of competition."

"A cutthroat one, by all accounts." Penelope was engaged in hunting out the raspberries in her bowl.

"Mind you," Griselda said, "while the competition rages fiercely at the family level, the staffs view the antics of their betters with general amusement that borders on bemusement."

Stokes frowned in open puzzlement. "Why would an adult brother and sister behave like that?"

"Ah." Having emptied her bowl, Penelope set down her spoon. "Remember my earlier conjecture, based on, I might remind you, your own observations from your meeting with the family—that there was an intense competitiveness between Mortimer and Cynthia that I attributed to them being so close in age and therefore vying for their parents' attention?"

When both Barnaby and Stokes nodded, Penelope grinned. "I was right about the competitiveness— although it's even worse than I guessed—but I wasn't *entirely* right about the reason for it. And despite the Halsteads and the Camberlys largely falling outside the sphere of the grandes dames, both Lady Osbaldestone and Caro had significant insights to share."

Penelope proceeded to present a concise summation of the pertinent observations those ladies had imparted. "So, to bring it all down to a nutshell, it's a combination of personal ambition and intense inter-sibling rivalry that drives all the Halstead children—Mortimer and Cynthia especially, but I doubt either Maurice or William are unaffected, at least with respect to the rivalry."

Stokes and Barnaby had been following the ladies' revelations with all due concentration.

After several moments, Stokes slowly nodded. He met Penelope's eyes, then looked at Griselda. "Thank you. Courtesy of your efforts, we now have a very firm idea of what these people are like, of what's important to them. And through that, you've solved one looming difficulty about motive—it's rare for anyone to commit matricide, especially without any strong degree of personal animosity between mother and child. We know there was no strong antipathy between Lady Halstead and her children, so, if the family had been otherwise normal, it should have required a motive of immense weight to force one of her children to kill her. But they aren't a normal family, and with the degree of parental neglect described by Lady Osbaldestone, the reason behind Lady Halstead's murder at the hands of one of her children wouldn't need to be so overwhelmingly powerful." Stokes's lips curved in almost feral anticipation. "Your information puts us on a much firmer footing with regard to the Halsteads. That's going to be a considerable help when next we interview them and ask for their alibis—which is going to have to be soon."

"Apropos of that next meeting," Penelope said, "in light of the usefulness of the information Griselda and I gathered, I really think that, if at all possible, she and

I should be present." Undeterred when neither Stokes nor Barnaby looked enthused, Penelope stated, "We see more than you do."

That was uncontestable. Stokes shifted. "I can't imagine how we might arrange that—the family will question your presence."

"Actually," Penelope said, "Lady Halstead's funeral is to be held the day after tomorrow. The notice was in *The Times* this morning. As far as I can see, there's nothing to prevent me and Griselda from joining the mourners, or attending the wake afterward, and I'm sure if we have a word to Miss Matcham, we'll be able to pass ourselves off as her supporters and, with any luck, attend the reading of the will as well."

Barnaby eyed his wife's irrepressible smile and inwardly shook his head. She had it all worked out, and as there was no danger involved . . . he glanced at Stokes. "It's a good idea." He could see in Stokes's gray eyes that, despite his reservations, he agreed. Looking back at Penelope, Barnaby said, "If nothing else, you and Griselda will be able to monitor the family's reactions and emotions while Stokes and I deal with the alibis."

"Exactly," Penelope beamed. She looked at Stokes. "So it's settled. Griselda and I will accompany you to the funeral and the wake."

"**I have** to admit," Penelope said, leading the way into their bedroom several hours later, "that I am very much looking forward to attending Lady Halstead's funeral, and even more her wake."

Following his wife into the room and shutting the door, Barnaby grinned. "Only you, my love, could say such a thing, and with such jubilant, jaunty expectation."

Penelope shot him a grin of her own. "It's . . . *engaging* to be involved in an investigation like this." Turning to the mirror set above her dressing table, she started pulling pins from her dark hair, which had been anchored in a complicated knot on the top of her head. "I'd forgotten how enthralling it can be. Identifying a murderer, especially one in a case such as this, is such a complex puzzle, one made even more absorbing and challenging because one needs to learn about people, to understand them, their aspirations and motivations, and put those all together in order to find one's way through the maze and reach the conclusion."

Barnaby shrugged out of his coat and draped it over his dressing stand, then unknotted and unraveled his cravat. While he understood—few better—Penelope's attraction to investigations, especially those of the criminal variety, he still wasn't entirely sure of how he felt about her plunging back into that arena.

"I know Griselda and I helped a bit with that business with Henrietta and James, but that was primarily by way of planning and organizing, which is all very well but lacks the challenge of an investigation." Her dark hair swinging loose, Penelope removed her necklace and earrings, then picked up her brush and started drawing it through her lush locks.

His shirt hanging open, Barnaby found himself, as ever, drawn by the sight. Walking slowly to stand behind her, he set his fingers to the long row of tiny buttons running down the back of her gown.

Feeling the tugs, after a moment Penelope set down her brush and stood straight and still, her hands on her hips, making it easier for him to slip the tiny loops over the rounded buttons.

"That said," she declared, "we—Griselda and I—are both still feeling our way, at least as to how much of our time we are willing to devote to investigating. Clearly, there has to be a balance struck, a weighing up, if you will, between all the other things we value in our lives, against the intellectual stimulation we derive from investigations."

He found knowing she was thinking along those lines comforting, yet . . . still engaged with her buttons, he murmured, "You and Griselda did well today." After a moment of inner wrestling, he added, "I hadn't realized you were going out again, that you had such an excursion in mind."

"We hadn't thought of it before you left, but once we did . . ." She shrugged. "It was something Griselda and I could do that you and Stokes couldn't. And, even better, it required no special consideration."

He frowned. "Special consideration?" The last button undone, he looked up.

She slid the sleeves of the gown down her arms, pushed and wriggled until the skirts shushed to the floor, then stepped out of them. Tossing the gown over her dressing table stool, she set her spectacles on the table and, clad only in a gossamer-fine chemise, turned to him. "Special consideration as to whether there was any danger involved."

"Ah." He reached for her and she came into his arms, her small hands slipping under the hanging halves of his shirt to spread, tactilely greedy, over his chest, even as his fastened about her waist, the sleekness of her skin screened from his touch only by the finest silk.

Tipping back her head, she looked into his face, then arched a questioning brow.

They hadn't bothered to light any lamp. Through the dimness, he met her gaze. "While I'm glad—and

254 · STEPHANIE LAURENS

relieved—to know that you do, in fact, stop to consider that point, I have to admit that the key issue for me, and Stokes, too, in you and Griselda involving yourselves to a greater extent in our investigations is the question of the danger such involvement may bring. The risks you might, even unwittingly, take, the physical threats that might eventuate."

She tilted her head, a particular habit, as she studied his face, reading not just his eyes but his expression, then her lips gently curved. "You might be interested in a particular insight Lady Osbaldestone shared with us today. While she was speaking of the Halstead family, both Griselda and I took due note—as one needs to do when a lady as old and wise as Lady Osbaldestone shares her views."

"Indubitably," Barnaby said, the cynicism in his tone quite clear.

Penelope grinned. "Regardless, I—and Griselda, too—believed this was one time, one revelation, that was too apt not to give due weight. In describing how the Halstead family, the current generation, came to be such a fractious brood, Lady Osbaldestone pointed to the single fact that, as children, they did not have the direct presence of their parents. Their parents weren't dead, but they were not there. Not present to guide and steer, to act as examples. In Lady Osbaldestone's view, that's the reason why, despite the senior Halsteads being exemplary people, their children are anything but."

Barnaby arched his brows. "And the lesson you and Griselda took from that?"

"Is that whatever balance we strike between investigating, and, indeed, all the other endeavors of our lives, it's our responsibility, and even more our duty, to ensure that, regardless of all those other distractions, we give our children the time with us they need." She arched a brow back. "And, incidentally, as the Halstead example also illustrated, that mandate applies as much to fathers as mothers."

Barnaby held her dark gaze, saw, investing her expression, the commitment to finding her way forward, her balance, her wish to engage in investigations already tempered by her devotion to their son—and to any other children that might come—and with equal commitment, inclined his head. "I have no wish to argue that."

Penelope smiled. Reaching up and wrapping a hand about his nape, she stretched up and brushed her lips over his. "So, you see, you and Stokes have nothing to be concerned about."

His lips were hungry, following hers. "Why's that?" he murmured, then closed the gap to sample the sweetness of her delectable mouth.

When he raised his head, she murmured, her tone suggesting impatience, "Because, having taken Lady Osbaldestone's dictum to heart, we've agreed, Griselda and I, that, regardless of temptation, we will never do anything that might keep us from returning safe and sound to our children every night."

"Ah. I see." There were times, especially when she was explaining the intricacies of feminine thought, that he felt quite dense, but as the links between all she'd said finally formed, he realized . . . and did, indeed, feel relieved.

Shifting to raise her other arm and drape both about his shoulders, she stepped closer still, pressing her luscious curves against the spare planes of his harder frame. "And just to settle the matter, I promise we won't go beyond the fashionable areas without Phelps and two grooms, exactly as I used to do before Oliver came along." Tightening her arms, she brought her lips to his. "So you can stop worrying."

He pulled back just enough to meet her eyes, to read in them her inherent understanding.

To appreciate anew that this was one of their strengths, their empathetic connection; it still made him uneasy at times to know how lacking in barriers he was when it came to her, how accurately and effortlessly she read him, yet there were benefits, too, and this was one.

She understood, and because she did, they would walk hand in hand through the minefield of their emotions. Of her wants and his needs. And they would find the balance.

A balance that would allow them both to enjoy their lives to the fullest, to exercise to the utmost the talents they'd been blessed with so that they gained the greatest, the deepest, and broadest satisfaction from their days. From the contributions they made, to themselves, to their family, to society.

He saw and appreciated, and inwardly acknowledged. Holding her gaze, he murmured, "Thank you."

Her lips curved. "Perhaps," she whispered, as at her command he bent his head, "you might express your gratitude in a way that doesn't involve words."

His laugh rumbled in his chest but never made it past his lips. She sealed them with hers, drank in his delight, and gave him her own, her passion and her joy, in return.

They moved into the dance in concert, in effortless accord.

Shedding their clothes, they let their hands roam, let them shape and sculpt, possess and surrender.

They found their way onto the bed, rolled and writhed, arched and gloried.

Delighted anew, as they did every time, in the passion-filled, desire-laced moments. In the exquisitely intense intimacies.

Heat rose as the last barrier fell.

Their bodies came together, merging on a single shared gasp.

Eyes closed, fingers laced, lips brushing, kissing, mouths melding, then parting, they journeyed through the familiar landscape that, as always, bloomed anew.

He'd wondered if they would lose this, if with the familiarity bred of matrimony this intimate intensity would fade.

It hadn't. If anything, the wonders of the journey had grown richer, more vibrant, more varied, more pleasure-laden.

More shattering.

When at the last he hung poised above her, muscles like iron, veins cording his arms, the heat of their striving bodies nothing less than a furnace as he drove into her willing body and took them through the last veil into paradise, he knew beyond words, beyond thought, beyond understanding that this wonder, this joy, this aching togetherness would never end.

Not in this lifetime, and if they had any say in it, not in the next, either.

Chapter 9

Violet was late down to breakfast the next morning. She walked through the door still sliding the last of her pins into her bun. "I couldn't sleep, then I overslept."

Cook, seated at the table and crunching a slice of toast liberally spread with her marmalade preserve, nodded dourly. "Know just what you mean. Took me ages to drop off, and I feel right lethargic this morning."

Violet poured herself a cup of tea from the pot left on the warmer. Setting the cup and saucer beside her plate, she slipped into her chair. "Where's Tilly?"

"Not down yet, either."

Violet and Cook sipped and munched, needing no words to share the moment. Violet welcomed the normalcy of the simple meal; last night, alone in her room, she hadn't been able to stop thinking about the fate that had overtaken Runcorn—a hale and healthy man several years younger than she. If the villain could so easily snuff out the life of such a robust man, what of her? How safe was she?

Such thoughts had gnawed at her until nothing would do but for her to get up and push and shove and shift her small dresser across her bedroom door.

She'd felt silly. She'd told herself it was an overreaction, yet once the barricade had been in place, she'd been able to fall asleep.

Of course, pushing the dresser away from the door had delayed her even further that morning. And then she'd discovered that her door had been fractionally ajar; she'd assumed Tilly had stopped by on her way downstairs from her attic room and had expected to have to make an embarrassing explanation . . . she frowned and glanced at the clock. "Tilly . . . perhaps we'd better go and wake her. She might be unwell."

Cook's blue eyes met Violet's; from their expression, Violet realized Cook was thinking much the same as she was—that it was strange that Tilly had not come down, no matter her state. Nothing short of complete incapacitation would have kept her from making her way to the kitchen, especially given the warmth there compared to the chill—real as well as imagined—that pervaded the rest of the house.

A whisper of unease slid through Violet's mind, leaving behind the first stirrings of trepidation.

Cook compressed her lips, then stated, "I'll come with you."

Violet nodded and rose. She led the way out of the kitchen and up the stairs. Reaching the first floor, she paused at the head of the stairs; along with Cook, she strained her ears but heard nothing—no footsteps, no rustling.

No hint of life.

Trepidation welled; foreboding settled like a leaden cloak about her shoulders.

Exchanging a worried, increasingly fearful look with Cook, Violet walked slowly to the narrow door at the end of the corridor. As with her bedroom door that morning, it, too, stood slightly ajar. Dragging in a breath, Violet reached out with one hand and pushed the door fully open. Beyond, the stairs to the attic lay shrouded in perpetual gloom.

Again they listened, and heard nothing.

"Tilly?" Cook called.

No sound.

They climbed the stairs, Violet first, Cook on her heels. Stepping into the narrow corridor that led to the three small bedrooms tucked under the eaves, they halted at the first door.

The door was closed but not shut. Violet tapped. "Tilly?"

The door swung further open; when no sound came from within, Violet pushed it wide.

They didn't need to go in to see what had happened.

Tilly lay on her back on the bed, her limbs twisted and tangled, her sightless eyes staring straight up at the ceiling.

Her mouth was open in a ghastly rictus, as if she'd been screaming to the last.

Violet stared at her friend—at the body that was all that was left of her. An icy chill bloomed at Violet's nape, then swiftly spread over her shoulders and sank into her. Her eyes still looked, but her brain refused to see.

"Oh-my-God. Oh-my-God."

The horrified whisper dragged Violet back, into the moment. She looked at Cook. The normally ruddy woman was parchment pale; eyes wide, she had her hands pressed to her face and was whispering through her fingers.

Without looking back at the bed, Violet swallowed, dragged in a short breath—all she could manage—then put an arm around Cook's shoulders and turned them both from the room, away from the doorway and the sight beyond. "There's nothing we can do." Her voice sounded far calmer, far more composed and controlled than she felt. "Come—let's go downstairs and send for the authorities."

There was nothing they could do for Tilly other than seek justice.

The journey back down the stairs and into the kitchen passed in a blur; when next her mind reengaged, Violet found herself in the kitchen, pouring cups of strong tea for herself and Cook, who had collapsed into her chair in a storm of noisy weeping.

Grabbing the rough pad of paper and the pencil Cook kept for making shopping lists, Violet sat at the table, took a gulp of her tea, then started to write.

Cook lifted her blotchy face from her folded arms. "Don't you dare send for that idiot doctor—he'll just say Tilly died of old age!"

"I'm not." Violet hadn't even considered sending for Milborne. She continued writing. "I'm sending for Inspector Stokes. And Mr. Montague—her ladyship trusted him, and I do, too."

She had no idea if Montague could do anything to help, but . . . she wanted him there. She just needed to see him, to sense his rock-solid certainty again, to let it settle her and anchor her. Without that . . . the instant she stopped doing something specific, she felt like her mind would splinter apart.

Cook sniffed, then in a watery voice asked, "You need two boys?"

Eyes on her writing, Violet nodded. "One for Scotland Yard, and the other for Chapel Court in the City."

Heaving a heavy sigh, Cook dabbed at her eyes with her apron, then pushed back from the table and got to her feet. "I'll get Tommy and Alfie from next door. They'll do it and be quick."

"Thank you." Violet kept writing. Kept her mind ruthlessly fixed on what she could do, rather than on what she couldn't.

She couldn't go back to the night before and confess to Tilly that she was afraid—afraid enough to put a dresser across her door.

Her fear had been the only thing that had saved her—but she hadn't been brave enough to let it save Tilly.

Stokes could barely believe it. He stood in the open doorway of the tiny attic bedroom and stared—glared—at the body on the bed.

He'd brought the Yard's surgeon, Pemberton, with him. At the side of the narrow bed, straightening from his first cursory examination, Pemberton shot Stokes a glance. "Same as the other one. Smothered with a pillow." Pemberton waved at the pillow that had been tossed onto the wooden chair in the corner behind the door. "That one at a guess."

Stokes humphed. "What's your best guess as to when?"

Pemberton grimaced. "Sometime in the wee small hours, but that is just a guess."

Stokes continued to stare at the bed. After a moment, he said, "The old lady was weak—this one wasn't."

"No." Pemberton nodded. "The maid fought back as hard as she could, but whoever stood above her holding down the pillow was stronger than she was."

"So in your opinion, the murderer's unlikely to be a lady."

"A female of any sort." Pemberton glanced down the body, visually assessing the limbs partially revealed by the disarranged sheets. "This victim appears to have been a hale and hearty woman. She wouldn't have been easily overcome."

Stokes grunted. "Anything else you can tell me?"

Pemberton shook his head. "Nothing else you don't already know."

"I'll leave you to it, then." Stokes had already searched the small room, but the murderer hadn't helpfully left a calling card or anything else resembling a clue. The room was spare and held little in the way of possessions; he doubted the murderer had bothered rifling through them, and there were no overt signs that anything had been disturbed.

Descending the narrow stairs to the first floor, then heavily going down the long flight to the ground floor, Stokes shook his head and muttered to himself, "He came to murder her, that and nothing else. But why murder the maid?"

Reaching the hall, he crossed to the constable he'd left guarding the front door. "Anything or anyone?"

"Just Mr. Adair, sir, and his missus and yours, like you expected. They went back to the kitchen—said they'd wait for you there."

Stokes nodded, rather surprised that Barnaby hadn't come straight upstairs . . . but then, he'd had Penelope and Griselda with him, and if Barnaby had come up to view the body . . . so no, he shouldn't be surprised that his friend had chosen the less disturbing path. "Pemberton's crew will be along shortly, but at this point I'm not expecting anyone else. Let me know immediately if anyone arrives."

"Aye, sir."

Stokes headed back through the house to the kitchen. Montague had been on the doorstep when he'd arrived, and he'd been glad to leave the other man to calm Miss Matcham and the volatile cook while he took care of business upstairs. Before he'd left the Yard, he'd sent a message to Barnaby, conveying the news and suggesting he join him at Lowndes Street—and having escorted Griselda to the Albemarle Street house on his way into work that morning, he'd extended the invitation to Penelope and Griselda, too.

Given how much the pair had learned yesterday, and accepting that they approached most situations from a different perspective, and therefore saw things neither he nor Barnaby did, he'd swallowed his natural resistance and included them . . . because he knew he'd have been a fool not to.

And not just in a professional sense.

He walked into the kitchen, and six pairs of eyes swung to fix on him. They'd all gathered in chairs about the kitchen table.

"So?" Barnaby prompted as Stokes lifted a chair from beside the fireplace and carried it to the table.

Setting the chair beside the one Griselda occupied, Stokes sat, met Barnaby's gaze, then looked at Violet—Miss Matcham—and the cook. "As you've no doubt guessed, she—Tilly Westcott, Lady Halstead's maid—was killed in the same way her ladyship was, smothered by a pillow placed over her face while she slept."

"Was anything different?" Barnaby asked.

"Not in the murderer's modus operandi, but there was one significant difference, one Pemberton—the police surgeon—just confirmed." Stokes glanced at Violet and the cook. "Was Miss Westcott in good health?"

"She was fit as a fiddle yesterday," Cook said.

Violet nodded. "She was entirely well as far as we knew."

"Would you say she was a strong woman?" Stokes asked.

"Strong as a horse, she was," Cook averred. "She could lift and carry things that'd make my back ache."

Violet glanced around the table. "Tilly was taller than me, strapping and rather raw-boned. So, yes"—Violet looked back at Stokes—"she was quite strong."

Stokes inclined his head. "So Tilly was much stronger than Lady Halstead, and she fought back—that much is obvious. But the murderer still successfully smothered her."

"So the murderer couldn't have been a woman—not in this case." Penelope glanced at Barnaby, then looked down the table at Stokes. "How likely is it that Lady Halstead's murderer and Tilly's murderer are *not* the same person?"

"Not very likely at all." Stokes paused, then said, "So the murderer is a man, one strong enough to over-power a strong woman."

"Any guess as to when it happened?" Barnaby asked.

"Pemberton says in the very early hours." Noise reached them from the front hall. Stokes rose. "That will be more constables. I'll send them to ask around the neighborhood in case anyone saw anything, but given the time and the weather last night, I'm not expecting that we'll have any luck." He walked out of the kitchen, leaving everyone else thinking; he returned two min-utes later and resumed his seat.

"So how did he get in?" Penelope looked from Stokes, to Barnaby, to Montague, and Violet beside him. "Any ideas?"

Barnaby straightened. "That was one issue we never resolved about her ladyship's death—how the murderer got into the house." He met Stokes's eyes. "There was heavy rain last night, just before mid-night. If we search now, we might get lucky and find some sign."

The winds that had whipped through the city the previous evening had been the harbingers of a storm with attendant downpour, and it was October; there were leaves everywhere. Stokes looked at Violet.

"When you first approached the front door this morning, did you notice any dampness or leaves, any sort of detritus, in the front hall?"

Violet shook her head. "The first time I went that way was when I let you and Mr. Montague in, but I wasn't looking all that closely—I'm not sure I would have noticed."

"And we've had too many people come in and out of the front door since to bother checking now," Stokes said.

"But coming in via the front door—that would be a truly arrogant act." Penelope looked at the cook. "Where's the back door?"

The cook swiveled to point. "Over there. But"—she looked up at Stokes as he rose to his feet—"I've been through it this morning to fetch the boys to take Violet's notes."

"That's all right." Stokes headed for the archway into the back hall. "Barnaby? The rest of you, please stay here."

Together with Stokes, Barnaby searched, but there was no sign of anyone with damp shoes going deeper into the house from the back door. Not even the cook had left any visible trace.

As they returned to the kitchen, Stokes grimaced. "No luck, so that's the doors ruled out—"

"No—there's a side door." When they all looked at her, Violet explained, "There's a door to a narrow alley that runs between the street and the mews." She pushed back her chair. "I'll show you."

Montague rose and gave her his hand to assist her to her feet.

She thanked him with a smile that felt weak, then went around the table. She led Stokes and Adair out of the kitchen, into the rear of the front hall, then through a narrow archway under the stairs. Two turns and she halted in the short, dark corridor that ended in the side door. She nodded toward it. "That's it."

She stepped aside to let Stokes and Adair past. Stokes took one step down the corridor, then halted. Adair remained in the rear. "Light," he said. "We need at least two lamps before we go any closer."

Stokes nodded and turned to Violet. "I take it that door is usually locked?"

She glanced down the corridor at the shadowy panels. "Usually."

"Who has the key?" Stokes asked.

"Lady Halstead has—had—a ring with the keys to all the doors. As far as I know, that ring is still in her dresser, where she usually left it. There's a key to the side door there, and there's a second one on the rack in the kitchen." Without waiting to be asked, she went on, "The door is only occasionally used, mostly for deliveries from milliners, dressmakers, and shops like Hatchards. Food goes to the back door, but other deliveries were directed to the side door."

"When was it last used?" Adair asked. "Do you know?"

Staring at the door, Violet cast her mind back. Eventually, she said, "As far as I know, it hasn't been used for several months, possibly not since last Christmas."

Stokes nodded and looked at Adair. "Let's get those lamps."

They did, then, with Violet holding one and Montague the other, Stokes and Adair carefully started down the corridor toward the door, meticulously searching the floor as they went.

Inch by inch, foot by foot, they progressed down the narrow hallway.

Six feet from the door, Adair, searching to the left with Violet holding the lamp over his shoulder, shining the beam ahead of him, paused, then glanced at her. "Can you angle the light into the skirting? Into the crevice between the skirting and the floor . . ."

As she did as he asked, he crouched and peered, then reached out with one finger. "Got you!"

Stokes swung around to look. He studied the single brown leaf Adair held up, balanced on the tip of one finger.

Adair met Stokes's eyes. "And it's still damp enough to stick."

Stokes quivered like a powerful wolfhound on a leash but paused to glance at Violet. "You're sure no one has come through that door this morning?"

She nodded. "I'm perfectly certain."

The smile that curved Stokes's lips was more menacing than comforting. "So," he said, "we now know that the murderer is a Halstead male who has a key to the side door."

Stokes and Adair examined the door, confirming there was no evidence it had been forced in any way, then, as a group, they returned to the kitchen. Walking ahead of the three men, Violet sensed a change in atmosphere, in them, as if previously they'd been unsure, uncertain, casting about, but now they'd caught the scent of their prey and were keen to follow the trail.

Their renewed determination spread and infected the others about the table as they resumed their seats and Stokes told the others of what they'd found.

Cook had withdrawn from the circle about the table but had made two fresh pots of tea; Violet sensed Cook was somewhat taken aback to find herself serving such company about her kitchen table. Adair had introduced his wife and Stokes's wife when they'd arrived; at the time, Violet had been too distracted to properly register the strangeness of their presence. Yet both women had been sensible and supportive, and she'd been grateful for their warmth when all else about the day—barring only Montague's presence—had left her feeling so cold. So isolated.

So alone.

They all paused to sip the tea Cook had dispensed. Violet could almost hear the thoughts whirling.

Then Stokes's wife—Griselda, as she'd told Violet to call her—set down her cup, a faint frown tangling her black brows. "What I don't understand is, why kill the maid? How could she possibly have been any threat to the murderer?" Griselda looked across the table at Violet. "Forgive me for asking, but she—the maid—couldn't possibly have been in league with the murderer, could she?"

"Absolutely not!" came from both Violet and Cook, who had retreated to stand before the stove.

Adair added, "And I would have to agree. I simply cannot imagine that Tilly had any hand in her mistress's murder, much less Runcorn's."

"Which," Adair's wife, Penelope, said, "brings us back to Griselda's question. Why kill the maid?"

After a moment, Stokes said, "Perhaps it's something similar to what happened with Henrietta Cynster." He glanced at Violet. "Another recent case."

"Hmm." Eyes narrowing, Penelope set down her cup. "You mean that Tilly had seen something or knew something that, while of itself of no particular moment, if put together with other information—"

"For instance," Montague said, "the sort of information that might come out through Lady Halstead's affairs being put in order."

Penelope nodded. "Exactly—if put together with that, then what Tilly knew would assume much greater significance—"

"To whit, that it would point a finger at the murderer." Somewhat grimly, Stokes nodded. "Yes, that's what I meant. All things considered, I believe Tilly was murdered because she knew something the significance of which she had not yet realized."

"He's protecting himself," Adair said. When they all looked at him, he went on, "All three murders can be explained by that—I don't think we need to invoke any other motive. He used Lady Halstead's account to hide the proceeds from his recent and ongoing involvement in some illegal enterprise, and in order to keep that illegal association concealed, he killed first Lady Halstead, then Runcorn, and now Tilly."

Stokes regarded Adair for several moments, then nodded. Then he frowned, and his gaze shifted to Violet.

Before Stokes could ask the question clearly forming in his head, Montague placed a hand over Violet's, where it rested on the table between them. "I think you must tell Stokes what you told me when I arrived."

Violet looked at him; although she had to be aware that everyone else was now studying her, she held his gaze. In response to the uncertainty in her eyes, he nodded encouragingly. An instant passed, then, making no move to draw her hand from under his, she drew breath and looked across the table at Stokes. "Mr. Montague called yesterday evening and told me of the progress of your investigation. Specifically, he told me that Mr. Runcorn had been murdered." She paused when Stokes glanced at Montague and arched one black brow.

Unapologetically meeting Stokes's gaze, Montague gently pressed Violet's hand, and she drew another shaky breath, reclaiming Stokes's attention, and continued, "This morning, when Mr. Montague arrived, I mentioned how unsettled I had been after learning of Runcorn's death—that I'd felt rattled enough to push my dresser across my door before I fell asleep last night."

Montague felt Violet's gaze briefly touch his face, then she faced Stokes again. "This morning, when I moved the dresser back, I discovered the door to my room was ajar." She paused to allow the ripple of shock that traveled around the table to subside, then went on, "It was most definitely closed when I went to bed, but this morning . . ."

Her hand turned beneath his, her fingers convulsively clasping his as she drew in another tight breath and raised her chin. "I suspect that if Mr. Montague hadn't told me of Mr. Runcorn's death, and I hadn't felt frightened enough to block my door, then I would now be as dead as Tilly."

Unsurprisingly, that declaration prompted a round of shocked and concerned exclamations.

Penelope caught Violet's gaze. "I don't suppose you know what you know, so to speak?"

Violet shook her head. "Rest assured, if I knew anything that might identify Lady Halstead's murderer, and now Runcorn's and Tilly's, too, I would instantly tell . . . well, anyone and everyone."

Penelope grimaced. Various murmurs of support and conjecture floated around the table.

Stokes had been frowning blackly at the table; raising his head, he rapped a hand on its surface. When everyone quieted and looked at him, he grimly stated,

"We now have three murders and a missing sum of cash, much of it likely ill-gotten gains. We have reason to suspect that the villain is a member of the Halstead family—not only was a man of a description that would fit several of the Halstead men seen in the vicinity of Runcorn's office on the night of his murder, and also seen meeting the lady who removed the money in question from the bank, but we now know the murderer gained entrance to the house to kill Lady Halstead's maid by using a key to the side door. Most likely he used the same entrance when he murdered Lady Halstead herself." Stokes looked around the table, meeting everyone's eyes. "I think," he said, "that it's time we interviewed the family again."

Chapter 10

Stokes had sent formal requests for the Halsteads and the Camberlys to assemble at the Lowndes Street house at two o'clock that afternoon.

As Penelope had said, "At that hour, they can't fob you off by saying they have to attend a luncheon, or any other pressing social event."

Stokes wondered if it was the lack of a viable excuse that saw all the Halstead brood trooping into the drawing room at the appointed time—or curiosity. Watching the arrivals from the rear of the front hall, he murmured to Barnaby, standing beside him, "That rivalry of theirs could work to our advantage."

Barnaby's lips lifted in a cynical smile. "You mean they've come to learn what you've uncovered about the others?" Watching Constance Halstead whisper to her daughter, Caroline, as they passed through the door, he nodded. "You may well be right."

After a moment, Stokes said, "I wish I could believe that Montague's searching might give us the answer, but I can't imagine our villain being silly enough to put his cash anywhere it might be found. Especially not after this business with her ladyship's accounts."

"No. He won't be that stupid." Montague had told them that it would take several days for him to hear back about the current state of the Halsteads' bank accounts. "I agree with Montague that it's one of those things we need to check, on the grounds that we would be stupid not to, just in case, but from the start this villain was cagey enough to know he needed to conceal that money—even more now than before, he's not going to allow it to be found and connected with him."

Stokes snorted. "If I were him, I'd put it in a tin under the bed."

"On top of the wardrobe," Barnaby murmured back. "Maids eventually find things hidden under beds."

Stokes's teeth flashed in a grin.

But he was severely sober when, with Barnaby and Montague, he walked into the drawing room. Violet, Penelope, and Griselda had gone into the room before any of the family had arrived; if anyone had questioned Penelope and Griselda's presence, Penelope had intended to adopt her most haughty manner and inform them that she and Griselda were there supporting Violet. As Stokes noted all three ensconced on a chaise beneath the windows opposite the fireplace, a position that afforded a clear view of the family members gathered in the chairs and on the twin sofas flanking the hearth, he assumed that any who had dared dispute their right to be there had been duly put in their place.

The three ladies were specifically charged with observing, both the individual reactions and the family interactions; Stokes didn't anticipate them contributing to the proceedings and fervently hoped they wouldn't. Explaining why their wives were posing questions in an interview would, he felt, tax even Barnaby's ingenuity.

After surveying the family and confirming all were present, Stokes crossed to take a position before the fireplace, from where he had an excellent view of all in the room. Barnaby and Montague followed; Barnaby halted on Stokes's right, with Montague beyond him. They, too, could see everyone's faces, could watch and note every reaction.

Two constables unobtrusively came into the room and, after quietly shutting the door, took up stations to either side.

They'd decided to use the drawing room rather than the dining room for this confrontation purely because the setting gave Stokes, and Barnaby and Montague, the advantage of height. They were standing, while, of course, the Halstead men had claimed prime positions on the sofas and in the armchairs.

Stokes was determined to shake the family and see what fell out of their tree.

"Well, Inspector," Wallace Camberly said, "what news?"

"I do hope you're here to tell us that the police have our mother's murderer behind bars." Mortimer Halstead all but sniffed. "God knows Peel's force has been endowed with sufficient resources."

Cynthia Camberly, née Halstead, smiled somewhat unctuously at Stokes. "Don't mind my brother, Inspector—he tends to be rather bureaucratically minded. But I take it you have news to impart?"

Stokes had shifted his gaze from Wallace to Mortimer; now he allowed it to rest on Cynthia for a moment too long to be comfortable—for his scrutiny to edge into insultingly superior—then, slowly, he surveyed the circle of faces. Only when his visual claiming was complete did he say, "I've summoned you here to inform you that Mr. Andrew Runcorn, of Runcorn and Son, whom Lady Halstead had requested to review her affairs, was murdered two nights ago."

Barnaby concentrated on the younger men—on Walter Camberly and Hayden Halstead—leaving Montague to watch their fathers, Wallace and Mortimer. As far as Barnaby could see, both young men's reactions fitted with their characters and ages—Walter, some years older, looked faintly shocked and a touch puzzled, while Hayden, although noting the information, continued to look quietly, rather sullenly, bored. Walter hadn't expected to hear such news and didn't know what to make of it, while Hayden really didn't care—Runcorn's death meant nothing to him.

Whoever had murdered Runcorn, Barnaby decided, it wasn't either of them.

After an initial moment of faintly shocked surprise, Cynthia leaned forward. Fixing Stokes with a commanding eye, she asked, "Are you suggesting, Inspector, that Mr. Runcorn's murder was in some way associated with his work on my mother's affairs?"

Again, Stokes was deliberately slow in answering, but eventually, he said, "As your mother's papers were scattered over Mr. Runcorn's desk and had obviously been searched, it's difficult to avoid that conclusion, ma'am."

"Well!" Constance Halstead's bosom swelled. "I really cannot see why anyone would have any interest in Mama-in-law's affairs. It must have been purely coincidental that her papers were on Mr. Runcorn's desk at that time."

"Indeed." Wallace Camberly's tone was clipped. "As her ladyship *had* requested Mr. Runcorn to review her affairs, I cannot see that there's any great significance in her papers being on his desk at the time of his murder." His gaze flat, Camberly met Stokes's eyes. "I believe you are making too much of a deductive leap, Inspector. Runcorn doubtless had many clients, and who are we to say who he might or might not have crossed through his work? His murder might have come about through his association with any of those others. As far as I can see, there's no reason whatever to suggest that his unfortunate murder was in any way connected with his work for Lady Halstead."

Unperturbed and imperturbable, Stokes regarded Camberly for a long moment, then raised his gaze and again swept the gathering. "You might also be interested to learn that, on the morning following Mr. Runcorn's murder, a large sum of money was withdrawn from Lady Halstead's bank account."

That caused a far more acute reaction.

"Who by?" Mortimer demanded.

"The devil!" Maurice shot upright in the corner of the sofa in which he'd been sprawled. "Do you mean that we—Mama—have been robbed?"

Cynthia's expression shifted from shock to calculation. "How much was taken?"

"And how?" Wallace Camberly's question was more in the nature of a peremptory demand. "Great heavens—the banks are supposed to have procedures in place to prevent this sort of thing."

"Indeed—and they do." Mortimer huffed. "Just what is going on here, Inspector? Is the bank itself somehow involved?"

Comments, conjecture, and speculation came from all quarters; even Caroline was moved to exclaim over the lost funds.

Stokes decided they'd gone on long enough—that his observers had had time enough to observe. He shifted—a single, forceful, menacing movement that instinctively had everyone glancing at him—then waited until the babbling ceased and their attention was once again his. "The police have established that the bank acted properly. They fulfilled a request submitted in writing by Lady Halstead. The bank was unaware that her ladyship was deceased. As Runcorn had not yet been informed of Lady Halstead's murder, then he, as her ladyship's man-of-business, had not yet informed the bank of the change in his client's situation. On close inspection, the letter presented to the bank was discovered to be a forgery, but a very good one. Whoever wrote it was extremely well acquainted with her ladyship's hand."

"Who presented the letter to the bank?" William asked.

Stokes regarded him for a moment before replying, "A veiled woman, thought to be a lady, although her station was purely an assumption."

A puzzled silence fell. Constance Halstead was the first to turn her head and look across the room at Violet, sitting on the chaise flanked by Griselda and Penelope.

Constance's daughter, Caroline, noticed, and she, too turned to look.

One by one, the others realized, and then all were staring at Violet, varying degrees of speculation verging on imminent accusation in their faces.

"Why wear a veil?" Cynthia mused.

Mortimer took her question at face value. "Obviously," he retorted, "to conceal her identity."

Cynthia's lips curved sarcastically as she glanced pityingly at Mortimer. "Precisely. Which suggests she expected to be recognized." Cynthia lifted her gaze to Stokes's face. "Does that not suggest, Inspector, that the veiled woman was in some way connected with my mother?"

Constance Halstead turned from her pointed scrutiny of Violet to add, "Especially with the letter being such a close match to Mama-in-law's hand."

"That," Stokes gravely conceded, "is one possible interpretation, but as the police have already discounted the members of her ladyship's immediate household, I would be interested in hearing of which other females linked to Lady Halstead you think might warrant further investigation."

Both Cynthia and Constance immediately pulled back. They exchanged glances but kept their lips shut.

Wallace Camberly shifted restlessly. "To return to more pertinent issues, Inspector, how much was stolen from the account?"

"I'm afraid," Stokes smoothly replied, "that I am not yet at liberty to disclose that information."

Barnaby had been observing Walter and Hayden throughout; Walter continued to look puzzled, while Hayden had resorted to studying his fingernails.

They'd decided to withhold the information that a gentleman fitting a description that matched five of the family had been seen at Runcorn's office and outside the bank at the critical times, judging that if they revealed that card, the family would band together, put up their shields, and become even more defensive and unhelpful.

They were unhelpful enough as it was.

Stokes had been consulting his notebook. Now he raised his gaze and, his voice hardening, said, "I have also to inform you that, this morning, Tilly Westcott, her ladyship's maid, was discovered murdered in her bed upstairs."

That jolted even Hayden into attentiveness; while his face revealed no sympathy, much less sorrow, his expression displayed a certain startled, prurient interest.

Walter's eyes had grown round, but he remained silent, allowing his parents, aunt, and uncles to put voice to the family's response.

Which could be summed up by an unvoiced *What has that to do with us?* Their expressions remained largely blank, some a touch bewildered, as if waiting for Stokes to explain the connection, to elucidate why they should be concerned with the maid's death.

Stokes obliged. "Miss Westcott was murdered in precisely the same manner as Lady Halstead." He paused, then went on, "We—the police—therefore believe that Miss Westcott was most likely murdered by the same villain, and most likely because she knew something that, at some point, would have identified Lady Halstead's killer."

Barnaby was rapidly losing interest in Walter Halstead and Hayden Camberly. All he was observing in either man was either bewilderment or curiosity. Neither showed any sign of knowing anything, of having any awareness at all, of any of the three murders.

Wallace Camberly was frowning. "In that case, Inspector, is it not reasonable to suppose that this maid, having over the years no doubt learned much from her ladyship concerning her wealth, was an accomplice to her ladyship's murder, and indirectly to that of her ladyship's man-of-business, and then, in disguise, assisted in the theft of the funds from the bank, only to subsequently be murdered by her partner in crime?"

"Indeed, Inspector." Mortimer Halstead unbent enough to stiffly incline his head to his brother-in-law. "Such a scenario admirably accounts for the facts." Mortimer raised his gaze to Stokes's face and arched an arrogant brow. "It's certainly more believable than any suggestion that any member of this family had anything to do with any criminal act."

Stokes held onto his temper and, his expression unreadable, blandly asked, "One aspect remains to be adequately explained, even by that scenario. Namely, how the murderer gained access to this house on two separate occasions via a key to the side door." Stokes swept the family with a sharply questioning gaze. "As we've come to that point, allow me to ask: Who among you has keys to this house?"

A ripple, not so much of unease as of annoyance, spread around the gathering.

Camberly glanced sharply at his wife. "As far as I am aware, we don't have one."

Cynthia's lips compressed, as if the question had prodded a sore spot, but she nodded. "We don't." As if compelled, she looked up at Stokes and snippily added, "And as far as I know, no other among this family does, either."

Mortimer, too, appeared irritated. "My mother, Inspector, was . . . independently minded. Even after my father died and she elected to remain here alone, she did not, as far as I am aware, distribute keys to this house." Mortimer again looked at Violet. "I daresay Miss Matcham can confirm that."

Across the width of the room, Violet met Stokes's eyes and reluctantly nodded. "I'm not aware that Lady Halstead gave any of her family a key to this house—she told me she didn't see the need."

"Precisely!" Cynthia nodded and looked at Stokes. "So you see, Inspector, there's no question of any family member being involved."

"For once I must agree with my sister, Inspector." Mortimer's expression suggested that doing so was akin to sucking a lemon. "Which brings me to ask what the police are doing to catch this murderous thief."

Refusing to respond to the undisguised jab carried in the tone of Mortimer's demand, Stokes smoothly replied, "The investigation is proceeding on several fronts. The family will be informed in due course of the outcome, but at this stage, our immediate next step is to establish the alibis of all those who are, by virtue of their association with the victim, potential suspects. Anyone who might, directly or indirectly, gain from her ladyship's death is, in the eyes of the law, a potential suspect. Consequently, while I assume it will be a mere formality, I must ask each of you for an accounting of where you were on the three evenings on which the murders took place."

The gathering erupted in protest, the ladies feigning shock and incipient outrage, the three Halstead brothers blustering and disputing the necessity.

Neither Walter Camberly nor Hayden Halstead added their voices to the clamor, but Barnaby noted that both looked uneasy. However, their wariness was focused on their respective mothers, which, Barnaby suspected, suggested guilt not over the murders but over something else. Something possibly entirely understandable and not at all villainous.

Wallace Camberly, too, did not bother verbally protesting; he sat in the corner of one sofa, his lips compressed, his expression that of a man whose temper was being sorely tried. He radiated irritation and severe annoyance, but, unlike the others, he gave the impression he fully understood that, in this instance, there was nothing to be gained from resistance.

292 • STEPHANIE LAURENS

Unruffled, stoic, Stokes waited out the protests, but Camberly reached the end of his patience first.

"Inspector—I'm a very busy man." Camberly straightened and met Stokes's gaze. "As I can see you are bound and determined to take our alibis, might I ask that you take mine first? There's a debate in Parliament later this afternoon that I wish to attend."

As all the other comments faded, Stokes inclined his head, but before he could say anything, Mortimer declared, "I, too, am expected elsewhere." He caught Stokes's eye. "I must return to my desk and my duties. The wheels of government will not pause for something as minor as domestic murder."

Barnaby suspected that Stokes, like he, might argue that last, but . . .

Stokes, no doubt quite pleased but hiding it, inclined his head to Mortimer, then glanced at Camberly. "Perhaps, Mr. Camberly, you would step this way?" Stokes waved to a round table with two chairs that sat in an alcove at the end of the long room. "And after I have your statement, I can deal with Mr. Halstead."

"Indeed." Camberly rose, straightened his jacket, settled his sleeves, then followed Stokes to the end of the room.

Mortimer Halstead watched them go.

His wife and his sister drew deep breaths, then started to argue over which of them was most urgently expected elsewhere such that they, and not the other, should follow Mortimer in giving Stokes their alibis.

Barnaby battled a grin. He glanced at Montague. Under cover of the din, Barnaby murmured, "Any insights?"

Montague shook his head. "Both Camberly and Mortimer Halstead are too accustomed to guarding their expressions. They were too often blank, or held rigidly to blandness—I couldn't identify any specific reaction to any of the revelations, or rather, none that would denote guilt."

Barnaby grimaced lightly. "Let's hope the ladies had more luck."

Across the room, Penelope turned to Violet. "Did any of them behave in a manner you hadn't expected?"

Violet considered, then shook her head. "I was mildly surprised that Caroline actually spoke, but what she said wasn't out of character. She, Hayden, and Walter usually attend this house under sufferance because their parents insist they must. They rarely contribute to any discussion and, I often think, are usually absorbed with thoughts of other things. Today . . . I would say all three were attending, concentrating on what was said, but . . ." She grimaced. "I sensed their interest stemmed more from curiosity—that sort of horrified fascination violent death tends to evoke."

Her gaze moving over the gathering before the fireplace, Griselda nodded. "Indeed—that's precisely how I read it, too." Glancing across Violet, she met Penelope's gaze. "I didn't detect any suspicious reaction, did you?"

Penelope wrinkled her nose and looked back at Lady Halstead's assembled family. "No." After a moment, she added, "That said, having now seen and observed them all, and thus finally comprehending just how overwhelming their self-interest and self-absorption truly are, I'm even more convinced that someone here, someone presently in this room, is indeed the murderer"—she looked back at Violet and Griselda—"for the simple reason that I cannot imagine any other person having a sufficiently good motive for killing first Lady Halstead, then Runcorn, then Tilly the maid, and going one step further and attempting to murder Violet, too." Penelope looked back at the Halsteads and Camberlys. "So it's someone here, but which one?"

"Perhaps their alibis will give us some clue." Griselda studied her husband, presently seated at the round table writing in his notebook as Mortimer Halstead, with a patently dismissive air, recited his whereabouts on the nights in question. Wallace Camberly had completed his turn and, with a brief nod to his wife, had departed, leaving through the door one of the constables had opened for him; Griselda knew there were two more constables in the front hall, waiting to ensure the family members quit the house directly and weren't tempted to stray into the sitting room or upstairs.

Mortimer Halstead rose from the table; after surveying the room, his expression cold and closed, he headed for the door. His wife, Constance, replaced him at the table, having stolen a march on Cynthia, who had been delayed by her son, Walter; the pair stood together, heads bent close, by the fireplace. Observing the quality of their exchange, Griselda murmured, "I'd wager Cynthia is coaching Walter on what he should say."

Penelope considered the sight, then snorted. "As if Stokes and his men won't check."

Constance rose from the table. Noticing, Cynthia whisked in to take her place, waving Caroline, who had intended to follow Constance, back. Although she scowled, Caroline gave way to her aunt and stepped back to wait her turn.

Constance Halstead paused to study the room. Her gaze came to rest on Violet, protectively flanked by Penelope and Griselda, and, head rising, much in the manner of a frigate under full sail, Constance swept across the room, bearing down on the chaise. Halting before it, she looked down at Violet. Ignoring Penelope and Griselda to either side, her expression that of a matron dealing with a household chore, Constance stated, "Miss Matcham, I believe you are better placed than any of the family to undertake the responsibility of dealing with this unfortunate occurrence of Miss Westcott's death. Indeed, I suspect it falls within the scope of your duties to her ladyship to do so."

Looking into Mrs. Halstead's face, taking in her somewhat petulant tone, Violet bit her tongue at that "unfortunate occurrence"; after a moment's consideration, she stiffly inclined her head. "As you say, Mrs. Halstead, on her ladyship's behalf I will contact Miss Westcott's family." She certainly wouldn't want to leave the matter of making sure Tilly's body and effects were properly dealt with to any of the Halstead brood. Glancing at Stokes, she saw him still busy writing as Cynthia rose from her seat at the table and Caroline swiftly took her place. Looking back at Constance, Violet amended, "Or at least, I will liaise with the police as to what should be done in that regard."

Constance's expression turned peevish. "I'm sure I don't know why the police are making themselves so busy over this latest murder—it's hardly of any great import."

Before Violet, Penelope, or Griselda could voice any of the retorts that leapt to their tongues, Cynthia Camberly halted beside her sister-in-law in a swish of stylishly subdued skirts. All three ladies of the family—Constance, Caroline, and Cynthia—had made some attempt to dress appropriately for mourning, but, of course, their orders for new mourning gowns were still with their dressmakers.

Unsmiling, her expression arrogantly superior, Cynthia looked down her nose at Violet. "As I'm sure you will understand, Miss Matcham, the family will wish to close up this house as soon as possible. Given her ladyship is gone, all reason for your continued employment has vanished, as, indeed, is true for the rest of the staff. Although her ladyship's funeral will be held at St. Peter's, we've agreed that it would be most convenient to host the wake here. After that, however, we would prefer to see the house closed."

"Indeed." Constance Halstead nodded. "So if you could inform Cook that you and she will need to make other arrangements commencing from tomorrow evening?"

"To ensure an appropriate standard, I will send my butler, two footmen, and a kitchen maid to assist with serving at the wake and with the subsequent clearing of the kitchen," Cynthia added. "However, both you and

Cook should consider your employment terminated as of the end of that day."

Keeping all reaction from her face, Violet studied the two harridans before her. She'd lived in the house, and had given exemplary service, for the past eight years, and Cook had done the same for even longer.

Violet felt Penelope's fingers tighten about her own in both support and warning; on her other side, Griselda shifted a fraction closer, without words signaling her support as well. Holding onto her composure with an iron grip, Violet stiffly inclined her head. As if from a distance, she heard herself say, "I will convey your instructions to Cook."

"Excellent." With a nod of dismissal, Cynthia turned, as did Constance, as Caroline joined them.

Constance and Caroline gathered their shawls and headed for the door.

Cynthia remained standing for several moments, through narrowed eyes watching her brother Maurice take his turn at the table with Stokes. Then she audibly sniffed, turned on her heel, and, head rising high, followed her sister-in-law from the room.

Griselda, Penelope, and Violet watched her go.

After a moment, Penelope observed, "I cannot recall ever meeting such dislikeable people."

Griselda smothered a cynical laugh. She looked at those still in the room. "I have to admit it's rare to meet such a universally unattractive group—there's not one my heart warms to."

"Are they always like that?" Penelope glanced at Violet. "Always so unlikeable?"

She thought back over the years, then nodded. "Yes. I've known them all for eight years, and they've always been as they are—coldly self-serving."

So self-serving she was going to have to find a new roof over her head . . . just the thought of trying to sleep upstairs, of being in this house when night again fell, sent a shiver down her spine.

Violet looked up and found Montague watching her; even across the room, she sensed his concern.

Once the ladies had departed, it didn't take long for the remaining men to give Stokes their alibis; as the last, Hayden, took himself off, Stokes rose and walked up the room.

Barnaby and Montague, who had hung back by the fireplace, observing the men, stirred and came forward to join the group as Stokes halted before the chaise Violet, Penelope, and Griselda still graced.

"Anything?" Barnaby asked, nodding at the notebook Stokes was perusing.

Stokes cast him a jaundiced look. "I asked for alibis for all three murders as well as the morning when the money was taken from the bank. With regard to the evenings, the ladies, unsurprisingly, have alibis of a social nature—messy, but they can be checked. However, as we've all agreed no female killed Runcorn or Tilly, and it was a male who met the woman from the bank, then our ladies are largely irrelevant." Stokes flipped over a leaf of his notebook. "The gentlemen's alibis are rather less specific, and much less easy to verify. For instance, all of them claim to have been either in bed, or walking in the park, or generally about on the morning when the money was taken from the bank. Their evening alibis are this club or that, this hell or that, this party or that. It's highly unlikely we'll be able to easily verify any of those." Stokes looked down the page and snorted. "William Halstead's alibis, while overtly the weakest, are probably going to be the easiest to confirm—he says he was drinking in a tavern by the docks on all three nights."

Barnaby nodded. "If it's his regular drinking hole, the barman and bargirls will know him and, most likely, be able to tell us if he was there."

Grimly, Stokes nodded. "Exactly." He glanced at the three ladies, then at Montague and Barnaby. "So other than predictably unhelpful alibis, what else did we learn from this exercise?"

Sliding his hands into his trouser pockets, Barnaby volunteered, "I doubt either Walter Camberly or Hayden Halstead is the murderer. Neither can yet control their expressions all that well—not like their elders—and neither reacted to the news of the deaths with any reaction that might suggest guilt."

Penelope and Griselda exchanged glances. "The ladies," Penelope reported, "also showed no consciousness or any awareness that would suggest they knew anything about the crimes."

"Unfortunately," Montague said, "the older males were impossible to read." Montague met Stokes's eyes. "In all my years of meeting with and assessing the reactions of clients, I have rarely met such . . . controlled façades."

Stokes nodded. "Indeed. William Halstead appeared to be the easiest to read—he appeared unconcerned and detached throughout—but was that a mask, or was that reality? Given the artfully crafted faces Mortimer, Camberly, and Maurice all showed, I can't have any confidence I read any of them aright."

Montague sighed. "So in terms of flushing out the murderer, this exercise fell somewhat short of our mark."

The others all rather glumly nodded.

Violet glanced at their faces, then rose. "I believe we can all do with some tea. Just let me have a word with Cook first—I have to tell her the family are letting us go and wish to close up this house tomorrow evening."

Stokes arched his brows.

Montague looked concerned.

Leaving them all to follow, Violet headed for the kitchen.

"Aye, well," Cook said when Violet informed her that they would have to quit the house. "That's no more nor less than what I'd expected from that lot, but, truth be told, wild horses couldn't keep me under this roof a single night more." Seeing the others coming into the kitchen, Cook turned to the stove, to the kettle she'd set boiling on the hob. She spoke over her shoulder as she filled the big teapot. "I'm off to me sister's this afternoon. I'll be back tomorrow morning to prepare the meats for the wake, but I'm already packed, and no amount of persuading will make me stay."

Setting aside the kettle, Cook cradled the teapot in her large hands; swishing it, she turned and met Violet's eyes. "You'd do well to do the same, Violet, m'dear—don't you stay here another night. Even more'n me, you have reason to go somewhere safe—some place no murderer will come skulking to your door."

Violet grimaced. Would that she had such a place . . . but just the thought of spending the night in the house alone was enough to stiffen her resolve. "Yes. You're right. Perhaps I'll find a small hotel nearby."

Montague had held a chair at the table for Penelope, and did the same for Griselda; Barnaby and Stokes were chatting in the doorway, still swapping opinions on the Halsteads. Drawing out a chair for Violet, Montague inclined his head to Cook, then met Violet's eyes as she moved to take the seat. "I agree with Cook. You must not remain here." If it had been at all acceptable, he would have offered her room at his apartment; regardless, he wouldn't be able to sleep if she attempted to remain at the Lowndes Street house. He eased the chair in as she sat. "If you need any assistance finding somewhere suitable to stay, I will be happy to escort you to any establishment you wish to consider."

"As to that." In the chair on the other side of Violet, Penelope shifted to face her. "I have a proposition to make."

Violet widened her eyes, inviting Penelope to share.

Penelope smiled and accepted the cup of tea Cook handed her. "Thank you." Setting down the cup and saucer, Penelope looked again at Violet. "I should first confess that, aside from occasionally involving myself in investigations, and, of course, seeing to my young son—Oliver is only eight months old—I am also something of a scholar. I specialize in ancient languages, and I correspond with other experts up and down the country. At the request of certain academic institutions, I occasionally take on translations of ancient texts. However, I've discovered that since the arrival of

Oliver, my correspondence has sadly fallen by the wayside, to the point that I really do need the services of an amanuensis to keep track of things." Penelope paused to sip her tea, then grimaced. "Believe me, this is not a fabricated need—both Barnaby and Griselda, let alone Mostyn, our majordomo, can verify that."

Capturing Violet's gaze, Penelope held it almost hopefully. "As I understand it, you are the daughter of a reverend and better trained in letters than is customary, and as part of your duties you acted as Lady Halstead's secretary. So . . . I wondered if you would be willing to move to Albemarle Street and take up the position of my secretary?"

When Violet didn't immediately respond, Penelope's gaze grew beseeching. "At least on a trial basis? I won't hold you to it if you find the work too onerous."

Violet had to smile. After a moment more of studying Penelope's eyes, and seeing nothing beyond sincerity in the chocolate-brown depths, she set down her teacup, hesitated, then asked, "You're truly not inventing this position because I so obviously desperately need one?"

Penelope placed her right palm over her heart. "I swear I really do need your help."

Across the table, Griselda leaned forward and caught Violet's eye. "She really does need help. Her desk has literally disappeared under a pile of letters and papers and open books."

"Besides"—Penelope's gaze went past Violet to Montague, currently conducting a quiet conversation with Cook—"I think you'll discover that your case is not anywhere near as desperate as you might suppose." Meeting Violet's eyes, Penelope smiled. "You have friends. We would help you regardless, but, as it happens, I really do need a secretary, and I suspect you'll be perfect for the post."

Griselda held up a hand. "I'll second that. Aside from anything else, you've already demonstrated that you will question Penelope when the situation calls for it, and, trust me, too few of her acquaintance will do that."

Penelope pulled a face at Griselda, but both women were smiling.

The chance to join with them, to be a part of a friendship that so effortlessly spanned the social strata, to have other ladies who understood her concerns and could sympathize . . . Violet blinked. When Penelope and Griselda both turned hopeful faces her way, she nodded and met Penelope's eyes. "Very well. I'll come to Albemarle Street and be your secretary."

"Excellent." Penelope drained her cup. "In that case, let's go upstairs and help you pack."

Violet paused to have a word with Cook, confirming that they would meet at the church the next day. Heading for the door, Violet was conscious of Montague's gaze following her; he had been delighted by her decision to accept Penelope's post, an emotion fueled rather transparently by relief. Relief that she would be safe.

While their husbands had joined Montague at the table to absentmindedly drink tea and chew over the investigation, Penelope and Griselda had waited for Violet by the kitchen door; climbing the stairs with the pair at her heels, Violet realized it had been a very long time since anyone had been concerned, personally concerned, over her safety. Since her father . . . despite her friendships with Lady Ogilvie and Lady Halstead, neither had been that close—in that way, to that degree.

Reaching the first floor and the door to her room, she led the way in. Her boxes and her small suitcase were stowed under her bed; it was the work of a minute to drag them out and wipe off the dust. Then Penelope and Griselda threw themselves into helping her gather all her belongings and pack them into the boxes and case.

Fifteen minutes saw it done. Violet paused, staring at the small pile of luggage assembled on her bed, her winter coat and bonnet waiting alongside. The sense of emptiness that now pervaded the house impinged, sank in. She glanced at Penelope and Griselda. "Tilly's things are in her room in the attic. She had even less than I. If you're not in a rush to be off, it might be better to pack her things now and take them with us so . . ."

"So you never have to set foot upstairs in this house again?" Penelope's glasses gleamed as she nodded. "An excellent idea."

"And yes," Griselda said, "we have time. We'll help."

Having the pair with her made climbing the attic stairs to the tiny bedroom tucked under the eaves somewhat easier. The door to Tilly's room had been left propped open. Violet entered, then stood transfixed by the sight of the narrow cot, which remained exactly as it had been when the constables had carried Tilly's body away, with the sheets dreadfully rumpled by Tilly's last desperate battle, the pillow still holding the impression of her head. The reality of Tilly's death rolled over Violet; a leaden weight settled on her shoulders, a chilly vise closed about her heart.

Tilly had been a good woman, a friendly face, a close colleague. A friend, albeit without the same sort of empathy Violet could already sense with Penelope and Griselda. Life was like that; some people were instantly within one's inner circle, while others were frequent and near, yet remained friends at a certain remove.

One still felt their loss.

Without a word, Penelope and Griselda moved past Violet and started to strip the bed.

That broke the spell. Turning to the old washstand, Violet bent and pulled Tilly's old, battered case from beneath it. Opening the case on the floor beside the dresser next to the washstand, Violet started transferring the contents of the dresser drawers.

She was emptying the middle drawer when footsteps, heavy and masculine, sounded on the stairs.

"Miss Matcham? Violet?"

Montague. "We're in Tilly's room," she called.

He appeared in the doorway and took in the scene. Violet rose and went to him.

Without hesitation, he reached out and took her hands, one in each of his. His thumbs moved over the backs of her hands, stroking, comforting; ignoring Penelope and Griselda entirely, he studied her eyes. Then he pressed her hands gently. "We'll find who did this—who killed Tilly, and Runcorn, and Lady Halstead. We"—with a tip of his head he included Penelope and Griselda, and by inference Stokes and Barnaby—"all of us, will not rest until he's caught. Until Tilly, and Runcorn, and Lady Halstead are avenged."

He held her hands for a moment more, then—to her intense surprise—he raised one and touched his lips to the backs of her fingers. Heat tingled where his lips brushed. Lowering her hand, he smiled faintly. "Have faith, my dear—we will find him."

With that, he stepped back; his hands reluctantly released hers and she had to fight not to curl her fingers and hold onto him. His eyes held hers. "I must go, but I'll see you tomorrow."

Looking beyond her, he dipped his head to Penelope and Griselda. "Ladies." Again, he met Violet's eyes. "I'll see you at the funeral."

She nodded. With a last, lingering look, he turned and left.

For several moments, she stood listening to his footsteps retreat, then she drew in a deep breath, turned, and went back to packing poor Tilly's belongings. Alongside her, Penelope and Griselda finished folding the covers and straightening the mattress and pillows, then, without waiting to be asked, they came to help her close Tilly's case.

"Our endeavors are evolving in ways I, for one, hadn't expected." Penelope, as usual, led the way into the elegant bedroom she and Barnaby somewhat unconventionally shared.

The evening was over and night had settled over Mayfair. Ambling in in Penelope's wake, Barnaby paused to shut the door, watching as Penelope, after setting her reticule on her dressing table, glided to one set of long windows. Beyond the glass, the night sky was a muddle of dark grays, a chill fog rolling in off the Thames. Reaching up, Penelope drew the heavy curtains closed, sealing them in with the comfortable and familiar.

With the warmth of shared lives.

Earlier, in the late afternoon, when they'd returned to Albemarle Street with Violet, Penelope had bustled about settling her new secretary into the household. Barnaby had checked through and dealt with his correspondence, spoken with Mostyn, then retreated to the nursery to share his thoughts on recent events with Oliver. Eventually, Penelope had joined them; she'd been enthused, engaged, and more energized than she'd been since Oliver's birth.

Leaving Violet to her own devices—something she'd assured them suited her perfectly—Penelope, Oliver, and Barnaby had spent the evening at a family gathering at Calverton House with the entire Ashford family, children and all, gathered about the long table, with Minerva, Dowager Viscountess Calverton, seated in the center and, gracious and delighted, presiding over all.

Everyone present had done all they could to please the ageing matriarch; Minerva had devoted her entire life to her brood, and in turn they were, one and all, devoted to her.

To Barnaby's mind, the illustration of the Halsteads' shortcomings could not have been more marked.

On returning from Mount Street, he and Penelope had settled a deeply sleeping Oliver into his crib, then had stood hand in hand looking down at their son for several of those precious minutes Barnaby was coming to treasure. Then, in silent accord, they'd turned away and come downstairs to their room.

With the curtains drawn over the second pair of windows, Penelope whirled, a delighted grin on her face. "But the excellent news is that we are, indeed, progressing."

Shrugging out of his coat, Barnaby demurred. "I wouldn't go so far as that—we've still no clue as to which of the Halstead men is the murderer."

Pausing to set the necklace and earrings she'd removed on her dressing table, Penelope threw him a pitying look. "I didn't mean progress with the investigation, but in how to manage investigating, how to balance it along with everything else."

"Ah." Barnaby nodded. "Your inspired idea of hiring Violet as your secretary."

"Precisely. You have to admit it was a masterstroke— multiple birds killed with one stone."

He smiled to himself, then confessed, "If you hadn't suggested it, I would have. Mostyn has even complained to me about the dust enveloping your desk."

She sighed. "Yes, well, I had no idea having a baby—or rather, said newborn itself—would prove such a very *distracting* distraction. You have to remember I'm the youngest of my family—I had no idea babies were so sweet and funny and altogether delightful. Oliver just has to start waving his hands and I'm enthralled, and an hour wings by before I even notice."

He humphed. "You can't claim any distinction on that score—I'm the same." Reaching out as she passed, he looped an arm around her waist and drew her to him—into his arms, into a kiss.

She kissed him back, her lips moving with familiar and confident ease beneath his, then, as he did, she drew back.

He looked into her eyes, so dark in the muted lamplight that their expression was impossible to read, then, very much feeling his way, he murmured, "I wonder if the effect will still be the same once our second child comes along."

Her hands gripping his upper arms, leaning comfortably back in his embrace, she studied his eyes, then her lips lightly quirked upward. "My guess would be probably not, for us—you and me—at any rate, but I daresay we'll find out—in good time."

Tilting her head, she went on, "I want to enjoy this time—this first time, with our first child—fully before we complicate matters further. I want to know, to feel confident that I've worked out this balance thing—that I've found the ways to organize all the facets of my life so that I can fully enjoy all of them, that I can get the most and give my best to each aspect without neglecting any other, rather than feeling as I have in recent times that all the aspects are constantly tugging at me, pulling in different directions, and that although I'm trying as hard as I can, I'm failing to properly succeed with any of them."

He studied her face. "I hadn't realized it was that . . . problematic. That it—everything all together—was tearing you apart."

She nodded, one of her usual decisive, definite nods. "That's exactly how it felt—like a mental drawing and quartering." She met his gaze, and her lips gently curved. Twining her hands at his nape, leaning back against his hold, she swayed a little, side to side. "But, as I said, we're making progress, and, indeed, we're well on the way to getting it right—to finding the way for me to keep my balance and be happy and satisfied in all areas of my life."

"That's why you're so pleased to have Violet as your secretary—she's a part of your plan."

"Exactly. The weight of papers on my desk is not something Griselda can assist me with, but Violet can—and, indeed, I rather suspect she, too, is one who would feel shortchanged by life and ultimately unsatisfied if her skills weren't appreciated and put to use." Pausing, she studied his eyes. "But what of you? What do you think of the new order taking shape, of my new and better balanced life? For, of course, *you* are one of the areas of my life I'm seeking to better service."

Knowing full well her choice of verb wasn't in the least accidental—a fact underscored by her pressing closer and suggestively continuing the side-to-side sway of her hips against his upper thighs, her taut stomach, encased in sleek silk, stroking over his already significant erection—he couldn't help but grin, yet he could see in her expression, tell from her watchfulness, that her question was serious and his answer important. He looked inward—and somewhat to his surprise found the truth waiting to be uttered, all but on his tongue. "I like it—I like having you beside me, mentally if not always physically, in an investigation." He paused, then confessed, "I didn't know how much I'd missed it—your involvement—not until you insisted and pressed, and forced your way back." An idea—a truth—occurred to him; for an instant, he considered holding it back but then drew breath and, with her warm and vital in his arms, admitted, "I suspect—I believe—that I need your intelligence, your mind, engaged and committed, to strike the brightest sparks from mine." His voice lowered; his next words came from somewhere so deep that their utterance felt like a catharsis. "Without you by my side, I will never be the best I can be."

Penelope read the truth in his blue eyes, the cerulean hue brilliantly bright even in the muted light. She heard the echo in his deep, rough tone, felt it in her heart, in her bones.

Letting the curve of her lips deepen, she stretched up and drew his lips to hers. Murmured, in the instant before their lips met, "We're a pair, you and I—just as well we're doing this together."

She pressed upward and sealed his lips with hers, kissed him—then let her lips part in invitation, let the reins slide from her grasp, and sensed him make the same decision, and surrender to the moment, to the night. To her.

To them, together.

Clothes fell to the floor, hands whispered over skin. Stroked, caressed, and kneaded.

Pleasure was their only goal—that, and togetherness.

Sharing, not just their bodies but each other's delight, the joys and the thrills and the passion-filled yearning, they divested each other of all restraint.

They knew the journey well, and neither saw any reason to rush. Crystal moments of sensation spun out, stretched, fragile and exquisite, before the next rush of heady, greedy desire surged, and shattered them.

Naked, bodies gilded by the lamplight, they swayed and danced, played and twined. Hands worshipped and lips paid homage; desire thrummed beneath their skins, heating, burning, while need sharpened passion's whip and lashed their flesh, their senses.

Then, at last, it was time, and he lifted her and they came together on a breathless gasp, a guttural groan, as the moment of joining seized their wits, their senses, their very beings. As the cascade of sensation and emotion ruthlessly focused each of them on themselves, on the other, on what together they were, could be, could create.

On the wonder.

On the indescribable, utterly overwhelming delight.

Catching her breath, she tossed back the tangling mane of her dark hair, brushed one damp curl back from his forehead, and looked down into eyes burning with the steady glow of his passion.

She read of his need, undisguised and viscerally real, saw the steadfast commitment, the devotion, the love.

Felt the complementary emotions surge through her in response.

Bending her head, she pressed her lips to his, merged their mouths, and gave herself—all she was, all her love—to him.

As he gave his to her.

Together in body, together in mind.

Together in bliss.

They had each other, and together they had everything.

Fog blanketed the streets, wrapping houses in gray clouds, impenetrable and disorienting.

Affected by the pervasive damp, the stairs in the Lowndes Street house creaked.

He paused, listened, but detected no movement from above, no sign that she'd heard him.

Drawing breath, he continued more carefully, keeping to the edge of the treads. Reaching the first floor, he paused again. Listened again.

When nothing but the echo of silence filled his ears, he drew another breath, a deeper one this time, to steel himself.

The doorknob turned freely. To his surprise, the door swung open.

Poised before the threshold, he stared at the half-open, freely swinging door, at the patch of moonlit floorboards now revealed.

He'd expected to have to push the dresser out of the way; he'd been willing to risk the noise, trusting to time, distance, and the cook's self-interest to be able to do what he'd come to do and quit the house without being seen.

Without risking being identified.

If push had come to shove, he'd been prepared to kill the cook, too.

He watched as one of his gloved hands reached out and pushed the door fully open.

Even as, still taking care to be quiet, he tiptoed into the room, some part of his mind already knew what he would find—had already understood what the absence of the dresser across the door meant.

The bed lay empty, the covers straight.

"She's not here." His whisper swelled to fill the room. Seemed to echo back and fill his ears, slide in and fill his mind.

Abruptly, he shook his head, shaking away the whispering.

Glancing around, he registered the absence of brushes, combs, all personal items.

Frowning, he stared again at the bed. "Where the devil has she gone?"

Chapter 11

Lady Halstead's funeral was held the following morning. Cynthia Camberly had prevailed, and the service was held at St. Peter's Church in Grosvenor Street, with the interment following immediately afterward in the graveyard beside the church.

Violet was glad Cynthia had won that round; many of the parishioners had been acquainted with Lady Halstead, and they filled the church to overflowing, their voices swelling the three hymns with genuine sorrow. The principal eulogy was delivered by the minister who had known her ladyship well. The large number of others who crowded into the church—older ladies and gentlemen both, many, judging by the gentlemen's unimpeachably conservative attire, from government and diplomatic circles—would have surprised Violet had Penelope not told her of the Halsteads' past status in that sphere.

All in all, Violet felt the event was a fitting tribute to Lady Halstead and her life.

From the second pew, with Montague to her left, and Penelope on her right, with Griselda beyond her, and Cook in the corner, Violet watched the casket carried up the aisle on the shoulders of Lady Halstead's sons, grandsons, and son-in-law.

Cynthia and Constance, both heavily veiled, followed, with Caroline, head dutifully bowed, close behind.

When the trio had passed, Montague stepped into the central aisle and gave Violet his hand.

She took it, felt his strength, that rock-solid certainty that was peculiarly his; she let her fingers curl, grasped, and let him anchor her.

He twined her arm in his, then escorted her up the aisle.

Penelope and Griselda, kindly supporting Cook between them, followed.

The interment was simple and rapidly done, laying Lady Halstead beside Sir Hugo in the family plot. Violet noted that Stokes, Adair, and several constables hung back at the fringes of the crowd; earlier they'd hovered at the rear of the church, watching and noting, although she hadn't seen anything worthy of their attention.

All went smoothly, uneventfully, unmarred by any bickering among the Halstead brood, for which Violet gave due thanks; despite the circumstances, she wouldn't have put creating a scene past any of them.

Then the first sod was cast by Mortimer—quickly followed by Cynthia.

Montague turned Violet away. "Come—let's head to the house ahead of the rush."

She nodded and allowed him to lead her down a side path to where their group had left their various carriages. Penelope and Griselda had already gone ahead with Cook in Penelope's town carriage, leaving the Stokeses' small black carriage for Montague and Violet.

As he handed her up, Violet murmured, "What about Stokes and Mr. Adair?"

"They've two carriages from Scotland Yard to ferry them and the constables." Montague settled on the seat beside her. He waited until the carriage had pulled out into the stream of traffic before saying, "Incidentally, you should be present at the reading of the will." When Violet looked at him, he met her gaze and nodded. "Lady Halstead clearly valued you, and Tilly and Cook, as well."

Violet blinked, then softly snorted. "The family won't be pleased."

"The family can like it or lump it." Montague felt uncharacteristically belligerent, but he rather liked the sensation. Rather liked the man he was discovering himself to be, courtesy of the lady by his side. Facing forward, he said, "I've seen the will—it's legally watertight. Any challenge will be a waste of time."

He felt Violet's gaze on the side of his face. "Will you be reading the will?" she asked.

"Given the letter of authority from Lady Halstead and my more recent acquaintance with the family, her solicitor, a Mr. Entwaite, has asked me to do the honors." He glanced at Violet. "Entwaite's a sound man, but he dislikes dealing with forceful people and unnecessary confrontations."

A smile curved her lips, dissipating some of the shadows that, today, had closed about her. Satisfied, he faced forward again and listened to the rattling of the wheels as they covered the short distance to Lowndes Street.

Once there, the volume of guests made it easy enough for their small band of investigators to gather in a corner of the drawing room without attracting undue attention.

Cook had retreated to her domain to oversee the presentation of the funeral meats. "She views it as her final duty for Lady Halstead," Penelope reported.

Both the Camberly and Mortimer Halstead's households had sent footmen to assist, but both had also sent their butlers. Inclining his head to where those two individuals were eyeing each other much in the vein of cocks about to fight, Montague murmured, "One can only hope the butlers don't come to blows."

Following his nod, the others looked, then Griselda, lips twitching, said, "Heaven help them if they do—can you imagine the apoplexy that would cause their mistresses?"

After an exchange of cutting looks, the butlers turned and stalked toward opposite sides of the room.

Penelope snorted. "Crisis averted. It looks like they've realized the limitations of their situations."

"Speaking of situations"—Barnaby caught Montague's eye—"what are the odds the family will ignore this crowd and, instead of acting as any manner of host, insist on having the will read immediately?"

Montague huffed. "That's not much of a wager, but apropos of that"—he looked at Stokes—"as I mentioned to Violet, at their solicitor's request and courtesy of that letter of authority, I will be reading the will. Violet and Cook should be present—the family can't argue that, as both are minor beneficiaries. And as Lady Halstead was murdered, I will propose that a representative of Scotland Yard has reason to be there—I imagine you would wish to attend?"

Stokes nodded. "Most definitely."

"Only one representative?" Barnaby asked, his tone a plaintive whine.

Montague turned his grin into a grimace. "Sadly, yes. One is easy to excuse, especially an inspector, but two is inviting the family to protest, and they could become difficult if they dig in their heels." He met Stokes's eyes. "My thinking is that there's no reason we wish to delay the reading of the will."

Stokes nodded. "The sooner the better. The more things that happen, and the more quickly they occur, the greater the pressure on our murderer. Who knows? There may be something in the will that casts some light, however murky, on his motives."

"From what I've seen of the will, that's unlikely—" Montague broke off, his eye caught by a beckoning wave from the ageing solicitor, who was standing in the doorway and craning his neck to look over the crowd. "Ah—here we go." Montague met Barnaby's eyes. "That didn't take them long at all."

To a chorus of "Good luck" from the others, Montague took Violet's arm and steered her through the considerable crowd.

As he fell in at their backs, Stokes murmured, his deep voice so low only they would hear, "I would appreciate it if both of you could keep your eyes peeled for whatever reaction we get from the five men we consider suspects. Given there's just the three of us in this meeting, let's concentrate on them.'"

Montague nodded. Glancing at Violet, he saw her jaw firm as she nodded, too.

The family had elected to use the sitting room for the reading of the will. As Montague ushered her through the door, Violet saw that the furniture had been rearranged. Lady Halstead's writing desk now sat before the fireplace; a small, neat, precise man in the dark garb favored by solicitors was just slipping into the chair behind the narrow desk. Settling, he perched a pair of gold-rimmed pince-nez on his nose, then rather nervously smoothed his thinning white hair over the sides of his head before somewhat trepidatiously surveying the family members seated in serried rows on more comfortable chairs set in an arc facing the desk.

Montague guided her past those chairs and on to two empty chairs set to one side of the bow window at the end of the room. As she whispered her thanks and sank down, she realized that the position, with the light streaming past her, gave her the best possible view of the family and the tableau before the fireplace.

Of course, the position also gave the family a clear view of her—and of Stokes, who took up a position standing to her left.

Having seen them installed, Montague went to the desk, to the second chair behind it.

Mortimer Halstead frowned at Montague. "What are you doing here?"

The solicitor—Entwaite—cleared his throat. "As Mr. Montague has a valid and wide-ranging letter of authority from my late client, and given his experience with complex estates, I have asked him to assist me in reading her ladyship's will and explaining its provisions if such explanations are required." Entwaite paused, then gravely added, "Such an arrangement is entirely within the scope of normal practice."

Mortimer's frown turned disgruntled.

"I believe," Cynthia said, her gaze fixed on Violet and Stokes, "that the reading of my mother's will should be restricted to the family."

Picking up what was obviously the will, Montague calmly replied, "All named beneficiaries have a right to be present at the reading of a will. In addition, in this case, given that her ladyship was murdered, Scotland Yard's interest in the contents of the will cannot be denied."

Violet noted the glib turn of Montague's phrases and, despite the occasion, inwardly smiled; all he had done was state the obvious, yet as he surveyed the assembled family, brows raised, clearly inviting any dissenter to speak up, although various family members shifted, none were so brave as to voice their opposition.

The door edged open and Cook slipped in, carefully closing the door behind her.

Montague smiled reassuringly and waved her in Violet's direction.

Cook all but scuttled down the room; Stokes held the chair beside Violet for her, and Cook sank onto it gratefully.

Violet patted Cook's hand. "Don't worry," she whispered.

"Very good." Montague glanced at Entwaite. "Everyone is present, I believe?"

Entwaite nodded. "Indeed. We may proceed."

Montague raised the will, transfixing the attention of every member of the family. In a clear, steady voice, he read the preamble, then passed on to the clauses giving effect to the distribution of the estate established under Sir Hugo's will, followed by the provisions detailing the disbursement of Lady Halstead's personal property.

Although he had read the will earlier in the day, he still had to pay attention to the words. He used the pause after each clause to quickly scan the faces turned his way.

There was nothing in the will to cause consternation; as expected, the combined wills of Sir Hugo and Lady

Halstead stipulated that the bulk of the estate, being the residue after all disbursements to the minor beneficiaries, be divided equally between their four children.

Said children heard the news, and—as might be expected of the Halstead brood—each appeared disappointed that their mother hadn't somehow favored them over their siblings.

Also as Montague had anticipated, the entire family paid close attention to what Lady Halstead had willed to others; when he named the sum of the annuity left to Violet—enough, if properly managed, to see her through the rest of her days in quiet but genteel comfort—the family threw darkling glances her way. The smaller annuities left to Tilly Westcott and Cook—Mrs. Edmonds, as she proved to be—elicited several mutters. He ignored the grumbling but took a moment to confirm aloud that, as Tilly had died after Lady Halstead, all that Lady Halstead had left to Tilly would pass on to Tilly's heirs.

Entwaite helpfully capped the comment by stating that he had located Tilly's brother, who was her legal heir.

Montague inclined his head in thanks. He scanned the family's faces once more, but as had been the case throughout, they all appeared faintly disgruntled, dissatisfied, but also detached; none appeared greatly exercised by anything they'd heard thus far.

Raising the will, he continued reading, listing the last of the bequests. Lady Halstead had—very sensibly in Montague's view—divided her jewelry piece by piece, naming which family member should receive each item. At the end of the list, her ladyship had left what she'd described as tokens of her affection to the three members of her household—a pearl choker to Violet—and that news made Cynthia Halstead suck in a quick breath through her teeth—a pearl brooch to Tilly, and a pearl ring to Cook.

Montague looked at Cynthia Halstead, wondering if she would protest, but although her face had set in lines of deep disaffection, her lips had compressed to a thin line, and she made no move to open them.

He was about to announce that that was the conclusion of the reading when Caroline Halstead said, "There's no sense in giving a pearl brooch to a dead woman, much less to her laborer brother." Fixing Montague with a stare every bit as arrogant as her aunt's, she stated, "As my late grandmother's only granddaughter, the brooch should instead come to me."

Montague had hoped—all but prayed—that someone would protest something. Caroline's objection gave him the chance to say, "If you wish to insist on such a redirection, you will need to contest the will, which, of course, will delay probate."

Mortimer frowned at him. "Delaying probate—what will that mean for the rest of us?"

Montague arched his brows. "In effect"—he cast his gaze over the faces turned his way, focusing on the men as he said—"not a penny of the estate will be paid out to anyone, not until the disputed matter is decided by the court and probate is finally granted."

As there was a good chance the murderer needed his share from the estate, Montague had hoped to jolt a telling reaction from the villain. Instead . . .

Cynthia swung to face Mortimer and shrilly declared, "I won't have my share held to ransom by your greedy daughter!"

Maurice half rose, his gaze locked on Caroline. "Don't be daft—it's just a brooch, you silly chit!"

William growled, "Have you lost your mind, girl?"

Camberly looked peevishly disgusted. Even Constance turned an appalled face to her daughter.

Who was already cowering under her father's black glare.

"We," Mortimer declared, his tone sharper, his voice harder than Montague had previously heard it, "are not going to hold up probate over a paltry brooch."

Caroline all but shrank into her seat and subsided.

Nothing more was said about the brooch.

Clearing his throat, Montague declared the reading of the will concluded. He handed the document to Entwaite, then looked blandly at the family. "Subsequent to Mr. Runcorn's murder, at the behest of Scotland Yard I currently hold, and will continue to hold, the Halstead financial records in my firm's vault until such time as you, via Mr. Entwaite, inform me whom you have appointed to deal further with the estate."

The family all blinked at him, then Mortimer frowned and said, "You seem capable—can't you deal with it?"

He could, especially as he'd decided to keep Pringle on, but he was far too experienced to touch clients like the Halstead brood with a double-length beanpole. "Sadly, no. My firm's client list is full. You will need to appoint some other man-of-business or similar agent."

With an abbreviated nod, he turned away and exchanged bows and farewells with Entwaite, then, leaving the solicitor gathering his papers, he walked down the room to where Violet and Stokes still lingered. Cook had already scurried out of the room, back, no doubt, to the relative safety of her kitchen.

Behind him, the arguments had already commenced.

Halting before Violet, still seated on her chair, Montague met Stokes's gray gaze. "I didn't detect anything—nothing that might point to one man over the others."

Stokes grimaced. "Nor I." He shifted so that, while appearing to converse with Montague, he could look past him to the family conclave raging before the fireplace. "Entwaite's getting out as fast as he can, although none of the family seem to be paying him any heed."

Violet shook her head. "They're already too engaged in arguing over how to divide the estate."

The three of them loitered, listening; in their usual manner, none of the family thought to temper either the substance or the level of their utterances. Along with Montague and Stokes, Violet heard the four Halstead children rapidly agree, somewhat amazingly, that none of them wanted any part of the two Halstead properties. That, however, was the limit of their consensus; Mortimer and Maurice were of the opinion the properties should be sold and the funds divided, while Cynthia and William, whether from true belief or simply to oppose the other two, insisted that they would be better served by leasing both properties.

After another three minutes of nothing but more argument, Stokes shook his head. "We're not going to learn anything useful here. Barnaby, Penelope, and Griselda were going to circulate among the guests and see what they could learn. I suggest we join them."

Violet nodded. Montague offered his hand, and she took it and rose.

Stokes stayed them with an upraised hand. His gaze had once again gone down the room. Violet followed it and realized he was looking at Caroline, predictably sulking, a bad-tempered glower on her face as she watched and waited for her parents to finish their arguments.

Glancing back at Stokes, Violet saw him exchange a look with Montague, then Stokes met her gaze. "I suspect it would be a wise idea for you, escorted by Montague, and perhaps Penelope and Griselda, too, to go upstairs to Lady Halstead's room and remove the bequests—the pieces of jewelry her ladyship left you, Tilly, and Cook."

Violet blinked, then glanced at Caroline. "I believe you're right." She looked at Montague. "I've written to Tilly's brother—he'll call at your office when he comes to town to fetch her body." She pushed the thought of Tilly's body away; she couldn't afford to dwell on that now, not here. Raising her chin a notch, she went on, "If you could send him on to me, I've already got Tilly's belongings, so I can add the brooch to them, and I'll give Cook the ring before I leave."

Both Montague and Stokes nodded.

"Come." Montague offered his arm. "Let's find Penelope and Griselda, then we'll go upstairs."

Stokes fell in behind them. "I would head upstairs sooner rather than later. The instant they stop arguing, they'll be up to sort that jewelry—you can count on it."

Knowing he was right, Violet quashed the impulse to look after what were, in effect, her ladyship's last guests—to cover the hostess gap neither Cynthia nor Constance had thought to fill—and instead allowed Montague to gather Penelope and Griselda, and escort the three of them up the stairs and into Lady Halstead's room.

She and Tilly had tidied the room on the day before Tilly had been murdered . . . Violet ruthlessly forced her mind back to her task and refused to allow herself to think beyond that. Crossing to the dressing table, she drew out the second drawer on the right. "Lady Halstead kept her pearls in here."

"Best to let me." Montague bent and drew the drawer fully out. Straightening, he set it on the table, then met her gaze. "If the Halsteads inquire—as they might—I can truthfully say that, as her ladyship's appointed agent and acting in accordance with her will, I took the pearls and gave them to you."

Although her lips wouldn't curve—not in this room—she smiled inside. "Thank you." Looking into the drawer, she pointed to a small box. "That's the brooch. And the choker is in that blue velvet bag. The ring . . . is that small box there."

Montague took the three items out, checked them, then handed them to her.

Leaving him to return the drawer to its place, Violet turned—and saw Penelope and Griselda peering into the wardrobe. Penelope was examining the gowns, while Griselda had bent to study Lady Halstead's boots and shoes. Violet frowned. "What are you looking for?"

Both glanced her way, then took one last look before stepping back. Shutting the wardrobe door, Penelope explained, "Trying to get some idea of her character—with women, clothes and shoes often say a lot." She waved at the wardrobe. "From her gowns, she seems to have been a soft, flowy, gentle lady."

Violet nodded. "She was. But she wasn't weak. She didn't like her children, but she couldn't change them, so she put up with them."

"That fits with her footwear," Griselda said. "Good quality and fashionable, but also functional. She liked fashion, but underneath, she appears to have been a sensible, practical sort."

Violet felt her features soften. "Yes—that was her."

They'd all gathered by the door. After one last look around, Violet led the way out and down the stairs.

In the front hall, she paused, looking at the open door to the drawing room, hearing the muted cacophony of the voices within; there were still a considerable number of mourners lingering over the refreshments.

Dragging in a breath, she turned to face the others. She glanced at Penelope, then looked at Montague. "I really don't wish to go in there and be sociable."

"There's no reason you should," Penelope stated. "You've done all and more than your association with her ladyship demanded."

Montague touched her arm—just a fleeting touch, but she felt his support. "There's no need for you to stay longer."

Violet glanced down at the three items in her hands. "Let me give Cook her ring and say good-bye, and then I would like to leave." *And never come back.* She didn't say the words, yet they resonated inside her. This was the end of one phase of her life; she could feel that in her bones. It was time to quit this house and move forward, into a future that was as yet nebulous, but she wasn't without friends, wasn't—thanks to Lady Halstead's generosity—without reserves.

The others trailed her to the kitchen. Farewelling Cook proved to be a teary undertaking, but, eventually, both she and Cook dried their eyes, and after exchanging their directions—Penelope helpfully supplied the address of her house, and Cook scribbled her sister's address in Bermondsley on a piece of paper—they parted.

Barnaby and Stokes were waiting in the front hall. "There you are," Barnaby said.

Violet felt Barnaby's keen blue gaze travel over her face; she had no idea what he saw there, but his voice had softened when he said, "Ready to go?"

She nodded.

Stokes, with Griselda on his arm, led the way out. Barnaby and Penelope followed. Montague gave Violet his arm and she took it, grateful, as they stepped out of the door and into a crisp breeze carrying the scent of dying leaves, for his support.

For his strength, and his willingness to lend it to her.

He steadied her down the steps and onto the short path. Barnaby held the gate. As she passed through, Violet was aware that the others were chatting softly about something—their observations, perhaps—but they made no demands of her and didn't look her way. As the gate swung shut, the other two couples started off down the street to where their carriages waited further along the curb. On Montague's arm, Violet followed.

Then she paused and glanced back. Back at the house she'd spent the last eight years living in, being reasonably content and settled in, caring for and working with two women she would never see again.

Montague had halted beside her, but he watched her, her face, not the house.

As she was about to turn and meet his eyes, Violet saw movement behind the sitting room window.

Mortimer was staring out—whether at her, the group, or unseeingly at the street she couldn't say. Even at this distance, his expression appeared pinched and peevish. Then he turned and walked away, deeper into the room.

Meeting Montague's eyes, Violet grimaced. "The family are still at it, still arguing, it seems."

Retaking her arm, Montague snorted. "With that family, they always will be."

There was no help for it, he would have to leave Miss Matcham for now. Aside from all else, he didn't know where she was staying, and if anyone heard him asking after her now . . . he couldn't afford that.

Best to lie low, at least for a little while.

Besides, he had other issues to deal with—and what the devil had been going on with the old lady's accounts?

Regardless, Wallace's suggestion that it was Tilly who had taken the money and subsequently been killed by her lover-accomplice, whom she'd previously assisted in murdering the old girl herself, had been beyond inspired. A gift from the gods, from his point of view.

And the police seemed to pose little real threat; they were scurrying around trying to find the thief, assuming whoever it was was also the murderer. Who knew? Their efforts might even provide a suitable scapegoat.

And thank heaven that man Montague had refused to deal with the old lady's affairs. Now he'd checked the man's credentials and had learned of his reputation, he realized how close a call he'd had.

But Montague had declined, and the old lady's papers were now in his firm's vault, no doubt pushed to the back wall. They could gather dust there until he located a suitable man-of-business, one he could influence or bribe, and inveigled the rest of the family to accept his choice. Which might well entail ensuring they never learned that the man *was* his choice, but he'd grown adept at such manipulations.

As his carriage rattled through the night, taking him home from his club, he reviewed the facts and measured them against his feelings. His compulsion to ensure, beyond all possible doubt, that he was safe. That nothing could possibly threaten his future.

No matter how he weighted the facts, regardless of that compulsion, this wasn't the time to act.

No, indeed. Things were going well—or, at least, better than he'd expected. Better than he'd had any reason to hope.

Now wasn't the time to senselessly rush ahead, put a foot wrong, and stumble.

He didn't—couldn't—question his certainty that permanently silencing Miss Violet Matcham was necessary for his long-term peace of mind, but he didn't have to act *now*.

If she had recognized the import of what he was certain she knew, she would have shared the information with the police, but she hadn't, yet, and to this point no one suspected him.

Keeping it that way was imperative.

So he would wait, and bide his time. And, eventually, an opportunity would arise and he would be able to silence Miss Matcham and finally win free of all possible threat to his future.

"Who knows?" Wreathed in shifting shadows, he arched a brow. "There may even be some way to twist the tale so that the maid's nonexistent lover-accomplice takes the blame."

Two mornings later, Violet entered the sunny breakfast parlor in the Adairs' Albemarle Street house to find Penelope already at the table.

Violet mock-frowned as she slipped into a chair alongside her new mistress—who didn't behave like any mistress ever known. "Are you always this early?"

Crunching on a piece of toast slathered with jam, Penelope nodded. She swallowed. "Usually. I was always an early bird, even as a child." She grinned. "Disgusting, isn't it?"

"I'll reserve my answer." Picking up the teapot, Violet poured herself a cup.

"I can recommend the jam." Penelope waved her toast. "Cook opened a fresh jar of her gooseberry preserve, I suspect in your honor, so you should try some so you can tell her how delightful it is. Which it is. If you like gooseberries."

Even though she'd spent only one day in the house, Violet had already grown accustomed to Penelope's sometimes disjointed and often unexpected utterances—enough, at least, not to be thrown. "I'll be sure to stop by the kitchen later."

For several minutes, they sipped and crunched in harmony, then Penelope pushed aside her empty plate. "I was wondering if there's anything specific you'd like to do today. Oliver has a small case of the sniffles, so Hettie has warned me off taking him out." Meeting Violet's eyes, her own impossibly innocent behind the distracting lenses of her spectacles, Penelope arched her brows. "So, is there anywhere you'd like to visit? Anything by way of entertainment you'd like to do?"

Violet looked into Penelope's chocolate-brown eyes and decided it was no wonder that she'd so taken to the other woman. She knew precisely why Penelope had made the offer; for Violet, yesterday had been both difficult and tiring.

Tilly's brother had called, sent around by Montague; Fred Westcott proved to have been Tilly's twin, and he'd been so much like her that Violet had had to expend considerable effort fighting to hold back her tears. Tears that would have made poor Fred even more bewildered and uncomfortable; he'd been having such a hard time believing his twin sister was dead.

He lived in Kent and had driven into town in a small wagon; he'd followed Violet's directions to Montague's office, and had been sent on to Albemarle Street to pick up Tilly's things en route to the morgue, where he'd planned to take possession of Tilly's body and drive it back in the wagon for burial in the little village graveyard beside their parents.

So Tilly was gone, and after Fred's departure, Violet had felt shattered.

Had truly felt and comprehensively understood the destructiveness of murder.

Penelope and her staff, and even young Oliver, had gathered around and done what they could to distract her; even Barnaby, when he'd joined them for dinner, had been almost unbearably kind.

When night had fallen, she'd escaped early to her bed, and in doing so had underscored that she, unlike Tilly, still had a place, a purpose, and a life to live.

This morning, when she'd woken, she'd discovered that her determination to expose the murderer and gain justice for Lady Halstead, Runcorn, and Tilly had only grown more steely.

Meeting Penelope's gaze, she said, "Actually, there's something curious I remembered this morning about the Halstead estate."

Penelope widened her eyes, her interest immediate. "Do tell."

"The family arguing about how to divide the estate jogged my memory—they mentioned the family's country house, The Laurels. It's part of the estate, and they were all arguing about whether to sell or lease it." Violet licked the last of the gooseberry preserve—it really was excellent—from her fingers, then, frowning, went on, "I have no reason to believe that this has anything at all to do with what's been going on, with those odd payments into Lady Halstead's account, but one of the factors contributing to her anxiety about the estate was that she'd received a letter from a neighbor in the country—the vicar's wife—about someone living at The Laurels." She met Penelope's gaze. "As far as Lady Halstead knew, The Laurels is closed up and untenanted, and has been for years."

"Ah." After a moment of considering her, Penelope asked, "I don't suppose you read this letter?"

"No." Violet held Penelope's gaze. "But I know where it is."

"Where?"

"In Lady Halstead's traveling writing desk, which is in the bottom drawer of that big chest of drawers in her room." Violet paused, then said, "While they might have taken the jewelry by now, I doubt the family will have bothered with the writing desk. It was old and not especially noteworthy."

"They might not even have stumbled on it yet." Behind her spectacles, Penelope's eyes gleamed.

Violet nodded. "And I remembered something else this morning that I'd forgotten."

Penelope's eyes widened even further. "What?"

"That I haven't handed Mr. Montague my keys to the house."

"Oh, my." A smile of quite remarkable energy spread across Penelope's face. "That settles it, I believe." She locked eyes with Violet. "Clearly, we are supposed to go to the house and examine this letter, and, if it proves to be interesting, remove it. Who knows? It might be vital evidence, even if we don't yet know what about."

Barely pausing to blink, Penelope continued, "I suggest, my dear Violet, that you and I have the carriage brought around, then take a trip to Greenbury Street to pick up Griselda—she'll definitely want to be a part of this—and then we can stop by in Lowndes Street and secure the letter before going on to the City and calling at Montague's so you can hand him those keys."

Penelope beamed. Violet couldn't help but beam back.

"And that," Penelope said, pushing back her chair, "sounds like an excellent way to spend our morning."

The Lowndes Street house already looked deserted.

When, at Penelope's direction, her carriage slowed to a halt by the curb in front of the house across the street, Violet peered out at the fully curtained windows. "They must have had the footmen and butlers draw all the curtains."

Seated opposite, Griselda gave a little shiver. "I hate it when they do that—it's as if the house dies, too."

"But there's not even black ribbon on the knocker." Penelope leaned closer to the window, scanning the house, then what she could see of the street. "Which is just as well, I suppose. Less reason to note us if anyone sees us going in."

She glanced at Violet. "Ready?"

Fishing the ring with the keys to the front and back doors from her reticule, Violet nodded. Jaw setting, she glanced at the house, then followed Penelope and Griselda from the carriage.

Leaving Penelope's groom with the carriage, they crossed the street—three ladies out for a morning stroll.

"Quick." Penelope swung open the gate. "There's no one about at the moment. Let's get inside."

Violet knew Penelope didn't mean her to hurry but rather not to dally. Very ready to oblige, she walked directly up the path, key already in her gloved fingers. Reaching the door, she slid the key into the lock, turned it, then twisted the knob, opened the door, and led the way inside.

Whisking around, she quietly closed the door immediately Griselda stepped past.

In the gloomy dimness of the hall, they all paused, listening, straining their ears for the least little sound that might indicate the presence of some footman or other servant left to watch over the house. If anyone arrived to question their presence, Violet would explain that she'd forgotten something from her room upstairs; she'd even brought a finely carved thimble so she could produce some real item as their excuse.

But no one came.

After a moment, Griselda shook her head. "There's no one here."

"I didn't really think there would be." Violet turned to the stairs. "This is a family that simply doesn't care about anything that isn't their own."

She led the way up the stairs. Penelope followed; Griselda brought up the rear.

Violet was grateful they were there, at her back, doing this with her. The deserted, empty, rather chill atmosphere that had spread through the house was unsettling. Faintly threatening. And made even worse by the dismal lack of light.

When they walked into Lady Halstead's room, it was immediately apparent that her family had visited. Even with the curtains tightly drawn, enough light seeped past for them to note the empty spaces.

Penelope waved at the dressing table. "The big jewelry box is gone."

"So are the silver-backed brushes and the ivory combs," Griselda said. "Along with the crystal tray they sat on."

"So—let's see." Violet went to the large chest of drawers, bent, and pulled out the deep bottom drawer. As the other two gathered around, she smiled. "As expected, they didn't get this far."

"Or simply weren't interested." Penelope stepped back as Violet straightened, the writing desk in her hands.

She walked to the bed and set the slanted-topped wooden box on the counterpane.

Griselda had already gone to the window; she eased one curtain back, allowing weak autumn sunlight to spill across the room to illuminate the bed and the writing desk.

"Thank you," Violet murmured. Opening the lid, with its worn leather inset, she set it fully back, revealing what lay in the cavity beneath—a loose jumble of letters covered in a variety of spidery hands.

She reached for the creased sheet lying uppermost. "This should be it."

Raising the letter, she angled it to the light, holding it so that all three of them could gather around and read.

The letter wasn't overly long, and from the easy salutation and the comfortable tone, it appeared that the wife of the vicar of Noak Hill, a Mrs. Findlayson, had been a longtime acquaintance of Lady Halstead. She wrote that Lady Halstead's Essex friends were somewhat curious about the fiercely reclusive people currently living in her ladyship's house. While Mrs. Findlayson had written nothing specific about what, exactly, had incited the locals' concerns, the implication that there was something of a dubious nature afoot came through clearly.

After perusing the letter twice, Penelope looked at Violet, then glanced at Griselda. "Noak Hill. I have no idea where that might be, precisely, but as it is in Essex, it can't be all that far."

"Perhaps," Griselda said, "we might ask your coach-man if he knows of it?"

Penelope nodded. "And, if so, how long it will take to get there."

"And back," Griselda said. "It's already eleven o'clock, and we won't want to be too late home."

"No, indeed." Penelope's expression had taken on a certain steely quality. "But I do think, Violet dear, that as Mrs. Findlayson and her friends have very likely not yet learned of Lady Halstead's death, you—accompanied by Griselda and me—should call on Mrs. Findlayson and let her know that her ladyship has passed on."

Violet met Penelope's gaze. "It would be the right thing to do. I'm sure Lady Halstead would wish me to inform her country friends of her death."

"Well, from all we've seen, her family won't bother," Griselda put in. "So I, too, vote yes—we should, if we can manage it within the day, visit Noak Hill vicarage."

"And, just possibly, pass by The Laurels, too." Penelope turned to the door. There, she paused, wait-ing for Violet to close the writing desk and, retaining Mrs. Findlayson's letter, return the desk to the chest of drawers. "Last item on this meeting's agenda," Penelope said as Violet straightened and Griselda closed the curtain again, plunging the room once more into gloom. "Do we tell Stokes, Barnaby, and Montague first, or later?"

Violet glanced at Griselda, then looked back at Penelope. "Actually, although the letter bothered her ladyship and she initially worried that the two issues might be connected, on reflection she decided that any problem at The Laurels was entirely separate from the odd deposits paid into her bank account—the sums involved were far too large to have been rent or anything like that. She decided that the people at The Laurels were most likely itinerants or something of the sort, and, relatively speaking, that that was a minor matter. As the bank account problem was her primary concern, she elected to concentrate—and have Runcorn and later Montague concentrate—on that, so she deliberately didn't tell them about the problem at The Laurels—she didn't want to distract them from the more pressing issue."

Violet paused, then more slowly went on, "More importantly, she didn't mention the letter or the problem at The Laurels to any of her family, so whatever the problem at The Laurels might be, it can't have any connection to the murders."

"Excellent!" Penelope said. "So as it's a side issue, and as such one our men don't have time to pursue, there's no reason we shouldn't, and see what we can learn. Especially"—turning, Penelope led the way out of the door and back toward the stairs—"as there's no reason to suppose that the strange people at The Laurels have anything to do with the murders."

"Regardless of what we might hope," Griselda wryly added.

Penelope nodded. "Precisely." She started down the stairs. "And anyway, it's an uncontestable fact that the three of us will make a much better fist of interviewing Mrs. Findlayson, the vicar's wife, than any man ever born."

Chapter 12

Penelope led the way into the office of Montague and Son. Montague's head clerk, Slocum, recognized her immediately and came forward with a smile.

"Mrs. Adair." Slocum's gaze went past Penelope to Griselda, whom he had never met, but then his eyes lighted on Violet and his smile deepened. "And Miss Matcham, isn't it?"

"And this is Mrs. Stokes." Penelope indicated Griselda. "You have recently encountered her husband, Inspector Stokes, I believe."

"Indeed, yes." Slocum bowed. "Good morning, ladies, and how may we help you?"

Violet smiled in return. "Good morning, Mr. Slocum. I'm here to deliver my keys to Lady Halstead's house to Mr. Montague. If he has a moment, I would prefer to give the keys into his hand."

"Yes, of course, miss." Slocum glanced over his shoulder at the door to Montague's office, presently closed. "He's with another client, but the meeting is in the nature of a lengthy review, so I will inquire if Mr. Montague can take a moment to meet with you."

"Thank you, Mr. Slocum—a moment is all that I need," Violet said.

Recognizing a familiar but unexpected face, Penelope left Violet and Griselda in the reception area before Slocum's desk and crossed to the smaller desk to one side. The clerk working there had glanced up at their entrance but had gone back to his papers. Penelope halted before the desk. "Mr. Pringle, isn't it?"

Pringle looked up and smiled a touch tiredly. "Yes, Mrs. Adair."

Slocum had disappeared into Montague's office; with a soft rustle of skirts, Violet and Griselda came to join Penelope. Turning to them, Penelope waved at Pringle. "Pringle was Mr. Runcorn's clerk." She looked back at Pringle. "You're working here now?"

Pringle nodded. "Mr. Montague was kind enough to take me on. His practice is quite large and varied, so there's plenty for me to help with—and I have to say it was a huge relief. Finding a new post at my age wouldn't have been easy. So few employers value experience these days."

"Indeed," Violet said. "I'm Miss Matcham—I was Lady Halstead's companion and met Mr. Runcorn several times. I was deeply saddened to learn of his death. Working alongside him, you must have felt the loss deeply—you have my sympathies."

Both Griselda and Penelope echoed the sentiment.

Pringle gravely inclined his head. "Thank you, ma'am, ladies." Drawing breath, he straightened. "As I said, in the circumstances it's been a great boon to be kept busy, so I'm doubly grateful to Mr. Montague in that regard."

Penelope angled her head, swiftly scanning the topmost documents. "So are you working on new clients, then?"

Pringle glanced down at the documents. "Not new ones as yet. My first task is to reassemble the Halstead file."

"And how is that proceeding?" Penelope asked.

Pringle sighed. "Slowly, I'm sorry to say. I'm aware the information might prove useful to the investigation, but Sir Hugo had quite eclectic tastes in investments, and therefore the documents are very varied, and often not what one might expect. Properly reordering them will take some time."

Behind them, the door to Montague's office opened. The three ladies turned in time to see Montague follow

Slocum into the main room. Montague's gaze, Penelope noticed, locked on Violet.

"Violet?" Concern, restrained but ready to leap to the fore, colored Montague's expression as he strode across the room. Then he noticed Penelope and Griselda, and, slowing, briefly inclined his head. "Penelope. Griselda." Halting before them, he returned his gaze to Violet's face; a fraction of a second passed before he asked, "What's happened?"

Violet smiled reassuringly. "Nothing of any great import." Raising a hand, she offered him the keys. "I remembered I hadn't yet surrendered these. They're the keys to the front and back doors of Lady Halstead's house. I thought I might leave them with you, to pass on when appropriate."

Montague took the keys. "Thank you. Yes, that would be best." His imminent concern evaporating, he glanced at Penelope and Griselda, then once again at Violet. "And what have you three planned for your day?"

Penelope smiled sunnily and leapt in to deflect his attention from the suddenly blank looks on her companions' faces. "Actually, we're off for a short jaunt into the country, and we need to be off."

"Indeed." Violet had recovered her composure. "We won't keep you any longer." She extended her hand.

Montague took it, held it, but his gaze returned to Penelope's face. "As it happens, my client of the moment"—he tipped his head toward his office—"is a relative of yours. Dexter. He's your cousin, I believe. Would you like to have a word with him?"

Dexter? Penelope's smile grew wider; she waved the notion away. "No, no—no need to distract him."

Dexter shared many similarities with her older brother, Luc; the two had been thick as thieves for most of their lives—they'd even married twin sisters. And, like Luc, on hearing that she, Penelope, was about to go for a drive in the country, Dexter would be instantly suspicious, and ask why, and where to, and what she thought to do there . . . and while Barnaby was well on the way to evolving into a modern man, one who didn't feel the need to hem ladies like her in at every step, Luc and Dexter were throwbacks to a more primitive—and much more protective—age.

Keeping her smile bright, Penelope added, "I'll see him at the next family dinner soon enough, but do give him my regards." Tugging her gloves on tighter, she turned to Griselda and Violet. "But now we really must be off."

The other two grasped her desire to leave; even though they didn't fully understand, both sensed her wish to avoid Dexter, so they smiled and immediately joined with her in taking their leave of Montague.

Penelope was the first out of the door; she didn't breathe easily until the carriage door was shut, the coach was moving, and they were safely on their way.

A more relaxed smile blooming, she leaned back against the squabs. "To Essex!" she declared.

"To Noak Hill," Griselda added.

"To The Laurels," Violet said, "and to whatever we find there."

Phelps, Penelope's coachman, had had to stop several times to allow the groom, Conner, to descend and ask for directions, but eventually the carriage rumbled up to a country crossroads and halted. Their last direction had come from the Bear Inn, less than half a mile back down the road, so this had to be it—Noak Hill.

The ladies peered out of the carriage windows. Griselda reported, "The signpost on this side says 'To the Priory.'"

Penelope nodded in the opposite direction. "The rest of the village looks to lie this way."

The carriage rocked as Conner jumped down. He came to the window and saluted; when Penelope let down the window, he asked, "Which way, ma'am? Church lies straight ahead, but most houses seem to be down there, to the left."

Penelope debated. "We're here to visit the vicar's wife, and I assume she'll be at the vicarage."

Conner nodded. "Looks like the vicarage is next to the church just ahead."

"Hmm, yes—but it would be useful to see if we can locate the Halsteads' house, The Laurels, first. From the look of things, it most likely lies somewhere along the village lane." Penelope looked at Conner. "Tell Phelps to drive slowly through the village, and if we spot the house—I would imagine it will have its name up somewhere—to roll past and come around again. We just want to get a good glimpse of it so we know what we're talking about."

Conner bobbed his head. "Yes, ma'am."

He climbed up to the box seat. A minute later, the carriage ponderously rolled forward, rounded the corner, and bowled slowly and sedately along the lane.

Violet and Penelope peered out of the windows on one side of the coach, while Griselda looked out at the opposite side of the lane.

"Cottages," Penelope reported.

"A set of three small terrace houses on this side," Griselda said. "The sort estates are building for their farmworkers these days."

They passed one larger house set back from the lane. "The Orchard." Violet pointed to the name on a brass plate embedded in one gatepost.

Several more medium-sized houses in their own yards followed. They were nearing the end of the village when Griselda said, "There it is!"

Violet and Penelope scrambled to that side of the carriage. They stared out at a substantial, free-standing house built of red brick, set back from the lane in a garden plot that had in large part been allowed to run to seed.

"The lawn—such as it is—has been recently trimmed." Penelope sat back as the house fell behind.

Across the carriage, Griselda met her eyes. "The curtains in several upstairs rooms are open, while in others the curtains are fully drawn."

"Odd if the house was closed up," Penelope observed. "I think it's safe to accept that the vicar's wife's intelligence is sound—someone is living there."

The house had been the last in the village. The carriage slowed, then turned as Phelps brought it around. Penelope rose and pushed up the trap in the coach's ceiling. "Back to the vicarage, Phelps, but as slow as you can past the house on our left."

Phelps complied, and, shifting to the other side of the coach, the three again peered out at the house. Ivy had completely overwhelmed a high, stone garden wall and was well on the way to claiming the tall wrought-iron gate set between a pair of pillars directly in front of the house's front door. Above the gate, a decorative wrought-iron ribbon carried the name The Laurels.

"The ivy's been cut back to reveal the name," Violet said. "But they've left it growing over the gate itself." She frowned. "How odd."

Beyond the blocked gate, a straight gravel path led directly to the narrow sweep of drive before the front door. Weeds strewed the path, and the lawn had encroached over its edges.

As the carriage rolled on, they drew level with the gates to the drive; of similar design to the smaller gate and also in heavy wrought iron, the much wider gates stood ajar. A gravel drive, clear of weeds and in reasonable state, led to the house; it ran along the front before curling around the far side of the blocklike building.

Penelope glanced up at the house, then sighed and leaned back as it passed once more out of view. "Three stories—there's dormers above that parapet around the top of the first floor. So it's of reasonable size, but not large—exactly what one would expect of a family of the Halsteads' means."

"So," Violet said, "the house itself holds no surprises—the only questions are who is using it, and for what."

Penelope nodded. "Let's hope Mrs. Findlayson can shed some light on those points."

It was early afternoon when they walked up the path to the vicarage front door. At their request for an audience, Mrs. Findlayson came to the door; she proved to be a kindly-looking woman of generous girth, with curly white hair surrounding a soft-featured face from which aging blue eyes looked upon the world with a certain calm serenity.

Violet took the lead, making the introductions and explaining that she was calling on Lady Halstead's behalf, having realized from Mrs. Findlayson's recent letter that Mrs. Findlayson had known Lady Halstead well.

Mrs. Findlayson was delighted to receive them. She insisted they join her in the comfortably cheery parlor; once they were seated, she ordered tea, then turned to Violet. "And how is dear Lady Halstead?"

Violet broke the sad news as gently as she could.

Mrs. Findlayson grew sad, then sorrowful. "Oh, dear. Murdered, you say? How very dreadful, to be sure. Such evil there is in the world these days."

The maid arrived with the tea tray and Penelope took charge, pouring a strong cup of tea and adding several lumps of sugar before handing it to Mrs. Findlayson.

The vicar's wife accepted the cup and saucer in something of a daze.

Penelope and Griselda busied themselves pouring their cups and handing Violet hers.

Her gaze on Mrs. Findlayson's face, Violet sipped, then murmured, "You knew her ladyship quite well, didn't you?"

"Oh, indeed." Her gaze unfocused, Mrs. Findlayson nodded. "We both came to the village at much the same time, both as new brides. We grew quite close over those early years, when she and Hugo spent more of their time here, but then he was posted overseas again, and they left the children—there were just the two then, Mortimer and Cynthia—at The Laurels with their nurses and a housekeeper and staff." Mrs. Findlayson pursed her lips in mild disapproval. "Of course, Agatha didn't wish to expose the youngsters to the dangers of life in all those dreadful foreign places Hugo used to have to go to, but over the years, I—well, all of us who knew them— did wonder if, after all, that decision was the right one."

Mrs. Findlayson looked at Violet and managed a weak smile. "As you knew her, dear, you will agree that a gentler, kinder lady would be hard to find, and I always suspected Agatha intended to come home frequently to visit the children, but with Hugo always being sent so far away, and the ships taking so long to make the journey, well, they didn't make it back, either of them, all that often."

Nodding to herself, Mrs. Findlayson went on, "Agatha returned to have Maurice, but then left soon after, when he was still just a babe in arms. William was born overseas—in India, I believe—but Agatha and Hugo brought him home, saw him settled in the nursery, and then they were off again."

Frowning, Mrs. Findlayson shifted in her chair. "I'm not one to speak ill of the dead, and heaven knew Agatha and I remained firm friends, but the way that poor mite howled for his mother—well, the whole village knew of it. And he ran away, several times if memory serves, but the tutors always went after him and caught him and dragged him back." Lips thin, Mrs. Findlayson carefully set her cup back on its saucer. "As in any friendship, there were some things Agatha did that I couldn't approve of, and that was one." Drawing in a breath, she lifted her head and met Violet's eyes, then glanced at Penelope and Griselda. "Against that, however, both Agatha and Hugo were delightful people and so very wedded to their duty to this country that it was all but impossible to hold such transgressions against them."

After a moment, Mrs. Findlayson smiled. "But I'm rambling on, and as both Hugo and Agatha are now dead, there's no point dwelling on the past."

"But it's right that you remember them, and comforting that your memories are so fond, at least of them." Violet paused, then said, "I'm tangentially involved with the sorting out of Lady Halstead's estate, and, as you might imagine, there's been considerable argument between her children as to the disposition of the assets. I wonder"—Violet met Mrs. Findlayson's eyes—"whether you could give me your opinion of them—the children? You must be one of the few who know all four well enough to comment on their characters, and it might help sort things out."

Mrs. Findlayson's expression, until then soft and gentle, hardened. She hesitated, clearly weighing the words that had come to her tongue, but then she looked at Violet and nodded. "Agatha's dead—murdered—and for all I know it was by one of them. Truth be told, I wouldn't put it past any of them. A more viperous brood would be hard to find—although I have to admit their stinging and biting was always directed at each other. All within the family, so to speak."

She paused, then went on, "William, for all his troubles, is the best of the lot of them. Followed by Maurice, although I wouldn't trust him with anything of value. Lacks morals in general, that one. But as for the elder two, Mortimer and Cynthia, if they weren't Agatha and Hugo's children, I wouldn't give them the time of day—not unless they've improved significantly since last I saw them. Cynthia is a self-absorbed harpy, and Mortimer . . . well, my husband once described him as a colorless egotist with no ambition beyond himself."

"They—Cynthia and Mortimer—seem very competitive with regard to each other," Violet observed.

Mrs. Findlayson nodded. "That was always a feature of life at The Laurels—the battles between those two. Over the years, my husband and I had countless consultations with the various nannies and governesses, and even some of the more concerned tutors. Many were driven to seek advice." Mrs. Findlayson frowned, patently sifting through her memories. Eventually, she said, "It was such a strange thing, to have children vying to be the most sanctimonious, the most priggish, the most conservative, the most religiously observant. It was almost impossible to upbraid them, you see? How can you punish a child for adhering to the rules too well? For taking those rules to extremes—and then further? And more, their actions, their behaviors, were never sincere—their apparent goodness was ever a product of ambition. For all their outward perfections, those two caused more gray hairs than Maurice, William, and all the other children in the village put together, all of whose transgressions were entirely normal and understandable. Everyone knew how to cope with the others, including the younger two Halsteads, even though they took matters to the other extreme, but the older two Halsteads were all but beyond our ken."

When Mrs. Findlayson fell silent, Violet was tempted to prompt, but then the vicar's wife stirred and said, "My husband once observed that what drove those two might initially have been a battle for parental approval—to be the best, better than the others in their parents' eyes, and recognized as such, and thus winning their private war, but with their parents never there, it became a battle with no end. That affected Mortimer more than the others—he was the oldest, and naturally expected to be the acknowledged leader, but Cynthia, for one, never accorded him that status, and the other two followed her lead, at least in that."

Mrs. Findlayson paused to sip from her cup, then, lowering it, concluded, "Mortimer lived here, at The Laurels, until he was in his early twenties, and by then he'd become the sort of man who is never satisfied with what he achieves but instead always wants to be more." Mrs. Findlayson shrugged. "For all I know, Cynthia might be the same—that wouldn't surprise me. As for the other two, I daresay they will have continued down the roads they'd started well along before they left here—and neither of those roads will serve them well."

Another silence fell while Violet, Penelope, and Griselda digested that, aligning the information with all they had themselves observed, then Violet set down her cup and saucer. "Thank you." She met

Mrs. Findlayson's eyes and smiled. "Your insights might, indeed, be of some help."

"I'm glad to do whatever I can," Mrs. Findlayson said, "especially if it will help catch Agatha's murderer."

"As to that"—Penelope shifted forward, drawing Mrs. Findlayson's attention—"you wrote in your last letter to Lady Halstead that you and others in the village had observed unusual activity at The Laurels. Although there's no reason to imagine it's related to Lady Halstead's murder, it did seem unexpected."

"Yes, well." Mrs. Findlayson arched her brows. "We were all quite surprised when the new people moved in."

"When was that?" Penelope asked.

"Oh, it would be well over a year now . . . perhaps fifteen months?" Mrs. Findlayson narrowed her eyes. "Yes, that's right. They'd been there for several months before Harvest Service. As no one from the house had yet attended at the church, my husband called a week before the service to formally invite them and urge them to join us, and, of course, by then everyone was wondering who was living there."

"And who is?" Penelope's eyes gleamed behind her glasses.

But Mrs. Findlayson shook her head. "The only people we've ever set eyes on are the odd manservant who answers the door and the pair who work in the kitchen. A man and a woman, but they're rather surly and keep entirely to themselves. Not so much as a nod if one passes them in the lane. Indeed, we never see them out and about except when they head down to Romford in their cart to bring in supplies for one of their evening entertainments."

"Entertainments?" Penelope's eyes widened.

"Indeed." Mrs. Findlayson nodded. "That was what prompted me to write to Agatha, because, really, these odd events have been going on for long enough. Every month, or thereabouts, carriages—all black and with curtains drawn—come rolling up and turn in at The Laurels. Eight or more carriages, every month, but they always arrive very late, usually after ten o'clock at night." Mrs. Findlayson primmed her lips, then opened them and confided, "Even the lads who've climbed the nearby trees to look over the walls say they've not been able to see anything of the goings-on inside the house, because even though the whole ground floor looks to be well lit on those evenings, the curtains are all drawn tight."

"How long do the carriages stay?" Griselda asked.

"Only two hours or so—we usually hear them roll past again about twelve or just after."

Penelope frowned, then asked, "And when the carriages leave, all their curtains are drawn?"

Mrs. Findlayson nodded. "Every single time, every carriage. So, you see, we have no idea who is living in that house and holding these odd events, and we also have no idea who is attending, much less what's going on in the house on those evenings."

Violet leaned forward. "You said these events happen monthly? On a specific date?"

"No, not exactly. It's roughly every month, but we never know the exact date—not until we see the two staff head out in their cart for Romford."

"When was the last entertainment at The Laurels?" Penelope asked. "Or, more pertinently, when do you anticipate the next event will be?"

"I can't remember the date of the last, but the next event will be tonight." Mrs. Findlayson met Penelope's eyes. "My gardener saw the pair from the house head off to Romford this morning."

They'd thanked Mrs. Findlayson, promised her that they would convey all she'd told them to those dealing with the Halsteads' affairs, then hurried back to Penelope's carriage, where they'd piled in as Penelope had directed Phelps to drive back to The Laurels.

Now the three of them stood just outside the overgrown front gate and, using the dense ivy as a screen, peered through the leaves at the house.

"Curtains are still open on the second floor," Penelope said, "but all the ground-floor rooms have curtains fully drawn."

Violet glanced at the trees in what appeared to be a dense wood growing along the side wall of the garden. "Even from high in those trees, no one could see into the first-floor rooms."

"Hmm, no." Penelope humphed. "No sense sending Conner into the wood to see what he can spy." After considering the house for a moment more, she said, "So what do we do? We're here, the house is here. If Mrs. Findlayson's information is correct, if we go to the door and knock, we'll either meet this odd manservant or . . . there'll be no one at home."

Griselda snorted. "And if there's no one at home, you'll want to look around, and possibly find your way inside—"

"Which might give us some clue as to what these peculiar entertainments are all about." Penelope nodded. "Exactly."

Violet drew back to stare at her.

Feeling her gaze, Penelope turned her head and met it.

Violet read the determination in her new employer's face . . . then she blinked, and nodded. "What an excellent idea."

Penelope grinned. "I knew you'd fit in with our little band."

Griselda was still studying the house. "There's no movement visible at all, either upstairs or down." She glanced at Penelope and Violet. "I can't see any point in going back to London without at least knocking on the door and seeing what more we can learn." She focused on Penelope. "So how are we going to do this?"

Penelope thought for only a moment, then turned back to where the carriage stood a little way along the lane. "We do it in style. It's the only sensible way."

They climbed back into the carriage, and, following Penelope's directions, Phelps drove up to the gate. Conner jumped down and pushed the gates wide, then swung up behind as Phelps sent the fashionable carriage sweeping through and up and around the drive, eventually slowing his team to halt the carriage before the two steps leading up to the porch before the front door.

Penelope waited for both Conner and James, the footman, who, in keeping with her promise to Barnaby, she'd had join their company for the day, to descend to the gravel. Conner went to the horses' heads while James, at his most regal, paused, then opened the door, let down the steps, and, terribly formally, handed her down.

Head tilted high, Penelope descended, hoping very much that someone was watching to appreciate their performance.

Violet followed to stand just behind her, then Griselda joined them, taking up position beside Violet.

Penelope nodded to James, and, in formation, they ascended the steps, James in the lead.

Halting before the door, Penelope raised her head, and nodded to James.

James pulled the chain dangling to one side of the front door. Deep inside the house, they heard a bell clang.

Seconds ticked past.

His hand still on the chain, James arched a brow at Penelope. She was about to nod when she caught the tramp of feet on carpet. With her eyes, she signaled James to take up his correct position to her right. He did, to the sound of bolts being drawn.

Several—and from the sound of them, rather heavy—bolts.

The door swung soundlessly inward, and a man—thin, only a few inches taller than Penelope, who definitely didn't qualify as tall—looked out at them, the expression on his distinctly weasel-like features declaring he was supremely bored. "Whatever you've come to suggest, we're not interested."

His accent suggested he'd spent much of his youth in the London slums, but although there were telltale broken veins decorating his face and nose, he did not appear to be inebriated at that moment. Regardless, he would never qualify as a butler, nor even a respectable manservant.

Penelope looked down her nose at him, something her breeding allowed her to accomplish despite her lack of inches. "I beg your pardon?"

Her tone, that of a daughter of the nobility addressing an abject serf, made the man blink, and rethink his approach. "Ah . . . what would you be wanting, miss—" His gaze took in Violet, Griselda, James, and the men and the carriage behind them, and he amended, "ma'am?"

Penelope waited with quite awful patience until he brought his gaze back to her face. "I wish to speak with your master. Please conduct us to the drawing room and inform him we are here."

The man frowned. "And you would be?"

Penelope's brows rose. "A lady from London—that is all you need to know."

She went to sweep forward, but the man, eyes widening, leapt to swing the front door half closed.

Penelope halted, then drew in a breath, clearly outraged.

Before she could wither him, the man hurriedly said, "My master—he's very particular-like. Doesn't let just anyone inside. Worth my job, it'd be, to let you in." His eyes flicked to James and the other men. He swallowed. "If you'll give me your name, I could see if he'll make an exception for you."

Penelope narrowed her eyes. "Who is this man you call your master? If he's the man I think he is . . . well, clearly he can't be, for he would never hire such an ill-informed manservant. So, sirrah, his name if you please. If he is who he should be, I will give you my name to take to him."

Violet had to admit that was a masterstroke, but, sadly, it didn't get them anywhere.

Edging the door even further closed, the man shook his head. "Only people the master knows come here. You don't even know who he is."

"I know who the owners of this house are," Penelope declared. "And I seriously doubt they're your supposed master. Does this man even exist?"

"He exists, all right, and there's nothing havey-cavey about us being here. We rent the place, all right and proper."

"No, you don't," Penelope stated. "I'm acquainted with the Halsteads, the owners of this house, and they know nothing about your tenancy."

That piece of information rocked the man; he pulled back for an instant, then, jaw clenching, growled, "You don't know what you're talking about, but I can tell you this—you're trespassing! And I don't have to answer to trespassers!"

With that, he slammed the door shut.

Immediately, they heard the bolts rammed home.

Penelope stared at the door. "Well!" She swung around and, leading the way, marched back down the two shallow steps and headed across the gravel to the waiting coach.

Griselda and Violet had fallen in behind. They were halfway across the stretch of gravel when Griselda murmured, "Don't turn around and look, but there's a girl at the first-floor window at the far end—I think she's trying to attract our attention."

"Indeed?" Penelope tossed her head as if flinging the comment over her shoulder. As she faced forward again, pausing before the carriage steps to sweep up her skirts and take James's hand to steady her, she said, "Yes—I saw."

Violet followed Penelope into the carriage; sinking onto the seat, she looked for the girl, but from where she was, the light reflected off the window. "Damn!" she muttered. "I can't see past the glass."

Penelope looked across the carriage at Griselda, who met her gaze. James shut the door, then the carriage dipped as he and Conner climbed up.

With a sharp crack of Phelps's whip, the carriage started rolling, slowly turning, gravel crunching loudly under the wheels.

Penelope ducked her head and peered up at the house again, then sat back. Again she met Griselda's now very serious and sober gaze. Penelope waited until the carriage rolled out of the gates and was bowling freely down the lane before nodding. "Yes, I saw—the poor thing looked quite desperate."

"Indeed," Griselda rather grimly said. "And I just realized something else. All the windows had bars—not just the downstairs windows but the first-floor windows as well."

Penelope stilled. "We're so used to seeing bars on windows in Mayfair that we don't register them anymore."

"But," Violet said, her expression turning as grim as Griselda's, "why would they have bars on windows in the country?"

"And even more to the point," Penelope said, "why does one have bars on windows on an upper floor?"

The three women exchanged glances, then Penelope stood and pushed up the trap in the ceiling. "Phelps?"

"Yes, ma'am?"

"Back to London with all speed—don't spare the horses." Penelope exchanged another look with Griselda and Violet. "We need to alert the Inspector and your master that there's something very wrong going on up here."

Chapter 13

"So, you see, we have to act tonight." Halting before her drawing room fireplace, Penelope looked from face to face around the circle of her assembled colleagues. Barnaby and Stokes were present, along with Montague, each seated in one of the large armchairs, while Griselda and Violet had sat on the chaise, allowing Penelope to claim center stage as she'd paced before the fireplace and described in succinct and factual fashion all she, Griselda, and Violet had discovered that afternoon.

It was already early evening, and time was slipping away.

After racing back to town, they'd let Griselda down in Greenbury Street, then Penelope and Violet had driven straight on to Scotland Yard. There, they'd found Stokes and Barnaby rechecking statements taken from witnesses about Runcorn's murder. After listening to a brief account of what the ladies had discovered, Stokes had sent a runner to summon Montague, and they'd repaired to Albemarle Street.

Griselda, with Megan and her nursemaid, Gloria, had arrived shortly after, closely followed by Montague. In keeping with her new policy of balance, Penelope had decided that the proud fathers should entertain Oliver and Megan. Leaving the gentlemen, supervised by Griselda and Violet, thus engaged, Penelope had consulted with Mostyn and organized a simple dinner of cold meats, bread, cheese, and fruits, which, given the early hour and the relaxed company, they'd consumed en famille in the dining room.

Once the meal had been consumed, and Oliver and Megan had been handed to their respective nursemaids, the company had regrouped and repaired to the more spacious drawing room. There, aided by Violet and Griselda, Penelope had described all they'd discovered that day, from Violet's recollection of the letter, to their brief visit to Lowndes Street, and their subsequent journey into Essex, capped by their unexpected discoveries at Noak Hill.

To her mind, and Violet's and Griselda's, the need to act now, tonight, was self-evident.

In response to her summation, Stokes exchanged a look with Barnaby, then looked back at her. "Tell me again the reasons you believe we must move on this place tonight."

Penelope stared at Stokes, amazed that he hadn't seen the obvious, but then she realized he wasn't disputing her conclusion but instead was asking her to restate and reinforce the arguments he would need to convince and win over his superiors.

She blew out a breath; where to start? "Well, I suspect the first point we need to make is the intuitive connection Lady Halstead drew between what was going on at her country house, The Laurels, and the odd payments into her bank account." Resuming her pacing, Penelope continued, "Although she subsequently downplayed it, that connection was instrumental in pushing her ladyship into having her affairs examined by Runcorn—and we are all in agreement that that action is what led to Lady Halstead's, Runcorn's, and Tilly's murders. So the strange entertainments, as Mrs. Findlayson terms them, being held at The Laurels appear critically connected, motivewise, to the three murders."

Pausing, Penelope arched a brow at Stokes.

Fingers steepled before his face, he nodded. "That's good as far as it goes. But why now—why tonight?"

"Because," Penelope continued, "according to the signs the locals have noted, there will be another such entertainment held tonight. The timing of these entertainments appears to mirror the odd payments—another, more definite link—but, therefore, after tonight there will not be another such entertainment for another month. *However*"—she held up a finger—"we know that the murderer is aware that the police are now involved, so there is every reason to suppose that tonight's event will be the last—his last hurrah, as it were, at least at The Laurels."

"Why," Barnaby asked, taking on the role of devil's advocate, "if he's worried about police attention, would he even bother to hold an event tonight?"

Penelope looked at him, momentarily at a loss, but then she grimly smiled. "Because he has wares to clear." Confidence escalating, she looked at Montague. "The items Montague has deduced he's selling, each worth two hundred and fifty pounds." She looked back at Barnaby, then shifted her gaze to Stokes. "And those items aren't the sort one can lock in a cupboard and leave until later."

Stokes nodded. "Very good." He was clearly formulating his approach to his superiors, an urgent request that, given all they'd learned, needed to succeed.

Barnaby glanced around at the others. The atmosphere in the room, between the six of them, had been progressively changing ever since their ladies had arrived back from Essex with their news. The more he, Stokes, and Montague had heard of what Penelope, Griselda, and Violet had uncovered . . . while some part of their initial response had been faint and, as far as they'd been able to manage, well-concealed horror at the ladies' glib and apparently carefree plunge into active and independent investigation, none of the ladies' actions had been reckless, and, at all times, as Penelope had promised, they'd had support and protection in the form of her coachman, groom, and footman—all men Barnaby himself had vetted and on whom he and Stokes knew they could rely. Their initial instinctive horror had been quickly submerged by building excitement, by increased focus and eagerness.

Their ladies had found the key to the murders, and neither he, Stokes, nor, he judged, Montague, were the sort of men to deny approbation and applause where it was due, much less hesitate to seize the information the ladies had assembled and use it to push the investigation along.

And the ladies were with them every step of the way. This investigation was now very much a fully fledged joint effort involving all six of them; each of them had a personal interest, had committed themselves to seeing it through.

As a group, together.

It was a heady, exhilarating, stimulating situation.

Stokes looked up at Penelope. "If, as Barnaby and I have already reported, he—whoever he is—is primarily driven by a wish to keep his identity a secret, isn't it likely that you three turning up at the door of The Laurels this afternoon will have put our bird to flight? Why, knowing you had called—and you did state you were acquainted with the Halstead family—would he remain, waiting for the authorities to turn up and expose him? Isn't it more likely that he would take his wares and run?"

"No, he can't." Barnaby couldn't help himself; the excitement of pulling the strands together was too great a lure. "The event has already been advertised." He met Stokes's eyes. "All those carriages that turn up to every event—they're not local. They have to come from somewhere. Those people—his customers, if you will—have already been notified that there's an event, a sale of some sort, on tonight. He can't just up and shift the location and time, not without risking a great deal, especially given that those he's dealing with are unlikely to be your average merchant."

"Indeed." Penelope sank onto the arm of Barnaby's chair. "And I believe you can be confident that although he—whoever he is—presumably knows by now that some lady is likely to pass on to the Halstead family the fact that someone is using The Laurels, he won't imagine that lady will be moved to do so tonight, or even tomorrow, much less that her information will occasion immediate action by Scotland Yard." Raising her hands, palms up, she looked at Griselda and Violet. "We were just three females, after all—hardly likely to be an imminent threat."

Montague and Stokes both snorted.

"However," Violet said, her clear voice a contrast to Penelope's forceful tones, "I would wager that if you sent men up there tomorrow, they'll find nothing more than an empty house."

Barnaby nodded. "That's all but certain." He met Stokes's eyes. "He—whoever he is—is locked into holding his entertainment tonight. For multiple reasons, he can't call it off, and although he must know by now that he won't be able to continue with his business, at least not from The Laurels, from his point of view, his best—indeed, most obvious—course will be to continue with tonight's event, and then relocate with all speed."

Stokes held his gaze, the expression in his gray eyes distant as he re-trod their case. The case he would lay before his superiors in support of his request for the authority and men to mount a raid on The Laurels tonight. Slowly, Stokes nodded. "So if we leave it, even until tomorrow, we'll almost certainly lose him. A man who has committed three murders—three murders the commissioners would like to see solved before the news sheets get wind of them and the Halsteads, and even more the Camberlys, come under public scrutiny. The commissioners want a result, and this is clearly an excellent chance to leap ahead several steps in our investigation—all the way to identifying this not-so-easy-to-identify villain."

Barnaby tilted his head. "That should shift them, don't you think?"

Stokes grimaced. "I hate politics—I'm sure all the commissioners as well as the Chief will want to agree and give the go-ahead, but . . . I fear they'll hesitate. Even with your father there, and Peel, too, the others will want to weigh up the pros and cons, to assess how the case weighs in the public scale. And with Camberly and Halstead involved . . ." Leaning forward, Stokes clasped his hands between his knees. "If there was something—just one more thing that would be certain to keep the public on the police's side, even if this raid proves to be a complete waste of time—"

"There is." It was Montague who spoke. When all eyes turned his way, he met their gazes gravely. "We haven't dwelled on it, but all of us can guess what 'items' the villain is selling." He looked at Griselda. "You saw one at the window—a young, desperate girl. According to my analysis of the sums he's cleared every month, he'll have at least four others in that house, very possibly more." Montague swept the group with his steady hazel gaze. "And none of us have to think too hard to guess to whom he's selling such wares."

Stokes's face slowly transformed into a mask of almost vicious, delighted triumph. "That's perfect," he growled. All but springing to his feet, he looked around at the others. "I'll go to the Yard and—"

"Wait, wait, wait!" Rising, Penelope waved her hands. "We need to work out a plan first." Hunting in a pocket, she drew out a crumpled sheet. Smoothing it, she shifted to show it to Stokes. Barnaby rose and looked over her other shoulder. "This," Penelope explained, "is a map Griselda, Violet, and I drew of The Laurels—as much as we could deduce from what we could see of the house and the immediately surrounding areas. See"—she pointed—"there are thick woods on this side, which should be useful, and—"

Ten minutes later, with the plan for the raid on the late Lady Halstead's country house fully detailed and defined, Stokes shrugged into his greatcoat and left to summon the commissioners, to lay out his case, gain their approval, and gather his constables, leaving Montague and Barnaby to arrange transportation for the rest of their company to the agreed rendezvous in the woods alongside The Laurels.

Waiting in the front hall for the carriages to be brought around, Penelope all but jigged with happiness. Not one of the men—not even Montague—had made any attempt to dissuade the ladies from attending, much less questioned their right to do so.

Their new investigating team was well on the way to becoming a fully functioning reality.

It was a cool night in Essex. A pale sliver of moon showed fleetingly through the canopy, concealed, then fitfully revealed by the low clouds scudding across the sky and the restlessly shifting branches of the tall trees in the wood. Although the majority of leaves had yet to fall, enough already had to provide a soft carpet underfoot, sufficiently thick to deaden the clomp of heavy boots as Stokes issued whispered orders and his men spread out, circling the house as silently as they could, as far as possible keeping under cover.

Violet wasn't sure such caution was truly necessary. As arranged, they'd gathered in the wood at half past nine—the six of them, plus Penelope and Barnaby's two coachmen and four grooms and footmen, as well as a good score and more of Scotland Yard's finest. From what Violet had made out from the earlier whispered exchanges, several of the young Turks on the detective side of the force, all of whom clearly held Stokes in some awe, had volunteered to assist him. Stokes had organized his force into smaller groups, assigning two detectives to a cohort of constables; he was presently engaged in dispatching the groups to positions around the house.

As far as Violet could see, no one in the house was watching, was in any way on guard; no one was expecting any interruptions to their proceedings, whatever those were.

Their force had assembled before any carriages had appeared, but even then all the curtains in the house, on both upper and lower floors, had already been drawn. Light shone through them, softer lamplight upstairs, while the downstairs rooms appeared to be ablaze—exactly as if a major social gathering was underway.

The carriages, all black and heavily curtained, had started to arrive at ten minutes before the hour; by ten o'clock, nine had pulled up, had disgorged their passengers, then been drawn to a halt along one side of the drive. The coachmen, all of them, had tied up their teams and gone inside, too, somewhat unexpectedly following their masters through the front door. The door had opened to every coachman's knock but was always swiftly closed after every admittance.

After ten minutes passed and no further coaches had rattled along the lane and in at the gate, Stokes had started sending his men out from the cover of the wood.

From her vantage point perched on a sturdy branch high enough to see over the wall, more or less in line with the front porch, Violet, along with Penelope, Griselda, and Montague, all similarly clinging to branches and tree trunks, had studied the "guests" who had arrived in the nine carriages. Both men and women, roughly an equal number of each; all had climbed down and walked quickly but not hurriedly inside, sparing not so much as a glance at their surroundings.

Although the light was poor, all the attendees had appeared fashionably, even elegantly, dressed. The ladies had worn dark gowns; some had carried shawls and reticules. Most of the males had sported coats and cravats, and some had carried canes and fashionable hats.

The confidence, the assurance, with which each had approached and entered the house was, Violet thought, telling. Leaning closer to the trunk of the tree, closer to Montague, standing on a lower branch on the tree's opposite side, she whispered, "All of those who arrived have been here before—probably many times."

Through the dark shadows, Montague met her gaze; after a moment, he nodded. "Yes, you're right." He glanced back at the house. "Anyone who was new to the place would have glanced around, at the very least shown some sign of hesitation, of taking stock. None of them did."

"Nor did their coachmen," Penelope whispered from the next tree. She started wriggling along her branch, clearly intending to jump down. "Whoever they are, they're all a part of this—there's no innocent bystanders in that lot."

Griselda humphed an agreement as she carefully stepped down, branch by sturdy branch, from her perch.

"Wait!" Montague hissed as Penelope prepared to jump.

When she stopped and looked at him, he hesitated for only a second before saying, "You might slip and twist your ankle, and then you'd have to stay here and miss all the excitement."

Penelope studied him for a moment, then softly laughed. "Oh, you are good. You, Montague, are a very welcome addition to our band of investigators. All right. I'll wait."

Montague clambered down, and Penelope allowed him to lift her down from her perch.

Violet, meanwhile, had edged to the trunk, but before she could start to climb down by herself, Montague returned and, with no more than a glance by way of requesting permission, reached up and lifted her down.

Somewhat to her surprise, her lungs stopped working—seized up in a most peculiar way in response to the feel of his hands about her waist, to the sense of strength as he so easily lifted her down and gently set her feet on the leaves. He hesitated for a second, a telltale moment in the dark of the woods when he stood and looked down at her, their shadowed gazes locked even though, in the poor light, they couldn't see—but they could sense, and they did, then he drew breath, and, sliding his hands from her waist, he stepped aside, out of her way. But he remained close beside her.

Stokes and Barnaby had been overseeing the disposition of their troops; they returned, two rather large shadows moving surprisingly silently, weaving through the trees.

Joining them, Stokes nodded. "We're ready." A flash of teeth in the darkness was a sharklike smile. "Our group will go in via the front door." A contingent of the burliest constables, as well as the six men from Penelope and Barnaby's staff, waited a few feet away. "Although I've got a warrant, I want Montague to lead the way using his letter of authority—the more confusion we can create over what exactly is going on, the better, and the easier it will be to break up the group inside and take everyone into custody."

Stokes's gaze shifted to Penelope, Griselda, and Violet. "I want you three, along with your coachmen, grooms, and footmen, to follow us through the gates and take up position on the lawn directly opposite the front porch." He paused, his shadowed gaze touching each of their faces in turn. "If this business is as we suspect, I want to be able to get the girls out of there as quickly as we can. I've told our men that they'll be able to steer the girls out of the front door and they'll be able to see you from there." Stokes tipped his head to the coachmen, grooms, and footmen. "Your men will stay with you, and help shepherd the girls from the front door to you. I don't want to risk any of the blackguards inside thinking to take hostages—not of any sort."

Even Penelope saw the sense in Stokes's plan. They all nodded and murmured agreement.

Stokes lifted his head. "Right then." He glanced at his men. "Let's get this raid underway."

They followed Stokes out of the wood, into the lane, and, falling into the requested formation, marched through the gates, presently set wide, and up the gravel drive. Violet had to admit it was a stirring moment; the crunch of so many heavy booted feet sounded like a drumbeat—the march of justice.

On reaching the area before the porch, their small party diverged from the rear and took up their appointed positions.

Montague, she saw, fearlessly led the way up the steps. Halting before the front door, he nodded to Stokes, who pulled the dangling chain. Montague waited for a heartbeat, then raised his fist and thundered on the door.

When the door failed to open, at Stokes's nod, Montague knocked heavily again.

Half a minute passed, then the door eased open.

Up on her toes, Violet could just glimpse the curious manservant as he stood blocking the doorway. His "Yes? Can I help you, sir?" floated over the many burly shoulders between them.

Montague flicked out the letter of authority he held in his hand. "I am empowered by the owner of this property, the late Lady Halstead, to investigate the use of her house." When the man simply gawped, Montague had no compunction in raising a hand, palm out, and shoving the villain backward; the man staggered back several paces, and Montague seized the opening and strode over the threshold into the front hall.

The door to his left was closed; directly ahead a wide staircase led up to the first floor, while a narrow corridor beside it gave access to the rear rooms of the house. To his right, a pair of doors stood wide, showing a section of what was plainly the drawing room. Pivoting in that direction, Montague strode forward, feeling decidedly more pugnacious than he could recall ever feeling as he took in the two couples beyond the doorway.

They might have been mistaken for guests attending a fashionable soiree if not for the hardness in their eyes and the signs of dissolute living etched in their faces.

Both couples had frozen, their expressions blanking, their eyes widening as their gazes locked on the men at Montague's back; ignoring the couples, Montague marched into the room and looked down its length.

And saw Walter Camberly, his eyes rounding, his mouth agape, standing alongside a round, raised dais—the sort of thing Montague had seen in dressmaker's shops. Atop the dais, tears streaking her face, stood a girl of some twenty summers, utterly naked.

Montague finally understood. Walter was *auctioning* the girls.

"Stokes."

"Yes. I've seen enough." His gray gaze locked on Walter Camberly, his face the definition of grim, Stokes moved up beside Montague. "I'll take care of him, you get the girl out of here."

"Done." Montague strode forward, shrugging out of his greatcoat as he went, barely registering the other people, men and women both, scattered about the room.

Walter Camberly's mouth opened and closed, but no sound issued forth. As Stokes reached him and seized him by the arm—ungently—Walter managed to croak, "Here! I say—"

"If you've got any brains, you'll keep your trap shut," growled a man—well-dressed, but clearly no gentleman—standing a few paces away.

Montague shut his ears to the mounting exchanges of pleasantries as Stokes's men moved through the room and introduced themselves to Walter's "guests." Raising his greatcoat, Montague held it up to screen the poor girl. "Here, my dear. Wrap yourself up, and let's get you out of here."

Tentatively, as if hardly daring to believe what was taking place before her very eyes, the girl slowly took possession of the coat; Montague averted his eyes as she slipped properly into it and hugged it about her body.

"Excellent." Montague held out his hand to assist her down from the dais. "Come along, my dear—you're entirely safe, and there are ladies waiting outside to help."

Blinking huge blue eyes, the girl took his hand and, holding the coat tight with her other hand, clambered down. Once she was on her feet, she met Montague's eyes. "There's others like me—upstairs."

Montague nodded, gently urging her forward. "Yes, we know. Others will be bringing them down momentarily." Shielding her from the jostling of the many bodies—police and their captives—now crowding the room, he guided her out into the front hall. There they found other girls being brought down from upstairs and led outside by solicitous constables. Barnaby had been in charge of that group, all of them older men with daughters of their own.

Remaining with his charge, Montague joined the exodus, escorting her across the porch, helping her over the gravel—although she was barefoot, she seemed unconcerned by the small stones—and then they were on the lawn and he handed her into Violet's care.

With a smile and a comforting embrace, Violet led the girl to join the others, gathering in a small circle inside the protective cordon of Penelope's men. The men were all studiously watching the house, showing the scantily clad girls as much courtesy as they could.

As Montague watched, the girl he'd escorted out was welcomed with cries of "Hilda!" Several of the other girls threw their arms around her.

Penelope waited for the hugs and cries to subside, then asked, "Girls, is this all of you?"

There were seven girls in all. They looked around, then Hilda raised her head and nodded, "Yes, miss. There were seven of us they'd caught this month. I heard him as was in charge"—with her chin, she indicated the house—"say as they usually had more, but tonight, this month, there was just us seven." Hilda's voice lowered, trembled. "We're all girls from the country, miss, good girls an' all. Each of us came down to try to find honest work in the city, but he came along with his lies and his promises of a good place to work that he knew . . . and then he brought us here and locked us up." Her voice dropped lower. "He were going to sell us for ravishment and worse."

"Yes, well," Penelope said, "you can rest assured that he won't be doing that, or much of anything else, not where he's going. Those gentlemen over there"—with a wave she indicated the constables marching the arrested "guests" out in a steady stream to the police wagons that had drawn up, having waited down the lane to the priory until they'd been summoned—"are from the police, and they will ensure that those dreadful people get their just deserts, which, trust me, won't be sweet." The words and Penelope's tone combined to help the girls relax just a little, their tension fractionally easing. "Now," Penelope continued, "do you know where your clothes are? If you'll give me instructions, I'll send my husband and Mr. Montague here to fetch what they can find."

Supplied with instructions in short order, Montague returned to the house and found Barnaby in the front hall; they went through the rooms upstairs, gathering up the bags they found in each room and filling them with whatever belongings they could find.

"The girls were maids from the country," Montague told Barnaby when he rejoined him at the top of the stairs. Montague had four bags, two under his arms and one in each hand, while Barnaby carried three similar cases. As they started down the stairs, Montague continued, "They came to London looking for honest work. From what I gather, he—by which I believe they mean Walter Camberly—met them soon after they arrived and offered them employment. He then brought them here."

Barnaby nodded. "I'd wager he hung around near the coaching inns. Easy enough to spot the wide-eyed innocents who've never been to town before."

Reaching the hall, they paused, and Stokes joined them, Walter Camberly in tow.

Walter still looked stunned, still uncomprehending as, hands bound before him, propelled by a burly sergeant, he stumbled along.

When the sergeant halted Walter a pace away from Stokes, Montague fixed Walter with a witheringly condemnatory glare. "You disgusting excuse for a gentleman—you preyed on innocent girls for your own gain."

"And," Barnaby said, his tone equally hard, "you then murdered your own grandmother to hide your crimes."

"Not to mention murdering your grandmother's man-of-business, Mr. Runcorn, and her ladyship's maid, Tilly Westcott," Stokes said.

Walter's face lost all color. His jaw dropped, hung open for several seconds, then his eyes bulged and he snapped his mouth shut. He looked at them, at their expressions, then vehemently shook his head. "No." With every evidence of desperation, he raised his bound hands as if pleading his case. "No—I didn't."

His face graven, Stokes signaled to the sergeant. "Take him away." As the sergeant shoved Walter on, Stokes added, "Just make sure you keep him well away from the others. No telling what they might do."

"Aye, sir," the sergeant replied, pushing Walter through the open doorway and onto the porch.

Twisting around to look back at them, desperation in every line of his face, Walter Camberly wailed, "I didn't murder anyone! That wasn't me!"

It was a long and busy night, but not one of them begrudged the effort.

Buoyed by triumph and the deep satisfaction of knowing they'd saved seven, at least, of Walter's victims from violation and misery, the six intrepid investigators banded together to take care of all the issues arising from the evening's raid.

Albemarle Street became their headquarters. Penelope, Griselda, and Violet returned there with the girls; Mostyn and the rest of the household rallied around, finding beds, comforting the girls with hot milk, then settling them to sleep. They put the girls in three bedrooms, two in each of two rooms and three in the other, so none of them would be alone.

Griselda descended the stairs with Penelope and Violet after they'd assured the girls that help would be forthcoming to find them honest work on the morrow, and then had bid them a good night. "I daresay tonight will be the first decent night's rest they've had since they reached London."

"Poor things." Violet sighed. "What Walter did was simply unconscionable."

"Indeed." Penelope was unusually somber. "I don't like to think about how many more he sold off over the last—what was it? Fourteen months?"

"Dwelling on the number won't do any good, but," Griselda said, "given they caught the brothel owners involved, and with any luck that will be all of them, then I suspect Stokes and his men will be closing down several such enterprises and freeing the girls shortly. Not that that will ameliorate the damage done, but at least they will be free again."

Penelope halted, head tilting as she considered that prospect. Then she nodded and continued down the stairs. "Fingers crossed, but it may well be that because of Walter's crimes, we might end up freeing many more girls than those he himself sent to hell."

As matters transpired, it wasn't going to be Stokes and his men who closed down the brothels. When he, Barnaby, and Montague finally returned to Albemarle Street, Stokes slumped in an armchair, accepted a glass of brandy from Barnaby, and answered Griselda's eager question. "Not me, love, but my peers in Manchester, Leeds, Birmingham, and Coventry." He sipped, sighed, then met the ladies' encouraging gazes with a half smile. "Walter Camberly stumbled on a lucrative non-London market. The brothels in those lesser cities can't keep enough girls—those that way inclined who have any sense move to London and the better pickings here. We snared nine brothel owners and their madams—the Chief's in alt. Usually, it's easy enough to catch the madams, but the owners . . . they are rarely to be found, and are even less easy to charge with any crime.

"This time"—with his glass, Stokes waved—"we have them all singing. And they're all giving us the same song. Cromer—he was the man you took to be a man-servant, but in fact he was more deeply involved in the racket, a full partner—was the connection. Through him, Walter Camberly approached the brothel keep-ers in those four cities and offered to sell them country girls—fresh, clean, unsullied country girls. Not being complete flats, Cromer and Camberly took the precau-tion of insisting they had to be paid in cash, and that the brothel owners themselves had to be present to take possession of the goods immediately after the auction."

Penelope shuddered. "Evil—simply evil." She looked at Stokes. "But how did Camberly find the girls?"

"It seems," Barnaby said, "that Walter stumbled onto the value of being innocuous. According to him, ever since he was a boy he would occasionally loiter about the coaching inns simply because he liked watching the coaches and the horses and the travelers—he said he used to imagine running away, the usual adolescent dreams." Barnaby paused to sip, then went on, "But as he grew older, and looked more mature, on and off over the last years, he would be asked by fresh-faced coun-try maids just off the coaches for directions. Sometimes even recommendations as to where they might find work, or where they might stay." Barnaby paused, then said, "Eventually, an evil scenario took root and blossomed in his brain."

"It sounds like his parents keep him on a very tight rein." Stokes knocked back the last of his brandy. "We haven't formally interviewed him as yet. I wanted to let him stew through the night." Stokes looked at Griselda, then Penelope. "What of the girls?"

"Thankfully, we got there in time for these seven. I've already sent a note around to Phoebe Deverell's agency, and I received an immediate reply. The woman in charge—a Mrs. Quiverstone—wrote that she and the agency will be happy to take all seven girls in and keep them under their wing, assess and train them, and make sure they get appropriate positions." Penelope leaned back in her chair. "So they are saved, safe, and well on the way to getting back their lives."

"Indeed," Violet said, "and from what the girls said, they do appreciate that, the horror of the last weeks aside, they might well end up in a better situation than they might have had Walter Camberly not interfered in their lives." Violet smiled. "They are very resilient, which is all to the good." She met Montague's eyes. "They're already looking forward, not back."

Penelope heaved a tired, but clearly satisfied, sigh and locked gazes with Barnaby. "Excellent, excellent, and excellent! We"—she waved one hand, indicating the six of them—"have notched up a major success. All that remains is to confirm that Walter Camberly committed the three murders, and it'll be time to celebrate."

Stokes looked at Barnaby, then Montague, then stoically said, "There's just one problem—Walter Camberly continues to insist that he hasn't murdered anyone."

Chapter 14

Stokes formally interrogated Walter Camberly the next morning at Scotland Yard. Barnaby, in his role as consultant, sat to Stokes's right, while Montague, courtesy of Lady Halstead's letter of authority, occupied the chair on Stokes's left.

Walter Camberly sat in a single hard chair on the opposite side of the table. Two large and grim-looking sergeants stood at ease behind him, staring over his head at the opposite wall.

His wrists and ankles shackled, Walter, disheveled and pale, sat with his head bowed, staring at his hands clasped on the table before him.

Tapping a finger on the table, Stokes considered him, then, in a noncommittal, nonjudgmental tone, said, "Care to tell us why you did it?" When Walter glanced up at him, puzzled by the tack, Stokes elaborated, "You're the only child of affluent, well-to-do parents. Your father's an up-and-coming politician. You've been given everything, have lacked for no comforts. You've been sent to good schools, had every opportunity. Courtesy of both your parents' families, you had the entree into society. You could have been anything you wished, could have made your mark in countless socially acceptable ways, yet instead you chose to throw in your lot with criminals—more, with elements that rank among the most despicable." Folding his hands, Stokes leaned forward, his eyes locked with Walter's. "With those dregs of humanity who prey on the most defenseless."

Stokes studied Walter's eyes, then softly asked, "So why? Why did you do it?"

Walter held Stokes's gaze, then drew a shuddering breath. "Because it was the only way to make my parents see me. To get their attention."

Stokes sat back, his expression reflecting his lack of understanding.

Immediately, Walter leaned forward, almost eagerly explaining, "You don't know what it's like—I'm *nothing* to them." Bitterness drenched the words. Walter studied Stokes, then Barnaby and Montague. "You look in from outside and see what they want you—what they want all society—to see. The perfect family—father, mother, and son. It's always been that way—it's always been about my father's ambition, which, of course, my mother fully shares. They don't care a fig for me other than that I fill that last position, that I stand by their side like some"—contempt and disgust rising in his voice, he gestured—"shop mannequin. Not a real person, just the representation of one. I'm nothing more than a stage prop to them."

Slumping back in the chair, Walter sneered, although the expression was clearly not directed at Stokes, Barnaby, Montague, or anyone else in the room. "Let's see how they deal with this—they won't be able to simply not notice, will they?"

Stokes inclined his head. "Probably not. So in that way, at least, you've got what you wanted."

Walter blinked, then slowly nodded. "Yes. I have, haven't I?"

But at what cost? Montague wondered.

Stokes let a moment elapse, then said, "I'm curious about why you organized the payments as you did—why use your grandmother's bank account?"

Walter snorted. "I don't exist other than as an extension of my parents, remember. I don't have any income other than what my father allows me—and he gives me my allowance in cash every month, so I never have any decent amount, just enough to get by for the month." Dropping his gaze to his hands, he raised a shoulder. "Why would they give me more? My tailor's bills, every bill I have, has to go to my father. That way, he—and through him my mother—keeps complete control. *They* decide how I dress, what style of hat, what type of boots. As I said, I'm nothing more than a tailor's dummy to them. But, of course, most importantly, by not giving me access to any decent amount of money, they limit what I can do socially—I can't wager, I can't go carousing with friends, I can't go and visit anywhere or do anything unless I ask for and receive their explicit approval and extra funds. I can't belong to any club because they don't believe it necessary, and it might result in me making undesirable acquaintances."

Studying his hands, Walter went on, "The only life I had was what they allowed me." He looked up and met Stokes's eyes. "So I didn't have a bank account. I never had the money to need one." He paused, then added, "And when I did start getting money from the sales at The Laurels, I didn't want to put it anywhere under my own name, in case it somehow got back to my father. It was clear the money would mount up, and I didn't dare hide it in my room or anywhere in the house, so . . . I used Grandmama's account." He met Stokes's eyes.

"I didn't think she'd notice. I didn't think she would ever even look at the amount in there, and as I was only putting money in, and I never took any out, then she would always have her expected amount there. If there was more, even if she noticed, I didn't think she'd worry—certainly not enough to look into it."

"How did you find out the details of her account?" Montague asked.

Walter shrugged. "Easy enough. One evening when we were there for dinner, I slipped away and searched Grandmama's desk in the sitting room. I found her account details as well as old letters she'd sent to the bank—instructions for withdrawals that had been paid out. I took several of the oldest letters so I'd be able to copy them and get my money out when I wanted it."

"As you did," Barnaby said, "when you learned your grandmother had instructed Runcorn to review her affairs." When Walter nodded, Barnaby clarified, "So you wrote a letter of withdrawal to close the account, removing all the funds in it, not just your money, and then . . . who was the woman who presented the letter and collected the cash?"

"That was an actress I hired—I promised to pay her well, and I gave her the forged letter. I'd practiced copying Grandmama's hand for months, off and on, so

I was sure the letter would pass, and it did. I used the actress because, of course, I didn't want to be seen, and if the letter had been genuine, then Violet would have been the one most likely to present it."

"Why take all the money," Montague asked, "rather than just your own?"

"I wrote the letter after Grandmama died—I'd meant to do it earlier, but with her gone, I knew I had to get my money out right away . . . and as she was gone, I thought I might as well have it all, rather than leaving it for the others."

"Did you like your grandmother?" Stokes asked.

Walter arched his brows. "She was all right. I never spent much time with her, but she seemed a decent sort." He shrugged again. "I didn't know her that well."

"Which," Stokes said, his tone growing grim, "presumably made it easier to murder her."

Walter's eyes flew wide. "No! I told you." Wild-eyed, he looked at Barnaby, then Montague. "I *didn't* kill her. I had nothing to do with that—with *any* of the murders." He glanced from one to the other, taking in their hard eyes, their grim faces. "Well, why would I? I had money of my own, and that was what I wanted. I didn't have to kill her to get it!"

A pause ensued, then Stokes looked at Barnaby, then at Montague. Then, slowly, he brought his gaze back to

Walter's face. "Why don't you tell us exactly what you did?"

With the threat of being blamed for the murders acting as a potent inducement, Walter recounted all the steps he'd taken, all his actions from the moment he'd learned at Lady Halstead's last, fateful family dinner that her ladyship was intending to get her affairs in order.

"I didn't kill her. I didn't kill any of them. I didn't need to. It never even occurred to me."

He made a convincing case.

And when he saw them still hesitating over exonerating him, at least with respect to the murders, he sighed, and said, "The money—all of it—is in a tin on the top of the wardrobe in my bedroom in my parents' house in Belgrave Square."

Barnaby shot Stokes a glance. Stokes caught it and fractionally tipped his head to Barnaby.

"As for the alibis I gave you . . ." Walter's lips tightened. "My mother told me what to say, so what I told you before is rubbish. My real alibis are, on the night my grandmother was murdered, I was drinking in the public house on Grosvenor Street, The Royal, not far from my parents' house. I'm a regular, and I stayed, as I usually do, until they closed at two o'clock." Walter's lips twisted. "Also as usual, I was utterly inebriated when I left—I was only just able to walk the short distance to my parents' home before passing out. I would never have made it to my grandmother's, much less been able to do . . . well, whatever was done."

Walter paused as Stokes, lips thin, pulled out his notebook and flipped to a new page. Stokes scribbled, then nodded, and Walter continued, "On the evening the man-of-business was murdered, I was at a small theater off Leicester Square—The Poulson. I went there to talk to and hire the actress. I was at the theater for the six o'clock show and stayed there, or with her, for most of the night. The actress's name is Lily Cartwright—she can tell you the names of the stage manager and the theater owner, both of whom saw me. On the night the maid was murdered, I met Cromer in a tavern in Tothill Fields to plan last night's sale." Walter paused, then glanced at Stokes. "With my grandmother dead, it was clear we wouldn't be able to use The Laurels anymore, so we needed to find some other place. We were at the tavern until the small hours—the barkeep and girls will remember us. We'd met there before."

Walter leaned further forward; when Stokes glanced up, Walter met his eyes. "Can't you see? My grandmother's death completely disrupted my dealings—my way to get sufficient funds to be shot of my parents' prison forever. It was all going swimmingly. Yes, I had to move the money out of her account, but I now have sufficient funds to be able to open an account of my own, and through Cromer I'd learned how to do it under another name." Walter spread his hands. "Why would I kill my grandmother? Let alone the other two?"

Stokes held his gaze for a long moment, then nodded. "You'll be charged with the offences arising out of your kidnapping and selling of the girls. If your alibis are sound, perhaps you'll escape the gallows." Rising, Stokes spoke to the sergeants. "Take him to the cells and tell the duty-sergeant I'll file the papers later today."

Barnaby led the way out of the interrogation room; Stokes joined him, and Montague followed.

They didn't say anything until they were in Stokes's office, sitting around his desk.

Barnaby met Stokes's eyes. "He's not the murderer."

Stokes grimaced. "No, he's not."

Montague was nodding. "But . . . where does that leave us?" He looked at Stokes, then at Barnaby. "What do we do next?"

Stokes blew out a breath. "Next, we make sure he's told us the truth. I'll get his alibis checked and search his room—not just to retrieve the money but also to see if he has a key to the side door of the Lowndes Street house."

"I'd better assist with the latter." Barnaby met Stokes's eyes. "We'll have to inform the Camberlys just what their son has been up to."

Stokes shook his head. "With families like this . . . it's as if a rot got in at some point, and then it spreads, not just through one generation but into the next as well." He noticed Montague's frowning, somewhat distant expression. "What about you?"

Montague met his gaze, then arched his brows. "Runcorn was murdered. When one considers the matter, killing Runcorn was far more risky for the murderer than his killing of either Lady Halstead or Tilly—and yet Runcorn was indeed murdered, almost certainly by the same man. Yet the only motive I can see for murdering Runcorn is the same motive we've had all along—the concealment of something in the accounts."

Barnaby was nodding. "We thought the mystery payments into Lady Halstead's bank account was that something, but if, as seems to be the case, it isn't that—"

"Then there must be something else." Montague lifted his hat from the corner of Stokes's desk. "I'm going to go back to my office and think about what else might be hidden in her ladyship's, or, more likely, the estate's, accounts—and what the fastest way to uncover it will be."

"Adair. Inspector." Standing behind the desk in his study, Wallace Camberly nodded to both men, then waved to two chairs set before the desk. "Please be seated."

They'd only just settled when the door opened and Cynthia Camberly came in. They all rose again as she shut the door and came to join them.

"Gentlemen." She eyed them curiously, then glanced at her husband.

Camberly waved her to an armchair to one side of the desk. As she moved to take it, he looked at Stokes. "I hope, gentlemen, that this won't take long." As they sat once more, Camberly continued, "As I daresay you know, Parliament is exceedingly busy at this time."

Cynthia leaned forward. "I take it you have news?"

"As to that"—Stokes made a show of consulting the notebook he'd drawn from his pocket—"with regard to your son, Walter Camberly—"

"Walter's out of town, visiting friends." When Stokes glanced up, Cynthia caught his gaze and smiled, although the gesture came nowhere near her eyes. "If there's been some question about his alibis, I'm sure I can help."

Stokes held her gaze for an extended moment, then transferred his attention to Camberly. "Mr. Adair and I have come to inform you that, as of last night, your son, Walter Camberly, has been taken into police custody. He is charged with crimes relating to the abduction of at least seven girls, their subsequent imprisonment at the house known as The Laurels, in Noak Hill in Essex, a house owned by the late Lady Halstead, and with the attempted sale of said girls into prostitution, along with several other crimes relating to those activities." Stokes paused to take in Camberly's stunned, utterly stupefied expression, then glanced at Cynthia—and saw the same reaction, but also desperate calculation already emerging. Looking back at his notebook, he continued, "Your son has admitted to all the crimes with which he is presently charged."

Cynthia's face contorted, but as if she was suppressing some scornful outburst rather than in any form of sympathy or concern.

"Good *God*," Wallace finally got out. He all but goggled. "Do you mean to say he's the murderer? That he murdered his own grandmother?"

"We are presently checking his alibis for the nights in question." Stokes turned to Cynthia. "If you have any information regarding your son's whereabouts on those nights, ma'am, it would be best to tell me now."

Cynthia's eyes fractionally widened as she sat back, sat straighter. Her gaze shifted, rapidly passing from her husband, to Barnaby, then to Stokes, and back again—then she drew in a deep breath and held it for a second before saying, "I'm sorry, Inspector. I had thought I knew, but clearly"—she gestured—"I have no idea what my son has been about."

Stokes paused to let the echo of her earlier comment color the silence, then he inclined his head. "If you say so, ma'am."

No doubt scenting the subtle threat, Camberly stirred. "I'm sorry, Inspector, but you have to forgive me—indeed, us—if we appear somewhat discombobulated. We are, of course, totally dumbfounded by your news." Reaching out, Camberly closed one hand about one of his wife's and squeezed—in comfort, or as a signal? "We had no idea Walter was involved in any less-than-acceptable activity, much less anything illegal—indeed, criminal."

"Much less murder." Cynthia straightened, her back now poker-straight, her head held high. She'd patently decided that outraged matriarch was the most appropriate role for her to play. "I am shocked and saddened beyond measure, Inspector. To think that we have nurtured such a fiend, one who has murdered and committed such unspeakable crimes . . ." She glanced briefly at Camberly, then went on, "We can only pray that you will find your final proofs quickly, and that the matter can be dealt with as expeditiously as possible—this is going to be such a difficult time for the family. All the family. And all on top of Mama's murder, too."

Barnaby wasn't at all surprised when, leaving one hand in Camberly's clasp, with her other, Cynthia pulled a lace-edged handkerchief from her pocket and, bowing her head, touched the lace beneath her eyes. Dry though Barnaby would swear those eyes were.

Wallace shifted, drawing Barnaby's and Stokes's attention from the not-so-convincing show. "Is there anything more we can help you with, gentlemen? As my wife intimated, while the situation wounds us deeply, we, of course, hold ourselves ready to assist in whatever way we can."

Stokes nodded. "We need to search Walter's room. Other than that"—tucking his notebook back into his pocket, Stokes rose—"I don't believe we require anything further from you or Mrs. Camberly at this point."

Barnaby got to his feet, as did Camberly.

Camberly glanced at Cynthia, still seated with head bowed. "I'm busy at the moment, but my wife, I'm sure, will show you to Walter's room."

Cynthia raised her head, her face a mask of martyred duty. "Yes, of course." She rose and waved to the door. "Come this way, Inspector. Mr. Adair."

418 · STEPHANIE LAURENS

With nods to Camberly, Stokes and Barnaby followed Cynthia from the room and back into the front hall.

As they climbed the stairs behind her, she stated, "I am devastated, of course, but, in hindsight, Walter was always a secretive child, very quiet about his own actions. We had no inkling whatever of these hideous activities of his." Gaining the first floor, she turned and led the way through a short gallery and on down a corridor. "Obviously, there's nothing my husband or I can do to in any way put right the damage Walter has done." Pausing outside a door, her hand on the knob, she swung to face them. "I can only pray, Inspector, that justice is served swiftly, and the damage to the Camberly name, and, indeed, that of the Halsteads, is minimized. There is, after all, no need for Walter's trial to cause pain and harm to those who, through no fault of theirs, share his name but were entirely innocent of all knowledge of his crimes."

She blinked, then her hard gaze fixed on Stokes's face. "If I understood you correctly, Inspector, Walter has admitted to the bulk of your charges. Presumably, there's no reason he can't appear before a judge and be sentenced in camera, as it were."

"As to that, ma'am, I'm sure I can't say. That will be a matter for the judge."

"I see. But if that were to come to pass, and Walter was dealt with adequately and removed, and you had proof of his guilt with respect to the murders, would there be any further need for another trial to settle the matter of the murders? You would already have dealt with the murderer—he would be transported, after all, would he not?"

Stokes remained silent; he honestly didn't know how best to respond—wasn't sure whether he could while remaining appropriately polite.

Barnaby stirred. "Again, ma'am, that's a decision for the judiciary, rather than the police."

Cynthia nodded. "Very well." Opening the door, she set it swinging wide. "Search as you will, gentlemen." She glanced once around the room. "Please remove anything you wish to preserve. After you've finished, we'll be burning everything."

Barnaby and Stokes stood back to let Cynthia leave; they watched as, walking swiftly, she returned to the stairs, then disappeared down them.

Stokes glanced at Barnaby. "I've never seen anyone disowned so quickly—or so ruthlessly. I wouldn't have thought it possible, but I actually feel almost sorry for Walter."

Barnaby nodded. "Indeed." He met Stokes's eyes. "Lovely family."

Montague joined the group of five he now regarded as his colleagues-in-investigation at the Adairs' house for dinner that evening. Penelope had intended the dinner to be a celebration of their success, but, instead, they were all in a most peculiar mood—elated on the one hand, and disgruntled and deflated on the other.

"Walter is not the murderer." Stokes sank into an armchair in the drawing room, a glass of Barnaby's brandy in one hand.

After their initial exchange of disappointing information when they'd first gathered in the drawing room, they'd decided to postpone further discussion of the murders until after they'd eaten and their minds had had time to digest what they'd learned.

Stokes swirled the amber liquid in his glass. "We found the money—all of it—exactly where Walter said it would be, and although we searched every nook and cranny in that room, we didn't find any key to Lady Halstead's house." He sipped, then went on, "And while I haven't yet checked the alibis he's now given us, those new alibis are detailed and, more, perfectly fit his story. Everything he's told us hangs together as one cohesive whole—and that whole does not include the murders."

Barnaby nodded. "I agree. And as Walter himself pointed out, he had no reason to murder Lady Halstead, and every reason not to. Her dying only further inconvenienced him by forcing him to stop using The Laurels."

Violet sighed. "So Walter as the murderer makes no sense."

Penelope pulled a horrendous face. After a moment, she said, "I hate to point this out, but we haven't simply eliminated Walter as the murderer—we've also lost our motive. Walter and his doings have accounted for everything *except* the murders. Everything about the odd deposits into Lady Halstead's accounts is now fully explained, as is the withdrawal of the money from that account. So the murders were never to do with that money." She looked around the circle of faces—at Barnaby, Stokes, Griselda, Violet, and Montague. "So what was the motive for the murders?"

Stokes glanced at Montague. "Any hints yet?"

"Yes and no." When Penelope, Griselda, and Violet all turned questioning faces his way, Montague explained, "If we go back and eliminate the odd payments from our deliberations, then regardless, we had assumed that Lady Halstead was murdered because someone in her family did not want her looking too closely into her financial affairs. That deduction still stands, and the motive behind the murderer's actions has been to compromise any detailed financial review by killing Lady Halstead, and then Runcorn, the two people most familiar with the estate—and we have reason to believe that Runcorn's murderer was one of the Halstead men."

"We now know," Barnaby said, "that it wasn't Walter."

Stokes nodded. "If we eliminate him, pending his alibis proving true, then that leaves Mortimer, Maurice, William, and Hayden. My men are still checking their alibis, none of which have proved straightforward bar William's, and even his are questionable, not good enough to eliminate him."

"Are you saying"—Violet looked at Montague—"that there's something *else,* some evidence of some financial crime, buried in her ladyship's or the estate's accounts? Something Mortimer, Maurice, William, or Hayden might have killed to conceal?"

Montague nodded. "Most likely it's something to do with the estate. Lady Halstead, and even Tilly, might have been murdered for other reasons, but there's simply no reason to kill a man-of-business, especially not one as relatively unacquainted with his client as young Runcorn was, unless there is, indeed, *something* hidden in the accounts. Something that would have been uncovered during an extensive review—possibly something Lady Halstead would have known to question. And no"—Montague glanced at Penelope—"as yet I have no idea what that something might be."

Penelope sighed heavily.

Griselda eyed her friend, then glanced at the others. "The girls we rescued last night have all settled in with Mrs. Quiverstone and her people at the Athena Agency. Mrs. Quiverstone is sure they'll be able to find suitable and safe employment for all the girls."

"I had no idea such places existed," Violet said.

"Oh, the Athena Agency has been in business for . . . well, it must be nearly two decades now." Montague glanced at Violet and smiled. "I recall being consulted over it by Deverell before he married his wife—Miss Phoebe Malleson, as she then was. It was she and her aunt who founded the agency, and it's now supported by quite a large network of fashionable households."

Reaching out, Stokes linked the fingers of one hand with Griselda's. "Despite not having yet caught our murderer, we shouldn't lose sight of what would otherwise rank as a signal success." His gaze traveling the group, touching on each face, he raised his glass. "To us, to the girls we've rescued, to the good we've done, to the villains we have succeeded in putting behind bars."

"Hear, hear," Barnaby said, raising his glass in response.

The others drank, then all lowered their glasses.

A short silence followed, then Penelope said, "All right. Now let's find the murderer."

Chapter 15

The following morning, as soon as the last member of his staff had come through the door of Montague and Son, Montague called everyone into his office and explained his current thinking regarding the Halstead file.

"So," he concluded, "we need to ascertain if any documents are missing, and if none are, we'll need to cross-check everything to determine if there's some other irregularity."

"But there has to be, doesn't there?" Gibbons said from the chair beside Montague's desk. "If, as you say, Runcorn was murdered because of something to do with the accounts, then somewhere buried in all of that"—Gibbons nodded at the three large piles of documents sitting on Montague's desk, the accumulated financial records of the Halsteads—"there must be some trace, some clue. No matter if the murderer did attempt to remove the evidence, no matter how thorough he thought he was, unless he was a man-of-business, too, he would have overlooked something."

Phillip Foster nodded. "Quite a challenge, even for one of us, to eradicate all sign, all the footprints of any particular transaction." Raising his gaze from the piles of documents, he met Montague's. "So where are we at present with our searching?"

Montague glanced at Pringle.

Pringle grimaced self-deprecatingly. "I'm still less than halfway through reassembling the main file. I've been working backward, but thus far I haven't found any document that's missing."

Slocum looked at Montague. "So where would you like us to start, sir?"

Montague considered, then said, "Let's see what we can accomplish today. I need you and Foster to take on as much of our scheduled work as possible. Gibbons and I will need to attend any meetings we have scheduled, but beyond that . . ." Montague considered the stack of papers, then said, "Pringle can continue reassembling the file, searching for any missing document, working backward. Mr. Slater?"

Montague's junior clerk straightened, his expression eager. "Yes, sir?"

"You will watch Mr. Pringle until you have the knack of what he is doing, how his numbering system works, then, under Mr. Slocum's oversight, in the time in which he doesn't require your services, you will commence reassembling the file, but working from the earliest documents forward." Montague looked at Slocum and Pringle. "At this point, we have no notion of when in the timeline of the Halstead documents the vital clue resides, so by having Slater work through the documents from the other end, as it were, we should double our chances of discovering if any documents are missing, and subsequently which documents they are."

Slocum, Pringle, and Slater all nodded.

Montague glanced at Foster. "Your first task, along with Slocum, is to keep the office functioning as usual, servicing all our other clients."

Foster grinned and saluted.

"If you have any time left over after that, you can help Gibbons compile a complete listing of the Halsteads' investments, past as well as present." Montague glanced at Gibbons. "Fred, you'll have to work with the file as Pringle reassembles it, and also with the earlier documents as Slater gets those in order."

Gibbons nodded. "How detailed a list?"

"Everything you stumble on, regardless of whether it paid a dividend, was sold at a profit or a loss, or was simply held and forgotten about. Cross-check with the bank accounts, all of them." Montague paused, then added, "Given there's nothing obvious about this—given we have no idea what particular investment or even type of investment, or style of fund or instrument, was of interest to our murderer—then we have to cover absolutely everything. Something that may appear minor and of no real account to us might, for reasons we do not know, be of vital importance to him."

"Right then." Gibbons rose. "I'd better get started."

"So what angle will you be tackling, sir?" Foster asked as he straightened away from the bookshelf he'd been leaning against.

Montague hid a wry smile; Phillip Foster was keen and eager to learn, something Montague was happy to encourage. "I'm going to work my way through the copies of the documents Runcorn had Pringle make for me. Those copied documents should at least touch on all the active sources of income to the Halstead estate." He paused, then explained, "What I identify through income and expenditure should reconcile with what Gibbons and you put together. If we come up with any anomaly, then we'll be on to something. But it's possible we'll end with a complete match, in which case, it'll come down to whether Pringle and Slater find something missing. Essentially, I will be working on the money itself, while you and Gibbons identify the sources, and Slocum, Pringle, and Slater will analyze the documentary records. Somewhere in all that, there has to be something missing."

"Indeed." With a nod, Gibbons led the way out.

Slocum, Pringle, and Slater gathered the three large piles of documents in their arms and carried them back out into the main office.

Leaving Montague considering the smaller pile thus revealed—the copies Runcorn had had Pringle make for him. That pile might have been smaller than the others; regardless, combing through it wouldn't be any small task, especially as he had no idea what he might be looking for.

Glancing at his appointment book, he confirmed he had a morning meeting with the Earl of Meredith, who was currently in town. As the earl spent most of his time at his estate in Somerset, that wasn't an appointment that could easily be rescheduled.

Montague glanced at the pile of documents on his desk, then, with an inward sigh, rose, lifted his hat from the hat stand, plucked the current Meredith file from his shelves—he'd already reviewed it—and headed for the door.

He returned two hours later, unexpectedly more enthused. Hanging up his hat, then replacing the Meredith file—there had been no surprises there—he returned to his desk. Looking down at the Halstead papers, he went over the plan of attack that had popped into his head as he'd traveled back from Mayfair. The approach was sound. Reaching for the pile, he set it squarely on his blotter, pulled up his chair, sat, and proceeded to sort the documents.

Distantly, he heard the main door to the offices open. An instant later, Slocum said, "Good morning, Miss Matcham. Can I help you?"

Before he'd even thought, Montague was on his feet and striding to the door, propelled by a species of fizzy emotion he'd never felt before. To his rational mind's surprise, he rather liked the feeling. Passing into the outer office, he saw Violet smiling at Slocum.

As he crossed the room, she turned to him and her smile changed—to something warmer, more personal. More for him.

"Miss Matcham. Violet." He took the hand she extended, held it. His gaze searched her face; from the calmness investing her features, he knew there was nothing wrong. "Has there been some development?"

"No." A faint frown swam through her fine eyes. "And that's why I'm here." She glanced around the office, at the evidence of their industry. "Stokes and Barnaby are off checking the men's alibis, and Penelope and Griselda are doing the same with the ladies—we thought it wise to be complete. But"—she raised her hands, palms up—"that left me with nothing to do, no way to contribute." She brought her gaze back to his face. "So I thought I would come here and see whether there's anything I can do to help you with your researches." She paused, then, head rising a trifle, said, "I've acted as a secretary for all my adult life, so I am good at reading and organizing documents."

Montague immediately saw opportunity and moved to seize it. "As it happens"—he waved at the rest of the office, at all his staff, most of whom had glanced up to exchange a smile with her—"I have all these others working in teams, tackling the problem from different angles. I've just returned from a meeting and was about to start on my own pile of documents." When her gaze returned to his face, he met her eyes. "I was going to handle it on my own, but coming back just now I realized there are two separate aspects, two different arms that I need to concurrently investigate—you could help me with one of those if you like?"

Her smile blossomed into delight, and she inclined her head. "I would be happy to assist."

Ignoring the interested, faintly intrigued, looks from his staff, reining in his own smile as best he could, he ushered Violet into his office. After helping her remove her coat and hanging her bonnet opposite his hat on the hat stand, he settled her in a chair on the client side of his desk and cleared a space on its surface for her.

"Right, then." Rounding the desk, he opened a drawer and retrieved several sheets of paper, as well as a handful of the sharpened pencils Slocum made sure were always there. Dividing the supplies between Violet's impromptu blotter and his own, he sat in his chair and faced the Halstead papers anew. Then he looked at Violet, met her encouraging gaze. "These documents are the copies Runcorn sent me. They should contain information on all the dealings required to generate a comprehensive review of the Halstead estate—the financial side of it, certainly. What we—you and I—need to do is list every item of income and every item of expenditure, and link each to a specific source. Gibbons out there, aided by Foster, is combing through the original documents and making a list of all the investments—the sources."

"So Gibbons's list and ours should match?" Violet asked.

"Exactly."

"And if they don't . . . then whatever point on which they don't match will be a clue?" When Montague nodded, Violet felt a surge of enthusiasm buoy her. Straightening the sheet of paper before her, she picked up a pencil. "So"—she met Montague's eyes—"where do we start?"

He hesitated for only an instant. "You can list the income—that's actually easier than determining what an expense might be. I'll take care of the expenses." Picking up the document on the top of the pile, he glanced at it, then replaced it and turned the entire pile upside down. "Pringle reordered these for me, and he put the most recent on top. For our purposes, it'll be easier to work from the earliest records on. So." Lifting the top sheet, he turned it over and handed it to her. "You start. Scan each document for any information on income. Whatever you find, note it down—where it was from, the date, and the amount—then hand the document on to me."

Taking the sheet, Violet scanned it. It was the receipt for a deposit into a fund made by Sir Hugo over three decades previously. "No income here." She handed the document to Montague.

He scanned it and smiled. "Correct." He reached for his pencil and nodded at the pile in the center of the desk. "Help yourself."

Feeling happily involved, Violet did.

They worked steadily through the papers. Mr. Slocum brought them tea and small cakes, which proved to be surprisingly delicious.

"There's a tiny bakery tucked away at the end of Chapel Court," Montague said in response to her query.

Licking crumbs from her fingers, Violet nodded and returned to the statement she was perusing. She felt no inhibition over asking questions, checking when an entry wasn't, at least to her, clearly income or expense. The further through the pile they worked, the more she understood the purpose of what they were doing.

Income and expenditure. When it came down to it, that was all money truly was. All it meant.

When the City's bells tolled twelve, Montague rose, went into the outer office to consult with his staff, then came back to inform her he'd sent his young clerk, Mr. Slater, and the office boy, Reginald Roberts, for sandwiches for the whole office.

Violet approved. "There is something of a sense of urgency, isn't there?"

Dropping back into his chair, Montague nodded. "Indeed." He didn't add that, for him, the thrust of that urgency derived from his fear that, in seeking to protect himself, the murderer would continue to seek to silence Violet. Not for one moment had Montague forgotten the chill he'd felt when he'd learned that her bedroom door, too, had been opened on the night the blackguard had killed Tilly. He'd come to kill Violet, too, but had been thwarted.

The only way to permanently thwart such a villain was to expose him and catch him.

Lifting the next sheet he needed to scrutinize for expenses, he returned to that task.

The sandwiches came and were consumed in a silence broken only by the occasional rustle of paper.

Just before three o'clock, Gibbons tapped on the door frame and entered, carrying a sheaf of papers in one hand. He raised the papers. "All the investments and every last source of income. Foster and I have been through all the documents. Slocum, Pringle, and Slater have nearly met—they say they need another hour or two, but they will get the entire file re-sorted by day's end."

"Excellent." Montague considered the documents he and Violet had yet to assess. With her helping, the pile had dwindled at literally twice the rate it would have had he had to do it on his own. "Another half hour, and we should be done." He glanced at Gibbons. "I'll call you when we are, then you and Foster can read through your list, while Violet and I check to confirm that we've got the expected income and expenses."

Gibbons nodded. "Call when you're ready. I've got a meeting at five o'clock—I'll be preparing for that, but there's not much I need to do for it."

Montague nodded and turned back to his task with renewed mental vigor; reaching the end of his analysis of the Halstead accounts by the close of the day was a very real carrot.

Finally—*finally*—he slapped the last of the documents back on the pile. "Done!" He looked up at Violet; after finishing with the last document and handing it on to him, she'd risen, stretched, and walked over to look out of the window.

Turning to him, she smiled. "Now what?"

"Now . . ." He looked at the sheaf of papers stacked on her side of the desk and waggled his fingers. "Let's see what you've got."

What she had was a neat list, ranging over several pages, of sources of income with the relevant amounts and dates of payment noted against each. And she'd organized the sources in alphabetical order.

As he'd done the same with the expenses—the original and any subsequent costs for each investment—it was easy to align their lists. "Wonderful." Standing, he lifted the original pile of copied documents they'd worked through and carried them to a chest nearby. "Let's get these out of the way." Returning to his desk, he picked up his listing of expenses and laid the pages out, from A to Z, across his side of the desk. Then he interspersed Violet's somewhat larger set of pages so that the income derived from each source lay next to the purchase and subsequent expenses for that source.

He surveyed the result with considerable satisfaction. Coming around the desk, Violet joined him. Glancing at her face, he saw much the same emotion reflected there. His lips curved and he looked back at their combined efforts. It was refreshing to discover that her mind was as tidy as his, that she took a similar delight in bringing order to complex matters.

"Now!" Turning, he strode to the door and looked out. "Fred? Phillip, if you're free. Let's see what we've got."

Gibbons and Foster came in, both eager to assess the results of their labors. At Montague's suggestion, the two men took the chairs on the client's side of his desk, while he positioned a deeper armchair for Violet alongside his admiral's chair.

Gibbons had picked up the lists he and Foster had assembled. "So how do you want to do this?"

"Start at the earliest record we have," Montague said. "We'll work forward from there."

The first investment Sir Hugo had made dated back more than thirty years. Gibbons read out the name, and Montague confirmed the expense, ticked it off, then crossed to Violet's accompanying list and read out the income. All agreed the income was as expected, and Montague then ticked that off, too.

They proceeded through the years of Sir Hugo's investment life, steadily ticking off the entries as they verified them. Initially, the investments were modest, and few and far between, but in the latter two decades of his life, Sir Hugo had been very much more active. "That was when he returned from overseas," Violet said.

They'd accounted for the investments made up to 1823 when Gibbons paused to note, "Actually, this is building into quite a nice portfolio—Runcorn Senior did well by Sir Hugo."

Montague nodded. "Indeed. Very sound, and with just the right amount of speculation for that style of client." He saw Phillip Foster taking mental note.

They continued on through more investments, many more in each successive year, in all cases verifying the purchase and the resulting income. They reached the year of Sir Hugo's death, and the number of new investments dramatically decreased, but Runcorn Senior had clearly continued to wisely advise Lady Halstead, and, each year, she had added a few new items to the portfolio.

"All very solid," Gibbons murmured. They continued cross-checking and verifying each investment, its purchase price and the income paid. Nothing was out of order; no alarm bells rang.

Until they reached 1833 and Gibbons read, "A parcel of twenty shares in the Grand Junction Railway."

Violet watched as Montague scanned his sheets. Sir Hugo had made a significant investment in the Liverpool and Manchester Railway in 1826, and that had been paying quite a nice income since the railway had opened in 1830; it was no great surprise to discover that Lady Halstead had bought shares in a second railway.

Pencil halting over an entry, Montague nodded and read out a sum.

"That's correct," Phillip Foster confirmed.

"And . . ." Montague tracked across to Violet's listing of income. And frowned.

Thinking back, Violet frowned, too. She leaned forward and looked at what she'd listed under the sources starting with *G.* Frown deepening, she said, "I thought I heard that the Grand Junction Railway opened earlier this year." She looked at Montague. "Perhaps they haven't made any payments as yet?"

Montague continued to stare at the sheets. "But they have." Raising his head, he looked at Gibbons. "And a very nice dividend it was."

Eyes widening, Gibbons nodded. "August, wasn't it? Unexpectedly large."

Montague pushed back his chair and rose. Retrieving the Meredith file he'd recently returned to the shelf, he opened the ledger, flicked through the pages, then, finger on the relevant entry, nodded. "Yes. It paid a very large dividend in late August this year, eight weeks after opening. Those shares should be returning . . . a very large amount."

Both Gibbons and Foster sat up, focused and ready to pounce. Montague held up a staying hand. "Before we get too excited, we should check that Runcorn, thorough though he appears to have been, didn't simply miss putting that page into the pile to be copied for me."

Returning the Meredith file to its place on his shelves, he led the way into the outer office. Gibbons and Foster followed close behind. Montague glanced back and saw Violet on her feet; across the office he met her eyes, smiled, and nodded. She had, after all, been instrumental in getting them to this point.

Reaching the long table Slocum, Pringle, and Slater had commandeered, spreading the pages of the huge file out across the surface so they could steadily add to their ordered piles, Montague halted, and, when the three glanced up at him, said, "We're looking for a statement of income, a dividend which should have been paid into the Halstead estate somewhere—we don't know to which account—in late August this year."

Slater, seated at one end of the table with three neat piles of documents before him, peered over them at Pringle, at the table's other end. "You should have that."

Already searching through one of the two piles before him, Pringle nodded. "This August . . ." Carefully, he drew out a small stack of papers from toward the very bottom of one pile. He held it out to Montague. "This is what we have for August this year."

"Barring anything still left in the mess." Slocum reached for the now very much smaller melee of papers in the middle of the table, those yet to be correctly re-filed by their dates. Picking up a handful, Slocum quickly checked the dates.

Pringle grabbed another handful, as did Slater.

Spurred by the hope that they'd finally stumbled onto something, Gibbons and Foster joined them.

Montague, meanwhile, stepped back from the fray, the already ordered documents for August in his hand. Waving Violet, who had hung back, to join him, he retreated to Foster's nearby desk. With Violet's help, he checked over those documents . . . and found nothing to indicate that any income had been paid to the Halstead estate from the Grand Junction Railway Company.

Meeting Violet's gaze, he saw the speculation rising in her eyes.

"Have we found it?" she asked.

He pressed his lips tight but couldn't quite suppress his excitement. "We might have."

Turning, they watched as, one after the other, the rest of his staff set down the papers they held. The last to do so was Slater. Looking up, he met the others' gazes and shook his head. "Nothing."

Everyone turned to Montague.

Returning to the table, he handed the papers he and Violet had checked back to Pringle. "There's nothing here, either. So . . ." He met Gibbons's gaze. "It appears that the Halsteads haven't been paid for their shares in the Grand Junction Railway. Our next step is to locate the share certificate." He looked at Pringle. "Do you know who held their certificates—was it Runcorn, or did Sir Hugo keep them?"

Pringle blinked, then he rose. "One moment." Going to his desk, he pulled out a drawer and lifted from it a small black notebook. "I took this from Mr. Runcorn's office, because without it . . . well, no one would know what was where."

Opening it, he flicked through the pages. Slocum, curious, went to look over his shoulder.

"Here it is," Pringle said. "The Halsteads." He ran his finger down the page, then stopped. "It says here that Sir Hugo kept his share certificates."

Montague frowned. "Does it say if he kept them at his bank, or at his home?"

"It doesn't say," Pringle reported.

"Try some of the other entries," Slocum suggested.

Pringle flicked slowly through several more pages. "Ah, yes—this is mostly notes from the older Mr. Runcorn, but he does say for others 'kept in bank.'"

Montague nodded. "So we can assume, therefore, that Sir Hugo kept his share certificates at home." He looked at Violet. "Have you any idea where? Was there a safe?"

She shook her head. "No safe, of that I'm sure. But . . ." She frowned. "What do share certificates look like?"

Montague held up a finger, asking her to wait. He strode into his office. Through the open doorway, she saw him walk to a section of bookshelves, press some spot, then swing the bookcase back to reveal a very large wall safe. The door was the size of a room door. Montague quickly spun dials, then turned the handle and pulled open the heavy door. He stepped into the dim space beyond but almost immediately reappeared, a stack of papers in his hand.

Returning and halting beside her, he showed her the papers. They were somewhat larger than bank notes but were covered in much the same elaborate writing and had a seal attached. "These," he said, fanning the papers, showing her various different styles, "are share certificates. They constitute proof of ownership."

Reaching out a hand, Violet ran her fingers across the papers. "Oh, I recognize these. I know where Lady Halstead kept them." She met Montague's eyes. "They're in the locked middle drawer of the chest of drawers in her bedroom."

Montague didn't look impressed. He glanced at his staff. "I'll need witnesses for this. Fred—you have your meeting. Pringle—you should come. And Foster, if you're free?"

Both Foster and Pringle were eager to assist.

Violet hurried back into Montague's office, donning her coat and tying on her bonnet as Montague, who had followed her, returned the share certificates to the safe, closed and locked it, and swung the bookcase back. Then he shrugged into his greatcoat, picked up his hat, and retrieved the keys to the Lowndes Street house from his desk drawer.

A minute later, he guided her out of the office and down the stairs to the street, Foster and Pringle following close behind.

The house in Lowndes Street was as dismal and chilly as the last time she'd been there, but Violet barely registered the gloomy atmosphere. Having let them in via the front door, Montague waited only until Pringle shut it behind them before waving her up the stairs.

She led the way to the first floor and Lady Halstead's bedroom. Entering, she went straight to the chest of drawers.

"The lock," Montague said.

She threw him a look, pulled out the small drawer that formed the base of the mirror sitting atop the chest, reached inside, and drew out a small key.

Montague looked disgusted. As she fitted the key into the lock in the middle drawer of the three that formed the top level of the large chest, he glanced at Foster. "*That's* why I do not allow my clients to keep their own share certificates unless they possess a safe."

Stifling a smile, very conscious of the excitement bubbling through her veins, Violet turned the key, heard the lock click open, then she tugged on the round wooden handle, and slid the drawer out.

Everyone crowded around to peer inside.

Three thick rolls of share certificates, each tied with a ribbon, lay neatly aligned, filling the bottom of the drawer. "Well," Montague said, studying the evidence, "we knew Sir Hugo had purchased lots of shares."

Reaching inside, he lifted out the three rolls, confirming just how thick each was. "Going through these is going to take time." He met Violet's gaze. "I'll be taking these with me when we leave—they are far too valuable to be left in an empty house. Close the drawer, and let's go downstairs."

She did, and they did; repairing to the dining room, they used the table to unroll and spread out the certificates. Pringle commandeered the salt cellars and some cutlery to act as paperweights.

They searched through one roll, then the second, and finally the third.

Montague laid the last certificate down. "No certificate for those Grand Junction Railway Company shares."

After a moment, he looked at Foster and Pringle. "Gather these up and take them back to the office. Pringle, I want you and Slocum to take an official inventory before Slocum locks them away, then, Foster, you can check the inventory against the list you and Gibbons prepared. If you find any further discrepancy, send word to me at Albemarle Street."

"Yes, sir." Both Foster and Pringle started to gather the certificates.

Montague rose and drew back Violet's chair.

She searched his eyes. "Where are we going?"

Montague met her gaze. "To tell Stokes, and the others, too. This is far too important for them not to know."

At eleven o'clock the next morning, Montague left his office and took a hackney to Albemarle Street.

On leaving the Lowndes Street house the previous afternoon, he and Violet had gone to Scotland Yard, but Stokes and Barnaby had been out; Stokes's sergeant had recognized Montague and told him that Stokes had said that he and Adair would be visiting various locales to check Walter Camberly's alibis.

Denied the most appropriate outlet for their building excitement, Montague and Violet had headed for Albemarle Street. There, they'd had to wait for Penelope and Griselda, who had earlier returned from an outing aimed at verifying the alibis of the Halstead and Camberly ladies, but had subsequently taken their children for an airing in Grosvenor Square. Rather than chase after them, Violet had suggested a late afternoon tea; suddenly realizing he'd been famished, Montague had agreed. They'd sat in the pleasant parlor and sipped and nibbled, and he had started to think through his next steps aloud.

Then Penelope and Griselda had arrived; not having any news of their own to impart, they'd been keen and eager to hear what Montague and Violet had together discovered.

Immediately grasping the significance, Penelope had sent a summons to Stokes and her husband, enticingly stating that a breakthrough had occurred and that they needed to return to Albemarle Street forthwith to learn its substance.

Then, of course, the four of them had had to wait with mounting impatience for Stokes and Adair to arrive. Once they had . . .

In the end, they'd all stayed to dine, the discussion over the dinner table rife with supposition, hypothesis, and suggestions as to how they might best proceed. Everyone had agreed that the missing share certificate was a major clue and that they needed to learn who presently held it—who had received the recent large dividend—with all possible speed, but at that point, the group had divided into three camps. Stokes and Penelope had been all for barreling ahead regardless of how much noise and dust they raised. Montague and Barnaby, however, had urged caution and care in taking their next steps, while Violet and Griselda had sat back

448 · STEPHANIE LAURENS

and weighed the merits of both arguments. Ultimately, it had been agreed that, despite the acknowledged urgency over identifying the villain—already a murderer three times over—before he either murdered again or, alternatively, fled, caution and circumspection were nevertheless required in dealing with such a matter.

As Barnaby had said, "The police marching into a share registry and demanding to see their books—even assuming you can—will only cause outrage and resistance on many fronts, none of which are pertinent to this investigation, and none of which will help us in the least."

Montague had nodded. "Indeed. It may not seem so, but in such a case, asking one question at a time will get us further faster, without unnecessarily raising anyone's hackles or alerting anyone beyond the most discreet officials to our inquiries."

Reluctantly, the others had agreed and had left it to him to formulate and ask the questions about the shares.

Meanwhile, Stokes and Barnaby would pursue the alibis of Walter and the Halstead men, while Penelope, accompanied by Griselda, would confirm Constance Halstead's, Caroline Halstead's, and Cynthia Camberly's alibis, purely to ensure they hadn't missed some connection.

As Stokes had somewhat grimly growled, "After this business with Walter, I wouldn't be surprised if we found some other irregularity within that family, something else that has nothing to do with the murders."

That comment had strengthened the argument for care in pursuing the question of the missing share certificate. Once burned, twice shy; they had no reason to feel certain that the missing share certificate was, indeed, the critical issue behind the murders.

Of course, they all believed it was, but . . . pedantic caution and care had become their new watchwords.

The hackney rocked around a corner. Glancing through the window, Montague saw the familiar façade of Carlton House roll by, then the hackney headed smartly down Pall Mall.

He'd spent the last hours identifying the firm that held the registry for the Grand Junction Railway Company shares. Unhappily, that firm was located in Manchester; he'd drafted a formal query and had sent it off by courier. He couldn't expect to hear back until at least the next day.

Now, as he'd promised, he was reporting his progress to Albemarle Street—to Violet, who had been designated their central contact. Although none of the others had voiced their concern, no one had wanted Violet to go out of the house alone.

The simple fact that she—and, it seemed, no one else still alive bar the murderer—had known where Lady Halstead's share certificates had been kept had escalated their fears for her safety. Montague's fears, certainly, and he'd seen a similar understanding in Stokes's, Adair's, Penelope's, and Griselda's eyes. None of them wished Violet to come to any harm; none of them wanted her to be unwittingly exposed to the murderer. If they could have, they would have hemmed her in with protections, but they were all rather too intelligent for that. Instead, they'd crafted a role for her that would keep her safely within the Adairs' house, and Montague would have wagered his last guinea that Adair's staff had been alerted to watch over her.

Montague was therefore unsurprised when, having climbed down from the hackney, paid the jarvey, and ascended the steps to the Adairs' door, he was admitted by their majordomo, Mostyn, who greeted him with a knowing smile and the words "Miss Matcham is in the parlor, sir."

"Thank you, Mostyn." Handing over his hat and cane, Montague settled his cuffs. "No need to show me in—I know the way."

"Indeed, sir." Mostyn hesitated.

Montague cast him a questioning look.

"I was just thinking, sir," Mostyn said, "that if you were so inclined, you might escort Miss Matcham for a walk in the park. Don't want her feeling cooped up and deciding to go for a walk on her own."

Montague arched his brows. "No, indeed." He inclined his head. "Thank you for the suggestion, Mostyn. I believe I will take it up."

As he walked down the corridor to the parlor, Montague noted that although the weather had been somewhat dismal of late, today the sun was doing its best to make an appearance, and there seemed little imminent threat of precipitation.

Violet was seated on one of the sofas plying her needle on some mending; she'd heard his footsteps and looked up. The expression that suffused her face, that lit her eyes, made him feel . . . special. Setting aside the mending, she rose. Smiling, she held out a hand. "Mr. Montague."

As, halting before her, he closed his hand about her fingers, she studied his face. "Do you have news, sir?"

It wasn't his news, or the investigation, that filled his mind. He looked down at her for several seconds, then quietly said, "My given name is Heathcote, although most call me Montague." Indeed, there was no one still alive who called him Heathcote. "I wonder, Violet, if you could see your way to calling me Heathcote."

She held his gaze, and through that simple connection told him that she, too, felt the link, the quiet but steady, unobtrusive but very real connection that was forming between them. Then she dipped her head in acquiescence. "I would be honored to call you Heathcote."

Another second passed, then she drew her fingers from his clasp and waved him to a chair. "Please, sit, and tell me what has happened."

"As to that, I wondered if you would care to take the air? We can talk as we walk. Green Park isn't far, and, indeed, I have little to report." Smiling a touch tentatively, he added, "It would be pleasant to get more from my journey here than just a few minutes of your time."

She laughed, twin dimples appearing in her cheeks. "Indeed, sir, and I would welcome spending more minutes with you in a gentler setting."

"We're in agreement then." Smiling more confidently, he offered his arm. "Let's send Mostyn to find your coat and bonnet, then we'll set out to indulge ourselves."

Five minutes later, her hand tucked in the crook of Montague's arm, Violet paced down Albemarle Street and around the corner into the busier thoroughfare of Piccadilly. The closeness engendered through their mutual endeavors of the previous day had developed further, and, it seemed, strengthened, and not just on her part, but on his—on Heathcote's—too. She felt a silly, giddy recklessness at the feel of him so close, so protectively strong by her side, a sense of solid male that played, alluring and comforting at the same time, on her female senses. As for the implication of his request that she call him by his given name, she decided she couldn't dwell on that—not while she was in public. Later, she would indulge, when she was on her own and there was no likelihood she might have to behave with any sense.

There were too many others strolling the pavements for them to safely speak of the investigation; instead, they walked, taking in the sights of the fashionable carriages that rattled over the cobbles, some ferrying ladies, others tooled by exquisites of varying degrees, all drawn by high-bred horses. They crossed Berkeley Street and paced past the long façade of Devonshire House, then at Clarges Street, they waited for an opening between the carriages and crossed the road, and walked on through the gate giving access to Green Park.

Immediately faced with the Reservoir, they turned right; eventually passing the fountain that marked the Reservoir's western end, they headed into the quieter walks beyond. The trees lining the walks were large and old; their leaves had already turned, and many had fallen, creating a carpet of golds and browns.

After glancing around and confirming that there were no others near enough to overhear, she looked up at Montague. "So, my dear Heathcote, what information do you have to report?"

His lips lifted and his eyes met hers, and for a moment they indulged in an unvoiced understanding, but then he looked ahead and dutifully divulged, "As discussed last night, I've located the firm that holds the registry for those shares. Had they been a London firm, I would have had more to report today, but, sadly, they're located in Manchester, so I've couriered a request to them."

She arched her brows. "What, exactly, did you ask for—and how likely are they to respond with the information we need?"

He glanced at her. "You're right—normally, a request to know who holds a particular share certificate wouldn't get far. The firm would treat that as confidential information. However, I called their attention to the fact that Sir Hugo Halstead had previously owned that certificate, which is a fact they'll be able to verify. Each certificate is numbered, so we are asking after a particular certificate—they are not interchangeable, like bank notes." When she nodded her understanding, he went on, "I explained that consequent to Lady Halstead's recent death, I was assisting in a review of the Halsteads' affairs prior to the same being submitted to the court for probate, and that I needed to clarify and provide proof of the transfer of that share certificate."

Meeting her eyes, he grinned. "No firm operating in the financial arena will unnecessarily allow their name to be cited in court proceedings, certainly not in relation to any unresolved question. They will want this matter clarified and dealt with before the estate is passed in for probate. I fully expect them to respond to my request with the name of the current owner, but, as they are in Manchester, that information won't reach me until tomorrow at the earliest, and perhaps not until the next day."

They strolled on; after several minutes, she asked, "Is there anything else you—we—might do to learn what happened to that share certificate?"

He shook his head. "It's as I explained last night. If we start asking openly, trying to locate the current owner, we will almost certainly find that person alerted to our inquiries before we learn his name. If it's the murderer who is the current owner, then we can all but guarantee he'll flee, and that long before we can get to his door." He glanced at her. "Asking in the way that I have, within the fraternity, so to speak, and we are, after all, a very discreet lot, then the Manchester firm will think to protect the current owner from having to deal with whatever court mess might otherwise ensue and so will give me his name, assuming I will then simply find proof of a chain of transfer, all legal and aboveboard, and no one will hear of the matter again."

"Ah—I see." After a moment, she met his eyes, quiet amusement showing clearly in her own. "I will be sure to repeat that to Penelope—who is certain to champ at the proverbial bit when she hears of the delay."

He laughed and closed his hand over hers where it rested on his sleeve. In pleasant and mutual accord, they ambled on beneath the autumnal trees.

But by the time they turned and headed back toward Albemarle Street, along with a sense of regret over soon losing Montague's—Heathcote's—company, Violet's mind had thrown up an even darker thought. And once she'd thought of it, it blossomed, overriding all else, all other considerations.

She waited until they were once more back in the front hall, and Mostyn left them, giving her privacy in which to bid Heathcote farewell. Holding out both hands to him, she caught his gaze as he took her fingers in his warm and comforting clasp. "These inquiries of yours . . ." She paused, then quietly said, "I cannot forget that Runcorn was murdered, and, it seems, the motive was to conceal who stole this certificate." She let her concern—real and welling—show in her eyes, then simply said, "You will be careful, won't you?" Feeling she'd pressed too far, she hurried to add, "I know it's not my place, but—"

"On the contrary." He held her gaze, then, very deliberately, he raised one of her hands and pressed a kiss—a gentle, warm, but entirely chaste kiss—to the backs of her fingers. "If there is any right in question, then, my dear Violet, I freely cede it to you."

The ensuing moment grew intense. Locked in each other's eyes, searching the other's eyes, they each looked for, and saw, found . . .

He hesitated, then said, "Now is not the time. But after this is over and all is settled . . . ?"

She hesitated not at all. She nodded, and for good measure stated, "Yes. When this is all over . . . we will talk about this then."

His lips eased into a slow, gentle smile.

She returned it. Her heart gave a silly little leap when, releasing her hands, he raised one finger and with its back lightly caressed her cheek.

The breath he drew in as he lowered his hand seemed tight. "I must go."

Wordless, she nodded. As he set his hat on his head, she moved past him and opened the door.

As he crossed the threshold, she said, "I'll be sure to pass the gist of all you said on to Barnaby, and Stokes, if he calls."

Gaining the pavement, he turned and flashed her a smile. "And you'll have to tell Penelope and Griselda, too, because if you don't, they'll drag it from you."

Violet laughed. With a jaunty salute, Montague strode away down the street.

She watched him go, then closed the door on a happy sigh.

"Well, well, well! Who would have thought it of Walter?"

He certainly hadn't. He'd always imagined Cynthia's get to be a mere cypher, little more than a stuffed doll—the expected heir—that she and Wallace trotted out for public consumption whenever a son's existence might improve their standing.

"I would never have imagined that Walter would have the intestinal fortitude to do anything so wonderfully, *outrageously* criminal. And so very socially unacceptable! And now . . ." His smile knew no bounds. "Oh, how the mighty are fallen!"

Even he could hear the gloating joy in his voice, the sound filling the quiet of his dressing room with openly malicious glee.

He reveled in it.

"And, oh, joy of joys, how *terribly perfect* if Walter is blamed for the murders, too!"

He honestly couldn't imagine any happening that would more delight him.

It took several minutes before the euphoria engendered by that prospect drained sufficiently for his underlying, ever-present obsession to resurface. But once it had . . . he still wasn't safe.

He had yet to fully secure his future.

He grimaced, but then turned thoughtful. "With the police focusing on Walter, perhaps now is the time to silence Miss Matcham?" He considered his reflection in his shaving mirror, tipping his head as he considered. "On the other hand, perhaps that's a sign to hold back for just a little longer." Eyes narrowing, he murmured, "But it would be unwise to wait too long—best if Miss Matcham's death can be made to appear connected in some way . . ."

Several minutes ticked by, then his expression started to lighten. "Perhaps Miss Matcham might have an 'accident'—something that will suggest that she might have killed herself out of remorse for the old lady's and the maid's murders . . . what if Miss Matcham was the one who'd had a lover? And that lover had, with Miss Matcham's connivance, killed the old lady, the man-of-business, and the maid, but, in the end, the murders prove too much for Miss Matcham's delicate sensibilities, so she kills herself, but takes the name of her lover to the grave . . ." He smiled. "Oh, yes. That will do nicely."

He stood before his mirror and watched himself think things through.

Miss Matcham had yet to remember anything relevant, or, at least, she had yet to say anything to the police, or they would have come knocking at his door asking very awkward questions. He had no way of knowing whether the matter of the share certificate he'd stolen would ever surface, but if it did . . . the maid had surprised him in the old lady's room; she'd seen him going through the share certificates, so she had had to die.

Given Miss Matcham and the maid had been close, he had to assume that the maid had mentioned finding him doing something she didn't understand with her mistress's papers to her friend.

Hence, for his peace of mind, Miss Matcham, too, had to depart this earth.

Until she did, until he could be certain there was no threat of exposure hanging over his head, he would never be able to relax and enjoy the fruits of his considerable labors.

So Miss Matcham had to die. The only questions remaining were: When? And: How?

Chapter 16

Two days later, Montague called in Albemarle Street in the afternoon. As he'd secretly hoped, he found Violet alone, sorting through Penelope's correspondence.

When he halted before Penelope's desk, Violet closed the leather-bound notebook she'd been jotting in and smiled delightedly up at him. "Penelope was summoned to bring Oliver to some family afternoon tea at her mother, Lady Calverton's house, and Griselda seized the opportunity to catch up with her shop." Violet surveyed the piles of letters haphazardly stacked all over Penelope's desk. "I thought to make some inroads here, but it's heavy going."

"Come for a stroll." Montague held out a hand. "We can walk around Berkeley Square while we share our reports."

Violet's eyes lit. "What an excellent idea!"

Five minutes later, with her rugged up in her pelisse, her bonnet tied firmly over her hair, and a scarf wound about her throat to ward off the brisk chill in the breeze, they set off along the pavement.

As they neared the square, she glanced at Montague—Heathcote. "Have you heard anything, learned anything more about the share certificate?" She was impatient to get on, to reach the end of the investigation so they could turn their minds to more personal pursuits, and she sensed, very clearly, that he felt the same.

He grimaced. "Not really. Initially, the share registry helpfully confirmed that I was correct in thinking that the Halsteads no longer owned those shares, but the registrar imparted nothing more. It required further, rather delicate, persuasion, including invoking the specter of an official demand from Scotland Yard, to convince the registrar to divulge who currently holds those shares." Pausing to open the gate to the park that filled the center of Berkeley Square, he waited until they were strolling the gravel walks, side by side, with her hand tucked in the crook of his arm, before continuing, "I trust I've now achieved that task—it was rather like chipping away at a stone, but I'm hopeful the next communication I receive from Manchester will contain the critical information. That said"—he met her eyes—"I seriously doubt the murderer will be the current owner."

"You think he'll have sold the shares?"

"I can't see why he would have taken the certificate if he wasn't after the money. And to convert the certificate to cash, he has to have sold it."

For several minutes, they paced in silence, then she asked, "Is there any way you can trace such a sale?"

"Courtesy of the share registry, I've confirmed that the Halsteads' ownership of the shares ceased approximately eleven months ago—meaning the new owner presented the certificate and registered the transfer of ownership at that point. But he might have bought the certificate earlier—not everyone is prompt in registering such things, and as there were no dividends paid until very recently, I can't tell from anything in the Halsteads' accounts exactly when the certificate passed out of their hands."

"When it was stolen."

"Correct." He hesitated, then said, "What I have done—the only thing I could think of to do to advance our cause while waiting for news from Manchester—is to estimate how much money the shares might have been exchanged for, and I am presently engaged in checking whether any such sum was deposited into any of the Halstead or Camberly accounts between fifteen months and nine months ago."

"Do you think they—the murderer, whoever they are—would have put the money into one of their accounts?"

He grimaced. "It's a long shot, but given this family's arrogance, I suspect they might not realize that bank accounts are records that can be searched, at least by the right people if approached in the right way."

"And you know the ways."

He nodded and met her eyes. "But don't tell Stokes—or at least, don't labor the point. He won't be grateful."

"Ah, I see." She smiled, looking ahead, idly surveying the numerous nursemaids and their charges with whom they presently shared the park.

They'd circumnavigated the park; as they approached the gate through which they'd entered, he said, "You should probably warn the others that while I will check, I don't expect to find any hint of the money in any of the family's accounts."

She studied his face as she passed through the gate he held for her. "You think they'll have used the money for something else?"

Joining her on the pavement, he nodded. "I can't see why they would have gone to the bother of stealing the certificate if they weren't in need of the money they could raise with it—and if they needed money, then, presumably, there was a reason for that need, something that made it imperative for them to get their hands on that much cash."

Tucking her hand once more in the crook of his arm—something in her delighting in the familiarity, that he expected and accepted that she should—she nodded. "That makes sense."

He glanced at her, his gaze traveling her face. "So that's my news. What of you and the others?"

She sighed; leaning on his arm, she tipped her head closer to his to say, "Sadly, the rest of us have even less to report. Stokes and Barnaby are now convinced that Walter's alibis are sound for all three murders, so he has been officially struck from the list of suspects. And while they are not overly impressed by the caliber of his witnesses, they are inclined to believe William's alibis for at least two of the murders."

"So William is still a possible culprit if the murders were the result of a conspiracy—if it was more than one of them doing the killings."

She nodded. "I believe that's what Stokes and Barnaby think at present. And from what I know of them, I could readily imagine William and Maurice working together, or even William and Hayden. Or even William and both those two. As for the female half of the investigation, Penelope and I completed a very discreet review of the three Halstead and Camberly ladies' alibis this morning. All appear to be sound, although as Penelope said, it's still possible that one or other played some supporting role. Regardless, we no longer believe it would have been possible for any of the three ladies in question to have been present at any of the murder scenes at the times of the murders."

Montague digested that. As they neared Penelope and Barnaby's house, he murmured, "So it keeps coming back to the Halstead men—Mortimer, Maurice, William, and Hayden. Each of the three murders was committed by one of them."

"Indeed." Climbing the steps to the Adairs' door, Violet plied the knocker, then turned to him. "And we still have yet to discover which one, or more, were involved."

He nodded. "Whether there was more than one acting in concert, or whether the theft of the share certificate and all three murders can be laid at one man's door."

At that point, Mostyn opened the door. Meeting Violet's eyes, Montague arched a brow and saw her smile in understanding; inwardly relishing the instinctive connection, feeling oddly domesticated, he followed her inside.

———

The following morning, Barnaby and Stokes called to see Montague.

As they settled in the chairs before Montague's desk, Stokes put their first and most burning question. "Have you heard who owns those shares yet?"

Leaning back in the admiral's chair on the opposite side of the desk, Montague grimaced. "No. But—damn it—that registrar will have to bend soon." Montague studied Stokes. "Either that, or you'll have to go up there and loom over him."

Stokes grunted. "For his sake, I hope it won't come to that." He paused, then said, "Send word as soon as you do hear. This case is dragging on too long, and the Chief is getting anxious."

Montague inclined his head. "So how goes your hunting?"

"Mixed," Barnaby said. "Violet said she'd mentioned our progress with William's alibis. Two—those for her ladyship's murder and Tilly's murder—we're inclined to accept. We found several others as well as the tavern staff—others William hadn't known about and who he doesn't know well enough to bribe—who could confirm that he was there on those two nights, at times that make it implausible that he could have reached Lowndes Street in time to commit the murders."

"But," Stokes said, his voice turning darkly grim, "William's alibi for the night of Runcorn's murder is too reliant on good friends of questionable character to pass muster. And none of the others—not a one—have alibis that are sound for any of the three murders." Stokes leaned forward; as if reading from a list, he recited, "Maurice Halstead says he was engaged with a lady whose name he declines to provide on two of the nights in question, and on the third, he believes he was visiting some den or hell, but he separated from the friends with whom he went there and can't remember when he left, or with whom, or where he went after that."

"In other words," Barnaby dryly interjected, "he was inebriated to the point of having no clear memory of where he was or what he did, much less who he was with."

"So Maurice remains a suspect for all three murders. Then we come to Mortimer Halstead—a fairly simple case, you might think. But no—Mortimer attended a dinner with his wife on two of the nights in question, but in both cases, his wife returned home in their carriage alone, leaving Mortimer in impromptu meetings that evolved out of the post-dinner conversations, and he subsequently made his way home on his own. On the night of Runcorn's murder, Mortimer attended some formal embassy soiree that commenced early in the evening and to which his wife did not go. He says he was home in good time, but the Halsteads have separate bedrooms, so Mrs. Halstead cannot verify when her husband got to bed on that night, or on any other."

"Hayden Halstead," Barnaby said, "proved to live a rather more interesting life than he attempted to lead us, and his parents, to believe. His stated alibis were that he was at home on each of the three nights, and retired to bed and slept the sleep of the innocent all night long." His expression serious, Barnaby shook his head. "I donned an everyman disguise and consorted with the Halstead footmen at the local public house. It seems all the Halstead staff are well aware that Hayden retires to his rooms—and then sneaks down the back stairs and goes out on the town. When we taxed Hayden with our insights, he wilted and corrected his statement."

Stokes snorted. "But the alibis he gave this time are no better than the first lot—he was out with friends carousing, he has no idea where, and as for the time . . . not even the friends we hunted down and spoke with have any real clue."

Barnaby grunted. "Indeed, the friends were so clueless it was impossible to be sure that Hayden remained with them each night, through the hours the murders were committed, nor is it possible to say whether Hayden was truly inebriated to the point of being incapable, because all his friends certainly were."

Stokes shook his head. "You would think that with three separate murders and three different nights it would be an easy matter to discount at least one of them, but no. And, worse, given that they are all family, all related, in this case we have to allow for a very real possibility of some level of conspiracy." Stokes straightened, exasperation clear in his face. "And if *that's* the case, then we're never going to be able to get far with these alibis."

"And," Barnaby said, "as soon as you start to entertain the possibility of a conspiracy—and yes, I absolutely agree we must—then you bring Camberly back into the picture."

When Montague frowned, Barnaby explained, "We'd discounted Camberly as a suspect because of the involvement of a Halstead male in Runcorn's murder, and because we assumed we were only dealing with one murderer. If there's a conspiracy, then Camberly might have murdered Lady Halstead or Tilly."

"We have Camberly's alibis," Stokes said, "but have yet to check them."

"That said," Barnaby countered, "Camberly's alibis appear more substantial, or at least more likely to be able to be substantiated. He said he was in late sittings, or at meetings with other politicians, and those meetings do frequently run until four in the morning or later. His alibis might well be sound, but we haven't yet checked." He met Montague's gaze. "That's next on our list. But have you learned anything further regarding the Halsteads' and Camberlys' finances?"

Montague nodded. "I had word first thing this morning that a quiet perusal of the Halstead and Camberly bank accounts shows no large sums of a size that might be all, or even a large part, of any payment received for the shares."

Stokes grimaced. "Well, that was a long shot."

Montague shrugged. "Presumably whoever took the share certificate sold it and used the money for whatever reason he had for stealing the shares in the first place."

Barnaby nodded. "He—at least one of the Halstead males—needed money desperately."

"Maybe so," Stokes said, "but why murder, not once but three times—"

"And try for a fourth victim in Violet," Montague reminded him.

Stokes inclined his head. "Indeed—four times. So why is he so willing to murder again and again to hide . . . what? Stealing a share certificate from his mother?"

"No." Barnaby's blue gaze locked on Stokes's face. "Not simply to hide the theft but to protect his station, his reputation—which the theft alone might threaten, but, even more, I'd wager he doesn't want the reason he was forced to steal coming out."

Stokes weighed the words, then nodded. "That sounds more like it. There's something more than just the theft—there's whatever necessitated it."

"In one way, that motive's reassuring." When Stokes cocked a cynically disbelieving brow, Barnaby grinned. "It means that our murderer—indeed, all our suspects, all the actors in this drama—are unlikely to run away, much less vanish. Not when the principal motive for this murderer is to ensure he can cling to his social position, that nothing damages it."

Montague said, "I don't disagree, but such a motive makes it less likely that William is the murderer."

"The principal murderer," Barnaby conceded, "but it doesn't mean that he, for whatever reason, didn't help Maurice, or Mortimer, or Camberly, by killing Runcorn."

Stokes groaned. "My head's spinning with this family and their alibis and the potential for conspiracy." Heaving a sigh, he rose and looked at Barnaby. "Which, I suppose, means you and I better get back to sorting said alibis out."

With a matching sigh, Barnaby uncrossed his long legs and got to his feet. He looked at Montague, then at Stokes. "One way or another, we will get there—and given that he won't run, we'll catch him."

"Amen." Stokes saluted Montague, then headed for the door.

With a nod and a smile for Montague, Barnaby followed.

Montague watched them go, then uttered his own sigh and, pulling forward the papers he'd pushed aside, got back to business.

There was nothing more he could do, not until he heard back from Manchester. Hopefully this time the registrar would come through.

The couriered message arrived at four o'clock that afternoon.

Slocum, on receiving it, almost ran in his hurry to ferry it to Montague.

Setting aside the ledger he'd been checking, Montague took the packet, picked up his letter knife, inserted the tip, and slit the envelope open.

Withdrawing a single sheet, he unfolded it and scanned its contents. Then he blew out a breath and sat back, his gaze fixed on the name inscribed on the page.

"Well?"

Glancing up, Montague saw Gibbons—it was he who had spoken—standing behind Slocum, who was hovering by Montague's desk. Foster looked over Gibbons's shoulder, expectation in his face, while the rest of Montague and Son's small staff were gathered about the doorway to the inner office, waiting to hear the news.

Montague's lips twitched; he looked back at the letter. "The registrar of the Grand Junction Railway Company formally verifies that the share certificate in question, that previously was the property of Agatha, Lady Halstead, is now registered to . . . the Earl of Corby."

Gibbons blinked. "Good God."

"Indeed." Montague nodded, in complete accord with that sentiment. "Furthermore, the registrar states that the earl, or, rather, his man-of-business, registered the shares eleven months ago. Therefore, as far as the registry is concerned, the shares passed directly from Lady Halstead to the Earl of Corby, with no other owner being registered in between."

Montague set the letter on his blotter. He stared at it for several seconds, then said, "Slocum—"

"I believe the Earl of Corby's man-of-business is Mr. Millhouse, sir. His offices are just around the corner in Throgmorton Street."

"Excellent." Montague glanced toward the door. "Reginald?"

"Yessir!" The young office boy all but bounded into the room.

Hiding a smile, Montague beckoned him forward. "Mr. Slater can deliver my letter to Mr. Millhouse, but before I write that, I need to send a message to Inspector Stokes at Scotland Yard."

Already scribbling, at the sudden silence, Montague glanced up—to discover Reginald standing stock-still before the desk, his eyes on stalks and his mouth agape.

Foster, grinning, dropped a hand on Reginald's shoulder. "No need to catch flies, Reggie. Do you know the way to the Yard?"

Reginald blinked, then his expression tended toward panic.

"Don't worry," Gibbons said. "It's at the start of Whitehall. Mr. Slocum will give you directions."

Reginald perked up, then Montague handed him the folded note. "No need to wait for a reply. Once you've seen that into the hands of the sergeant on the front desk at Scotland Yard, you can hie away home."

"Thank you, sir." Reginald took hold of the note as if it was solid gold. "I won't let you down."

Montague smiled. "I'm sure you won't. But hurry now—it needs to be there as soon as possible."

Reginald spun away and ran. Pausing only to drag on his coat and get directions from Slocum, he rushed out of the office.

"Ah, the exuberance of youth." With a nod, still smiling, Gibbons ambled out, followed by Foster. Slater and Pringle had already returned to their desks.

Slocum looked in. "Just checked my book, sir—it is Mr. Millhouse, at number six, Throgmorton Street."

"Thank you, Slocum." Montague set a fresh sheet on his blotter. "Tell Slater this might take a few minutes."

"Aye, sir."

It took him a full half hour before he was satisfied with the wording of his request to Mr. Millhouse. Millhouse was a few years younger than Montague, and while Montague was considered by most to be the preeminent man-of-business in London, there was a certain degree of professional courtesy and rivalry involved; striking the right note with his first communication on this matter with Millhouse was important. Especially as Montague fully expected the first communication would, inevitably, be followed by several others; getting all the answers he wanted couldn't be done with a single note.

If he baldly listed all the questions he—and Scotland Yard—needed answers to, Millhouse would balk, and his noble client would be even less inclined to be helpful.

Reining in his own, very real, impatience wasn't easy, but he'd been in business—had been dealing with business and the men involved—for too long not to play by the rules, unwritten though most of those were. Indeed, he'd built his considerable reputation on his precise understanding of those rules.

So his letter to Mr. Millhouse of Throgmorton Street was a masterpiece of understated respect and carried within it a subtle invitation to Millhouse to join with Montague in unraveling a minor mystery as to the transference of the Grand Junction Railway Company share certificate in question.

Rereading the missive, imagining Millhouse reading it and his reactions, Montague let his lips ease into a smile. "Done." Carefully blotting his penmanship, he folded the letter, inscribed the direction on the front, then sealed it. "Slater!"

Slater had clearly been waiting for the summons. He already had his coat on when he looked in through the doorway. "Ready?"

Montague held out the letter. "Try and catch him before he leaves for the day, then go on home yourself. He won't reply tonight."

Slater nodded, took the letter, and departed.

Montague glanced at the clock and saw that it was nearly six o'clock. He listened, and realized that most of the others had already left.

As if to confirm, Slocum put his head through the doorway. "I'm off now, sir."

"Very good, Slocum." Montague stood. "I believe I'll go up myself."

He followed Slocum from the office. After locking the door, he turned and climbed the stairs to his apartment, very conscious of a wish to—like the rest of his staff—find that intangible thing called "home" waiting for him there.

But Violet was in Albemarle Street, and although he wanted, very much, to share this latest discovery with her, to sit by her side, relax in the glow of what he'd accomplished that day and look forward to the challenges of the morrow, it was already six o'clock. By the time he reached Albemarle Street, it would be too close to dinnertime, and, besides, although he would be happy to share this latest development with the others, he didn't want to share Violet's company with them.

That wasn't what he craved.

Reaching the door to his apartment, he went in and instantly smelled the scents of roasting beef and baking. From the kitchen, Mrs. Trewick's usual greeting floated out. "Dinner's ready and waiting, sir! If you'll take your seat at the table, Trewick will bring it out."

Montague walked into the sitting room and halted. He looked around the room—the empty room devoid of all companionship—and vowed to himself that it wouldn't remain so for long.

He'd waited long enough, and at last he'd found Violet.

As soon as they identified who the murderer was, and saw Lady Halstead, Runcorn, and Tilly avenged, he would ask Violet to be his.

He needed her here; he'd had enough of living alone.

The reply from Millhouse arrived at eleven o'clock the next morning. Reading the careful phrases, Montague couldn't help a cynical smile; he would take an oath Millhouse had labored over his reply for even longer than he himself had worked on the phrasing of his request.

Slocum was hovering; Gibbons and Foster were leaning in the doorway.

Montague glanced their way, then said, "After various preliminaries, Millhouse writes that he understands that the share certificate in question was acquired by the earl when it was tendered in lieu in settlement of a debt of honor."

Hands sliding into his pockets, Gibbons let out a low whistle. "Some debt!"

"Indeed." Montague scanned the subsequent lines a second time and inwardly sighed. "And, as one might expect, Millhouse doesn't know and therefore cannot answer as to the identity of the gentleman who surrendered the share certificate."

"Well," Foster said, "other than that it was a gentleman the Earl of Corby deigned to gamble with."

Eyes narrowing, Montague looked at Slocum. If he was remembering aright . . .

Slocum nodded. "The earl's a big gambler, sir—known to care little about who he gambles with, as long as they can pay."

Montague grimaced. "That was my understanding, too. So the fact that this gentleman owed the earl many thousands of pounds doesn't actually tell us all that much about said gentleman."

Slocum made a rude sound. "Other than that he was stupid enough to sit down with Corby and a pack of cards—the earl's reputation for winning isn't exactly a secret."

"True." Montague considered, then grimaced. "That still gets us no further. Any of the Halsteads, or Camberly, for that matter, might, for some reason, have been moved to engage with Corby."

"What now?" Gibbons asked.

"Now . . ." Montague stared unseeing at his blotter for several moments, then, chin firming, he reached for a fresh sheet of paper. "Now I see just how persuasive I can be with regard to a competitor like Millhouse."

Montague's second letter to Millhouse took more than an hour to craft. He didn't expect a reply that day, as it seemed fairly clear that Millhouse, if he deigned to pursue the matter at Montague's behest, would need to consult with the earl.

Montague was therefore surprised when Slocum hurried—definitely rushed—into his office, waving—definitely waving—an envelope.

"A reply from Mr. Millhouse, sir." Slocum laid the envelope on the desk as Montague reached for his letter-knife.

The rest of his staff congregated about the doorway; everyone had become infected with the scent of the chase.

Retrieving the short missive from the envelope, Montague scanned it. "Halstead."

Cheers erupted from around the door.

Without looking up, Montague said, "Don't get too carried away just yet. All Millhouse has written is a Mr. Halstead—he doesn't know, or at least hasn't said, which one."

But from the tone of the letter, Montague could tell that he'd succeeded in engaging Millhouse's curiosity with his previous missives and their tantalizing hints of a major Scotland Yard investigation.

Laying aside the letter, Montague glanced at Slocum. "Get Reginald—I want him to run a message back to Millhouse immediately."

The gathering about the door scattered.

Montague's next note was succinct and clearly intimated that he considered Millhouse a peer of equal standing—one equally interested in bringing miscreants who dabbled in their world of finance to justice. Especially miscreants who had any dealings with their major clients.

Quickly blotting the note, he was folding it as Slocum returned with Reginald in tow.

Montague grinned at the lad, who grinned back. He handed over the letter. "You know where to go?"

"Yessir—Mr. Slocum told me."

"Right then, off you go. And this time inquire if there will be a reply, and if there is, wait and bring it back." Millhouse would appreciate not having to use his own runner.

Montague watched Slocum usher Reginald out, seeing the boy down the stairs before shutting the door and returning to his desk.

For a moment, Montague dwelled in the moment, appreciating all that was right and good within it. The satisfaction of knowing their small group of investigators were on the right track—that it was one of the Halstead men behind the theft of the share certificate, and therefore most likely behind the murders. He savored the welling swell of familiar excitement—of being on the hunt, of scenting his financial prey. Yet in all the investigations he'd previously engaged in, he'd been involved at one remove, acting at the behest of one of his clients. This time, he was personally as well as professionally involved, and that heightened the emotions, setting a keen edge to the drive to find answers and see justice done.

To see justice triumph.

More immediately, he felt the engagement and support of his staff; their actions, their interest, made it very clear that they understood that commitment to justice, that they shared it and would stand behind him in seeing the job done.

Their understanding and support warmed him.

They sometimes made him smile, yet he knew how lucky he was in having such an intelligent and devoted group at his back.

He took a moment to appreciate them, and the blessings of his day, of his life, then he reopened the file he'd been assessing and settled to steadily work his way through it.

Twenty minutes later, Reginald burst through the office door. He waved a letter, then, with a flourish, presented it to Slocum.

Who checked the direction, then rose and brought the missive to Montague.

The rest of the staff craned their necks to watch and listen.

Montague read the note, then called out for their benefit, "Millhouse will have to ask the earl directly, which, as he notes, will take a certain amount of finesse, but he—Millhouse—hopes to have an answer for me by sometime tomorrow. He can't say when, but he doubts it will be before noon at the earliest."

With a nod, Montague set the letter down and smiled at Reginald, then at Slocum. "It's the best we could hope for—there's really no way for Millhouse, or, indeed, anyone else, to extract that information other than from the earl—and Millhouse will get the answer easier, and sooner, than anyone else."

The others absorbed that; Montague glanced through the open doorway, and from their expressions he knew both Gibbons and Foster were taking mental notes. They were learning the ways, as they should.

Slocum and Reginald retreated to the outer office, leaving Montague to repeat his words to himself.

Although he felt rather like a terrier must when wanting to maul a bone, he'd reached his present eminence in the fraternity of men-of-business in the great City of London precisely because he did know when he could push, and when pushing would be counterproductive.

Ultimately, if Millhouse couldn't induce the earl to part with the required name, Barnaby would no doubt mobilize his father to approach the earl—earl to earl, as it would be—but that would necessitate explaining far more to the Earl of Corby than might be wise, and they had no notion of the relationship between the earl and whichever Halstead had circled within his orbit.

Montague spent several more minutes considering if there was any faster way forward, but none presented itself. He was about to send Stokes a missive but then recalled that, along with the others, he had been summoned to dinner in Albemarle Street that evening.

Smiling to himself, he settled back in his chair and returned to his work—to his files and their figures.

He would tell the others of the breakthrough in person.

Chapter 17

When Stokes and Barnaby walked into the drawing room, joining Penelope, Griselda, Violet, and Montague, who had arrived moments earlier, Penelope swept the gathering with an imperious eye and demanded, "Has anyone identified the murderer yet?"

When Stokes pulled a face, both negative and disgruntled, Barnaby shook his head, and Montague said, "Not yet," Penelope paused with her gaze on Montague's face, but then she waved her hands in a warding gesture and decreed, "No talking about the murder until after dinner. Let's enjoy the meal first."

No one argued; indeed, all six fell in with the suggestion, and a gentle, convivial dinner among friends followed.

Violet appreciated Penelope's tack; even though she'd spent most of her day sorting Penelope's correspondence, the murders had constantly lurked in the back of her mind, the question of the murderer's identity nagging like a toothache. Penelope and Griselda had spent their day in non-investigative endeavors, Penelope attending a meeting at the British Library, and Griselda at her shop, but they, too, had confided that the murders had never been far from their minds.

By unvoiced consent, no one mentioned the murders or anything to do with the investigation until they had returned to the drawing room and settled in their now accustomed places on the sofas and chairs—Penelope and Griselda on one sofa, Montague and Violet on the sofa opposite, and Barnaby and Stokes in the armchairs flanking the fireplace, long legs stretched out before them, glasses of brandy in their hands.

"So," Penelope finally said, "where are we now with this tiresome murderer? Have we unearthed any further clues?"

Lowering his glass, Stokes reported, "We haven't got any further with their alibis—they're the sort we can't prove true or false, so they get us precisely nowhere."

"But," Griselda said, "alibis, the checking of them, has allowed us to confirm that Walter is not the murderer, that William did not murder either Lady Halstead or Tilly, and that none of the three ladies were actively involved in the murders."

"Sadly," Stokes said, "with this family, that doesn't get us all that far. The only one of them we can definitely rule out of having any involvement in these murders is Walter. Any or all of the others, including the ladies, could have been involved as accomplices, and any of the remaining five men, Camberly included, could have been guilty of one or more of the murders."

Penelope grimaced. "In general one assumes that it would be emotionally very difficult, and commensurately very unlikely, for a child to murder their mother, and the notion of a *number* of children conspiring to kill their mother seems even more far-fetched. In this case, however, given the lack of emotional connection between Lady Halstead and her children because of her long absences abroad . . . well, it's possible that the normal, natural barriers against matricide might not have been there."

"More," Griselda softly said, "it's possible Lady Halstead's children, some of them, at least, might have resented a mother who put them so very far behind her husband and his career."

Both Violet and Penelope nodded. The men soberly absorbed the insight.

After a moment, Barnaby stirred. "To return to specifics, for Runcorn's murder, at least, the villain remains a Halstead male, so regardless of the existence of any family conspiracy, at least one Halstead male is involved." He glanced at Montague. "Have you got any further as to who sold the shares to Corby?"

Montague nodded. "According to Corby's man-of-business, the earl acquired the shares by way of payment of a gambling debt from a Mr. Halstead."

"Good God, man!" Stokes sat upright. "Which one?"

But Montague had held up a staying hand. "Corby's man-of-business, a Mr. Millhouse, knew only that Corby got the shares from a Mr. Halstead. However, Millhouse has agreed to inquire further of the earl, but it will be at least noon tomorrow before he expects to have any answer—and that, I suspect, depends on when he can get an audience with Corby."

Stokes glanced at Barnaby.

Before Stokes could voice what was clearly in his mind, Montague continued, "Should the earl decline to identify the specific gentleman to Millhouse, then perhaps an approach at a more exalted level—for instance, Adair's father, the Earl of Cothelstone, who is also widely known as one of the peers overseeing the Metropolitan Police—might be in order." Montague's lips twisted wryly. "However, experience suggests that Millhouse will have more luck, and that more rapidly. Noblemen like Corby have a tendency to believe that they should not divulge the names of those who lose to them to others of their station, but that the same prohibition does not apply to men of lesser station, such as Millhouse, especially not when, as I suspect he will, Millhouse suggests that the earl should furnish him with the name as a way of ensuring the taint of theft and consequent murder never comes anywhere near the earl's good name."

Barnaby chuckled. "You and your peers have a very fine appreciation of the nobility's foibles." He looked at Stokes. "Montague's correct—Millhouse will have a better chance of getting that name than my father. If the pater approaches Corby, Corby will demand to know every little detail about the case before divulging the name, and if we're trying for discretion—and we must not forget that, despite Walter's sorry exploits, we have no evidence that Camberly, MP, is involved, nor Mortimer Halstead, Home Office official, either, much less the ladies—then telling Corby all in exchange for a name is not a good way to proceed."

"Indeed," Penelope said. "We do need to protect the innocents. This case is not going to end well for the family in any case, but the less speculation over who is actually guilty, the better."

Stokes looked around the circle, then slumped back in his chair. "Very well." After a moment, he cocked a brow at Barnaby and Penelope. "So exactly where are we in terms of identifying who, exactly, are the guilty parties here?"

Penelope promptly replied, "On two counts now—Runcorn's murder and the man who gave Corby the stolen share certificate—we know the guilty party was a Halstead male."

"We've ruled out Walter," Violet said, "but in terms of who among the others is increasingly unlikely, I doubt William would have moved in Corby's circles, and, truth be told, I've never heard that William gambles, not to any extent. He might not have a great deal of money, but at the level he's chosen to live, he doesn't really need much to get by."

Stokes nodded. "Of the Halstead men, I agree that William is the least likely to have been involved."

"That leaves us with Mortimer, Hayden, and Maurice as the most likely culprits," Montague said.

"And as to that . . ." Barnaby shifted to better face them all. "After Montague sent word that it was Corby who now owned the shares, since I knew the earl to be a heavy gambler, I spent the day ambling around the gentleman's clubs, those I suspected Corby frequents. Through chatting with the doormen and the concierges, I confirmed that the earl was a member and known to play at a number of establishments, and I subsequently inquired whether any Halstead or Camberly was a member of those clubs."

"What a brilliant notion!" Penelope beamed at her spouse, then impatiently gestured. "And . . . ?"

Barnaby grinned at her. "And, as I was about to divulge, one of Corby's favorite haunts does indeed boast a Halstead as a member."

"Which Halstead?" Stokes demanded.

Barnaby met his eye. "The one we might have suspected—Maurice."

"That doesn't surprise me," Violet said. "Maurice has always been the spendthrift, the profligate. He's a peacock, and throughout the years I was with the family, everyone knew he gambled heavily."

After a moment, Griselda said, "So does this mean Maurice is the murderer?"

Stokes grimaced. "From what I've seen and learned of him, he's a devious, calculating sort—he could be behind all three killings. I wouldn't put it past him."

"However," Barnaby said, much in the manner of continuing Stokes's train of thought, "given the issues with this family, and the twists in this case, we need to be wary of leaping to conclusions, of making judgment calls rather than relying solely on facts. Our judgment, in this case, might lead us astray. The facts won't."

"But," Stokes said, "we are making progress. We are closing in." He looked at Montague. "I want to know the instant you hear from Millhouse as to which Halstead handed Corby that share certificate." Stokes snorted. "With this family, we can't even take it for granted that the Halstead who handed Corby the certificate was the same Halstead who owed him the gambling debt."

Penelope frowned. "This family gives me a headache—our final breakthrough can't come fast enough."

"Hear, hear," came from all the others.

Mostyn chose that moment to bring in the tea tray and as a group they turned their attention to other things, but once the tea had been consumed and everyone rose as Stokes, Griselda, and Montague prepared to take their leave, their progress with the case again claimed their minds.

"I know I shouldn't," Stokes said, meeting Barnaby's gaze, "yet I'm back to thinking we've been making this a lot more complicated than it needs to be." He glanced at the others, his gaze touching all their faces. "The chances are that, once we confirm that it was Maurice who gave Corby the share certificate, we'll have our man, and he'll prove to have committed all three murders." Stokes met Barnaby's gaze. "You said it earlier—the murders were all about our man protecting himself from exposure over something, and now we know that something was the debt to Corby and the theft of that share certificate to cover it."

"From all I've heard over the years," Violet said, "Maurice is barely tolerated on the fringes of the social circles to which he aspires to belong." She glanced at the others. "If it came out that he'd gambled with Corby and, after he'd lost, had stolen from his mother to cover the debt, and, more, had then passed off a stolen share certificate to Corby . . . well, he wouldn't be welcomed even within the gentleman's clubs, would he?"

"Exactly," Stokes said. "We have sound motive, and the means, now all we need is the final proof. One man, one Halstead—despite all the distractions, we don't need more than him to account for all the crimes."

After a moment, Barnaby nodded. "Agreed. The possibility of a family conspiracy might be there, but we've found no evidence that such an unholy alliance actually occurred. One man, one Halstead—and Maurice Halstead seems to be our man."

The six of them massed in the front hall, those departing putting on their coats and saying their good-byes.

Griselda had brought little Megan with her when she'd arrived earlier in the afternoon. Hettie, Oliver's nursemaid, brought the sleeping bundle down from the nursery and gently placed her in Griselda's arms.

"There now." Smiling, Hettie stepped back. "She was right as rain the whole time. She and Master Oliver played for a while, then out like lights, they were."

"Good." Tucking a fold of the blanket over Megan's dark head, Griselda smiled at Hettie. "Thank you for watching over her, Hettie."

Hettie beamed, bobbed a curtsy, then went back up the stairs.

Stokes, who had hovered at Griselda's elbow, bent to check on his daughter, then, satisfied she was sleeping soundly, he straightened and turned to shake Barnaby's hand and exchange a brief hug with Penelope, while Barnaby peeked at Megan and gave Griselda's shoulders a gentle squeeze. "Safe journey home," Barnaby said. He nodded to Mostyn, who opened the front door.

Stokes shook Montague's hand. "Let me know as soon as you hear."

"I will," Montague assured him.

With a smile and a salute for Violet, Stokes gathered Griselda, who had already touched cheeks with Penelope and Violet, within one arm and ushered her down the steps to their small black carriage, which was waiting by the curb.

Montague watched Stokes, a powerfully built man with considerable standing, hover protectively over his wife and daughter, and acknowledged the visceral tug, the deep-seated yearning, not a jealousy but the recognition of an emptiness he now knew he needed to fill. He might be London's most lauded man-of-business, but in the final weighing, his life would be worth very little if he didn't make a push to secure and embrace all he'd thus far lived without.

Not out of choice so much as out of negligence. Of always having work to do.

Montague was about to turn to Violet, when Barnaby swung his way.

A chill breeze whisked through the door, and Mostyn quickly shut it.

"I have to admit," Barnaby said, a touch of self-deprecation in his expression, "that I hadn't truly registered that stealing the shares and having that come out might be sufficient motive for murder in and of itself, but for such as the Halsteads, with their social aspirations"—he glanced at Violet, who had drawn nearer with Penelope—"the threat of being identified as such a thief would loom exceedingly large."

Montague nodded. He glanced around the faces. "Rest assured I'll send word the instant I have confirmation."

With a smile, Barnaby shook his hand; Penelope squeezed his arm, then stepped back. Leaving Montague to finally turn to Violet.

He discovered her tightening a warm shawl about her shoulders. She smiled. "Let me walk you out through the garden."

His answering smile felt like sunshine on his face. "Thank you. I'd like that."

With the briefest of nods to Barnaby and Penelope, he followed Violet into the garden parlor and out onto the side terrace.

They both paused on the terrace and looked up at the sky. It was chilly but crisp, a fine October night, with the scent of wood smoke on the air and a black velvet sky above.

"We're nearly there, aren't we?" Violet asked.

"Yes." He offered his arm and she tucked her hand comfortably in the crook of his elbow. As he steered her down the shallow steps to the lawn, he added, "After Barnaby's discovery, the information from Corby will merely be the final confirmation—the last piece of evidence needed to convict Maurice Halstead."

She shivered. "They truly have proved to be a malignant brood. I will be glad to have this ended, to be able to face forward and look ahead without the specter of a villain lurking in the shadows, waiting to pounce, hanging over me." She glanced at him, her lips curving. "I have realized that you—and the others, too—have been most assiduous in keeping me company whenever I step out of the house, out of Mostyn and company's care."

He shrugged. "We value you. We . . ." He paused, then, voice lowering, went on, "I don't want to lose you—not even to risk it." He met her gaze. "Not now I've found you."

Her smile grew more mysterious; as they strolled slowly down the side lawn toward the garden gate that gave onto Albemarle Street, she murmured, "Rest assured my sentiments are complementary." She held his gaze. "I don't want to lose you, either—not now I've found you."

Their steps slowed even more. "Tell me," he said, "what do you seek of life? Courtesy of Lady Halstead, you will shortly have sufficient funds to live comfortably for the rest of your days."

She nodded, her expression serious as she said, "The one thing I would choose is to not live alone." She glanced at him. "Not if I didn't have to—not if there was someone I wished to share a life with."

He halted, drawing her to face him. "You know I would gladly share my life with you—that out of all this, that's the hope, the reward, that for me shines most strongly."

"As it does for me." Her sincerity rang in her tone, invested her expression. She paused, then, drawing breath, continued, "When this is ended—"

"The instant it is."

She nodded, more confident, growing more assured. "As soon as we are free of the tangle of the Halsteads, we—you and I—will . . ." Her hand slid from his elbow to his palm; they both looked down, watched as, driven by their unvoiced need, their fingers twined. She looked up, and hope shone in her eyes.

Raising their linked hands, he brushed a kiss to her knuckles. "We will speak, and talk, and discuss—and we will figure out the ways so that we can live together, so that we can grow together in the ways that best suit us. We are both our own people—we can do as we wish. But for the record, my dear Violet—"

"No!" Slipping her fingers from his, she placed them over his lips. "Don't say it." Then she smiled, taking all sting from her words. "I'm . . . a little superstitious. Saying it seems like tempting Fate, and with the likes of Maurice Halstead hovering . . ." She blew out a breath. "My dearest Heathcote, I'd rather not risk it."

He laughed softly, eyes aglow with a joy she could see even in the shadows. "Very well—until it's done, I will wait. But for not a minute longer."

"No, indeed." She nodded. "I hereby give you permission to speak the instant we are free of this coil."

"I'll hold you to that." He didn't let go of her hand. "But if I may ask a purely curious question, are you enjoying working for Penelope? Do your talents actually lie in that direction?"

She nodded. "To my surprise, they truly do—and, trust me, she truly is in need of the sort of help I can give."

"Another pair of intelligent eyes."

She smiled. "Something like that. I may not be able to translate the obscure languages that she can, but I do know how to keep an appointment book, and that is one skill Penelope sorely lacks. She nearly missed an important lecture that she'd agreed to give at the library today. She'd forgotten to note it down, and if I hadn't unearthed the letter confirming the date from the stacks on her desk, she would have embarrassed herself dreadfully. So, yes, she does need my help on a continuing basis."

"Hmm . . . but, perhaps, not on a live-in basis." He arched a hopeful brow.

Chuckling, she inclined her head. "No, indeed—I could quite easily travel here for a few days each week, and that would be sufficient."

"And, after all, the City isn't all that far. Just a short hackney ride."

She tilted her head. "Is that where you live—in the City?"

He hesitated, then admitted, "I live in an apartment over the office. It's quite spacious, and the nearness means I'm home very soon after the close of business every day, but—"

Again she placed her fingers over his lips. "No—don't say anything else. You will have to show me this apartment of yours, and we'll work things out from there." She smiled. "I really don't have any firm views against living in the City."

He nodded. "Good. That will give me a chance to convince you."

Her expression grew serious. "You won't have to do that—where you are, wherever you choose to live, that place will contain the most important element I want—that I rather think I need—to make the rest of my life complete."

Understanding, pure and true, all but shimmered and glimmered between them, a clarity in their gazes, a seeing with no screen, no veil to dim the reality.

Locked in the other's eyes, each saw and knew the possibilities, each recognized the potential.

The moment tugged. Montague bent his head, and Violet stretched up. Hands found hands and locked, holding them together, steady and anchored as their lips touched, brushed, then met.

Held.

The kiss was simple, unadorned, bare of anything save their feelings—and what they each intended the contact to convey. A pledge, a promise.

His lips moved on hers, seeking, yearning. Slipping her fingers from his, she reached up, wound her arms about his strong neck, pressed closer and kissed him back.

Gently, his hands rose to grip her sides, then he spread palms and fingers over her supple back, supporting and holding, keeping, but not seizing.

Glorying in her giving.

And his.

Eventually, he lifted his head. And felt faintly giddy in a dizzyingly pleasant way.

With a warmth that bloomed in his chest and spread as he saw the delight in her eyes, saw his own satisfaction mirrored there.

"Soon," he said.

She nodded. "Soon." With that, she drew back and, reluctantly, he let her go.

Drawing her shawl more tightly around her shoulders, Violet turned to the gate. Heathcote walked with her the few steps further, waited while she slid the bolt back and swung the solid panel open. She looked up at him—her man, the one man she'd been waiting all of her life to find—and smiled softly. "Good night, Heathcote."

His answering smile held a touch of possessiveness. "Good night, my Violet." With a dip of his head, he stepped through the gate. "Good night."

On a sigh, she shut the gate, listened—and realized he was waiting for her to lock it. She did. A few seconds after the bolt slid home, she heard his footsteps slowly walk away.

Smiling, her expression incapable of adequately reflecting the joy buoying her heart, she turned and walked back to the terrace.

Walking up the shallow steps, she murmured to herself, "And how I'm going to manage to fall asleep I truly do not know."

Smiling even more widely, she went indoors.

"How absolutely lovely!" On a happy, satisfied sigh, Penelope turned from their bedroom window that overlooked the side garden.

Into Barnaby's arms. He had come to look over her shoulder to see what she was so avidly watching below.

He'd taken one brief glance, then had transferred his gaze, and his attention, to his wife. Meeting her dark eyes, he smiled. "You're rather lovely, too." He hesitated, then, more soberly, said, "Have I told you that recently?"

She tilted her head the better to search his face, his eyes, then the subtle curve of her full lips deepened. "Not recently enough. Perhaps you should remind me?" Her hands had come to rest on his chest; sliding them slowly up and over his shoulders, she moved nearer, pressed artfully closer. "Of that, and all associated sentiments."

He felt his lips curve with sexual intent, then he bent his head and set them to hers. Matched them to hers.

For a heartbeat they held still, then she parted her lips, and he angled his head. And took advantage of her flagrant invitation and filled her mouth, took, possessed, and savored.

And she savored him with an open, undisguised appreciation he'd come to treasure. One of the many joys of marriage, of a connection that had grown, one that had deepened and broadened, and, to his secret relief, had, if anything, returned stronger than ever after Oliver's birth.

There was a confidence there, between them now, that spoke of mutual experience, of a degree of intimate knowledge of the other that could never be achieved with anyone else. For him there was her, and for her there was him, and both of them lived with that mutual certainty anchoring their hearts.

Their foundation.

Rock-solid and sure, unwavering and immutable, it promised them all the strength they would ever need.

In the here and now it gave them the understanding and ability, and even more the reason, to go slow.

To take each moment and stretch it, expand it to the fullest, and squeeze from every heartbeat of the interlude every last drop of pleasure.

From the first brush of his hands over her silk-clad curves, to the pressure of her hands easing his coat off his shoulders, through each choreographed beat of a dance they knew by heart, they immersed themselves in each instant.

Each tick of their sensual clock brought delight.

Fed desire.

Invoked, provoked, and stoked their passions.

Divesting her of her gown became a tempting, alluring, irresistible prelude. Ultimately revealing her breasts was a special delight; now their son was weaned, her breasts had softened into lusher, utterly sumptuous mounds, ones he could now reclaim, could once again feast upon.

She gasped, and clung, and held him to her, urging him on not with words but with deeds, fluent in the unspoken language of loving as they both now were, but, as ever, she refused to cede her share of the reins.

She demanded, and took her turn at stripping him, revealing, rejoicing in, and then feasting.

With her small hands, with her lips, her hot mouth, and her teasing tongue.

With every last one of her senses.

As he had with her, she explored, claimed, and possessed, and set fires beneath his skin.

Then she slid to her knees and took him into her mouth, and razed his senses utterly.

Devoted herself wholeheartedly to the task.

When he could withstand her sensual torture no longer, not for another heartbeat, he broke, and drew her up, drew her fully into his arms—and they both froze, and together seized the moment to absorb, to appreciate to the fullest that excruciatingly evocative instant of naked bodies meeting, of bare skin sliding, gliding, her silken sleekness stroking against his harder and rougher, hair-dusted limbs as their bodies instinctively adjusted and accommodated each other's in their intimate embrace. Instinctively, together, they drank in the free, unfettered giving—and the consequent eruption of mutual delight.

Mutual pleasure.

That was their goal as he bent his head, as she stretched up and their lips sealed in a kiss of blazing, aching, unforgiving need.

They let the flames rage; they held to the kiss and let passion's flames lick, spread, then coalesce and roar.

Breaking from the conflagration, he raised his head and lifted her.

On a desperate gasp, she wound her arms about his shoulders, clasped her hands at his nape, shook back her tumbling curls and, raising her legs, wrapped them about his hips.

And sank down as, gripping her hips, he drew her down.

They came together on a sensual sigh.

In a moment of aching togetherness. Of acute, unfettered, unrestrained intimacy.

Lids falling, they savored the inexpressible delight.

Absorbed the welling pleasure.

Then they let the surging, driving need take them. Have them, capture them, whip them on.

And from somewhere amid all the passion and the fire and the heat and the urgency, from beneath their sensual desperation, joy, effervescent and unstoppable, unquenchable, bubbled up.

And filled them.

Merging with the sweeping tide of their sensual pleasure, with their driving need for completion, that joy, brilliant and acute, wound and twined and added another dimension to their experienced joining.

And opened their senses to another dimension of delight.

Penelope felt like she was close to bursting with the welling, surging, geysering emotions; never had they been this strong, this powerful, this glittering and engaging.

Dragging her lips from Barnaby's, she tipped her head back, then, all but bubbling with that swirling delight, she framed his face between her hands, found his heavy-lidded eyes with her gaze, and gasped, "The bed."

She didn't have to ask twice. In three swift strides, he was by the bed's side, then he tipped them both down.

They bounced once, then sank into the billows of their featherbed, and she reached for him as he drew her fully beneath him; she wriggled and then arched, and on a glorious gasp took him in, took him deep as, on a guttural groan, he thrust powerfully into her.

Then they rode the racing tide of their uninhibited, unfettered passions.

When the peak appeared before them, they raced on without check, in concert, together, in unshakeable accord.

Up and over the sensual cliff, and into the void they flew.

Striving to reach their sensual sun.

Hands gripping, fingers twined, bodies cleaving, hearts beating as one they stretched, touched, and let

the implosion take them. Let ecstasy break them, frag-
ment, and remake them.

As it had so many times before, but this time, in that
infinite instant of searing togetherness, of emotional as
well as physical melding, from under heavy lids their
eyes met, held, and they both saw, both knew, both
sensed the subtle addition that extra joy had brought to
them—to their union.

Another strand woven into the emotional rope that
linked them.

Another element of their love.

An additional strength that would hold them together
over the years to come.

Heavy-lidded, passion-spent, their gazes held for an
instant longer, then she let her lids fall, felt a smile—full
and open—curve her lips.

Felt its mate curving his lips as he touched them
to hers.

And they let go and sank into the glory, into the bliss
that was theirs to claim.

Later, they shifted and settled amid the rumpled
sheets, wrapped in each other's arms. His head on the
pillows, Penelope slumped against him, her head resting in the hollow beneath his shoulder, Barnaby stared
up at the shadowed ceiling and, without conscious

intention, found his mind sorting through all he'd felt. All he'd sensed.

All that had come to be, settling like an additional layer of experience between them.

Raising one hand, he stroked the rumpled silk of her dark hair. He knew she wasn't yet asleep. "You're happy, aren't you?" She'd grown more settled, more assured and content, over the last weeks. "Happy with the way things are working out."

It was that happiness he'd sensed running through their loving.

Without raising her head, she nodded. "We might not have caught our murderer yet, but in a personal sense, we've already succeeded—or so I believe." A second ticked past, then she lifted her head; looking into his face, she met his eyes. "I've found the balance I was searching for—I don't just think that, I know that. It feels *right*. My studies, my lectures, my helping others with translations—that's all still important, still speaks to a certain part of me, of my mind—and you, Oliver, and this household, and to a lesser extent our wider families, will always come first, have first claim on my time and my energies, yet still I truly need that extra element that comes through investigations."

She paused, eyes on his; after several seconds of considering, she stated, "It's not just the intellectual challenge of solving a mystery, of ferreting out all the facts and putting them together in a jigsaw of events to clearly define what took place. That's a part of it, true, but, ultimately the highest calling, the strongest motivation, is to see justice done. Through helping with investigations when the opportunity is there, contributing to the overall justice of our world is something I can do, and therefore should do."

Her lips curved lightly as she added, "The pursuit of, and support of, justice. That's why you do what you do, and why I should, and need to, assist whenever I can. Whenever Fate lays the opportunity before me, I should, and need to, respond."

He paused, studying all he could see—all she let him see—in her eyes, all that he could feel through her gaze, read in her expression, then he murmured, "I see it, too—that you have found your balance. And it's one I understand, a stance I can—and will happily—accommodate and support."

Her smile was the definition of radiant. "Excellent!" Snuggling back into his arms, settling her head as she liked, in the hollow beneath his shoulder, closing her hands over his as he settled his arms about her, she sighed deeply and relaxed. "Now we just need Corby to confirm that Maurice Halstead is our murderer, and all will be completely well."

Chapter 18

The following morning, seated before a delicate escritoire set in one corner of the parlor, Violet was drafting a letter Penelope needed to send to a scholar in Aberdeen when, in the distance, she heard the front doorbell peal. Knowing Mostyn would take care of whoever had called, Violet continued carefully scribing.

It had taken her days, but she had finally succeeded in completely organizing Penelope's huge desk, in the process uncovering several matters Penelope had forgotten to address. With Penelope's blessing, nay, encouragement, Violet had taken on the role of communicating with the various scholars involved, styling herself as Mrs. Adair's secretary.

She smiled whenever she thought of the title; in many ways, it was more to her taste than that of companion.

The door opened and Mostyn looked in. When Violet looked up, he tipped his head toward the front of the house. "A Mrs. Halstead to see you, miss. I told her Mrs. Adair's not in, but she insisted it was you she's come to see. I've put her in the drawing room."

Violet blinked, then set down her pen. Penelope had gone to meet with her sister Portia, and Griselda had decided that trimming bonnets in her shop was the best way to spend the time while they waited for Corby's confirmation of Maurice Halstead's guilt.

But why on earth had Constance Halstead come to see Violet? Today?

Rising, Violet smoothed down her skirt. "Thank you, Mostyn. I suppose I must see what she wants."

Noting her lack of enthusiasm, Mostyn trailed her into the front hall. "I'll be just out here, miss, should you need anything."

Meeting Mostyn's eyes, Violet smiled her thanks, then, pausing before the drawing room door, she drew in a breath, raised her head, and nodded as Mostyn reached for the doorknob. He opened the door, and, head high, she walked into the room.

To her mind, she owed the Halsteads nothing. Certainly not more than a moment of her time, and, truth be told, she was driven more by curiosity than any real wish to speak with Constance Halstead.

Constance had been sitting on one corner of one of the damask-covered sofas; she was still wearing her half-cape, still had her bonnet and gloves on, and was clutching her reticule tightly in her lap. Seeing Violet gliding toward her, Constance quickly stood.

Violet inclined her head. "Mrs. Halstead."

With severe civility, Constance stiffly returned the gesture. "Miss Matcham."

Violet waved to the sofa. "Please, do sit."

"Actually, I won't, if you don't mind." Constance's gaze shifted over the furnishings, the fashionable, undeniable elegance of the decor. "This . . . ah, won't take long."

With a sudden spurt of insight, Violet realized Constance felt out of her depth. Although the Adairs didn't flaunt their wealth and aristocratic backgrounds, there was an indefinable, intangible air that marked the household as being of the upper echelon of the ton. Several degrees above the circles in which Constance and her family moved.

Violet's station fell somewhere between that of the Halsteads and that of the Adairs; she could move in both circles—one higher, one lower—with reasonable assurance, certainly without suffering from the nervous uncertainty currently afflicting Constance.

Telling herself she should take pity on the woman, Violet remained standing, too. "In that case . . . what brings you here, Mrs. Halstead?"

Constance's lips pinched, her expression reverting to her customary, fussy, never-satisfied mien. "I have come to request your assistance in sorting through Lady Halstead's things. Now that the police and that Mr. Montague have finally deigned to give the family the keys to the house, we wish to ensure that everything is appropriately dealt with—we don't want anything vital being accidentally thrown out." Constance paused, her expression hardening. "What with Tilly gone—"

Violet noted that Constance managed to make it sound as if Tilly had deserted her post, rather than been murdered.

"—then you are the one who knows her ladyship's belongings best." Tipping up her chin, Constance somewhat belligerently stated, "I require your help to get her things together so that we can properly decide what should be done with them."

Violet had no wish whatever to return to the Lowndes Street house. "I'm afraid I'm currently engaged—"

"Miss Matcham." Constance drew herself up and made a valiant attempt to look down her nose. "Lady Halstead gave you employment for more than eight years. I would have thought simple loyalty alone would move you to perform this last task—this last duty—for her. Only you know where her belongings—those she held dear and would wish passed on—are stowed. Only with your help can we be certain we've adequately dealt with such items as she would have wished."

Violet drew in a breath but continued to hold Constance's gaze. Her increasingly belligerent gaze.

Constance had been quick to attempt to evoke Violet's guilt, but the precipitousness didn't make the sentiment, once called into being, any less effective. Lady Halstead deserved to have her belongings treated with respect and a degree of understanding and compassion her children and their spouses unquestionably lacked. And while there seemed little doubt that Constance wanted to leave this drawing room, to quit what was for her a subtly unnerving stage, equally clearly she was determined to take Violet with her.

Inwardly sighing—knowing Constance's stubbornness of old—Violet slowly inclined her head. "I can spare you—or rather, Lady Halstead—a few hours. But I will have to return here by one o'clock."

Constance waved the qualification aside. "We can see how far we've got by then." She turned toward the door. "But as you are pressed for time, I suggest we don't waste any. My carriage is waiting outside."

Resigning herself to spending the next two and more hours in Constance's aggravating company, Violet turned and led the way to the door. Opening it, she let Constance precede her into the front hall.

Closing the door behind her, she caught Mostyn's eyes. "Mostyn—I'm going to go to Lowndes Street, to Lady Halstead's house, to assist Mrs. Halstead in sorting through her late ladyship's things."

"Indeed, miss." Mostyn glanced at Constance, then looked back at Violet. "I'll inform Mrs. Adair when she returns."

"Please tell her I will be back by one o'clock." Violet glanced at Constance. "If you'll wait while I fetch my bonnet and pelisse."

It wasn't a question, but Constance replied, "I'll wait in my carriage." Turning to the door, she added, "Don't be long."

Raising her eyes to the heavens, Violet turned and went quickly upstairs.

Two minutes later, when she returned downstairs, her bonnet on her head, gloves and reticule in one hand, and her green pelisse neatly fastened over her pale green gown, Mostyn was waiting before the closed front door. "Are you sure this will be all right, miss? Going back to that house with one of that family?"

The thought had already occurred to Violet; she gave Mostyn the answer she'd given herself. "It seems all but certain that the murderer is Maurice Halstead— we're only really waiting for confirmation—and believe me, Constance positively loathes Maurice, and

I'll be with her the whole time." Pausing before the door, she met Mostyn's gaze. "And Lady Halstead does, indeed, deserve to have her belongings dealt with by someone who loved her, rather than one of her noxious brood."

Mostyn briefly studied her eyes, then bowed. "Indeed, miss." Opening the door, he added, "I'll keep an eye out for your return."

Stepping outside into a gusty autumn breeze, Violet clamped her hat on her head and, lifting her skirts, hurried down the steps to where Constance Halstead's carriage waited.

Millhouse's runner appeared at Montague's office a few minutes after the City's bells had tolled eleven o'clock.

Montague, working at his desk, heard the boy's voice pipe, "From Mr. Millhouse for Mr. Montague," and only just restrained himself from leaping to his feet and striding out into the outer office.

Through the open doorway to his inner sanctum, he saw Slocum receive a simple missive. Noting the eager, inquisitive glances thrown his way by Gibbons and Foster, and the others, too, he jettisoned all attempts at nonchalance and, rising, met Slocum in the doorway.

Slocum handed over the packet.

Everyone in the office watched, breath bated, as Montague broke Millhouse's simple seal, unfolded the single sheet, and read.

"Good God!" Head rising, Montague stared blankly across the room as he rearranged the pieces of the jigsaw in his mind . . . then, jaw firming, he nodded decisively. "Yes." He looked back at the note. "That *does* fit."

He had to tell Violet and the others.

Folding the note and slipping it into his pocket, he returned to his office for his hat, saying to Slocum as he did, "Send a brief note to Millhouse thanking him for his help. Tell him it's been invaluable and I'll be in touch to explain as soon as I'm able." Noting Millhouse's boy hovering by the door, eyes wide, Montague added, "And give the boy half a crown."

"Yes, sir." Slocum followed as Montague strode across the office, heading for the coat-stand by the door.

"Who was it?" Gibbons called out. "Don't leave us in suspense."

Shrugging on his greatcoat, Montague told them, adding, "I'm heading to Albemarle Street—depending on who is there, I'll most likely go on to Scotland Yard."

Leaving his staff speculating as to the ramifications of the truth, Montague went out of the door, clattered down the stairs, and, setting his hat on his head, strode into Bartholomew Lane in search of a hackney.

At last, they had their man.

Violet followed Constance Halstead into the dimness of the front hall of the Lowndes Street house. As had been the case when Violet had slipped in with Penelope and Griselda, and later with Montague, the house was dark, all the curtains drawn tight.

"Faugh!" Constance dropped the keys she'd used to unlock the door on the hall stand and reached up to untie the strings of her bonnet.

Violet noted that the keys were her old house keys; Montague must have sent them to the Halsteads. Deciding that she would rather keep her reticule, bonnet, gloves, and pelisse with her so she could more easily leave when the time came, she wondered, "Where should we start?"

She hadn't really meant to speak aloud, but Constance glanced at the jeweled watch she wore pinned to her collar, then looked up the stairs. "I daresay we should start in Mama-in-law's bedroom."

A fraction of a second was enough consideration for Violet to verify her deep antipathy to going anywhere upstairs. "Actually"—turning, she boldly led the way into the sitting room—"if you wish to make best use of my time, then we should start in here." Crossing the room toward the windows, she glanced back at Constance, who had come to hover in the doorway. "There's far more of her ladyship's things tucked away down here than there are in her bedroom."

Constance's lips thinned. She looked as if she wanted very much to argue, but she couldn't find any real grounds on which to do so.

Looking away, smiling to herself, Violet grasped the curtains and pulled them wide; enough light streamed in through the panes to allow them to work without lighting any lamps. Returning to the sofa, she set down her reticule, then reached up, undid her bonnet strings, and lifted the bonnet from her head. Setting it down on the sofa, she started unbuttoning her gloves. The house had grown cold and somewhat damp; she decided to keep her coat on. "So"—she looked at Constance— "where should we start? With the bureau, or the writing desk?"

Frowning, Constance came into the room. "The writing desk, I suppose."

Inwardly shaking her head at the woman's grudging tone, Violet turned to the desk, opened it, and started to pull out the top row of tiny drawers.

She tried not to listen to the ghosts of countless memories, of the happy times she, and often Tilly, too, had spent with Lady Halstead in this room, when her ladyship had been moved to show them the small trinkets she'd kept and tell them of her travels and the strange places she'd seen, the exotic adventures she'd had.

Lady Halstead had lived a full life, but she hadn't deserved to have it end as it had.

At the hands of her son. Gasping her last under a pillow Maurice had held over her face.

A chill touched Violet's heart, but then Constance joined her before the desk, and Violet dragged in a deeper breath and focused her mind on the task at hand—on fulfilling her last duty to her late employer.

Montague leapt from the hackney before it had halted, tossed the crown he'd had ready to the jarvey, then, hat in hand, strode up the steps of the Adairs' house and rang the bell.

Mostyn opened the door and immediately stepped back. "Mr. Montague, sir."

Montague strode across the threshold, eager to see Violet, to tell her the news—to learn what she thought of it. "Good morning, Mostyn. Miss Matcham, your master, and mistress—are they at home?"

"No, sir." Closing the door, Mostyn faced him. "Mr. Adair went to the Yard to consult with Inspector Stokes, and Mrs. Adair went to meet with her sister, Mrs. Cynster, but I expect her back for luncheon."

None of that surprised Montague, but . . . "And Miss Matcham?" Violet was supposed to have remained indoors, or alternatively have gone out only with those they trusted.

"A Mrs. Halstead called and asked Miss Matcham to go with her to the Lowndes Street house to help sort through the old lady's things." A slight frown bloomed in Mostyn's eyes. "I did ask if that was wise, sir, but Miss Matcham assured me that Mrs. Halstead loathed Maurice Halstead—him who's the murderer—and so she'd be safe with Mrs. Halstead."

Montague felt a chill touch his soul. Instinct reared, but not one he recognized. He was accustomed to dealing with intuition, with flashes of insight born of experience, of simply knowing through recognizing some pattern . . . but those familiar instincts involved money and investments.

This one told of life and death.

This one screamed of danger.

Of murder.

He swore and swung toward the door.

"Sir?" Mostyn instinctively reached for the doorknob.

Montague paused. His face felt graven, his mind awash with a torrent of emotions, of cascading thoughts and conjecture. He dragged in a breath and forced himself to think; Violet might not survive if he made a mistake. "Send word—urgently—to your master and to Inspector Stokes. Tell them to bring constables to the Lowndes Street house." He swallowed, had to force the next words out. "I believe the murderer has lured Miss Matcham there to do away with her." He met Mostyn's wide eyes. "I'm going there directly."

He moved to the door. Mostyn opened it wide. "I'll take the message myself, sir."

Montague nodded, slapped his hat on his head. "Pray I'll be in time." With that muttered injunction, he hurried down the steps.

The jarvey who'd brought him from the City was on the verge of rolling on again. Montague hailed him. "Lowndes Street, Belgravia—at the best pace you can manage." Opening the hackney door, he added, "A sovereign if you get me there in record time."

The jarvey flashed him a grin. "Then hop in, guv, and hold onto your hat."

Montague tumbled onto the seat, grabbed the door, and hauled it shut as, true to his word, the jarvey sent the carriage all but careening down the street.

Hanging onto the swinging strap, Montague ignored the mayhem left in their wake as the jarvey tacked and weaved and drove like a demon through the late morning traffic. He didn't care about causing a public ruckus;

all he cared about—the entire focus of his being—was on reaching Violet and keeping her safe.

Giving Mostyn those orders had required a leap of faith. In truth, Montague had no notion if his call to action would be an embarrassing false alarm, but . . . he couldn't take the chance.

Not when Violet's life hung in the balance.

What did his dignity, his reputation, matter against that?

Clinging to the strap as the hackney veered dangerously around some dowager's carriage, then rocketed ahead along Piccadilly, Montague suffered a moment of utter self-astonishment. Of looking at himself and seeing . . . someone he hadn't realized was there, lurking beneath his reserved, conservative, deliberately mild exterior.

He'd never thought of himself as a man of action, yet here he was, racing through Mayfair to rescue a lady.

Compelled to do so, even if it meant making an abject fool of himself.

He truly didn't care.

All he cared about was Violet.

The thought, and all it meant, resonated in his brain.

Then he drew breath and grimly focused on the Lowndes Street house, and what he might find when he reached there.

They'd been in Lady Halstead's house for barely half an hour when Violet saw Constance check her tiny watch for the third time.

They'd finished emptying the writing desk of its contents and had sorted the keepsakes into various piles. In a rare burst of familial feeling, Constance had remarked that she supposed she'd better let Cynthia look at things before she threw anything away. Of course, Constance had immediately marred her performance by making a snide, gloating comment about Cynthia no doubt having much to cope with in the wake of Walter's spectacular fall from grace.

Ignoring the remarks, Violet had moved on to the bureau. It contained significantly more by way of personal mementos than the desk had. Three long, deep drawers' and three smaller ones' worth, to be precise.

She and Constance worked steadily through the drawers, top to bottom. They'd started on the first of the long drawers when Constance once again checked her watch.

Hands inside the drawer, Violet paused, assembling the words for a polite inquiry as to what Constance was waiting for, when the sound of the front door opening had them both looking up, then turning to face the sitting room door.

Violet in surprise, but, she immediately saw, Constance in relief.

"Thank heavens." Constance went to the side table, where she'd left her reticule.

Before Violet could ask what was going on, the sitting room door opened and Mortimer Halstead walked in. He, too, was consulting his watch.

"About time!" Constance's exasperation rang clearly. "I *told* you I was expected at noon for luncheon with Mrs. Denning, and that's all the way out at Twickenham!"

Tucking his fob-watch back in his waistcoat pocket, Mortimer raised his gaze to his wife's face. "Indeed. My apologies, but I was delayed by some accident at Hyde Park Corner—all the traffic is banked up."

Violet experienced a sudden pang of memory; the detached, disconnected, subtly dismissive expression on Mortimer's face—entirely usual for him—was one Lady Halstead had described as "Home Office neutral." It told the world precisely nothing about what was going on in his mind—indeed, it raised the question of whether anything was going on in his mind at all.

Entirely accustomed to her husband's unresponsive demeanor, Constance humphed. "Lucky, then, that I'm headed in the opposite direction, or my day would have been a disaster." She glanced at the table before the sofa where she and Violet had arranged the piles of letters and mementos. "Miss Matcham and I have made a start in here, but she says her time is limited today, so I'll leave you to decide what most needs doing." Tugging her coat straight, reticule in hand, Constance nodded coldly to Violet. "Miss Matcham."

Violet didn't bother replying, not that Constance waited for any acknowledgment; she was already sweeping past Mortimer and on into the front hall.

A second later, the front door opened and shut. Leaving Violet alone with Mortimer Halstead.

It had happened so quickly, and distracted by the unexpected memory, Violet hadn't had a chance to consider . . . but Maurice was the murderer, not Mortimer. Nevertheless, she'd never liked Mortimer—if she'd had to choose the Halstead offspring she liked least, it would have been him—and, now she consulted them, her thumbs were pricking.

She didn't want to be alone in this house with Mortimer Halstead.

Even if he wasn't the murderer.

His gaze, slightly frowning, had fixed on the piles of his mother's belongings. Mortimer walked forward; halting before the sofa, he examined the various groupings, then sighed. "It's a start, I suppose, but . . ."

From outside, the sound of a carriage rattling off reached them; Mrs. Halstead making good her escape.

Violet inwardly grimaced. Should she have pro-tested against the impropriety of being left alone with Constance's husband? Could she have? Would Constance have listened?

No; Constance would have looked at Violet as if she'd been some species of insect far beneath her, much less her husband's, notice. Constance would have told her not to be ridiculous; she would have been no help.

And as for Mortimer . . . watching him, Violet knew that, innocent of the crimes though he might be, his only interest would be in seeing her do the work he wanted her to do, and that most expeditiously.

She therefore wasn't surprised when, a touch of pee-vishness now in his expression, he raised his gaze to her face and stated, "While I daresay this is all well and good, my mother kept her more valued and meaningful pos-sessions in her bedroom, and as I can only spare an hour away from the office—which, as I understand it, will also suit your timetable—might I suggest, Miss Matcham, that we continue these endeavors upstairs?"

Violet hesitated.

Mortimer glanced at the items they'd already sorted. "I'm really only concerned with items of consequence, not knick-knacks and keepsakes—if, instead of bother-ing with the rest of these, we can at least locate and gather everything stowed upstairs, it will greatly expe-dite this exercise." He looked at her. "Don't you think?"

Violet couldn't disagree, and she wanted to be finished and done with this task, with this house, as much as, apparently, Mortimer did. Lips tightening—she still didn't like any of this—she nodded. "As you say."

She looked at the letters she still held in her hands, then ran her gaze along the piles on the table. Selecting the most appropriate, she set the letters atop it, then looked at Mortimer.

Stepping back, he somewhat pompously waved her out of the room.

Stifling a flaring impulse to head straight for the front door, Violet led the way to the stairs. As she lifted her skirts and started climbing, she realized she'd left her reticule, bonnet, and gloves in the sitting room but decided they would be safe enough there; she would be leaving in an hour.

Halfway up the stairs, premonition—strong and absolute—swept her, chilling her nape, tightening her lungs.

Mortimer . . . how odd that he'd stood back, that he'd elected to follow her up the stairs rather than lead. He'd always treated her as a higher servant, one who should follow, not be deferred to.

Until now.

Her scrambling senses abruptly focused on the man behind her.

He was following two treads back.

Senses abruptly expanding, she registered that his footfalls had altered—not just in rhythm but in weight, from the lighter steps of the fussy, self-important, but, in reality, inconsequential Home Office bureaucrat to a heavy, deliberate, intention-filled tread.

Pressing one hand to her waist, she raised her chin, surreptitiously sucked in air.

And tried to steady her giddy head.

Tried to think through the instincts that were now screaming—that knew, simply *knew*, regardless of all their information to the contrary, that the murderer now walked at her heels.

She'd slowed, but she forced herself to keep climbing as steadily as she could.

How to get out of this? How to escape him?

How?

Reaching the top of the stairs, moving like an automaton, she stepped into the gallery. Sheer desperation gripped her, and she shoved her wits into action. Mortimer wasn't tall for a man, but he was taller than she was, and considerably heavier. Unquestionably stronger. As she walked steadily toward Lady Halstead's room, and very likely to her own doom, her mind frantically surveyed her late employer's bedroom, searching for something—anything—that might give her a chance.

Pausing outside Lady Halstead's bedroom door, Violet dragged in another breath, then opened the door and, deliberately leaving it set wide, walked in. She paused, making a show of considering where to start, but she'd already made up her mind.

Battling to show no hint of fear, much less suspicion, she went around the bed, heading for the bedside table that stood against the wall between the bed and the fireplace. "I know her ladyship kept her most recent and important correspondence in here. As well as other items she valued."

She clamped her lips shut. She couldn't afford to babble. Penelope hadn't expected to return to Albemarle Street until sometime after midday; she wouldn't receive Violet's message in time to grow curious and come to rescue her—not in time. Not before Mortimer killed her.

That he intended to do so Violet did not doubt—no longer harbored the slightest doubt. He had followed her into the room, his movements, his whole demeanor far different from his customary fussy vagueness; his dark gaze was focused and rested heavily on her. His expression was intent. A predatory stillness seemed to descend over him as, watching him from the corner of her eye, she drew out the top drawer of the small table and started lifting out the contents.

Laying the letters and notes, the ribbons and pins on the bed, she kept her gaze apparently on them, on her hands as she lifted, considered, and sorted each item. Again and again, her gaze flicked up, and from beneath her lashes, she checked on Mortimer, but he didn't move.

He said nothing at all.

Just watched her.

Minutes ticked past.

Her first handful sorted, she drew in a tight breath and turned again to the drawer. She was reaching in, grasping another handful of Lady Halstead's mementos, when she saw movement at the edge of her vision—she focused and saw that Mortimer had moved to the opposite side of the bed.

Straightening, she turned and looked at him—as, his gaze still locked on her, he lifted the pillow from that side of the bed.

His expression was set. His mind was made up.

Slowly and deliberately, he started to walk around the bed, his gaze rising to lock with hers.

Violet saw her death in the dark orbs, in his fixed and weighty stare.

She swallowed and took a step back. Found her tongue. "Is that how you killed her?" She nodded at the pillow. "Your mother? With that pillow?"

He blinked, slowed. "Yes." He hesitated, then added in a blandly conversational tone, "It was surprisingly easy."

He stepped around the corner of the bed, and she sidled another step, scrambled to say, "What about Runcorn? Was that you, too?"

Halting, turning the pillow so he held it crosswise, he frowned. "Of course. Once the old bat set him onto going through her affairs, eventually he would have stumbled across the missing shares."

"But Tilly." Keeping her eyes locked with his—if his gaze was locked with hers he wouldn't notice what lay beyond her—Violet clasped her hands before her, wrung her fingers, and hoped she was projecting a suitably helpless image. "Why did you kill Tilly? She was no threat to you."

"Ah—that's where you're wrong. Tilly surprised me while I was going through Mama's share certificates, looking for the one that would best serve my need. When the question of the missing share certificate arose, as it would have at some point, Tilly would have remembered, and I couldn't have that." Mortimer's gaze searched Violet's face, then his eyes narrowed.

Violet held her breath and prayed he hadn't guessed her plan.

She almost exhaled in relief when he asked, "Didn't Tilly tell you? Didn't she mention seeing me here, going through Mama's papers?"

Violet forced herself to shake her head. "No. She never mentioned it."

Mortimer stared at her for a long moment, then his brows faintly arched. "How sad for you that you're going to die essentially for no reason."

Eyes flaring wide, she opened her mouth to try to dissuade him, but he spoke first, his voice dropping in register as he murmured, "But, regardless, you are going to die."

"But how on earth will you explain it?" she all but blurted. She didn't know why she was so desperate to keep him talking; she knew there was no help on the way. But the longer she kept him talking, the longer she put off the final dreadful moment when she would have to fight for her life. "Your wife knows she left you here with me. How will you explain that away?"

The faint curve of his lips chilled her blood. "Simple. I'm running late for a meeting at the Home Office—I truly am. Suddenly remembering that meeting, and knowing of no reason I couldn't trust you, I left you here continuing to sort through my mother's things for the rest of the time you could spare us."

Shaking her head, she eased back another step. "But then how did I die?"

His gaze flicked to the window at the end of the room, then returned to her face. His smile grew even colder. "Again, what could be more simple? Overcome with guilt, because, of course, it was you all along—you who, with your lover-accomplice, stole the share certificate, then, when that threatened to come out, you let him in and he killed the old lady, and then Runcorn, and then Tilly. But in looking through my mother's things, here in the room where you watched her die by your lover's hands, guilt rose up and smothered you." He glanced at the pillow he held in his hand, and his smile grew. "Literally smothered, and then, of course, you do what any self-respecting lady like you would do—you jump out of the window to your death. The cobbles below should ensure that no evidence of you being unconscious, or having struggled before you fell, remains."

Such evil . . . Violet met his eyes and slowly shook her head. "It won't work. Too many people know me too well—and even now they're asking the Earl of Corby who he got that share certificate from. He'll identify you, and you will be caught."

Mortimer blinked; for an instant, the pedantic civil servant who was paranoid about his status, his social and professional standing, surfaced, but almost immediately he sank back behind the darker, somehow deader, almost certainly more genuine face of the murderer. "Montague." He paused, then shrugged. "I'll take care of him later."

What? "No!" She hadn't intended to point him toward Heathcote. "I mean, why add another murder to your list?"

Again, he shrugged. "Why not? Removing people one by one has proved easy enough thus far." His fingers flexed on the pillow. "And instructive though our little discussion has been, Miss Matcham, I regret that meeting of mine won't wait much longer."

Raising the pillow, he came for her.

Violet whirled. Grabbing the poker from its stand by the hearth as she turned, she swung it up and around—straight for Mortimer's head.

He saw the danger just in time to ward off her blow with the pillow.

Feathers flew. Mortimer cursed. Desperate, Violet yanked the poker free, hauled it back, and swung again.

Flinging the pillow aside, with both hands Mortimer caught the poker along the shaft.

Seizing it, he pulled.

Violet clung and refused to let go. If she did, she would die.

Mortimer cursed and hauled.

Locking her fingers about the handle, Violet grimly hung on, shifting to keep her feet as Mortimer tried to wrench the weapon from her.

He paused, clearly thinking of some way to dislodge her. Before he could, she kicked him in the knee.

Thunder rumbled.

Mortimer cursed and staggered but didn't let go of the poker. Regaining his balance, he set his feet and braced his shoulders, his features contorting in a black snarl as he tensed to, once and for all, wrench the poker from her.

The floor shook. From the corner of her eye, Violet saw a flash of movement in the open doorway. Heard a curse—not from Mortimer.

Wholly focused on her, Mortimer didn't register the intrusion. Jaw setting, he violently yanked—and wrenched the poker from Violet's grasp.

Immediately, he swung it high over his head, clearly intending to strike her down.

With a roar, Montague charged across the room, driving his shoulder into Mortimer's, barreling into him and knocking him away from Violet.

He and Mortimer ended on the floor, struggling in a heap beneath the window.

Vicious curses spewing forth, Mortimer struggled and fought to get free.

Montague wasn't having that. Jaw clenched, propelled by a potent mix of fury and fear, with a strength he hadn't known he possessed, he grabbed Mortimer by the lapels, and, twisting and shifting, he slammed the other man's back—and the back of his head—to the floor.

Swinging over Mortimer, straddling him, Montague planted a hand on Mortimer's heaving chest and held the man down while he prepared to rise—to check that Violet was all right.

It was her scream that saved him. "Heathcote—watch out!"

He saw the poker swinging at his head just in time.

Grabbing the iron bar in his left hand, he staved off the blow. Gritting his teeth, he held the poker back, raised his right fist, and slammed it into Mortimer's jaw.

Something crunched. Even though his hand throbbed, Montague realized on a flash of savage satisfaction that it wasn't his bones that had broken.

Mortimer groaned, then slumped, eyes closed.

Montague twisted the poker from Mortimer's lax grip, then slowly—watching to make sure the man truly was unconscious—he eased up and rose to his feet.

He turned to Violet—as she rushed into his arms.

He closed them around her, felt her arms go around him and crush tight.

Tossing the poker onto the bed, he hugged her even tighter, setting his cheek to her hair. "I was so frightened," he confessed. "All the way from Albemarle

Street, all I could think about was you—him hurting you. Possibly killing you. Then the carriage couldn't get through, and I had to leave it and run . . . I didn't think I would get here in time."

He heard the emotion investing his words, heard the inherent vulnerability exposed, and didn't care. Violet was in his arms, safe and whole, and nothing else mattered.

She tightened her arms, then eased her hold enough to lean back and look into his face. She met his eyes, and her face, her smile, was everything any knight could ever hope for; radiant, joyous, she held his gaze, her love shining in her eyes. "But you did arrive in time, and you saved me." She studied his eyes and her smile softened. "Actually, you did more than that. You lent me your strength so I could hold on until you came."

He arched his brows. "I did?"

She nodded. "When it came to that fraught moment when I had to face the reality of possibly losing my life . . . I discovered I wanted to live—so much. I wanted to live, was determined to live, because of you. You lent me your strength, even though you weren't here. You gave me the will, and therefore the where-withal, to fight, to resist, even though I had no idea anyone might arrive to help. But you did."

Lacing the fingers of one hand with hers, he raised her hand to his lips and tenderly kissed her knuckles.

"You fought, and held on, and I came, and so we've caught our murderer, and now we can go forward."

She'd agreed he could speak the instant this was over. Trapped in his gaze, Violet felt the moment close around them. The sounds of arrivals downstairs reached them, but neither paid the impending interruption any heed. Heathcote's gaze moved lovingly over her face, then, almost tentatively, he lowered his head.

Violet stretched up and, inwardly joyous, set her lips to his.

Kissed him as he kissed her, in an inexpressibly sweet exchange, an acknowledgment that they were there, together beyond the danger, alive and unharmed, able and ready to go forward hand in hand.

That they had found each other, had saved each other, and valued and wanted and desired the other above all else in the world—that was what their simple kiss said.

Eventually, he raised his head and she lowered her heels to the floor.

Still locked in each other's smiles, arms twined, they turned to the door—and found Stokes and Barnaby waiting, both trying to hide their smiles.

Keeping one arm around Violet, not even trying to hide his pride, Montague waved at Mortimer. "I"—he glanced at Violet, met her eyes, and amended—"we give you our murderer, gentlemen."

Resuming his usual stern mien, Stokes stalked forward and looked down at Mortimer Halstead, who was beginning to stir, to groan. "Not Maurice?"

"No. Millhouse sent me word earlier." Montague looked across the room at Barnaby. "You were right that it was Maurice who was a member of Corby's club, but you don't have to be a member to play at a club, much less lose to Corby."

Barnaby nodded, then ambled around the bed to join them, allowing two large constables, who had been waiting by the door, to respond to Stokes's beckoning; Stokes was still standing looking down at a semiconscious Mortimer.

Acknowledging Violet with a smile, Barnaby said, "And I suspect I know why he did it—why someone like Mortimer sat down to play with a notorious gambler like Corby. I've just been talking to the pater, and he mentioned that Corby was one of the peers sitting on an appointment board for the Home Office. Mortimer was due to appear before it in a week's time, seeking promotion."

Montague glanced at Mortimer, still stretched supine at Stokes's feet. "So he what? Intended to lose, or thought to win?"

"In Mortimer's eyes, I suspect either would have served," Barnaby murmured. After a moment, he went on, "All of this, from start to finish, has been about currying favor with Corby to ensure Mortimer's promotion."

Another moment passed, then Violet shivered. "It almost beggars belief that anyone would be so . . . cold-bloodedly self-serving."

A stir at the doorway had them all looking that way—to see Penelope poised on the threshold. She took all the elements of the scene in in one glance, then she looked at Barnaby, Montague, and Violet, and wrinkled her nose. "Damn! I'm too late." Walking forward, she gestured widely. "Clearly everyone is hale and whole, and, sadly for me, you appear to have everything well in hand."

Barnaby laughed. He held out one hand, and when she reached for it, he twined their fingers and drew her close.

Penelope took it further and linked her arm with his, but her bright, dark gaze wasn't distracted; it traveled to Violet's face, then moved on to Montague's.

Then Penelope smiled brilliantly; looking up, she met Barnaby's gaze. "And, equally clearly, everything has worked out wonderfully all around!"

Barnaby grinned. Violet and Montague shared a smile. And Penelope continued to beam delightedly upon them all.

Unsurprisingly, Mortimer, once he regained consciousness, didn't share Penelope's view.

"This is nonsense!" Marched down the stairs with his wrists shackled, then thrust into a chair at the dining room table, he huffed and puffed. "I'm an important senior Home Office official. I'll have you know that the Home Secretary himself is chairing a meeting at this very moment, one I'm supposed to be at, and instead—" With his bound hands, Mortimer gestured at Montague and Violet, who, along with Penelope and Barnaby, had followed Stokes and his men into the room, purely to see what transpired.

What sort of story Mortimer would concoct.

"*Instead,*" Mortimer all but spat, "I was set on by those two. I found them upstairs, rifling through my mother's papers. Doubtless trying to find something to steal—or perhaps trying to conceal something."

Stokes, who had halted, standing, at the head of the table, eyed Mortimer with a certain curiosity.

When Stokes made no response, Mortimer squirmed; his features contorted. "Get these shackles off me, I say! I've done nothing wrong!" With his head, he gestured to Montague and Violet. "It was them, I tell you!"

Stokes studied him some more, then in a perfectly equable tone asked, "Any more lies you'd like to get off your chest?"

When Mortimer glared at him, Stokes smiled his sharklike smile. "It's no good, Halstead. We have Corby's word, and when that's combined with everything else, all the evidence we've accumulated, it'll be more than enough to hang you."

Mortimer looked belligerently recalcitrant. He dropped his gaze from Stokes's face, but his eyes shifted back and forth, as if he was searching for some other way to excuse himself, or to talk his way out of his crimes.

Stokes arched his brows. "Nothing more to say?" When Mortimer didn't respond, not even by a look, Stokes glanced at his constables. "Take him to the Yard. Tell the desk he'll be charged with the murders of Lady Halstead, Mr. Andrew Runcorn, and Miss Tilly Westcott. Also the attempted murder of Miss Violet Matcham, and the theft of a share certificate from Lady Halstead." Stokes looked back at Mortimer; the man had hunched his shoulders and was looking down, occasionally shooting furtive glances to either side. "I'll be along shortly to finalize the charges. Meanwhile, put him in a cell and tell the desk he stays there until the Chief says otherwise."

Both constables snapped off salutes. "Aye, sir." With determined expressions, they closed in on Mortimer.

The others stood back and watched as, between them, the constables hauled Mortimer Halstead to his feet and marched him out of his mother's house.

They all trailed behind. Halting in the dim front hall, through the open door, they watched as Mortimer was escorted down the path and out of the gate.

When the constables and their prisoner had passed out of sight, Stokes turned to Violet, Montague, Barnaby, and Penelope. And grinned. "Got him. I'll have to go and formalize the charges, but after that"—his gaze settled on Montague and Violet—"I believe a celebration is in order, on several counts."

Chapter 19

Everyone had agreed with Stokes's suggestion, and plans were made for a celebratory dinner in Albemarle Street that evening. In the interim, Stokes and Barnaby returned to Scotland Yard to put the final touches to their case, while Montague took Violet and Penelope for a celebratory luncheon, then returned them to Albemarle Street and journeyed on to the City, to his office, to tell his staff the news.

The intrepid investigators regathered at six o'clock in Penelope's drawing room. Oliver and Megan were present, and were placed on rugs on the floor the better to entertain and divert their proud fathers while Penelope and Griselda demanded and received a full report of all the day's doings from Montague and Violet.

Like Penelope, Griselda was disappointed not to have witnessed the spectacular culmination of their investigation. While Penelope had pieced together most of what had occurred from comments the others had let fall, she, too, wished to hear the sequence of events properly related by those who had experienced said events firsthand. The two friends sat side by side on one of the sofas and interrogated Violet and Montague, extracting every last little detail of their thrilling, frightening, and ultimately wonderfully successful day.

Sitting beside each other on the other sofa, both still smiling, indeed, unable to stop, Montague and Violet bore with the inquisition with indulgent good cheer.

When they reached the end of their exciting tale, Griselda frowned. "Do you think Mrs. Halstead was . . . well, an accomplice? Did she know of Mortimer's actions? Did she support them?"

Stokes looked up from the blocks he was stacking for Megan. "It seems not. She was utterly shocked when we informed her of her husband's arrest, and I don't think she was acting."

"She came close to fainting when she realized that she had, however unwittingly, played a part in, as she subsequently described it, Mortimer's foul scheme by persuading Violet to go with her to the Lowndes Street house." Barnaby glanced up briefly from the tussle he was having with Oliver over a rattle. "I agree with Stokes. She was beyond aghast, and she wasn't acting."

"To her credit, once she grasped the reality, her first thought was for her children—about how their father's disgrace would affect them and their futures." Stokes grinned as, with one bat of her small hand, Megan set the tower he'd built crashing to the rug. All but bouncing on her plump bottom, eyes bright with glee, she chortled and clapped. Then she crawled to one of the blocks and retrieved it.

Stokes glanced at the others. "Incidentally, had there been any doubt as to who the murderer was, when we searched Halstead's dressing room, we discovered a key to the side door of the Lowndes Street house. It was made some years ago, so Mortimer has had some notion of stealing from his mother for at least that long."

"I noticed the keys he—or rather Mrs. Halstead— used to enter the house today were the ones I used to have," Violet said.

Stokes nodded. "Exactly. And we didn't find any other keys to the house, so his key to the side door—and it was well hidden, and why was that?—was his secret way into and out of the house. But to cap it all off"—Stokes's grin brimmed with satisfaction—"the curtain cord he'd used to strangle Runcorn was cut from one of the cords in his dressing room."

Barnaby snorted. "Believe it or not, he'd deliberately scheduled a clash of meetings at the Home Office so one group thought he was in the other group's meeting, and vice versa—and then he told his staff he'd been summoned by some ambassador and had to step out for an hour."

Stokes's chuckle was dark. "He's been so busy planning things, there's no chance he'll be able to plead insanity."

"So he will hang?" Violet asked. When Stokes glanced at her, she said, "I'm not normally so bloodthirsty, but he stole three lives."

Stokes merely nodded, his gray gaze direct. "He'll hang."

"I fear I have to ask," Penelope said. "How are the rest of Lady Halstead's children reacting to the news?"

"With all speed," Barnaby replied, his tone beyond cynical. "They are predictably horrified and cutting all ties, distancing themselves with all possible haste."

Penelope feigned a shudder. "What a terrible brood. They are the antithesis of what a family should be."

Barnaby arched his brows. "Actually, I wouldn't be surprised if this incident didn't draw the other three closer. Maurice and William were both truly shocked—and Cynthia seemed thoroughly shaken. And with her and Camberly already reeling from the impact of Walter's disgrace, well . . ." After a moment, Barnaby shrugged. "I got the impression the shock might, this time, have shaken the three remaining enough to make them grow up. Enough to make them realize that, to survive, they'll need to pull together, rather than pull apart."

A moment passed, then Griselda said, "For the sake of the Halstead children, I hope that proves to be the case."

Gurgles and the patter of blocks on the floor diverted everyone's attention. For the next several minutes, they all watched the antics of the pair of infants rolling and playing on the rug.

Montague watched as Violet, soft laughter and encouragement lighting her face, leaned forward to clasp little Megan's hands and help the tiny tot, who had crawled to Violet's feet, then had determinedly climbed, hand over hand, up Violet's skirts until she was upright, stand on her own tiny feet.

Megan rocked back and forth, weaving, then, with one of her signature chortling gurgles, she fell back on her bottom, hands waving, then batting in delight.

Stretched out on his stomach, Oliver watched, big eyes curious and wondering.

Smiling, Violet sat back. She felt Heathcote's gaze, turned her head, and saw him watching her, a curious, arrested look much like Oliver's in his eyes.

It took her only a moment to realize what he was thinking—imagining. She blushed but didn't look away. Instead, following his train of thought, she held his gaze, then, smiling still, reached out and lightly squeezed his hand.

Her message, one she felt sure he understood, was simple: They had so much to talk about, and now they could—but later.

Mostyn chose that moment to enter and announce that dinner was served. Hettie and Gloria followed at his heels, ready to retrieve their young charges and cart them off to bed.

The six stalwart investigators rose and, each couple arm in arm, went in to dine—to enjoy their celebratory dinner.

Penelope's cook had been informed of their news and had responded appropriately; the fare was festive and delicious. The conversation turned general, roaming freely from politics to the police force, to the continuing progress with the seven girls they'd rescued, to social news and around again to their families, their children.

To the future—a future built upon all that they already possessed.

When they reached the syllabub, Barnaby tapped his glass with his spoon.

At the tinkling, the others all looked up, looked his way.

"I have a toast," he told them, raising his wineglass, "and a suggestion. First, the toast." He lifted his glass high, let his gaze sweep their faces as they did the same. "To us—to the six of us. Working together, we've successfully brought a triple-murderer to justice and avenged the three innocents he killed. So—to us!"

"Hear, hear!" Everyone murmured the refrain and drank.

"And now," he said, lowering the glass, "to my suggestion." He looked at Montague, seated to his right. "Over the last years during which I've been a consultant to the Yard, Stokes and I have come upon several cases which have involved financial dealings, at least in part. On some, we had your assistance, while with others we muddled through. However, more than ever these days, criminal cases of the sort Stokes requires my help with are also those most likely to involve—" Barnaby gestured.

"Financial instruments of one sort or another?" Montague supplied.

Barnaby inclined his head. "Just so. Crimes within the upper echelons of society usually involve money, and ton money is rarely left under any bed."

"Or in a tin on top of some wardrobe," Stokes dryly added. While the others chuckled, Stokes met Montague's eyes. "What I believe my friend and colleague here is trying to say is that we—he and I—would be honored if you would consent to join with us in solving whatever such cases come our way."

Montague looked from Stokes to Barnaby, then glanced at Violet, seated opposite, and nodded. Looking back at Barnaby, he more formally inclined his head. "It is I who would be honored to join with you gentlemen in your endeavors."

"In seeking justice." Violet raised her glass. "To our three champions of justice."

Penelope and Griselda promptly raised their glasses. "Our champions! Hear, hear!"

Barnaby grinned down the table. "As it happens, that was only half of my suggestion. The other half"—he looked at Violet, on Penelope's right—"was to pay tribute to Violet's contribution to the investigation, especially her insights into the people involved, and to ask, if I may, whether you are intending to continue as Penelope's secretary?"

Violet blinked and looked at Penelope.

Who reached out and closed her hand over Violet's. "Oh, *please*, do say yes." Penelope's expression conveyed a hint of incipient desperation. "God alone knows what I might be forgetting these days—I do so need you, someone I trust, to take charge of things."

Violet smiled and closed her other hand over Penelope's, lightly squeezed. "Then of course I'll remain in the post—I'd be delighted to continue working with you."

"Excellent." Penelope beamed, then looked up the table at her husband. "But why did you want to know that?"

"Because," Barnaby said, "I wanted to suggest that, in support of yours and Griselda's reemergence into more active investigating, having Violet add her particular expertise would bring yet another dimension to our team."

"Of course!" Griselda turned an approving gaze on Barnaby. "How very insightful of you, Barnaby dear." Leaning forward to address Penelope and Violet, Griselda said, "Do agree, Violet—if you join us, we'll have an excellent base from which to understand all the victims and villains likely to come our way." Griselda waved. "Penelope knows all about the aristocracy, and I know all about the middle and working classes, but neither Penelope nor I have all that much understanding of the social layers that lie between."

"The gentry." Penelope had been nodding eagerly. "Indeed." She met Violet's eyes. "Do say yes, again,

Violet—we truly would welcome your input into our investigations."

Her smile growing deeper, Violet looked from Barnaby, to Griselda, then to Penelope. "As your secretary, I hadn't imagined sitting in the parlor and writing your letters all day. I had rather assumed I would join you—indeed, I'm not sure how you might manage to keep me away."

"Wonderful!" Penelope beamed up the table, meeting Barnaby's blue gaze and letting her very real appreciation of his tack—his suggestion—show. Having Violet join them was the perfect way to support and assist Penelope and Griselda in maintaining the new balance to which they were still making minor adjustments. The perfect way to set everything in place so they could go forward into the future with confidence.

Sitting back, letting her gaze travel the table, seeing Violet and Griselda talking about hats, and Barnaby, Stokes, and Montague exchanging comments about a recent political scandal, Penelope felt happy satisfaction well, then overflow. Reaching for her glass, she raised it. The action caught the others' eyes and they looked at her inquiringly even as they, too, reached for their glasses.

"I have a toast, too." So saying, Penelope raised her glass high. "To our new investigative team—may our future be bright!"

The "Hear, hears!" and echoing "To our futures!" were heartfelt and strong.

Looking up the table, Penelope met Barnaby's eyes, tipped her glass to him, and drank deeply.

They left the table for the drawing room, where the talk went on for some time. Despite their differences in station, they faced many of the same personal hurdles and shared many of the same aspirations, the same dreams, not just for themselves and their families but for wider society as well.

Eventually, Stokes raised his head, listening. "The rain's finally here." The clouds had been massing all afternoon, and from the drumming on the glass and the gurgling in the drains, had finally decided to spill their contents liberally over the city. Looking at Griselda, Stokes smiled, fondness and more in his eyes. "We'd better get on, my love, before the traffic slows even more."

Griselda glanced at the clock on the mantelpiece. "Heavens, yes! Look at the time."

Ten minutes later, Violet stood beside Heathcote, with Barnaby and Penelope near, all four hovering just inside the front door as they laughed and waved at, and called good-natured suggestions to, Stokes and Griselda, who, with Megan bundled up and hugged close in Griselda's arms and Hettie huddling near, were escorted by Mostyn and two footmen, all holding large umbrellas high, to Stokes's carriage, waiting at the curb. The rain was teeming down, drops glinting in the lamp-beams as they pelted to the ground.

Montague sniffed the air. "By tomorrow morning, the City will be washed clean."

A sudden gust of wind and a flurry of rain had the four hurriedly retreating back into the hall.

Leaving the door almost closed, Barnaby turned to Montague and held out his hand. "I sent a footman down to Piccadilly to find you a hackney. Can't have you going out in this and catching your death."

"Or drowning." Grasping Montague's arm, Penelope stretched up and planted a kiss on his cheek. "Thank you for saving my secretary—she's only been with me a short time, but already I don't know what I would do without her."

"More accurately," Barnaby said, "you do know, and that only makes you more determined to keep her." He smiled at Violet and took her hands in his. "If I may?" He bent and brushed a kiss to her cheek. Then he released her and, taking Penelope's hand, stepped back toward the stairs as he nodded to both Violet and Montague. "Good night to you both."

"Indeed." Allowing Barnaby to draw her up the stairs, Penelope sent an air-kiss winging Violet's way.

"I'll catch up with you tomorrow sometime, Violet dear."

Violet watched the pair disappear up the stairs. As she turned to Heathcote, the two footmen came back through the front door and walked on down the hall.

One nodded to Heathcote. "Mr. Mostyn said as the hackney will be just a few minutes, sir."

"Thank you." Montague waited until the pair had passed through the swinging door at the rear of the hall, then, turning to Violet, taking her hands—hands she readily surrendered—he looked into her face.

Her well-beloved face.

She looked up at him; the same hopes and expectations that were burgeoning in his chest were shining in her lovely eyes.

He smiled, gently, then raised one of her hands and brushed his lips to her fingers. "We need to talk—we have so much to say, to discuss." He searched her eyes. "To decide." He drew a deeper breath and faintly grimaced as the sound of the rain drumming outside increased—as if to remind him he needed to go. He sighed. "Sadly, however, this is clearly not the right time or, indeed, the right place." He hesitated, then said, "I would like, if you agree, to call on you tomorrow. There's somewhere I'd like to take you. To show you."

Her smile was all gentle understanding. "Of course. I'll be here, waiting for you. At what time will you call?"

His smile deepened. "I would say as early as possible, but . . . shall we say ten o'clock? At least that seems somewhat civilized."

Her smile broke into a soft laugh. "Dear Heathcote—ten o'clock sounds perfect." She held his gaze and quietly said, "I would wait for you for forever, but I'd really rather not. I've waited all my life for you, and now you're here . . ."

He nodded and pressed a more heated kiss to her other hand. "Indeed. Now we're here, we both want to get on."

On a waft of wet wind and a flurry of raindrops, Mostyn looked around the door. "Carriage is here, sir."

"Thank you, Mostyn." Releasing Violet's hands, Montague lifted his hat from the nearby stand. His eyes still on her, he nodded, then forced himself to turn to the door, set his hat on his head, and stride away, out into the night and the rain.

Alone, but not for long.

Slumping back in the dark of the hackney, Montague felt expectation well and realized he was grinning.

Griselda settled Megan in her crib, then, straightening, looked down at her sleeping cherub and smiled.

Standing alongside his wife, Stokes dipped his head and, glancing into her face and savoring the madonna-like quality of that smile, felt something inside him ease, and settle, too, just like his sleeping child. After a moment's hesitation, he took the plunge and murmured, "You're content with this, aren't you?"

Faint surprise in her face, Griselda looked at him, studied his eyes, then her lips curved again, reassuring and calming. "You mean being a mother, being a milliner, being the lady of this house, being Penelope's and now Violet's friend, and being an investigator, too, and working to somehow make everything fit?" Placing a hand on his arm, she steered him out of the nursery and toward their bedroom next door.

He nodded. "Yes—that. All of that."

Her fingers found his and twined, and she drew him into their room, paused to let him shut the door, then she went into his arms. "Yes." She met his gaze. "I'm content. It's not easy, and probably never will be, but the rewards are great."

Then she tilted her head, her eyes still searching his, a coy smile spreading across her face. "You didn't notice, but I left something out."

"You did?" Her list had sounded fairly comprehensive to him . . . his hands firming about her waist, he replayed her words, but he couldn't see it. "What?"

Her sultry chuckle reached to his bones as, stretching up, she wound her arms about his neck and smiled, all wifely indulgence, up at him. "I omitted to mention the best thing of all—the one that makes all the others worthwhile. Not because it's less than all the rest but because it's more—because it's the foundation all the other parts of my life stand upon."

Something in him quivered as he read the truth in her eyes, but he had to, needed to, hear it from her. To hear the words on her lips. "And that something is?"

Her smile turned radiant. "Being your wife."

She drew his head down, drew his lips to hers, and kissed him.

Stokes tightened his arms about her, drew her tight.

And decided that, after all, everything was, and would be, all right.

After checking on Oliver, then retreating to their bedroom, Penelope and Barnaby spent the next hour enthusiastically celebrating in their own private way.

Finally spent, her breasts still rising and falling deeply as she waited for her breathing to even out, her hair spread about her in tangled disarray, Penelope lay on her back and stared at the moonbeams playing fitfully across their ceiling. Slumped beside her, Barnaby lay on his chest with his face half buried in the pillow beside hers, one heavy arm flung across her waist.

His breathing was even more labored than hers—hardly surprising, given his recent performance.

The downpour had finally petered out, but the sense of everything outside having been washed and made new remained; the coming day held infinite promise.

She sighed, the sound redolent with happiness. "I'm so glad we didn't turn away from this chance—that we faced the challenge, rather than let it slide. We've worked our way through, to this—to my new state of equilibrium. And as we've done it once, we know we can do it again—that no matter what comes, we *can* adjust, find our new path, and go on. Together."

And in that, she felt she should give credit where credit was due. "I'm proud beyond words of you—and of Stokes, too. You both came through the challenge with colors flying." Lifting a limp arm, she gestured widely, if weakly. "You assimilated the changes and adjusted as necessary."

Stirring, Barnaby snorted, the sound muffled by the pillow. Shifting his head slightly, he said, "If you don't by now know that to keep you happy—to keep you engaged, enthused, and challenged, as I know you need to be—I would alter the way the moon revolves about the earth, then you need new spectacles."

She laughed. Turning to him, she stroked a hand down his naked side, and when, in response, with a

564 · STEPHANIE LAURENS

groan he turned over and shifted his arm, she snuggled closer, resting her head where she preferred it to be, in the hollow beneath his shoulder. Relaxing as he draped his arm around her, she pressed a kiss to his chest. "I have noticed, but, in all fairness, I should admit that you don't—and won't—need to go to the trouble of interfering with any celestial bodies. You just need to stand by me as you have in this. You just need to keep being you."

Lifting the hand she'd spread on his chest, Barnaby pressed a warm kiss to her palm before settling that palm once more over his heart. "That," he murmured, "I can do."

A second passed, then she murmured, "I love you, too."

Eyes closed, he smiled, and decided he could live with that.

Forever.

The next morning, Montague arrived in Albemarle Street at precisely ten o'clock. Leaving the hackney waiting, feeling oddly nervous, he ascended the steps to the Adairs' front door. He raised his hand to knock—and the door swung inward.

Mostyn grinned at him. "Been keeping an eye out." The majordomo stepped back, and Violet swept through.

Her gaze locked on Montague's face; she nodded to Mostyn without taking her eyes from Montague's. "Thank you, Mostyn. I don't know when I'll be back."

In light of her smile, in light of her words, Montague felt like a conquering hero. Offering his arm, he said, "You look lovely." To his eyes, she was radiant.

Her smile deepened. "Thank you. I have to admit that I did sleep well."

Guiding her down the steps, he dryly murmured, "Not having the threat of a murderer hovering over you must have been a great relief."

She glanced at him, then, smiling, allowed him to hand her into the carriage. He followed and, shutting the door, settled beside her. When the carriage rattled into motion, she reached for his hand and settled her fingers in his. "If you must know, it wasn't relief that the murderer was caught that made it so easy to fall asleep—it was happiness, pure and simple, at knowing what today would bring." Turning her head, she met his eyes. "I felt like a child waiting for Christmas morning."

The words warmed him; lightly pressing her fingers, he quietly said, "I hope what comes lives up to your expectations."

Her fingers tightened on his, returning the pressure. "Trust me, it will." After a moment, she said, "Tell me—were you born in London?"

As they rattled through the town, he told her of his past—of the parents he'd been close to despite the fact they'd been getting on in years before he was born, of the evolution of his business from the more conservative services his father had supplied to the more varied activities he now pursued. "I was the Son in Montague and Son—as figures and money always fascinated me, I started working alongside my father when I was fifteen. Eventually, my father drew back from the business, gradually passing his clients into my hands." Montague met Violet's gaze. "By the time he died, I was the de facto principal of the business and had been for several years." He shrugged and looked ahead. "Some might say I came to my position easily, that it was handed to me—and there's some truth in that."

Smiling, Violet shook her head. "No—the opportunity might have been laid before you, but what you did with it? That was all you." She met his gaze. "What you are now, the businessman, the man, is entirely due to you."

She thought he blushed, but then he glanced away. "And what of you?" he asked. He looked back at her. "Are you a Londoner, too? Or . . . ?"

"Not. I was born in Caversham, just north of Reading. My father was the vicar of Woodborough, and he held the living there until his death. My mother had died several years before, so I was left to find my way." The carriage rolled around a corner, and she briefly met his eyes. "I was lucky enough to find a position with Lady Ogilvie in Bath, and when she died, I moved to London to take up my post with Lady Halstead. She and Lady Ogilvie had been acquainted."

She looked ahead, but his gaze remained on her face.

"You were happy with Lady Halstead."

Statement, not a question, but after a moment she replied, "Not *happy*—now I know what happy is, I realize I haven't been that way in a long time." Lips lifting, she glanced at him. "But I was content—satisfied with my lot, certainly. I can make no complaints over those years—as with you, some might say I had it easy, too."

He returned her regard. "But life is, indeed, what you make of the opportunities that come your way."

The carriage slowed and they both glanced out. The familiar façade that included the narrow door that led up to Heathcote's office appeared, and the jarvey brought his horses to a halt.

Violet blinked, wondering; she looked about her as Heathcote handed her down.

Montague paid off the jarvey, then, taking Violet's elbow, he steered her across the narrow strip of pavement to the green-painted door with its inset window bearing the words *Montague and Son, Agents of Business*, in gold letters. Fishing in his pocket, he drew out his keys. As he found and fitted the right key in the lock, he noticed Violet glancing interestedly about.

"It's Friday," he said, nodding at the general bustle in the court. "In this area, that means it's extra busy as everyone rushes to get their week's financial transactions completed. Although most businesses open on Saturday, the major banks and the Exchange are closed."

"Ah." She nodded. Turning back to him, she said, "I hadn't really paid attention on the previous occasions I came here—I was too exercised by events." Swinging to face the door as he set it wide, she noticed the small Closed sign at the bottom of the window. "As you said, it's Friday, but it appears your office is neither open nor busy." Arching a brow, she entered.

He followed, closing the door and relocking it before turning to look at her. "In celebration of our success with the investigation, I gave my staff the day off—Lord knows, they earned it. Every one of them contributed in some way."

She smiled, turned, and started up the stairs. "That was nice."

"Perhaps," he said, following her, "but also necessary." When she threw a questioning glance at him, he said, "I told you I wanted to show you something."

Reaching the first-floor landing, she halted before the door to his outer office and turned an inquiring face his way. Joining her, he shook his head and waved her up the next flight. "My apartment's one flight up."

Her expression cleared as she remembered what he'd told her; flashing a fascinated look his way, she eagerly headed up.

"My parents," he said, following, "had a house north of Finsbury Square. When they died, I sold the house and bought this building instead—not just my offices but the whole block. It seemed a wiser investment. I rent out the rest of the space other than my offices." He looked ahead. "And the upper floor."

Joining her on the small landing before his apartment door, he selected the right key, then fitted it to the lock. Reaching for the brass doorknob, he met Violet's gaze. "This is where I live—where I've lived for the last ten years."

He set the door wide and watched as she looked into the small foyer. Then she walked in and he followed, shutting the thick door behind him.

Violet took note of the simple, plain, but high-quality finishes, immediately recognized the sound solidity of Heathcote Montague reflected in his home. Glancing back at him, she asked, "Do you live here alone?"

"I have a couple—Mrs. Trewick keeps house and cooks, and Trewick performs the duties of a general manservant. They have separate quarters off the kitchen."

Walking through the archway into what proved to be a long sitting room, Violet nodded. She paused to take in the furnishings and get her bearings, then asked, "Are they in—the Trewicks?"

Setting his hat on the hall stand, Heathcote looked faintly uncertain. "Ah . . . no. I gave them the day off, too."

Violet let all she felt inside invest her smile; delighted, she turned to him and met his eyes. "Good."

Faint relief showed in his face as he came to her. "I hoped you wouldn't think it too—"

Stepping into his arms, she placed her fingers across his lips, cutting off his words. "It isn't too anything." She trapped his gaze with hers, looked deep into his hazel eyes. "This is our time to talk, to discuss, to decide—all you did was ensure we have the privacy to do that, and for that . . ." As she removed her fingers, her gaze lowered to his lips. "I can only be glad." She breathed the last word as she stretched up and set her lips to his.

A wanton act, perhaps, but to her mind, he and she had already stepped past the social boundaries. The polite barriers no longer applied. Here, now, it was just her and him—a man and a woman, a gentleman and a lady. Here, in this private space, only the personal, what existed between them, remained.

Apparently, he agreed; she'd barely had a chance to kiss him before he took over and kissed her back.

His arms closed around her, drawing her close, not hesitantly but definitely. That warm, safe, reassuring cage made of his muscles and bones, and even more her reaction to it, told her where she stood. To her, this man was safety, security, a safe harbor through any storm—and more. With him, she could be . . . the woman she'd been born to be.

Opportunity.

She reached for it—without hesitation pressed closer, deeper into his embrace; sliding her arms over his shoulders, locking her hands at his nape, she held him to her. And when he tested her lips, she parted them and, boldly, without any guile, invited him in.

And delighted in his acceptance.

Never before had she communed with a man thus. She'd been kissed before, yes, but not like this—not when the exchange became a dialogue, a communication that passed back and forth, wordless yet so descriptive, silent yet deeply, profoundly evocative.

Meaningful.

Promise, and commitment.

Both were there in that kiss—him to her and her to him, and beyond that to what might be, to what they together might create and share.

Their exchange shaped the vision, enshrined it in their minds.

A clear statement—and they both wanted it.

Yearned for it.

Desired it.

Heat of a kind she'd never felt before rose and spread, heavy and lush, beneath her skin, a compulsive surge that for all its unfamiliarity she recognized instinctively. Rich and potent, it lured and beckoned, and she answered—and so did he.

Gently, with a reluctance that resonated within her, he drew back and broke the kiss.

He looked into her eyes, and she looked into his and saw him—the man she loved—clearly.

One large hand cradling the back of her head, his gaze traveled her face, her eyes, her lips, as if in wonder, then he brought his gaze back to her eyes. "I'm a simple man, Violet—I don't have fancy words. All I know is that I need you to make my life whole. All I know is that I want you as my wife, and that I will move heaven and earth to win you."

Her answer leapt to her curving lips. She held his gaze as she gave it. "I don't want heaven. I don't even

want earth. I do want you—and I do, more than anything else in life, want to fill the position of your wife."

"So you'll marry me?"

"Yes." Even she heard the joy in that word. "I'll
marry you, and be your wife, and have you as my
husband—nothing, simply nothing, could make me
happier."

He captured one of her hands and raised her fingers
to his lips. "I swear you will never regret accepting my
suit."

"I know I won't"—she held his gaze—"because I
love you."

She felt the ripple of reaction that passed through
him, as if those simple words had turned some key and
unlocked . . . something within him.

It felt as if shackles fell, as if her words had released
some long-ago binding, one he'd placed on himself and
had forgotten, or had never truly realized was there.
His commitment to his work had been that absolute,
that demanding. But now . . . he felt free—free to
speak, to say, to admit, "Love"—he searched her eyes
and saw that emotion shining—"is too simple a word
for what I feel for you. Admiration, adoration, worship—all that, and more."

Slipping her fingers from his, she laid her palm
against his cheek. "You don't need more—you

just need to be you, and to continue to love me as I love you."

"But . . . I want so much." He felt his lips wryly curve. "The businessman within me will never die—my heart seems such a paltry thing when placed in the scales."

She laughed. "Never that. You have the heart of a lion."

"But I want . . ." He couldn't, it seemed, stop himself from making a bid to have it all, all he now knew his soul yearned for. Craved. "You, by my side, and a family—if we're blessed." At the arrested look in her eyes, he hurried to explain, "I've already got the business, the position, the station—the wealth, the acquaintances, even the close friends. I have all the appurtenances of a successful life, but without a wife, and even more a family, all the rest means little." He held her gaze. "I know we're neither of us in the first flush of youth, yet . . ." He hesitated, then forced himself to say, to ask, "If you're willing . . . ?"

The smile that slowly bloomed on her face transcended joy. Her eyes shone with the same all-encompassing emotion. "You said it yourself before—we are our own people, you and I. We can be whatever we wish to be. Lovers, spouses, parents—we can, if we choose, have it all."

As he drew in a huge breath, she stretched up and, just before her lips touched his, she stated, "And we do so choose."

Then she kissed him, acceptance, agreement, and commitment reaffirmed—passionately—in the caress.

Without conscious direction, his arms closed around her and he gave her the same in return.

And let the moment lead him—and her—as it would.

When he lifted his head—separated their lips by a heated breath—and glanced at the door to his left, then arched a brow at her, her smile only deepened.

And she whispered against his lips, "Yes."

Violet didn't need to say more.

Not to him—the man who looked at her with love and passion in his eyes, solid and true and unwavering.

She could never question the rightness of this—could not doubt the sense of falling in with destiny as she let him lead her into his bedroom and close the door.

What followed . . . was a reflection of them, of who they were, the straightforward, honest, and true people they knew no other way to be. They offered themselves up—to each other, to the glory that erupted and swept through them.

In the soft sheets of his bed, in the soft light of a long, autumn afternoon, they found each other, and discovered themselves.

Discovered a wider view of all they could be—of all they could aspire to claim.

Passion and joy, heat and desire, and the culminating cataclysm of ecstasy—they found them all on that golden afternoon, found, seized, and made them theirs.

And when, at the end, Violet settled in his arms—a Violet unbridled, her lustrous hair rippling in a silken mass over his chest and arms—he smiled. On his back, eyes drifting closed, he recalled an earlier thought. "Before I met you and all this"—with a slight wave, he indicated them and their togetherness—"came about, I never thought of myself as a man of action. But courtesy of you, and all that's followed, I've discovered that when the need is there—"

"You very much rise to the occasion." She chuckled, soft and low.

He could feel the curve of her lips against his chest. "Believe it or not, I wasn't going to put it quite like that."

"That's why I said it—I knew you wouldn't." She shifted; lifting her head, she looked into his face. Smiled. "You haven't surprised me—I saw you, your potential, clearly from the first. You're the man I've been waiting all my life to find, and now I've found you and claimed you . . ." Stretching up, she touched her lips to his. "I'm never going to let you go."

As she eased down again, into the hollow by his side—a space, it seemed, perfectly fashioned for her—he tightened his arms around her. "Just as well, because you're everything to me."

Settling, she sighed happily, then spread her hand over his heart and lightly patted. "My Heathcote."

He smiled. Through the last hours, she'd said his name several times—gasped it, moaned it, sighed it . . .

Nestling his cheek against her hair, he closed his eyes.

Hearing her call him by his given name had already become his most treasured dividend.

HARPER LUXE

THE NEW LUXURY IN READING

We hope you enjoyed reading
our new, comfortable print size and found it
an experience you would like to repeat.

Well — you're in luck!

HarperLuxe offers the finest in fiction and
nonfiction books in this same larger print size and
paperback format. Light and easy to read, HarperLuxe
paperbacks are for book lovers who want to see
what they are reading without the strain.

For a full listing of titles and
new releases to come, please visit our website:

www.HarperLuxe.com